He closed the door, ~~~~ darkness. Faith lean~~~~ smooth steel finish ~~~~ back. The night had g~~~~ breeze stirred her hair, and goose bumps peppered her skin. In the shadowy blackness he caught her other hand in his, circled long fingers around her slender wrists and pinned them to the truck on either side of her head.

Behind his shoulder the night sky was inky-black and studded with stars. Anticipation was a heavy weight, low in her belly. Inside her chest, her heart pounded so hard she feared it would burst free and fly off into space to take its place among those stars.

"Alone at last," he said, and lowered his head to kiss her.

Also by LAURIE BRETON

MORTAL SIN
FINAL EXIT

*Watch for Laurie Breton's next
novel of romantic suspense*

CRIMINAL INTENT

Available March 2006

LAURIE BRETON

LETHAL LIES

MIRA®

If you purchased this book without a cover you should be aware
that this book is stolen property. It was reported as "unsold and
destroyed" to the publisher, and neither the author nor the
publisher has received any payment for this "stripped book."

ISBN 0-7783-2151-7

LETHAL LIES

Copyright © 2005 by Laurie Breton.

All rights reserved. Except for use in any review, the reproduction or
utilization of this work in whole or in part in any form by any electronic,
mechanical or other means, now known or hereafter invented, including
xerography, photocopying and recording, or in any information storage or
retrieval system, is forbidden without the written permission of the publisher,
MIRA Books, 225 Duncan Mill Road, Don Mills, Ontario, Canada M3B 3K9.

All characters in this book have no existence outside the imagination of the
author and have no relation whatsoever to anyone bearing the same name
or names. They are not even distantly inspired by any individual known or
unknown to the author, and all incidents are pure invention.

MIRA and the Star Colophon are trademarks used under license and registered
in Australia, New Zealand, Philippines, United States Patent and Trademark
Office and in other countries.

www.MIRABooks.com

Printed in U.S.A.

This one's for Samantha,
the brightest light in my life.

ACKNOWLEDGMENTS

Thanks, as always, to my husband, Paul, for putting up with the craziness when I'm on deadline, for sitting through book signings that were as exciting as watching paint dry, for driving me from bookstore to bookstore to sign stock, for tolerating my day trips for the sake of research, and for being my personal one-man publicity department. I love you.

Thanks to Dr. D. P. Lyle, M.D., for answering my questions about the effects of date-rape drugs on the body.

Thanks to my editor, Valerie Gray, for all the hard work, dedication and tough questions. You keep me on my toes!

Thanks to the MIRA art department for the fantastic covers. I'm always thrilled with the result.

Thanks to my agent, Ethan Ellenberg, for everything you do for me. Without you, none of this would have happened.

And last but definitely not least, thanks to my friend and boss, Grace Leonard, for her never-ending patience, understanding and support.

One

Rain drummed down in opaque sheets, and Chelsea squinted to see beyond the steady sweep of windshield wipers that barely kept up with the downpour. The state highway ran alongside the river, as crooked as a snake's back, and she reminded herself to keep it under sixty. It would be a hell of a thing if she hydroplaned off the road and into the Androscoggin before she could get to Ty.

Midnight wasn't exactly an ideal time to be paying a visit to Serenity's chief of police. More than likely, she'd be dragging him out of bed, grumbling all the way. But this wouldn't wait until morning, and she didn't trust anyone else. Besides, once Ty heard what she had to say, he'd stop grumbling.

She'd been working on this story for weeks, digging and poking into dark corners, building it up brick by brick. She'd deliberately kept the cops out of it until she was certain that what she'd been told was true. God forbid she should point the finger of guilt at an innocent party. But tonight, she'd seen the evidence with her own eyes, had confirmed for herself what her heart already knew to be the sickening truth.

It was time to bring this mess to the police. Time to turn over to Ty everything she'd uncovered. Then she would go home and write up her story. It wouldn't take long; she'd already written it in her head. Once Ty gave her the go-ahead, she'd file it—an exclusive that was going to make her career as a journalist.

This story would knock the town of Serenity on its collective ass. For the first time since she'd left her job at the *Boston Tribune* to return to this one-horse town at the end of the earth, Chelsea Logan felt alive. It was the thrill of the chase, the scent of danger, that brought the adrenaline junkie inside her roaring to life. She'd come back here a year ago with her tail tucked between her legs because Daddy was dying and she needed a change. She hadn't meant that change to be permanent. But the job offer from the *River City Gazette* had come at the right time. Daddy had left her the house, and she was tired of the hassles that accompanied working for a big-city newspaper. Besides, permanence was an illusion that lasted only as long as it took for something better to come along.

Right now, there was nothing better on the horizon. So she'd stayed here in the tiny Western Maine town where she'd grown up. She'd enrolled Jessie in the local high school, started renovating the house, and stayed to watch the town decay, day by day, inch by miserable inch, right before her eyes.

She fumbled in her purse for a cigarette, then remembered that she'd quit last week. Again. In her rearview mirror, headlights rounded the curve behind her. Too high, too far apart, too bright. A pulp truck. The damn things were everywhere. Day and night, big and ugly and noisy, a pox on the landscape.

Chelsea stepped down harder on the accelerator and roared into the straightaway. Ahead of her, the wet road suddenly shimmied and dipped. She blinked and adjusted her headlights to low beam to cut down the glare reflecting off wet pavement. The lights in her rearview mirror swelled, blended together and then separated again. She shook her head to clear her vision, then gasped as a sudden wave of nausea washed through her.

Her car wandered across the center line, and she yanked it back. Behind her, haloed in inky blackness and magnified by the rain, the pulp truck's headlights grew to monstrous proportions. Dizziness overwhelmed her, and Chelsea gripped the steering wheel hard, weaving back and forth across the center line as she struggled desperately to hold the Kia steady.

The pulp truck's headlights were directly behind her now, pushing her, blinding her. Chelsea's foot slipped off the accelerator, then regained its hold. Unable to distinguish pavement from soft shoulder, she slowed to a crawl. With a furious blare of his horn, the trucker blew past her, his massive tires hurling a wall of water across her windshield.

Weak and shaken, she fumbled for the window crank, lowered the window and gulped in fresh air. Something was terribly wrong, something had turned her stomach inside out and shoved its contents up into the vicinity of her tonsils. If she could just stop the car and get some fresh air, maybe upchuck whatever was pressing against the back of her throat, she was certain she'd feel better. *Food poisoning.* That had to be it. The veal must have been tainted.

Straddling the center line, she searched the darkness ahead of her for the rest area that should be coming up on her left. With immense relief, she recognized the narrow turn-out nestled along the riverbank. She turned the steering wheel, crossed the pavement and hit the hard-packed gravel with a jolt. *Thank God*, she thought. *Thank God.*

The car continued rolling, and she wondered muzzily which one was the brake pedal. Was it the one on the left? No, that was the clutch. *Left foot, clutch. Right foot, brake.* With renewed confidence, she stomped hard on the right-hand pedal. Too late, she realized her mistake. The Kia shot into black, empty space, then began falling in slow motion. It hit the water nose first, hard enough to snap her head back against the headrest. The car hesitated for a long instant, poised like a ballerina over the rushing river, then slowly tumbled forward onto its roof.

Water rushed through the open window. Her muzzy brain was still clear enough so she knew that air pockets would remain the longest at the highest point. But her reflexes were shot. Dizzy and disoriented, she fumbled with the seat belt. But it refused to respond to her clumsy fingers.

Panic slammed into her. She struggled to free herself, but her movements were awkward, and the stubborn seat belt held tight. It was her worst nightmare come to life. She was trapped, locked into place between the steering wheel and the seat, hung upside down from the strap like a side of beef, while around her, the water rose steadily.

This isn't an accident. She heard the words in her head, as clearly as though they'd been spoken. Frantic now, her heart hammering as her fingers battled the wayward seat belt, she groggily replayed the last few hours of her life. The cat-and-mouse game they'd been playing. Dinner at his place. Casual conversation. A bottle of wine. One for the road, he'd joked, while she sat there dry-mouthed, barely breathing, eyeing that bottle of Beaujolais like a leopard eyeing a gazelle on the hoof. Five years. Five long years of sobriety behind her. If she drank it, she might be plunged back into the hell where she'd dwelled for most of her adult life. If she didn't drink it, he might realize she knew him for the monster he was.

Truth or dare.

While her insides roiled with indecision, he'd opened the bottle, poured them both a drink, handed one to her. Watched her drink it.

And left his glass untouched.

The wine, she thought in disbelief. *Not food poisoning. The goddamn son of a bitch drugged me.*

Frigid water slapped at her face. Her fingers, numb from the cold and weakened by whatever he'd drugged her with, tugged uselessly at the jammed seat belt. She wanted to weep at the irony of it. She was going to die because of her scruples. She, Chelsea Irene Logan, who'd never had many of them to begin with.

Oh, God. What would happen to Jessie? Who would look after her baby when she was gone?

Davy, she thought. *Goddamn you, Davy.*

And the water swallowed her up.

The morning was miserable, cold and raw and damp, the kind of damp that ate into your bones and sucked out the marrow. It had rained for two weeks straight. The river was running high, the steep bank muddy and slick. Police Chief Tyrone Savage stood with a paper cup of tepid coffee in his hand and watched a yellow-slickered kid from Sonny's Towing attempt to hook a winch to one axle of the submerged Kia. Ty had been the first responder on the scene, and he'd slithered down there for a look even before the EMS crew arrived. Now he was caked with mud and wet up to his ass, and turning blue in places he'd never known a man could turn blue.

He knew the car. Everybody in town knew the car. Serenity was the kind of place where people knew what brand of toilet paper you used and whether you preferred single or double ply. If there was any possible doubt about the identity of the driver, the license plate shimmering beneath the surface of the water was a dead giveaway. CHELSEA-1. Ty knew exactly who and what they'd find when they pulled the car to the surface. What he didn't know was how the hell she'd ended up here. It looked as though she'd just driven off the edge and straight into the river. When she hit the water, the Kia had flipped, landing on its roof and settling into the mud a few feet from shore.

A gray drizzle peppered his skin. Along the riverbank, a grim-faced cluster of rescue personnel stood watching, augmented by the usual assortment of the morbid and the curious who'd taken time from their morning commute to stop and gawk. The kid in the raincoat and wading boots raised his arm in a signal to his partner, who eased the wrecker forward. With a mournful groan, the Sephia shifted position and began to rise, inch by painful inch, out of the Androscoggin's murky depths.

Ty tamped down the fury simmering inside him. Before

this day was over, some bureaucrat in Augusta would be sporting a new asshole, courtesy of Police Chief Tyrone Savage. It wasn't just the knowledge that the victim happened to be the girl he'd lost his virginity to eighteen years ago behind the high school bleachers that had him furious. Chelsea Logan had been a pistol back then, and he suspected he wasn't the only young buck who'd taken that particular ride with her. And it wasn't just that he hated traffic fatalities occurring in his town. They weren't frequent—the last one had happened on graduation night two years ago when seventeen-year-old Ryan Overton lost control on a curve and wrapped his Camaro around a tree—but Ty was resigned to the inevitability of them. As long as there were automobiles, there would be automobile accidents.

It wasn't even the fact that he would be expected to accede jurisdiction to the Maine State Police in the accident investigation that had him wild-eyed and furious. If they wanted the headaches that went along with trying to reconstruct Chelsea Logan's last moments, they were welcome to them.

No, it wasn't any of these things that had him so mad he could gladly wrap his fingers around somebody's throat and squeeze. What had him really ripped was the fact that he'd asked the Maine Department of Transportation no less than three times over the past twelve months to install a guardrail in this spot. This section of rural highway was an accident waiting to happen. The road closely followed the contours of the riverbank, with only the occasional tree to prevent a motorist who strayed onto the soft shoulder from tumbling headfirst into the turbulent Androscoggin. The posted speed limit was forty-five, but this part of Maine was crawling with pulp trucks that consistently did sixty-five to seventy on the two-lane blacktop. DOT had refused his request, claiming that since the road ran in a straight line for a half mile, this was a low-risk location.

Before he was done with them, the folks at DOT would wish they'd never heard his name. Now he would get his guardrail. A little late for Chelsea Logan, but better late than never.

Pete Morin sidled up to him, wearing a stupid-looking rain hat and an ugly green slicker the color of a Hefty bag. Around the toothpick tucked into the corner of his mouth, Pete said, "No skid marks. Doesn't look good."

He followed Pete's gaze to the state trooper who crouched by the roadside in the rain, patiently examining the Kia's tire tracks. "She could have fallen asleep. Wandered across the highway and over the edge."

Pete shifted his considerable weight onto his right leg. "Not at the angle she went in." He removed the toothpick and gestured with it. "Car woulda flipped on its side. Nope, she hit the bank nose-first and drove straight over the edge."

It was the same scenario he'd envisioned. Because it didn't set well with him, Ty took a sip of coffee before responding. It tasted like the mud that had seeped into every orifice in his body. "So what are you saying?"

"It's not my job to draw conclusions, boss. That's why you got that fancy criminology degree."

"Right. Thanks for the reminder."

The winch groaned as slowly, laboriously, it hauled the Kia up the muddy riverbank. The car jolted and bumped, water sloshing from every imaginable crevice. "She coulda been drinking," Pete said, and chomped back down on the toothpick.

"Maybe." But it didn't sound right. Chelsea had inherited her father's propensity for the bottle, and she'd nearly let it ruin her life. A few years ago, with the help of AA, she'd finally gotten sober. She'd worked so hard since then to rebuild her fragmented life that he couldn't imagine her getting sloshed and accidentally driving into the river.

Which left him with an alternate, even less believable option: that her actions had been deliberate.

Every instinct he possessed said that wasn't possible. It was unimaginable that Chelsea would have deliberately orphaned the fifteen-year-old daughter who'd been the center of her universe.

With a thump, the Kia landed on solid ground and bounced

on its tires. "Keep the gawkers away," Ty ordered, and strode to the vehicle, where paramedics Ron Steel and Jeannie Arsenault had already opened the driver's door and were leaning over the victim.

As a small-town cop, he witnessed death on a sporadic basis: accidents, suicides, house fires, the occasional heart attack or drug overdose. As a veteran of the Gulf War, he'd become intimately acquainted with death in all its insidious and unexpected forms. Death was never pretty, never easy. It was even less pretty when the deceased was a lifelong friend, especially one as vivacious and spirited as Chelsea Logan.

Her skin held a bluish tinge, and had begun to wrinkle, as though she'd spent too long soaking in the bathtub. Her honey-blond hair hung in wet strings clumped with debris from the river. Her body was limp, her head tilted at an impossible angle; either the cold temperature of the water had delayed the onset of rigor mortis, or else she hadn't been here long.

He cleared his throat. "Jeannie?"

In a pinch, Arsenault occasionally filled in for the county coroner, Keith Gagnon. Owner and operator of Eternal Rest Mortuary, Gagnon wasn't known for the haste with which he responded to emergency calls. After all, the dearly departed weren't going anywhere anytime soon.

"No pulse, no respiration, advanced cyanosis," the paramedic said. "She's definitely dead."

"Gagnon on his way?"

"He's been called."

"We'll need to transport the body to Augusta for an autopsy." Ty glanced over the roof of the car and his mouth thinned. "Don't these damn people have anything better to do?"

"Human nature," Arsenault said cheerfully.

"Close the door. Find a blanket or something to cover the window until the hearse gets here."

He turned abruptly and nearly ran brains-on into Lemoine, the state trooper, who stood with clipboard in hand, scribbling something on an official-looking sheet of paper. "We'll be impounding the vehicle," Lemoine said, still writing. "Checking it for defects." He glanced up. "Any ID on the victim?"

"Chelsea Logan. Local woman. I know her personally."

Something shifted in Lemoine's eyes. "Then you'll be notifying next of kin?"

Ty rubbed a weary hand across his brow and wondered if there was any easy way to tell a fifteen-year-old kid that her mother was dead. "I'll take care of it," he said.

There had to be somebody, some relative who could take responsibility for the girl. But who? Chelsea's mother had run off when she was a kid, and as far as he knew, they hadn't spoken in thirty years. Not that he blamed the woman. Cyrus Logan had been the meanest son of a bitch he'd ever had the displeasure of tangling with. Mean as a snake even on the rare occasions when he was sober, violent and uncontrollable when he wasn't. His meek little wife had shown an uncharacteristic glimpse of backbone the day she'd walked out the door. Too bad her single act of courage hadn't included taking her daughter along with her. Nine months ago, the old bastard had done himself and the world a favor by breathing his last breath. So Chelsea would leave no grieving parents behind. And she'd been an only child. No brothers or sisters. At least not legal ones, although rumor had it that old Cyrus might have fathered more than one unacknowledged offspring.

But that was just rumor.

Which, he supposed, left Davy. Even though Davy Hunter and Chelsea Logan were divorced, they'd maintained an on-again, off-again relationship for the better part of two decades. Serenity was a small town, and people liked to talk. The rumor mill had spent years speculating about the identity of Jessie's father. Was it Davy, or someone else, some shadowy unknown figure? Neither Davy nor Chelsea had ever bothered to satisfy the curiosity of those wagging tongues. Ignoring the gossip, they'd simply taken up where they'd left off when they both returned to Serenity last year. Some bonds, it seemed, were stronger than divorce.

But Davy wasn't exactly daddy material.

This just got better and better. Cussing under his breath, Ty yanked open the rear door of the Kia. Dirty water splashed around his ankles. He scooped up Chelsea's waterlogged purse from the back seat, shuffled through its contents and pulled out a small leather-bound address book.

She hadn't used indelible ink. Damned inconsiderate for a woman who, judging by the angle of her tire tracks, appeared intent on drowning herself. The pages bled blue and black, massive splotches that rendered much of the writing illegible. But the inside front cover was still relatively undamaged. He skimmed the personal information: address, date of birth, phone number. Doctor, dentist, religious persuasion. Next of kin.

The name jumped out at him. Not Davy Hunter, but another name, one he knew only too well, written in bleeding blue ink. Chelsea's cousin. *Faith Pelletier*.

His stomach went into free fall. Amazing, the power her name still had over him, even after all these years. As kids, they'd been inseparable, to the point where people came to refer to them as a single hyphenated unit: Faith-and-Ty, Ty-and-Faith. Throughout high school, they'd been part of a tight-knit foursome: Faith, the sweet-faced introvert; Chelsea, the girl determined to live life on the edge; Davy, intense and brooding; and Ty, the police chief's son who would have done anything to embarrass his parents.

For an excruciatingly brief time, he'd thought there was a chance that he and Faith might become more than friends. Until he'd done something incredibly stupid and ruined whatever might have happened between them.

Directly after graduation, Faith had kicked the small-town dust from her heels and headed off in search of greener pastures. She'd certainly found them. He'd seen her in the bookstores, read her name on the bestseller lists. He'd even caught a glimpse of her on one of those late-night talk shows. Raven-haired and sultry, she was a vision of cool, sleek sophistication. The transformation from painfully shy schoolgirl to glamorous bestselling author was nothing less than amazing.

Life had its little ironies. The kid who'd so hated being the son of a cop was now a cop himself, a cop who'd never quite managed to bury his feelings for Faith Pelletier. And now it was all up to him—he had the unenviable task of notifying Faith Pelletier that her cousin was dead and that, as Chelsea's only living relative, it was up to her to figure out what to do with fifteen-year-old Jessie.

Ty turned his back on the Kia. Above his head, the sky still wept. Thirty yards away, a tall, lean man shouldered his way through the crowd of onlookers, the tails of his red flannel shirt flapping with every step. The dark-blond ponytail that hung past his shoulders gave him the appearance of an aging hippie, although he'd been born a generation too late for true hippiedom. Even from this distance, even in this murky light, his pallor was clearly visible. As was his agitation. He gave Lemoine a brief glance and dismissed him. Fists clenched, he marched determinedly toward Ty.

Three feet short of a collision, he stopped. They eyed each other wordlessly, then he peered past Ty's shoulder at the Kia and studied it in silence.

His gaze swung back to Ty. And in a harsh, unrecognizable voice, Davy Hunter said, "What the hell happened?"

Two

"Three months." Faith Pelletier lifted her wineglass by the stem, took a healthy slug of sauvignon blanc, and tried to digest her agent's words. Outside the restaurant window, the New York City sidewalk teemed with people. Inside, the hushed murmur of conversation and the discreet chink of silver and crystal painted a hazy backdrop to Marie's pronouncement. Faith swirled the wine around inside her mouth, then let it trickle, cool and smooth, down the back of her throat. "They're giving me three months."

"It was the best I could do." As Marie Spinelli leaned over the table, her cell phone rang. Scowling, Marie swiveled in her chair, dark head lowering as she bent to fish the offending object from her purse. With the flick of a button, she silenced it and dropped the phone back into her purse. "They can wait," she said. "This is more important."

Taking a series of slow, deep breaths, the way Dr. Garabedian had taught her, Faith steeled herself against the anxiety that hovered, waiting to pounce, like some dark beast just outside the periphery of her vision. Her skin felt tight, as though she'd stayed too long in the sun and it had shrunk a couple of sizes. "They can't do this to me, Marie. This is the literary equivalent of a death sentence."

"Not if you can dig yourself out of this funk you're in and get back to work." Marie stabbed her fork into her salad and pulled out a cherry tomato. "Look, hon," she said, "the people at Moon and West have been more than understanding about your situation. When Ben got sick, they pulled *Blood Sport* from the schedule because they understood that he had to be your first priority. Nobody even questioned that your husband had to come first."

Faith sipped her wine. "Big of them to be so accommodating in my time of need."

"Not really. You've made them a healthy chunk of change over the years. They could afford to be accommodating." Marie eyed the miniature tomato impaled on the tines of her fork. "But they won't wait forever. They've already paid you a substantial advance for the book."

"Most of which went to pay Ben's medical bills."

"And Ben has been gone for eighteen months. The meter's ticking, sweetie. You haven't had a new book on the shelves in two years. Much longer, and readers will forget who you are."

Faith set her wineglass down hard on the linen tablecloth. "That's bullshit," she said. "I have a healthy fan base. I may not be John Grisham, but I'm not hurting for readers."

"Bullshit it may be, but it's the party line, and the party is who writes you those nice fat advance checks." Marie set down her fork and picked up a dinner roll. Tearing it in two, she reached for a butter packet. "I've done as much dancing around these people as I can. As it is, I practically had to promise them my firstborn male child to get the three months." She painstakingly unwrapped the foil-covered packet and generously applied butter to the roll. "This'll go straight to my hips," she said, "but do you think I can resist any kind of fresh-baked bread? When it comes to willpower, I'm as substantial as a marshmallow. Look, Faith." Her dark eyes, rimmed by sooty lashes, softened. "There won't be another extension. The bottom line is that you produce a publishable manuscript within ninety days or they'll sue you for breach of contract."

"Christ on crutches." Faith let out a breath and closed her eyes against the blinding pain worming its way into permanent residence behind her right temple. When she opened them again, Marie was shoveling salad into her mouth with ravenous enthusiasm. The woman was whipcord lean and had the appetite of a velociraptor. Faith opened her mouth, then closed it as panic worked chilly, treacherous fingers up her spine. Firmly, she said, "I can't do this, Marie."

"Stop." Marie swallowed and pointed her fork. "Stop right now. I swear to God, if I hear the words *writer's block* coming from your lips, I'm going to scream."

"It's not writer's block. I don't believe in writer's block."

"I know there's something in that statement that should comfort me. So why doesn't it?"

Marie's face was open and appealing, her zest for life etched in every line, and Faith tried to smother the guilt she felt at the prospect of disappointing the woman. Marie was more than a literary agent. She was a dear friend, not to mention an ardent fan. Faith searched desperately for the right words to explain something for which she, a woman who made her living with words, had none. "I can't feel the story anymore," she said. The blank expression on Marie's face reflected the inadequacy of her explanation. She tried again. "I don't have any emotional connection to it. I don't give a damn about any of my characters. I don't even remember why I wanted to write it in the first place."

It was the truth. Just not the entire truth. These days, she had no emotional connection to anything or anyone. Her inability to complete *Blood Sport* was merely a symptom of something larger, something that encompassed her entire life.

"Fake it," Marie said. "It's fiction. It's all made up anyway."

"And you know as well as I do that you can't write fiction without emotion. Not good fiction, anyway. Right now, Dr. Seuss has more depth than anything I could write."

Still waving her fork, Marie said, "Seems to me he did all right for himself with that red fish, blue fish jazz. Look, kiddo, at this point I really don't think Moon and West is looking for depth. They're looking for a finished manuscript. Something to fit into next year's fall schedule." Marie glanced at the slender gold watch on her left wrist. "Shit. I have to run. I have a two o'clock appointment and it's already quarter of." She set down her fork, dabbed at her lips with her napkin, and signaled the waiter for the check. "I hate being the bad guy," she said, "but you don't really have a choice. You're not in a position to pay back the advance, and if you fail to produce a manuscript…well, as they say in Tinseltown, you'll never work in this town again."

On the sidewalk outside the restaurant, Marie raised an arm, and a bright-yellow taxi pulled up to the curb. The woman had an enviable knack for hailing cabs that Faith had never been able to emulate. Marie opened the rear door of the cab, then paused beside it. "You can do this," she said. "I have absolute faith in you. All you have to do is put your mind to it. Practice a little positive thinking."

"*Rah-rah-rah,*" Faith said dryly. "I'm surprised you didn't bring your cheerleader sweater and pom-poms."

Marie grinned and climbed into the waiting cab. "I know you won't let me down," she said, smoothing her skirt around shapely knees, "because if you do, we'll both end up on a street corner, selling pencils from a tin cup." Marie slammed shut the door to the taxi, said something to the driver, and the Crown Victoria sped away from the curb, leaving Faith alone on the sidewalk, once again a victim of the whirlwind that was Marie Spinelli.

She knew what Marie was up to. The woman might have been playing the heavy, but her motives were as transparent as window glass. Marie had been right there while Ben was dying, had seen firsthand the hell that Faith went through. There was no way Marie believed that she was acting the part of the temperamental *artiste*. Underneath her tough exterior, Marie Spinelli was worried. The steamroller act was her unique form of tough love, predicated on the theory that the occasional swift kick in the ass never hurt anyone, and might just help restore Faith's equilibrium.

If only it were that easy, Faith would have gladly bent over and presented the aforementioned body part to Marie for enthusiastic kicking.

She set off on foot, automatically matching her stride to that of her fellow New Yorkers. Brisk, purposeful, unwavering. The only people who dawdled on the sidewalks of New York were muggers, dope dealers, and tourists. Pausing at a busy intersection, she glanced to her right and caught sight of herself in a store window. The woman who stared back was slender and petite, her dark hair a little wild, her blue eyes wide and direct. Not unattractive, if you discounted the tiny creases at the corners of her mouth. Anybody looking at her would have thought she was normal. Nobody would have guessed that like Humpty Dumpty, she'd been broken into a gazillion pieces, and nobody—not Marie, not Dr. Garabedian, not even Faith herself—could put her back together again.

The light changed, the walk signal lit up, and the crowd surged forward, carrying her along with it. The only writing she'd done in two and a half years was comments scribbled in the margins of student papers. *Sentence fragment. Misplaced modifier. Weak thesis statement.* Yet Marie—not to mention the entire editorial department at Moon and West— expected her to pull a completed *Blood Sport* out of a hat in a mere ninety days, as if the last eighteen months of her life hadn't been a train wreck punctuated by a pharmacopoeia impressive enough to turn Walgreen's and CVS both green with envy. One pill to help her fall asleep, another to help her wake up. One to raise her spirits, another to subdue them. Until Dr. Garabedian had begun weaning her off her vast array of medications two months ago, she'd been a walking, talking testament to better living through chemistry. Except that she wasn't really living, just marking time.

Until what? That was the sixty-four-thousand-dollar question. When she entered the foyer of her town house, she auto-

matically braced herself for the rush of padded feet, the clicking of toenails on polished hardwood, the joyful welcome
from a wriggling bundle of soft fur and wet, sloppy kisses.
Buddy launched himself at her, and she returned his greeting,
then struggled to disentangle herself from forty pounds of
blissful, mixed-breed mutt.

She'd never been much of a dog person. Buddy had belonged to Ben, had suffered from an unmistakable case of
hero worship, following him around everywhere he went.
For a long time after Ben died, Buddy had moped about the
house, lying for hours in sunny locations, all sad brown eyes
and long-suffering sighs. She'd considered giving him away
to some family in the country, someone with a half-dozen kids
he could play with and acres of fields where he could run.
But she couldn't bring herself to do it. Buddy offered her
unconditional love and friendship at a time when she sorely
needed both.

Vigorously rubbing him behind the ears, she said, "We'll
take a walk in a little while. Okay?" Flashing a wide doggy
grin, tongue lolling, Buddy wagged enthusiastic agreement.

She picked up her mail from the floor in the foyer and went
to the kitchen to make a cup of tea. The light on her answering machine was flashing red. Probably a telemarketer. These
days, telemarketers were just about the only people who
called. Faith filled the teakettle and set it on to heat, pushed
the button on the answering machine, and began shuffling
through the mail.

Junk mail. Bank statement. More junk mail. The first call
was a hang-up, followed by ten seconds of screeching dial
tone. Faith tossed the junk mail on the counter and tore open
the bank statement. The machine beeped, and the next message began to play.

"Faith? This is Chief Tyrone Savage with the Serenity Police Department."

Bank statement in hand, she froze. On the stove, the teakettle began to hiss as the water neared boiling point. The tinny

recording continued. "I need you to call me at 207-555-4528 at your earliest convenience. Again, that number's 207-555-4528."

The kettle whistled, and she reached with trembling hand to turn off the burner. Had he really said Tyrone Savage? *Police Chief* Tyrone Savage? Just to be certain she hadn't heard him wrong, she replayed the message. But it wasn't really necessary, for she would have recognized that voice anywhere. It was a little deeper than she remembered, his Maine accent a little more pronounced. Eighteen years had passed since she'd last heard it. But she couldn't possibly fail to recognize Ty's voice.

He'd broken her heart. Worse still, he'd never even known it. How could she tell the boy who'd been her best friend since childhood that one balmy spring Saturday, somewhere between Bald Mountain Road and the Dairy Queen, she'd fallen head over heels in love with him? They'd been just kids, barely eighteen years old, neither of them anywhere near ready for any kind of serious relationship. Besides, if she'd confessed her feelings to him and he hadn't felt the same way, she would have died of mortification.

So she'd kept her feelings to herself. And it was just as well, considering that a week before graduation, Chelsea had bragged to her about doing the nasty with Ty out behind the high school bleachers in retaliation for Davy's supposed infidelity.

Faith had been devastated. Just like every other boy in town, Ty had chosen her cousin over her. And who could blame him? Chelsea was beautiful and vivacious in a way she would never be. She'd wanted to hate Chelsea, but she couldn't even do that. It wasn't as though Faith had her name tattooed on his body. Ty Savage was a free agent, and if he wanted to sleep with her cousin, he had every right in the world.

So she'd taken her broken heart off to college and never looked back. But it had been a long time before she got over it, a long time before she trusted her heart enough to love again. She'd eventually met Ben. Everything had felt so right with him, and she'd put the memory of Ty Savage behind her.

She couldn't imagine why he would be calling her now, and she had half a mind to simply ignore his message. Talking to strangers wasn't high on her list of favored activities these days, and for all intents and purposes, Ty was a stranger. They'd known each other so very long ago.

But he must be calling for a reason. He was, after all, the police. There was a certain poetic justice to that, for he'd hated being the son of a cop. Perhaps he now had a son of his own who hated it just as much. The idea left a strange, tight feeling in her belly as she dialed the number and asked for Chief Savage.

She was immediately placed on hold. While she waited, phone braced between ear and shoulder, she made her cup of tea. She was swishing the tea bag around in the cup when he picked up and said, in a soft, low voice, "Savage."

There was something intensely sexy about that voice. Faith caught her breath and reminded herself that he probably had a wife and six kids, a potbelly and thinning hair, and lived in a rusty trailer with hay bales stacked around the skirting. "Ty?" she said in her most perky voice. "It's Faith. Faith Pelletier,"

There was the briefest hesitation before he said, "Faith. Thanks for getting right back to me. I called about Chelsea."

She let out a breath. *Hell and blast and damn.* She should have known that if the police were calling, Chelsea was involved. Ever since they were twelve years old, Chelsea had been getting into messes and she'd been bailing her out. Some things never changed.

With a sigh of resignation, she said, "What kind of trouble has she gotten herself into this time?"

Again, that brief hesitation. "I hate like hell to have to break this to you over the phone."

Dread slithered up her spine. Her fingers tightened on the phone cord. "What?" she said. "What's happened?"

He cleared his throat and said, "Your cousin was killed last night."

Three

She was afraid to fly, and since Buddy couldn't ride Amtrak, Faith packed the dog, her laptop, and a suitcase full of clothes and drove to Maine in Ben's Saab. It was a long trip, one that Buddy clearly enjoyed, sitting in the passenger seat with his chest puffed out like an admiral, grinning his goofy Forrest Gump grin. All the way to Portsmouth, she kept asking herself why she was doing this. She had a book to write. A deadline hanging over her head. She barely knew Jessie, and Davy was taking care of the funeral arrangements. He and Chelsea used to be married. Let him take responsibility for Jessie. She was probably his daughter anyway.

She stopped questioning herself once she crossed the state line and passed the sign that read: Welcome to Maine, The Way Life Should Be. Whoever came up with that slogan had obviously never visited Serenity. And now that she'd crossed that invisible line of demarcation, it no longer mattered why she was here, because somehow, in spite of her long-standing vow to never again set foot north of the Piscataqua River Bridge, Faith Pelletier had come home.

Home hadn't changed much. From Kittery to Portland, the Maine Turnpike still boasted the same stunning view of trees, trees, and more trees. Portland was a brief blur of shopping malls and motels. Then it was trees again, all the way to Auburn, where she clicked her blinker and exited the turnpike for the final leg of her journey.

"Keep your eyes open," she told Buddy. "You're about to get a rare treat. A firsthand look at the Maine the tourists never see."

He wagged agreement. Buddy always agreed with everything she said. In fact, he was the most agreeable traveling companion she'd ever had. Much more agreeable than Ben, who had hated to travel and had always grumped and sulked until they reached their destination.

After the endless monotony of the turnpike, the congested streets of Auburn were a welcome sight. Civilization, or what passed for it in these parts. She followed the river north to the outskirts of town, past car dealers and fast-food restaurants and shopping malls, and then she was out of the city and headed into the wilds of Western Maine.

The highway was in better shape than she remembered, the hum of her tires on the asphalt reassuring. After two decades of living in the skyscraper canyons of Manhattan, she found the open fields and the distant mountains foreign, almost otherworldly. But the back roads were still somewhat familiar, and there were enough major landmarks left standing to help her navigate. The scenery had changed a bit; in the years since she'd left, new homes had swallowed up more and more of what had formerly been undeveloped land, and trailers, much more aesthetically pleasing than their forebears, dotted the landscape. Nobody even called them trailers anymore. Gentrification had given them not only a new look, but a new name: manufactured housing.

Driving alongside railroad tracks that looked as though they hadn't been used in decades, she passed an auto supply store and a John Deere dealership. Here and there, she saw signs advertising names she'd nearly forgotten: Polaris, Jonsered, Husqvarna. Chain saws and snowmobiles were an integral part of life here in rural Maine. People depended on them for their livelihood, sometimes even for their lives. Logging was obviously still a major industry, judging by the number of loaded pulp trucks she saw headed for the paper mill in Rumford.

The river took a sharp turn, and she caught her first glimpse of Serenity, nestled into the valley spread out before her, the late-afternoon sun glinting off the windows of the triple-decker apartment buildings that marched in neat rows, like soldiers in formation, up the steep hillside east of town. From her vantage point, she could see the antiquated green iron bridge that spanned the river, overshadowed by the twin chimneys of the now defunct Mollyockett Manufacturing. For forty years, Cyrus Logan had worked in the spinning room at Mollyockett. Every morning, he would leave for work with coal-black hair. And every night, he would come home transformed, his hair, his beard, even his eyebrows turned white by cotton dust. Too young to understand the damage that repeated exposure to the ceaseless blizzard could do to a man's lungs, she and Chelsea used to giggle about it behind his back.

It had killed him in the end. He'd died last August of emphysema and sheer orneriness. She hadn't gone to his funeral. It had been less than a year since she'd lost Ben, and she was still dealing with the fallout. Besides, Cyrus Logan had been a miserable excuse for a human being. He'd been a horrid man, and she'd spent every day of the six years she lived under his roof planning her escape.

For Chelsea's sake, she'd sent flowers and a card instead. Through some unfortunate accident of birth, the old goat was, after all, Chelsea's father. And she and Chelsea had been close once, in some dim past that she'd struggled for years to put behind her. Now, due to a similar accident of birth, she was expected to take responsibility for Chelsea's teenage daughter. It was the right thing to do under the circumstances, and she kept telling herself that was why she was here. Just as Cyrus Logan had taken her in, she would do the same for his granddaughter. A family obligation, nothing more.

It had nothing to do with the fact that, although she had settled into a stable and comfortable lifestyle with Ben, she'd never quite been able to break her bond with the erratic and irresponsible cousin who'd once seemed as essential to her as her own right arm. It had nothing to do with the bleakness of those first few months after the sudden loss of her parents when she was twelve. Nothing to do with the fact that her first response upon receiving word of Chelsea's orphaned daughter was a wrenching stab of empathy, the first true emotion she'd felt since Ben died. Faith had once walked in Jessie Logan's shoes, and it hadn't been an easy walk. Nearly a quarter of a century had passed since that awful day when her parents died, and she still hadn't fully recovered from the loss.

But of course that wasn't why she was here.

She crossed the bridge, rattled over obsolete railroad tracks, and passed the mill, its brick chimneys inactive, its parking lot empty, the pavement cracked and choked with weeds. Some of the windows were broken, others boarded up. The gate was closed, its chain-link fence secured with a rusty padlock and a No Trespassing sign, the town's lingering death formalized by those two seemingly innocuous words.

Aside from a half-dozen empty storefronts where eighteen years ago there'd been none, Water Street looked pretty much the way she remembered it. Businesses had come and gone; a Subway shop now occupied the space where the pizza parlor had stood, and the pet shop had morphed into Information Systems, LLC. Even in this far-flung outpost of civilization, the advance of technology marched relentlessly onward. The real estate office, its window adorned with the biggest asparagus fern she'd ever seen, had changed hands, and Depositors Trust, the small local bank where her parents had done their banking, had been swallowed by the massive conglomerate that was Key Bank. But two doors down, Phil Bonner still cut hair in his barbershop, tucked in a narrow space between the *River City Gazette* and the police station. And halfway down the block, Lenny's Café still advertised the best breakfast in town.

Like the main thoroughfares in many New England downtowns, Water Street was limited to one-way traffic, and in order to get to where she wanted to go, Faith had to circle around behind the business district and backtrack. Here, the true face of Serenity became evident. The backside of downtown boasted a pawn shop and a video rental store, its windows gummed up with tape from old movie posters. Beside the regional Probation and Parole office sat an extinct mom-and-pop store that predated the convenience store era. Boarded up for decades, it still bore a rusted Pepsi sign.

But Androscoggin Street's biggest claim to fame was its half-dozen bars, their grimy windows blackened to keep daylight at bay, their presence announced by signs advertising Old Milwaukee, Schlitz, and Budweiser, king of beers. Blue-collar joints, blue-collar beers. No fancy microbrews here. Most of these establishments didn't even have names posted outside their doors. No names were needed; the locals knew they were here, and nobody else cared.

At the end of Androscoggin Street, she circled a small park where an American flag flapped proudly in the wind beside a square of polished granite embedded with a plaque that bore the names of local men who'd died in service to their country. Bright red tulips, most likely planted by the VFW, surrounded the flagpole and the stone that held the plaque. Taking a right toward Bald Mountain Road, she passed Food City, its parking lot half-full of dented pickup trucks and Detroit-made cars with a few years on them. Few people here drove new cars. Ben's Saab would stick out like the proverbial sore thumb.

Bald Mountain Road wound through the hills and valleys east of town, through dense woods and open fields greening up with spring. Three miles out, surrounded by acres of blueberry barrens and scrub vegetation, Cyrus Logan's turn-of-the-century farmhouse sat halfway up Bald Mountain. Faith pulled into the dirt drive and parked by the old chicken coop. Although the intervening years had turned it into a pile of rusted wire and silvered wood, the coop had once held chickens. It had been her duty to feed those chickens, and she'd hated them with a passion unparalleled in her young life. They'd been truly nasty creatures, dirty and smelly and mean, and she'd quickly learned to toss the chicken feed at them and run.

She got out of the car and turned Buddy loose. Nose to the ground, he scurried to and fro, lifted his leg on one corner of the chicken coop, then raced around the back of the house to see what trouble he could find there. Faith zipped her jacket against the brutal wind. She'd left her gloves in New York, where the temperature had been seasonal. She'd forgotten how late spring arrived in these Western Maine hills. Here in Oxford County, it felt more like mid-March than mid-May.

She was home. Odd, but it didn't feel like home. She'd spent six years of her life in this house, six excruciating years of putting up with Cyrus Logan's tyranny, yet she felt no connection to it whatsoever. She gazed emotionlessly at its weathered face. The house possessed no ghosts, other than the ghosts of those long-dead chickens. It was simply a house, one that could have used a new roof, decent siding and vinyl replacement windows.

Hands tucked into her pockets, she swung around, turning her back to the wind. The view to the west was breathtaking, hills and valleys stretching into infinity, a sweeping vista of light and shadow, greens and blues and blacks merging into the distant bluish peak of Mount Washington, still capped with snow and silhouetted against a bloodred sky. The view had been one of the few things that made living here tolerable. That, and Chelsea. For a time, she'd been obsessed with her cousin, who was so much prettier, so much more daring, so much trendier than she was. Chelsea was everybody's darling, the bird of paradise, while Faith was just the plain brown wren who fluttered along behind her.

Now, standing here in Uncle Cy's driveway as a northerly wind that carried the fresh, muddy scent of spring slammed into her with almost gale force, the truth struck her for the first time: Chelsea was gone. Chelsea, who'd been more of a sister than a cousin, who had kept her sane during those six dreadful years. Chelsea, who'd outshone her in every way, who had manipulated her, made unreasonable demands of her, walked all over her. Chelsea, who had protected her with all the passion and ferocity of a mother bear protecting one of its cubs.

Chelsea Logan had been her salvation. And now she was dead.

Faith whistled for Buddy, who came bounding jubilantly from somewhere in the back forty. She opened the door of the Saab and he scrambled up into the seat, muddy feet leaving a trail across the leather upholstery. Faith swiped at the mud, then got in behind him and turned on the heater.

Once her hands had warmed enough to be operational, she drove off in the gathering dusk to find Davy Hunter's place, where Jessie waited for her. Ty had given her detailed directions and then wished her luck. She hadn't been quite sure how she was supposed to take that. Had it been a warning of some kind? She'd finally decided to take his words at face value. What else could she do? This situation was not of her own making. Life had handed her a lemon, and she had no option but to make lemonade.

Davy lived on the other side of Bald Mountain, which wasn't really a mountain at all, just what passed for one in this neck of the woods. Faith crested the peak, then drove back down the steep, winding road to the bottom. Following Ty's directions, she took the dirt road at the foot of the hill. It led her past an antediluvian swamp that stretched on for half a mile, dark and eerie and ominous. Sasquatch country. Anything she might meet up with in a Manhattan alley was nothing compared to what she might find out here.

She tamped down her anxiety and kept driving. Daylight disappeared quickly here in the valley, and dusk had almost turned to darkness when she found his driveway, marked by a single blue reflector. It was little more than a narrow, rutted path, the undergrowth on both sides vying with it for survival. Faith followed it, cussing as she hit a pothole hard enough to slam her teeth together.

The driveway ended abruptly in front of an ancient trailer. No manufactured housing this. It was a trailer in the true sense of the word, the kind you could have backed some big-ass V8 station wagon up to and hauled away. Roughly eight feet wide, it might have been thirty-five feet long. Enough of the original paint remained to tell her it had once been green, but most of that green was gone. Where it wasn't green, it was gray, weathered by time and the elements. Where it wasn't gray, it was rust colored. The roof was lined with old tires to keep it from buckling in the wind, and one of the louvered windows above the trailer hitch had been broken and repaired with cardboard and duct tape.

An aluminum stovepipe stuck out the back wall, smoke drifting from the makeshift chimney. A satellite dish, incongruous in its setting, was attached to the roof of a plywood lean-to that somebody had tacked on as an entryway. If she hadn't seen the turquoise 1962 Biscayne abandoned in the weeds out back of the trailer, exactly where Ty had told her she'd find it, she would have thought she was in the wrong place. She considered the very real possibility of backing up the car and leaving. It wasn't too late to turn tail and run. Hard to believe that a little over twenty-four hours ago, she'd been sitting at Manhattan's trendiest new restaurant with Marie, sipping white wine. Now she was here, trapped on some distant, alien planet, with just Buddy for protection.

Christ on crutches. What had she gotten herself into?

She turned off the car. "You stay here," she told Buddy. He gazed at her through mournful eyes, probably wondering if she was going to leave him the way Ben had. "I'll be back," she said, "honest." He didn't look as though he believed her, but he laid his chin on his paws and stayed put.

She stepped out of the car and closed the door. The whine of a table saw drew her attention to a small outbuilding beside the trailer. She crossed the lawn and stepped up into the open doorway. Inside, beneath a single bare bulb that dangled from the ceiling, a man in a plaid flannel shirt guided a piece of lumber through the saw, releasing the pungent scent of fresh-cut cedar. Sawdust flew wildly in every direction. Above the screeching protest of saw blade on wood, a radio played some country song she didn't know.

Faith stood in the doorway and waited for him to notice her, reluctant to announce herself for fear that she'd startle him and he'd cut off some crucial anatomical part. He guided the wood with an expert hand while, in the background, a rumbly-voiced country singer crooned about love lost and found again.

The saw ground to a halt, and he finally looked up and noticed her. Eighteen years had wrought changes in his appearance. Wrinkles fanned out from the corners of his eyes, and his hair hung in a ponytail halfway to his waist. His eyes, red rimmed and tired, held a distance that was disconcerting. Davy Hunter looked like a man who'd seen too much of the hard life and was no longer interested in civilized human interactions.

"Faith," he said curtly.

"Davy." She hesitated, uncertain of how to proceed, not quite comfortable in his presence, even though she'd known him since childhood. "I'm sorry," she said finally. It wasn't enough, but nothing else seemed appropriate to the occasion.

He acknowledged her words with a brief nod. "I imagine you're looking for the girl," he said.

That was a dismissal if ever she'd heard one. "Is there anything I can do?" she said. "To help with the funeral? Or—" She paused, suddenly tongue-tied.

He stared at her stonily, blue eyes hard and inhuman. Abruptly turning his back on her, he picked up the piece of cedar he'd just cut, and ran his hands over it. "Arrangements are all made," he said. "Girl's in the trailer."

"Well," she said, tucking her hands in her pockets because

she didn't know what else to do with them. "I guess I'll see you tomorrow then."

"Nope."

That stopped her in her tracks. To his back, she said, "I won't see you at the funeral?"

"Nope." Davy bent and took his time selecting another piece of lumber from a neat stack beside the table. He turned it over in his hands, studying it closely, before abandoning it for a different piece. Apparently satisfied, he straightened and placed the slab of lumber on the table saw, lining it up carefully with the blade. "I won't be there," he said.

And he turned the saw back on.

Four

The aroma of meat loaf hit him the instant he walked through the door, reminding Ty that a cup of chicken noodle soup and a vending machine turkey sandwich were woefully inadequate to keep a two-hundred-pound man alive. He hung his coat in the hall closet, kicked off his size thirteens, then climbed barefoot to his second-floor bedroom tucked under the eaves of the little bungalow where he'd grown up. He locked his gun and holster in the cabinet where he kept them when he was off duty, then traded his uniform for jeans and a flannel shirt.

In the kitchen, Buck had the radio tuned to the local AM station. The Red Sox were playing a doubleheader tonight against Cleveland, and Buck's attention was divided between the potatoes he was mashing and the homer that Manny Ramirez had just hit. Ty took a can of beer from the fridge and went to the cupboard for a glass. He stood there for a moment in front of the open cupboard door, pondering the jar of relish that was tucked between the thirty-year-old Tupperware that wouldn't die and the inexpensive Wal-Mart glasses he had to keep replacing because Buck kept breaking them. Ty shot his father a quizzical glance. With a shake of his head, he took the relish out of the cupboard and returned it to its rightful place in the refrigerator.

"That Ramirez," Buck said, over the ball game and the buzz of the electric mixer, "he's some ballplayer."

Pouring beer into his glass, Ty mumbled something incoherent.

"Course, he's no Ted Williams," Buck said, setting the mixer on the counter and unplugging it. "Now *there* was a ballplayer. But the Sox have a strong team this year. They'll take the pennant, I guarantee you."

His father had been making this same claim every season for as far back as Ty could remember. Since the Red Sox hadn't won a World Series since 1918, he refrained from making a response. "Meat loaf smells good," he said instead.

Buck popped the beaters from the mixer into the sink. "Your mother always said my meat loaf was better than hers."

Ty held his glass of beer aloft in silent tribute to his father's culinary skills. It was a good thing Buck knew his way around a kitchen. If they'd had to depend on Ty's talents as a chef, they'd be living on pasta and scrambled eggs.

They ate at the kitchen table with the radio still tuned to the game. Not exactly conducive to stimulating conversation, with Buck's attention cemented to the Red Sox, just as it was every game night for six months out of each year. While Buck listened to the game, Ty mentally reviewed what he knew about Chelsea Logan's death. No matter how he looked at it, no matter what scenario he posed, no matter what questions he asked himself, he inevitably found the answers troubling. There was no rational reason Chelsea should have driven into the river at a ninety-degree angle on a straight stretch of highway unless she'd done it deliberately.

"I went down to see Spence Goodwin today," Buck said during a break between innings. "He said he'd give me a good deal on a truck."

Yanked abruptly from his ruminations, Ty raised his head and blinked a couple of times while he processed his father's words. "Why'd you do that?" he said. "I told you not to buy a truck from Spencer Goodwin. He'll screw you five ways to

Sunday. Go talk to Claude Larochelle. At least he won't steal your trade-in."

"Spence isn't that bad." Buck buttered a slice of bread. "He's selling a three-year-old F-150 that's only got twenty-eight thousand on her. Barely broke in. Four-wheel drive, plow attachment. And he said he'd give me a good deal on a trade."

Ty set down his fork. "Damn it, Dad, you didn't sign anything, did you?"

Buck braced both palms against the table and drew his bushy white eyebrows together. Not a good sign. "I've been buying cars since long before you were born, smart-mouth. I think I can handle it without any help from you."

"Dad," he said reasonably, "I'm just trying to keep you from being taken for a ride."

"Do I look like a goddamn idiot, Tyrone? I can read the fine print just as good as you can. Christ Almighty."

Before he could formulate a response, the game came back on. Buck got up from the table and scraped the remainder of his meal into the rubbish. Dropping his plate into the sink, the old man unplugged the radio and took it with him into the living room. A moment later, the game started up again.

Open mouth, insert foot. It seemed as though Ty couldn't say or do anything right lately. Buck was as prickly as a porcupine in heat. Not that they hadn't always had their differences. When Ty was a teenager and Buck was the police chief, they'd barely tolerated each other. But time, and some much needed maturing on Ty's part, had healed that earlier rift. He was only trying to help. Lately, Buck just hadn't been himself. At seventy-three, he wasn't as sharp as he'd once been. His memory was failing in little ways, things like the relish in the cupboard. It was probably a normal part of the aging process. But normal or not, it still made Buck a ripe candidate for exploitation, and Ty had no intention of letting anybody take advantage of his old man.

He finished his meal, then washed the dishes and put the

rest of the food away. His father would eat the leftovers for lunch tomorrow. There might even be enough left for Ty to make a meat loaf sandwich for his own lunch. It sure as hell beat the cardboard fare he got from the vending machine at the station.

He found Buck in the living room, ensconced in his recliner, feet up and an open book on his lap. His father was a big fan of Tom Clancy, but it seemed as though he'd been on page 238 of this book for a month now.

Ty sat on the couch and attempted civilized conversation. "How's the book going?"

Buck closed the thick paperback and smacked it onto the table next to the radio. "It's just like every other damn book of his. Read one, you've read 'em all."

He cleared his throat and tried again. "Speaking of writers, Faith Pelletier's in town. Pete saw her downtown this afternoon, driving a red Saab with New York plates. She's here for the funeral. And for Chelsea's daughter. I imagine she'll take Jessie back to New York with her."

"Red Sox are whipping the pants off of Cleveland," Buck said irritably. "Where's the friggin' fun in that? No challenge at all." He leaned over the arm of the chair and snapped off the radio. "That kid's been carted from pillar to post all her life. Be nice if she could stay put now that she's finally started to set down roots. I imagine she'll inherit the house."

"House isn't worth much," Ty said.

"Christ, where'd you get that damn cynicism of yours? Must've come from your mother. God rest her soul."

"Dad," he said gently, "Mom's not dead."

"I know she's not dead, you damn fool!" Buck lowered the recliner with a thump and placed both feet flat on the floor. "She's across town, living in sin with that snot-nosed Gilpatrick kid. I figure the harlot needs all the help she can get from God."

Ty closed his eyes. There wasn't even a remote possibility of coming up with an appropriate response to his father's words. Buck wouldn't appreciate anything he had to say on the topic anyway, and it wouldn't do anybody any good to remind him that Jeff Gilpatrick was hardly a snot-nosed kid. The man was a respectable fifty-six years old, just five years younger than Glenda Savage. Not exactly a gigolo.

And it was a bit of a stretch for Ty to imagine his gray-haired, matronly mother as a harlot, even if she and Jeff were living in sin. Their marital status, or lack thereof, was their own private business. She and Buck had been divorced for five years. If Glenda wanted to live in sin, or—God forbid—sleep with the entire graduating class of the U.S. Naval Academy, it was none of Buck Savage's business.

And sure as hell none of Ty's.

His stomach soured. Maybe it hadn't been such a hot idea after all, moving back home after he and Linda split up. It had seemed the ideal solution at the time. He was alone, and so was Buck. The house had plenty of room for both of them. Just two carefree bachelors, living it up together.

"I'm going out," he said. "I'll be back in an hour or two."

Buck glanced toward the window. "Lousy night to be going out if you don't have to. That wind's howling like it's February."

"I'll manage somehow, Dad." He went to the hall closet and took out his coat. Standing in the kitchen doorway, he said, "Anything I can pick up for you while I'm out?"

Buck lifted the television remote and clicked it on. Dan Rather's face filled the screen. "If I need anything," Buck said, "I can get it myself."

"Figured that's what you'd say," he told Buck, and let himself out the back door.

Jessie Logan was a silent little thing with limp brown hair and wire-framed glasses. She looked younger than the fifteen Faith knew her to be. The girl might be in deep mourning, but if she was, it was impossible to tell. She didn't make conversation, didn't show interest in anything Faith had to say and was polite to a fault.

Faith didn't claim to know much about teenagers. The

closest she'd ever come to motherhood was a week spent en-
tertaining Ben's twelve-year-old niece while the girl's mother
was away on a Caribbean honeymoon cruise with husband
number three. She realized that she and Jessie were virtual
strangers; the girl had been eight years old the last time they'd
seen each other. Still, she wasn't sure this was how teenagers
were supposed to act. Chelsea's daughter was so demure, so
staid, Faith found herself wondering if it was all an act. Did
Jessie let her hair down, drink and smoke and dance on table-
tops when there were no adults around? Was this somber
young sparrow dressed in monochromatic shades of gray the
real Jessie? Or was the kid simply going through the numbness, all too familiar to Faith, that accompanied the sudden,
unexpected loss of her mother?

Either way, it seemed she wasn't going to get an answer
from Jessie. When they reached the Logan place, the girl
climbed out of the car with her backpack slung over her shoulder, lowered her head against the wind, and marched stolidly
to the house. After unlocking the back door, Jessie stood in
the kitchen with her coat still on and said without inflection,
"You can sleep in the guest room at the top of the stairs. I'm
going to my room now." Without another word, she left Faith
standing alone in the kitchen.

Maybe she really was Davy's daughter after all.

Faith slogged back out to the car, dragged in her luggage
and her laptop, and carted it all upstairs to the guest room.
Years ago, this room had been a repository for the abandoned
belongings of Chelsea's runaway mother. When his wife left
him, Cyrus Logan simply boxed up her things and locked
them in this room, where he wouldn't be bothered by the
constant reminder of what he'd lost. Sometimes, when he
was out carousing with his drinking buddies or passed out on
his bed, Faith and Chelsea would sneak in here to look at the
possessions Adrienne Logan had left behind. A handful of
drab little dresses, a few pieces of costume jewelry, a box of
knickknacks, wrapped carefully in newspaper, all of it myste-

rious and exotic in the eyes of a pair of adolescent girls. There'd even been a sewing machine, one that must have cost someone dearly. Faith wondered now what had become of Adrienne's belongings. Had Cyrus disposed of them at some point before he died? Or had Chelsea finally given up on the childhood fantasies she'd woven around her mysterious, departed mother and donated the items to Goodwill?

Now the room held a twin bed with a white ruffled spread, a simple pine dresser, and an oval braided rug. Faith unpacked and hung her clothes in the tiny closet under the eaves, draping each item carefully on its hanger to prevent wrinkles. She scouted around the room for a telephone outlet, but there didn't seem to be one. Acting on a hunch, she got down on her knees and lifted the spread. Sure enough, there was the phone jack, dangling from the baseboard at the head of the bed. She crawled halfway under the bed to plug in her laptop, then brushed the dust bunnies from her knees and elbows and booted up the computer.

The gods were smiling upon her; the phone line was in working order, and she dialed in to check her e-mail. With a series of rapid mouse clicks, she deleted the various ads offering penis enlargement, guaranteed weight loss, and low-cost mortgage refinancing. There were several messages from fans; she skimmed each one briefly, then saved them all in a new folder to respond to at a later time.

She opened Marie's e-mail last. Being the utter coward she was, she'd e-mailed her agent instead of calling. Just a brief note to say there'd been a death in the family and she would be out of town for a few days. Marie's response was similarly brief: "My condolences. Call if you need anything. Stay in touch, and write, write, write!"

There was nothing else of any significance, so she shut down the computer and stood at the window, arms crossed as she gazed out into the utter blackness of the rural Maine night. She'd forgotten what it was like out here in the boondocks, with the nearest neighbor a half mile away and acres of blackness between her and civilization. The city girl she'd become found the absence of light and noise and people disquieting. There was something eerie about a darkness so absolute that, had she been standing in it, she wouldn't have been able to see her hand in front of her face. It frightened her. There, she'd admitted it. It was a damn-fool thing, but then most phobias were. Faith Pelletier, who'd never feared anything until her husband died, now slept with a night-light because she was terrified of what might be out there in the dark, just beyond her reach. Waiting to reach out for her.

Her chest tightened. *Stop*, she told herself. *Stop it this instant.* With slow, careful breaths, she suppressed the anxiety. Stepping away from the window, she gazed regretfully at her purse, sitting neatly on the dresser, the bottle of tranquilizers inside drawing her like a beacon. It was all she had left; Dr. Garabedian had taken away everything else. It was only a matter of time before he took the Valium away, too. "Use them only for emergencies," he'd told her. It was time, he said, to start backing off, time to learn to function again without their help. Sooner or later, he'd reminded her, she would have to reclaim her purloined life.

Her life. Faith absently rubbed her temple and thought longingly of home. She couldn't leave this place soon enough. But that wouldn't happen until she'd closed up Chelsea's house, hired somebody to keep an eye on the place, put it on the market if it came to that. She'd have to pack up all Jessie's things, pick up her school records and whatever medical records were available. She could be stuck here for a couple of weeks. Maybe even longer. All while she was supposed to be working on *Blood Sport*.

It was impossible. There was no way she could work on the book with so many other responsibilities tugging her in different directions. *Blood Sport* would have to wait until she got things settled here. She'd call Marie in the morning and tell her that things in Serenity were more complicated than she'd anticipated, and that it might be a couple of weeks before she could get back to the book. Once things were settled here, she and Jessie would climb into Ben's car—she still thought of the Saab as his—and head home to New York.

Faith wrapped her arms more tightly around her and rubbed her elbows. It was cold in this ark of a house. And her stomach was screaming to be fed. It was getting late; Jessie must be starving, too. Stepping into the hall, she glanced around, then moved toward the only door that was closed. Knocking softly, she said, "Jessie? Are you hungry? I thought I'd check out the fridge and see what I can find for us."

Silence. She waited, tried again. "How about a grilled cheese sandwich and a glass of milk?" Kids loved grilled cheese sandwiches. Didn't they?

"I already ate." Jessie's voice, coming from behind the closed door, was muffled. "At Davy's."

It wasn't much, but it was better than silence. Again, she hesitated. "You're sure there's nothing I can get you?"

"I'm not hungry. Thank you, anyway."

It was pointless to argue. She couldn't force the girl to eat. Where the hell was Ben when she needed him? He'd been a natural with kids. He would have known what to do. But Ben was gone, and she was on her own. Baby steps. That's what Dr. Garabedian had told her. *Think of life in terms of baby steps.*

"I'm going downstairs to find something to eat," she said. "If there's anything you need, you know where to find me."

She waited, but there was no answer. As she turned toward the stairs, she heard the unmistakable click of the lock being slid into place on Jessie's bedroom door.

Great. Now she had to decide whether to leave the girl there, behind locked doors, and hope to God she didn't slit her wrists, or demand that she open the door and become her sworn enemy forever.

It wasn't much of a choice, even for a woman who was whole. For one who'd been broken into pieces, it was more than she could handle. Running away was the only viable solution. Like Scarlett O'Hara, she'd think about it tomorrow.

She gripped the smooth wooden banister and started down the stairs.

She was halfway down when the music began, the sweet, haunting refrain of a violin playing an old Celtic lament she recognized but couldn't remember the name of. It was coming from Jessie's room, and it took Faith a moment to realize it wasn't a recording. Jessie was playing the violin.

She stood there on the stairs, transfixed by the sorrow that poured forth at the touch of rosined bow to those weeping strings. This, then, was how Jessie expressed her grief. Perhaps music was the only way the girl could communicate to the world that her heart was broken.

Or maybe, just maybe, Faith herself was projecting. Maybe she was the one with the broken heart, and not Jessie. Maybe she hadn't realized it until the first sorrowful notes drifting from a violin played by a motherless young girl pierced the hard outer layer of her heart and left it bleeding.

A shiver passed through her. Somebody walking over her grave. That's what her mother used to say. She hadn't thought of it in years, and had no idea why she'd remembered it now.

But she didn't waste time wondering. With the mournful keening of Jessie's violin dogging her steps, Faith fled to the kitchen.

She was leaning into the refrigerator, glowering at its paltry contents, wondering what kind of person didn't keep sliced cheese—a staple of the American diet, for God's sake—on hand, when a knock at the back door nearly sent her through the ceiling. Faith let out a yelp and slammed the refrigerator shut, then stood for an instant, hand over her racing heart, to catch her breath.

Buddy sprinted to the door and began barking. "Sit," she ordered. He stopped barking and sat, tail sweeping the floor behind him, eyes alight with anticipation as she walked to the door and peered through the window. A dark-haired, attractive man stood in Chelsea's dimly lit shed. Broad-shouldered

and square of jaw, he looked familiar in a hazy, half-remem-
bered way. Her heart stuttered and stumbled before settling
back into a steady rhythm. In one hand, he held a square, flat
box that bore a universally recognized red-and-blue logo.
Tucked under his elbow was a six-pack of Rolling Rock.
Faith peered past his shoulder and was just able to make out
the police cruiser parked beside Ben's Saab, its blue bubble-
gum lights faintly silhouetted against the night sky. She hadn't
heard him drive up, probably because the plaintive wail of
Jessie's violin had drowned out all other sound.

She opened the door, and for a full ten seconds, they simply stared at each other. There was no potbelly, no thinning
hair. If anything, he'd improved with age. A quick glance at
his left hand told her he wore no wedding ring. Not that it mattered. She felt none of the awkwardness she'd feared. They
might have last seen each other yesterday. Ty Savage was big
and handsome and he smelled of pizza, and she'd never been
so happy to see anybody in her life.

"How did you know?" she said. "How did you know I was
starving?"

"I'm psychic," he said. "Can I come in?"

"As long as you bring the pizza with you. Maybe you can
give me some pointers about dealing with teenagers while
you're here. Do you have kids?"

His smile carved twin dimples in his cheeks, deep furrows
that served to heighten an already considerable attractiveness. "Nope," he said. "Never got around to it."

"You're forgiven for that oversight. You brought pizza, and
you're the first friendly face I've seen since I got here."

While he made friends with Buddy—who always knew
which side his bread was buttered on—she found dinner plates
right where they'd always been. There didn't seem to be any
napkins, so she grabbed a fistful of paper towels instead. Ty
set the pizza and the beer on the kitchen table before glancing quizzically in the direction of the second floor. "What's
with the doom-and-gloom music?"

"It's Jessie. I'm starting to feel as though I've stumbled into the middle of some gothic novel. First, there was the mysterious recluse who lived in a hut in the middle of a swamp." She set two plates on the table and divvied up the paper towels. "Now I have a ghost who flits silently from room to room, playing heart-wrenchingly eerie music in the dark. I'm afraid to go into the attic for fear of running into the crazy lady who's undoubtedly chained to a rafter up there." She paused, ran a hand through her hair. "Sit. Make yourself at home. Do you need a glass?"

"The bottle's fine. You don't have to wait on me." He took off his coat and hung it on a hook near the door, then pulled out a chair and sat across from her. She nearly swooned at the luscious aroma that wafted from the pizza box when he lifted the lid. "I assume the mysterious recluse you're referring to," he said, tearing off the first slice of pizza and handing it to her, "is our good friend Davy."

"You assume correctly." She took the pizza wedge, loaded with mushrooms and olives and pepperoni. Heaven in a cardboard box. "We had a lovely conversation that consisted of my nervous babbling and his monosyllabic replies." She took a huge bite. The pizza tasted as good as it smelled. She peeled a string of cheese off her chin and surreptitiously fed it to the dog under the table. "The way he's living, I just can't imagine—" She broke off, shook her head. "And then he tells me he's not coming to the funeral. No explanation, nothing. Just that he wouldn't be there. What's happened to him, Ty?"

He handed her a bottle of Rolling Rock. "I think he's defected to the dark side."

She opened the bottle with a soft hiss and took a sip. "Seriously," she said.

He leaned back on his tailbone and stretched out his legs. "Seriously," he said, "I honestly don't know. He was gone for three or four years. When he came back last year, he moved into that hellhole out there in the swamp. The crowd he runs with these days—well, let's just say he could upgrade to a better class of associates. Other than his outlaw friends, he doesn't have much of anything to say to anyone. Except Chelsea. They were thick as thieves."

Remembering, she said, "Weren't they always?"

"Pretty much. Except when they weren't." He peeled a piece of pepperoni off his pizza and tossed it to Buddy. "How's Jessie holding up?"

"Who could say?" She raised her eyes heavenward, in the direction of the music that still floated wraithlike through the house. "This is pretty much the full extent of my interaction with her. The girl just lost her mother. She has to be hurting, but she doesn't seem to want any comfort. At least not from me. I offered her supper, but she very politely brushed me off. Do you know her well?"

He tore off a second slice of pizza and folded it so the toppings wouldn't fall off. "Not really. She seems to be a good kid. From what I hear, she gets straight A's."

"She comes by it naturally. Chelsea could have been a straight-A student if she'd chosen to focus her high school years on studying instead of socializing."

"Mmm," he said vaguely.

"So," she said. "You're a cop now. Imagine that."

His slow and easy smile warmed her. "That's me," he said. "The cop's son with an attitude who ended up following in his old man's footsteps. I'm practically a cliché."

"And you enjoy your work?"

"Amazingly enough, yes. It's a whole different thing, being on the other side of the badge."

"But you must have a terrific rapport with all those belligerent teenage punks out there. After all, you've walked in their shoes."

Those soft brown eyes widened. "Ow," he said. "That hurt. Was I really that bad?"

"To my recollection, you weren't so much bad as defiant. It must have been difficult, growing up as the police chief's son. All those expectations, most of them unrealistic. I'd say you were a normal teenage boy, chafing at the restrictions placed on you."

His smile lingered as he studied her face. "You always did have a way of making me feel better about myself."

"Did I?" His words surprised her, for in reality, in spite of the runaway feelings she'd never dared to express, neither of them had ever overstepped the boundaries of friendship.

"You did," he said. "If it hadn't been for you, I never would have made it through high school algebra. I felt like such an idiot. Bad enough that I was a math dummy. But it was even worse that I had to be tutored by a girl."

"Ah, yes. The shame of it, that a mere female could know more about math than a macho teenage boy. Sexism, alive and well in Serenity."

"Guilty as charged. But you never made me feel stupid, and I was always grateful for that."

"You weren't stupid. Math just wasn't your thing."

He grinned. "And it still isn't. So how are you holding up? You look tired."

"I am tired. Tired, and still in shock. Chelsea was such a scrapper. She's lived through things that would have flattened me. And then to die like that, in a pointless accident, at thirty-five. It's a tragedy, no matter how you look at it."

Ty set down his beer bottle and considered her at length. Her heartbeat took a sudden leap. "What?" she said. "What aren't you telling me?"

Upstairs, as if on cue, the violin playing ceased abruptly. Glancing in the direction of the staircase, he spoke in a muted voice. "I shouldn't say anything. I'm only telling you this because you're apt to hear rumors. Gossip. And because we used to be friends."

"What?" she said again, more sharply than she intended.

"I'm not saying I agree with this." He looked pained, and more than a little reluctant to divulge whatever he was about to tell her. "Right now it's only speculation, until the state police complete their investigation. But at this point, it looks like—"

Faith wet her lips. This wasn't going to be good news. "Like what?" she said.

Ty glanced toward the stairs again. And sighed. "Suicide," he said. "It looks like Chelsea killed herself."

Five

The usual breakfast crew had jammed Lenny's Café until the walls bulged. Every one of the pink-and-turquoise leather booths, circa 1958, was occupied. Lenny's was Serenity's morning hot spot, the only place to get breakfast unless you wanted to drive all the way across town for generic fast food. There was nothing generic about Lenny's place. The decor was cheerfully tacky, and the kitchen probably wouldn't have passed a rigorous inspection by the health department. But the prices were reasonable and the food was good enough to make it worth the remote possibility of salmonella infection.

A buxom redhead in a turquoise uniform trimmed with pink carried three plates piled high with bacon, eggs and toast. She smoothly wound her way between the tables that Lenny had crammed into the center of the tiny room to make space for as many paying customers as he could squeeze in. "Morning, Ty," she said over her shoulder as he came in the door.

"Morning, Maxine."

As he did every morning, the cop in him ran a quick scan of the room, checked out all the faces, familiar and unfamiliar. Not that there were many unfamiliar ones. He'd lived here all his life, and if he didn't know every single one of Serenity's five thousand residents, he came close. He exchanged greetings with several of them and made his way to the coffeemaker located at the end of the vintage turquoise-and-pink-speckled counter. Taking one of the heavy ceramic mugs stacked along the wall, he poured himself a cup of coffee from the pot that sat on the warming burner.

He slid onto a cracked leather stool crisscrossed with duct tape, lifted the smudged lid to a glass cake server, and helped himself to one of Lenny's fresh-baked chocolate doughnuts. Lenny made the best doughnuts in the world, soft and doughy in the center, crusty and nubby on the outside. And this morning, they were still warm. Heaven, all wrapped up in a four-inch circle of chocolate dough.

Maxine flashed by, pencil tucked behind her ear. "The usual?" she said.

"The usual."

He took a sip of coffee and watched her work, admiring the rapid efficiency of her movements and the way the tight bodice of her uniform outlined breasts that he knew from firsthand experience were still firm and high. At forty-two, Maxine Fournier had a few miles on her. Nobody would ever mistake her body for that of a twenty-year-old, but she was still a damn fine-looking woman. And she possessed something he'd found lacking in most younger women: a brain. She was somebody he could actually talk to, a quality he found infinitely preferable to a flawless twenty-year-old body.

She set three plastic glasses on a round tray and poured orange juice into them, then returned the pitcher to a small refrigerator hidden beneath the counter. Her eyes reflecting an emotion he couldn't identify, she said, "Damn shame about Chelsea."

He grunted noncommittally.

Maxine didn't say more. Even if she did hear every piece of gossip that passed for conversation in this town, she wasn't one to pry. Behind the grill, Lenny slid a couple of plates onto the pass-through shelf and jingled the little bell atop the counter. Maxine swung around with a precision that came from years of practice and swept the plates up. She added the mountainous stack of pancakes and the steak-n-eggs to the tray of juice and lofted it.

Ty swiveled on his stool and sipped his coffee. At their usual table in the center of the room, Roland Eugley and Floyd Moody were arguing heatedly about some occurrence long forgotten by the rest of the world. "I'm telling you," Floyd said, "it was 1979. February. Just after the big thaw." Propping a steel-toed work boot against the table pedestal, he rocked his chair back on two legs and crossed his arms over his considerable girth.

"Then you're stupider than you look," Roland said, and Floyd's chair thumped back onto solid ground. "The blizzard was in January of '78. Biggest goddamn mess I ever saw." He rested flannel-covered elbows on the tabletop. "They shut down every damn highway in the state of Massachusetts, and the milk trucks couldn't get through for a week. While we waited for the road crews to remember we were alive up here in no-man's-land, we poured our milk down the drain." He grimaced, apparently still traumatized by the memory of something that had happened when Ty was just a kid. "Like flushing dollar bills down the toilet. Came close to wiping us out. Took us two years to recover."

"Touching story," Floyd said, "but you're wrong about the year. It was 1979. Get on over here, Ty, and tell this old fool that he's wrong."

Ty picked up his coffee and his doughnut and ambled over to the two codgers whose constant bickering reminded him of the grumpy old men immortalized by Jack Lemmon and Walter Matthau. He pulled out a chair, swung it around and straddled it. "What seems to be the problem, gentlemen?"

Both men smelled of damp wool and eucalyptus drops. "He's the problem," Floyd said. "That's what."

"Help us settle this," Roland said. "You remember the blizzard of '78? Floyd here says it was '79."

"Roland," he said gently, "in 1978 I was in the fourth grade."

"Ah, hell," Roland grumbled. "What good are you anyway? You're just a pup. Bet your old man would remember. Buck's got a mind like a steel trap. How come he stopped coming by here in the mornings, anyway?"

Ty took a sip of black coffee. "Couldn't say. He's busy, I guess."

"Hah! More likely you won't let him out of the house, now that he's retired. Afraid he'll be making time with your girl behind your back." Roland cast an appreciative glance toward Maxine's shapely rear, lusciously delineated by her skirt as she bent to place a heavy plate of coronary suicide in front of Darrell Quirion. "Not that I'd mind making a little sweet music with Maxine myself, if I could remember how it's done."

"She's not my girl," Ty said amiably, and took another sip of coffee.

"That mean she's free and clear?" Roland said.

"I guess you'd have to ask her that, Rol. I'm not privy to that particular information."

The door opened and Newt Rollins, owner of the *River City Gazette*, stepped into the room. His skin was pasty, and he'd neglected to shave for a couple of days. Behind the wire-framed glasses, his eyes wore the glazed expression of a man who wasn't quite sure where he was or how he'd gotten here. The door closed behind him, and for an instant, conversation ceased as every eye in the room turned to the newcomer. Newt glanced around the room, spied an empty stool at the counter, and shambled toward it.

Conversation began again. "Cripes," Roland said, "Newt hardly looks like the end product of that expensive liberal arts education his folks sprang for."

"Cut the poor bastard a break," Floyd said. "He just lost his best reporter."

"He's lost himself more'n that," Roland said. "Look at him. I never saw a man look that sick over losing an employee. There must've been something besides work going on up there in that newspaper office." He sounded a little miffed to think he'd lacked knowledge of any clandestine goings-on that had taken place right under his nose.

"I dunno," Floyd said. "I hear she had eyes only for Davy Hunter."

"Just because a woman isn't looking back doesn't mean a man isn't looking at her in the first place. Isn't that so, Ty?"

"I'm afraid I wouldn't know about that," Ty said.

"No," Roland said, "I imagine you wouldn't, you lucky cuss. You prob'ly never looked at a woman that didn't look back."

"Newt's an okay guy," Floyd said.

"I got nothing against him personally, but it's a damn shame the way he's running the *Gazette* right into the ground. His old man ran a strong, conservative newspaper for forty years. In the past five years, Newt's managed to turn it into a wishy-washy, bleeding-heart liberal rag."

Ty hid a grin behind his coffee cup. "Don't be so bashful," he told Roland. "Tell us what you really think."

At the next table, Randall Bailey leaned toward Ty and said, "Think this weather'll ever turn, Tyrone? It's the frickin' middle of May, and I'm still wearing my long johns."

"Christ's sake, Randy," Floyd said, sounding as outraged as an old-maid schoolteacher, "that's way more information than any of us needed to know."

Both tables broke into good-natured laughter. Across the room, Maxine signaled to Ty that his breakfast was ready. He stood up, coffee mug in hand, and said, "You boys stay out of trouble now."

As always, they hooted at the idea of Buck Savage's wet-behind-the-ears kid telling them to stay out of trouble. Satisfied that he'd done his neighborly duty by providing them with their morning's entertainment, Ty wormed his way between tables to where Newt sat at the far end of the counter. He rested a hand on Newt's shoulder and said gently, "Hey."

Newt looked up, took a moment to focus on his face. Recognition dawned in his eyes. "Hey," he said.

"How you holding up?"

Newt shrugged. "It's been two days since they pulled Chelsea out of the river. How do you think I'm doing?" He shot a bleary-eyed glance around the room. "They're all talking about her, aren't they? Goddamn busybodies."

"I imagine most of them are," Ty said, remembering what Jeannie Arsenault had said to him. "Pretty hard to change human nature."

"I've heard what they're saying. They say she killed herself. It's not true, you know."

Ty didn't know what to say to that, so he said nothing. Newt returned his attention to the coffee mug he held in both hands. "You've obviously talked to Davy Hunter," he said. "What's he saying about it?"

"Not much," Ty said. "He's pretty broken up. About like you'd expect."

"He wasn't good enough for her, you know. She deserved better."

Ty squeezed Newt's shoulder a couple of times. There was really nothing more to say. It was a moot question now anyway, whose bed Chelsea Logan chose to park her shoes under. "Hang in there," he said inadequately, and moved on.

Maxine waited at the cash register with his breakfast in a white take-out bag. He drained his coffee and traded her the empty mug for the bag.

"You okay?" she said as he handed her a five-dollar bill.

"Me? I'm tough as shoe leather. But you might want to give Newt a little extra TLC. I've seen roadkill with better color than he's wearing this morning."

Maxine glanced down the counter to where the newspaperman hunched over his mug of coffee. "Yeah," she said. "I've definitely seen him looking better." She slammed the cash drawer shut.

Ty held the take-out bag aloft. "Thanks. Oh, and Maxine? Keep the change."

For the first time this morning, the shadows lifted and a

faint smile crossed her face. "Ayuh," she said in a mock Down-east drawl. "I always do, don't I?"

Ty was just finishing his breakfast when Dixie Lessard stuck her head through the door of his office. Part dispatcher, part secretary, part gopher, the blond, blue-eyed mother of three was the glue that held Serenity's tiny police force together. "I just got a call from Omar Abdallah," she said. "Seems he had a little visit from our neighborhood vandals last night. I could've radioed Pete, but I figured you'd want to take it yourself."

"I'm on it." Ty rolled his chair away from the desk and stood. "Thanks, Dix."

Omar Abdallah's variety store was at the far end of Water Street, on the opposite side from the police station. When Ty got there, he found the tall, slender black man standing on the sidewalk, assessing the damage. Some creative soul had decided to redecorate the front of Omar's store with a can of neon-green spray paint. A three-foot swastika now adorned the brickwork. Just in case the Nazi symbol didn't adequately convey the message, the would-be artist had added the words Nigger Go Home.

"Clever," Ty said. "And so creative."

"I found it this morning," Omar said, "when I came to open the store."

It was teenagers. He couldn't prove it, but his instincts told him that's who it was. There'd been a rash of vandalism over the winter and, although he didn't have any hard evidence, he had a pretty good idea who was behind it. He just had to find a way to nail the little bastards.

"This is troubling," Omar said. "There have been other incidents."

Racial tension had been taut in recent months, and Ty had heard rumors of such incidents. But they'd been only rumors, unconfirmed until now. "What other incidents?" he said.

"Name calling. Harassment of our wives and daughters on

the streets. Taunts thrown at our young men, bullies inciting them to fight. Merchants who refuse to do business with us. Small incidents, but troubling nevertheless."

Inside his stomach, a tiny ball of fire erupted. "Damn it, Omar, why haven't you come to me about this?"

Omar's smile held more irony than humor. "We have difficulty enough blending into the community. Running to the authorities will not improve the situation. We prefer to handle these incidents our way."

"Harassment is illegal. You don't have to tolerate it."

"True." Omar stood very still as he gazed at the graffiti his two scrawny young sons were trying to remove with soapy water and a wire scrub brush. Quietly, he said, "We saw more than enough vandalism in Mogadishu. We came here to find a safe place to raise our children. We weren't expecting to be welcomed with open arms." He watched emotionlessly while his sons continued to scrub away at the green paint. "Nor did we expect the kind of hostility too many of us have spent a lifetime facing."

"I'm sorry. This kind of thing shouldn't be happening to you." Ty rubbed absently at his gnawing stomach. "I thought we'd done a better job of educating people." When the Somalis first arrived, the high school had held a series of forums to educate the public about who they were, where they'd come from, and why they were here. Attendance at the forums had been spotty. *Diversity* wasn't exactly a household word in Serenity. "I'll tell Pete and the rest of the guys to keep a sharp eye out for troublemakers."

Omar held out his hand. "Thank you," he said.

Ty clasped it. "If anything else happens," he said, "I want to know. Immediately."

Not that he had any concrete idea of how to solve the problem. He supposed it was inevitable that the situation would eventually escalate beyond the vague grumblings of a bunch of cranky old men hanging around the checkout at the Big Apple convenience store on a Saturday night. This influx of

Somalis was too much of an adjustment, too big a change, for a town that had already undergone too many changes over the past few years.

Serenity had once been a solid, blue-collar mill town, just like dozens of mill towns across New England. Situated on one of Maine's primary rivers, the town had been built around the big brick cotton mill whose twin chimneys belched soot and smoke twenty-four hours a day. Mollyockett Manufacturing had been running three shifts a day since it opened its doors in 1882. There wasn't a family in town who didn't have somebody working at the mill. Mollyockett had fed and clothed generations of hardworking Mainers. Like the town itself, what the mill lacked in glamour it made up for with a strong work ethic and a face that wasn't afraid to show the world its bumps and blemishes.

But at some point midway through the 1980s, the world began to change. The siren call of cheap foreign labor lured greedy manufacturers elsewhere. Goods that had been produced at home for generations started being made overseas for a fraction of the cost. The state of Maine, with her previously strong manufacturing economy, gradually lost her shoe factories, her paper and textile mills. Mollyockett held out longer than most, but when the company announced its impending closure, nobody was surprised. The state had already lost mills in Lewiston and Saco and a dozen other places. Everybody had known it was only a matter of time.

The closing of Mollyockett Manufacturing had devastated the town's economy. Some people managed to find work at the paper mill in nearby Rumford, but times were hard there, too. A few found jobs slinging hash, punching a cash register or pumping gas. Several families packed up and relocated to Portland or Kittery or some other place where they could find work. But the majority of these former mill workers, trained for no other kind of work, were forced to depend on either unemployment checks or the state's welfare system. Some of them drowned their bitterness in a bottle. Others took out their frustrations on their wives and kids. Those were pretty much the only available options.

Then, six months ago, the Somalis had arrived. Five families, thirty-two individuals who'd moved upriver from Lewiston seeking a smaller, quieter, less hostile environment. Even if they hadn't been ebony-skinned in a tiny town located way out in the puckerbrush in the whitest state in the nation, they would have been looked upon with suspicion. They were Muslims, and therefore subject to keen scrutiny. No matter that they were African Muslims instead of Arab Muslims. In post-9/11 America, any follower of Allah was suspect.

And in an economically depressed little town of five thousand people, many of whom felt angry and cheated, an influx of thirty immigrants of any color or religious persuasion was bound to stir up trouble. There was already a shortage of jobs, and locals weren't happy about having to compete with these foreigners for the limited resources that were available.

Walking at a brisk pace, Ty exchanged greetings with Lauren Weiss, who was unlocking the door of the real estate office. He nodded to Phil Bonner, the town barber, busy behind the window of the barbershop giving one of Elmer Boynton's boys a buzz cut, the same cut Phil had given Ty every summer of his life until he turned eighteen and went away to college. Out front of the police station, Ralph Lessard, the department's part-time maintenance man and Dixie's father, was planting flats of pansies alongside the front walkway.

"If the weather doesn't warm," Ty said, "they're apt to freeze to death."

"We're past frost," Ralph said evenly as he tamped dirt down around the roots of the colorful cluster he'd just planted. "I figure spring'll get here sooner or later. It hasn't missed a year yet."

Halfway up the stairs, Ty said, "From your mouth to God's ear."

Inside the station, Dixie was on the phone. "Uh-huh," she said. "Uh-huh. I hear you." She rolled her eyes as she tapped manicured nails on the desktop and waved a pink message slip in the air with her other hand. He grabbed it on the way by and read it: "Call Detective Lemoine, Maine State Police re: Logan case."

While he waited for Lemoine to come on the line, he rummaged in his desk drawer for the bottle of Maalox that had recently become his best friend. He took a big slug, grimaced at the taste, and was just wiping his mouth when Lemoine picked up.

"Our people just finished with the car," Lemoine said. "No mechanical problems. And I have a preliminary report from the Medical Examiner. Cause of death was drowning. He's running toxicology tests. It'll take a while for those to come back. In the meantime, I intend to nose around, make a few routine inquiries. Try to find out if she'd been despondent. If she had money troubles or boyfriend troubles or some other kind of troubles."

Ty capped the bottle of Maalox, tightened the cap, and shoved the bottle back into the drawer. "I talked to Chelsea the day before she died," he said. "I didn't see anything indicative of problems in her life. As a matter of fact, she seemed pretty revved up about something she had going."

The open phone line crackled between them. "The problem," Lemoine said evenly, "is that so far, everything points to deliberate action. The lack of skid marks. The angle she went into the water, almost a full ninety degrees. There's no evidence whatsoever to indicate it was an accident."

Lemoine had a point. That didn't mean Ty had to like it. "I keep trying to put myself in her shoes," he said. "If I had any intention of ending it all, drowning would probably be my last choice."

"Gun's a lot quicker," Lemoine agreed. "Efficient and effective."

"But messy."

"Women," the trooper said. "You know how they are. They jump off bridges. Swallow pills."

"Drive cars into the river."

"Exactly. I'll be in touch."

Ty hung up the phone, tilted his swivel chair and propped his feet on the metal trash can under his desk. Everything Lemoine had said was true. Unless something else showed up, some problem with the car, something in the tox screens, then every shred of evidence pointed toward suicide. So why was he having so much trouble buying that theory?

Maybe because he'd known her since they both wore diapers. Chelsea's life had been turbulent. No argument there. Depending on the alignment of the planets at any given moment and on Cyrus Logan's transitory periods of sobriety, her upbringing had alternated between unconventional and truly dysfunctional. She'd spent the better part of her adult life struggling to accomplish a self-fulfilling prophecy, determined to live down to her father's rock-bottom opinion of her. For years, she'd bounced from bottle to bottle and from man to man. She'd grown a little hard, a little cynical. It came with the territory. But underneath that surface cynicism lived a woman brimming with passion, a woman determined to grab life with both hands and squeeze every last drop of essence from it.

A woman who didn't have a suicidal bone in her body.

Ty checked his watch. He still had an hour before the funeral. Because he couldn't seem to let it rest, he got in his cruiser and drove out to the accident site. He had no jurisdiction in this investigation; this was Lemoine's baby all the way. But he couldn't shake the feeling that they were looking in the wrong direction, missing something so obvious they should have tripped over it.

He parked in the rest area, got out of the car and stood near the riverbank, listening to the rush of the Androscoggin, still swollen from the spring rains that had finally come to an end. Somewhere nearby, a cardinal sang in its distinctive clear, sweet voice. Ty searched the treetops for a telltale flash of scarlet amid the vivid green spring foliage, but the cardinal wasn't giving away its location.

He walked the length of the narrow turn-out, shoes crunching on the gravel, and stopped to study the straight stretch of highway which, like the cardinal, refused to reveal its secrets. *Talk to me*, he thought. *Tell me what happened.* But the wind carried no answer to his ears, only the whine of an eighteen-wheeler grinding its gears as it wound down the twisting stretch of mountain road that connected with the state highway a half mile east of here. Ty took a hard, bracing breath and held it in his lungs for a long time before releasing it. Nothing here felt out of place. In this spot where time seemed to stand still, everything was just as it had been yesterday, last week, ten years ago. The river, the birds, the pulp trucks. For all he knew, nothing had changed here since men wore loin-cloths and carried wooden clubs.

Except that Chelsea Logan had died here. And Ty Savage wanted to know why.

Six

*A*shes *to ashes, dust to dust.*

Faith stood by the open grave and tried to concentrate on the minister's words as a gentle breeze, ripe with the scents of greening grass and freshly turned earth, played about her face. Such a mournful occasion called for gray skies weeping tears of sorrow. But nature, in its infinite wisdom, had chosen instead to present the most exquisite spring day imaginable. Not a cloud dared disturb the brilliant blue clarity of the sky. Above her head, leaves rustled in the chestnut tree that shaded the back corner of the cemetery adjacent to the First Methodist Church. Overhead, a robin warbled his paean to the sudden and dramatic return of spring. And one way or another, she just knew that somewhere out there in the Great Beyond, Chelsea was enjoying the irony.

Beside her, Jessie stood stiffly erect, dry eyed and stoic. Faith reached out a hand and rested it against the center of the girl's back. Jessie didn't respond, but she didn't push the hand away, either. They stood that way, like strangers pressed together on a crowded subway train, as the minister droned on in interminable prayer.

She was surprised by the turnout. The tidy white church had been filled to the rafters. Either Chelsea was well liked, or people were overcome by curiosity, for the citizens of Serenity, male and female, young and old alike, had come out to bid farewell to Chelsea Logan.

Many of the somber faces ringing the grave were unfamiliar. A gaggle of teenage girls who were probably Jessie's friends. A willowy black woman, draped from head to foot in some kind of traditional Eastern attire, standing out vividly against a sea of white faces. Faith focused on her for a moment before moving on to the man who stood beside her. Fortyish and pleasant of countenance, he had wheat-colored hair that fell in a cap of loose waves around his head. He wore wire-framed eyeglasses that were a perfect complement to his square face and even features. There was something vaguely familiar about him, something that tugged at the edges of her memory, but she couldn't seem to place him.

Other faces bore the stamp of familiarity. Lenny Nadeau had closed his café until noon so he could attend the funeral. Roland Eugley and Floyd Moody, inseparable as always, looked equally uncomfortable in suits and neckties. Linda Larochelle, still playing the role of prom queen eighteen years after graduation, was as stunning as ever in a stylish black dress and a tasteful silk scarf in varying shades of red. Her lips painted a glossy, dazzling scarlet, she bore an uncanny resemblance to some exotic bird of paradise, which Faith suspected had been her intent. Linda stood beside her father, Claude, one of Uncle Cy's longtime drinking buddies. He looked pale and a little queasy, and Faith wondered if he'd been in ill health or if he was just deeply affected by the sudden death of his old friend's daughter.

On the opposite side of the grave, next to a somber Ty Savage, stood old Mrs. Wing, who'd spent forty years as the town librarian. It had been Alma Wing who'd first encouraged Faith's love of reading. Mrs. Wing had enthusiastically recommended wonderful age-appropriate books—*Charlotte's Web*, *The Wind in the Willows*, *Jane Eyre*—opening new and exotic worlds to a young girl for whom real life seemed narrow and colorless. When, at a relatively early age, Faith's reading interests and abilities took her beyond the boundaries of the children's room and into the adult section of the library, Mrs. Wing had conveniently looked the other way and allowed the girl free rein to explore.

The final prayer ended. There was a murmured chorus of amens, and with a collective release of tension, the crowd began to disperse. The worst was over. Across the flower-strewn grave, she met Ty Savage's steady gaze. He acknowledged her with a nod and turned to exchange a brief word with Mrs. Wing. She nodded, and with a slow, even stride, Ty began working his way toward Faith.

Beside her, Jessie said, "I'm leaving now. I'm spending the night at Becca's house."

Still squeezing his way around the carpet of flowers designed to camouflage the open grave, Ty suddenly came up against a wall in the person of Linda Larochelle, former prom queen and all-around annoyance. Linda clutched his arm and leaned against him with intimate familiarity, then began talking in a rapid rush of words.

Faith tore her attention away from them and focused it on Jessie instead. "You're not coming home?" she said, surprised.

"Mom always lets me stay with Becca. She's my best friend. We practically live at each other's houses."

Jessie would be expected to attend the wake. People would want to offer their sympathies and gather information about her emotional state to share later over coffee and Little Debbie cakes. On the other hand, she was only fifteen years old, she'd been through a terrible ordeal, and there was no earthly reason why she should be forced to endure further torment at the hands of well-meaning but nosy neighbors. If she wanted the comfort of her best friend right now, she should have it. Besides, if the things Ty had said last night were true, if rumors really were circulating about Chelsea's death, the last thing Jessie needed right now was to hear them.

But Faith couldn't just let Jessie go running off willy-nilly.

She might not know much about parenting, but that much she was sure of. "You can go," she said, "but first I have to talk to Becca's mother. Is she here?"

"Right over there. I'll send her over."

Jessie walked away across the grass, pale and fragile and almost ethereal as she skirted her mother's grave to reach the group of teenage girls Faith had noticed earlier. They immediately surrounded her with an outpouring of hugs and sympathy.

Jessie would get through this. It would take some time, but as long as she didn't hear any of the ugly stories people were telling about her mother, she'd make it through. Damn gossips. As if Chelsea could possibly have driven into that river deliberately. The very idea was preposterous. Chelsea Logan might have possessed a number of faults, but she'd loved her daughter with almost rabid intensity, the same kind of intensity she brought to everything in life. Having grown up motherless herself, Chelsea would never, not in a million years, have intentionally left Jessie to struggle through adolescence alone.

Which was something Faith intended to tell Tyrone Savage if he ever managed to peel himself away from Linda Larochelle. They were still talking intently, heads lowered in intimate proximity. Faith studied them with rapt interest. They made a stunning couple, and she wondered if they were an item. It was certainly possible. Ty had told her he didn't have children, but he hadn't mentioned anything about a significant other.

Not that it mattered one way or the other to her.

"Excuse me, Ms. Pelletier?"

Embarrassed at having been caught, she yanked her attention away from her speculation about Ty Savage and the prom queen. She'd been back less than twenty-four hours and already she was developing a case of small-town nosiness.

The man who'd spoken was lean and muscled and tall, in his midthirties and darkly handsome, so handsome she wondered how she'd managed to miss seeing him until now. In spite of the day's warmth, he was wearing a suit and tie, but not a single bead of perspiration dared mar his perfection. "Skip Lombardi," he said, and held out his hand. "I'm principal over at Serenity High School."

"Mr. Lombardi." She shook the hand he offered. "Thank you for coming."

"It's Skip," he said, studying her at length through eyes as vivid a blue as the sky above their heads. "My condolences on your loss. This is such a shock. I knew Chelsea. We dated a couple of times when she first came to town. She was far too young and vital to…" He trailed off as though uncertain how to proceed. He cleared his throat. "Jessie's a good kid. She doesn't deserve something rotten like this. Of course, nobody does, but Jessie's sort of special." He flashed her a devastating smile, then grew somber once again. "I want her to take as much time off from school as she needs. When she comes back, her teachers will do whatever's necessary to help her catch up."

"Thank you," Faith said. "That's kind of you."

"If there's anything my teachers or I can do for you or Jessie, please don't hesitate to call." Lombardi discreetly checked his watch. "If you'll excuse me," he said, "I have an appointment in twenty minutes."

As she stood there watching him walk away, a voice from behind her said wistfully, "Woo-woo-woo. If only I were single again. And about twenty pounds lighter."

Faith turned around. The voice was attached to a short, heavyset woman who looked a little lumpy in her ivory linen suit. Her sandy-blond hair fell straight to her shoulders and was clipped across her forehead in bangs that nearly obscured her eyebrows. Beneath the bangs, her face was open and friendly, dusted with freckles, and in spite of the solemnity of the occasion, her vivid blue eyes danced with cheerfulness. "Dottie McLaughlin," she said. "Becca's mother."

"Of course. Thanks for humoring me. I didn't want to sound like a shrew, but I also wasn't turning Jessie loose without at least meeting you."

"I'd be the same way with any of my kids." When Dottie spoke, her freckles moved in an animated dance. "Jessie will be just fine at our house tonight. She's spent so much time there, I call her my spare kid. She's one of the family." Genuine distress dimmed the woman's smile. "I'm so sorry about Chelsea. I liked her. And I can't imagine what Jessie will do without her. I admire you for what you're doing, taking Jessie under your wing like this. But I can't help wondering…who's taking care of you?"

Faith took a deep breath and let it out. Sometimes the kindness of strangers touched her. "I've been through worse things and survived," she said. "But thank you for caring."

Dottie smiled sadly. "I know this is a difficult time, and the last thing you need is some stranger poking into your life. But I want you to know that if there's anything we can do to help—anything at all—we're just a phone call away. We're in the book. David and Dorothy McLaughlin, 38 Central Street. Listen, I have to scoot. I'm taking five teenage girls and a four-year-old boy to McDonald's for lunch. I can remember when that kind of thing qualified as a fun excursion." She shuddered, but her expression remained pleasant. "I'll bring Jessie home in the morning. I'm sure she'll want to take the rest of the week off from school."

"That's what I expect. Thanks again."

"Not a problem. Take care now. I'll see you tomorrow."

Dottie walked toward the knot of teenage girls who'd taken Jessie to their collective bosom, and Faith swung back around to see if Ty and Linda had finished their summit meeting. But they'd both disappeared. She scanned what was left of the crowd, but neither of them was anywhere to be seen. Even the pasty-faced Claude Larochelle, Uncle Cy's old drinking buddy, had apparently dissolved into thin air.

"Faith! There you are! I've been looking for you." Red of face and teetering on high-heel shoes that were at least a size too small for her plump little feet, Hilda Larson bore down on her with the grace and demeanor of a battleship. She wore a no-nonsense navy-blue suit with huge white buttons, and carried a gray purse large enough to give any would-be mugger second thoughts. If Hilda ever wielded the thing, it would pack one hell of a wallop.

"Come inside now, dear," she said. "We have finger sandwiches and casseroles and potato salad. We can sit and visit. It's been such a long time." Hilda took her hand, squeezed it, and smiled bravely. "Such a sad occasion. I knew Chelsea's mother when she was a young girl. This would break her heart, God love her. I've always wondered what became of Adrienne. The way she just took off like that, and never contacted her daughter again—" She shook her head in silent reproach. "It's just so tragic. Not that I blame her one bit for running away from that awful man. But just think." Hilda's eyes gleamed with excitement over the intrigue that surrounded the defection of Chelsea's mother. "Poor Adrienne is out there somewhere, and she doesn't even know her daughter is dead."

It was going to be a long afternoon. Faith plastered on the generic smile she reserved for public occasions—banquets, book signings, family funerals—and let Hilda lead her into the church basement, where trestle tables and wooden folding chairs had been set up. The mourners, at least those who didn't have jobs to get back to, were slowly gravitating in the direction of the buffet table. "Sit," Hilda said. "Let me get you a plate."

The last thing she wanted was food, but she didn't have the energy to argue. Hilda melted into the throng, and Faith was immediately surrounded by people who wanted to offer their condolences. While she scanned the crowd for Hilda's return, she endured an unending stream of people invading her privacy with hugs and handshakes and words of sympathy.

Her hands, clasped tightly around her purse strap, began to sweat. If ever there were a time to take a tranquilizer, it was now. But the constant barrage of faces made privacy impossible, and if she opened the bottle of tranquilizers and swallowed one in public, rumors of Chelsea's pill-popping cousin would be all over town by suppertime. The gossips would have a field day blowing the story all out of proportion. By nightfall, she'd be a recovering addict, a habitual resident of one of New York's pricey private rehab clinics who'd fallen off the wagon once again. It wasn't worth the effort of trying to explain the truth. People would believe what they wanted to believe. It was easier to get by without the Valium.

But she wanted one of those little yellow pills, craved the comfort, the freedom from anxiety that she knew it would bring. To her immense relief, she saw Hilda returning with two plates of food, parting the crowd like Moses parting the Red Sea. "'Scuse me," Hilda said, plowing past people with little regard to courtesy. "'Scuse me. Here you go, sweetie." She handed Faith a plate heaped with enough food to feed a family of three. "Sit down, honey. You look so pale. This is too much for you. All these people. And I know how close you and Chelsea used to be. I'd hate to see you pass out from grief." Her tone was all saccharine sympathy, but the gleam in her eyes belied her words. Had Faith passed out from grief—or from anything else, for that matter—it would have fueled Hilda's gossip supply for the next two decades.

Patting her hand, the plump matron said, "Eat. You'll feel better afterward."

Hilda's wisdom on that particular topic was questionable, but Faith took the path of least resistance and ate. The tuna was too oily. After a few bites, she moved on to the potato salad. It was delicious, seasoned with onions and chives. If she'd been at all hungry, she would have dug in with gusto. But her appetite had fled the instant she set eyes on Chelsea's coffin. Faith took another bite, then put down her fork. The oily tuna had made her queasy, and it was unbearably hot here in the church basement. It didn't help that she was sitting directly in front of a wall register that blew stale, dry air into a room where the air was already heavy and unbreathable.

What was it her mother used to say about Maine weather?

If you don't like the weather, wait a minute. Yesterday might have felt like February, but today felt more like July. Whoever was in charge of this little party had no business running the furnace on a day this hot. And all these bodies crammed into such a small space only added to the problem. Faith furtively wiped her sweaty palms on her skirt and tried to ignore the uncomfortable sensation that the walls were closing in on her.

Hilda was still talking, babbling about a series of stories Chelsea had written for the *River City Gazette* about the Somali immigrants. Faith pretended to understand what she was talking about, but for all the good it did, the woman might as well have been speaking Mandarin Chinese. With over a hundred people squeezed into a room designed to hold half that many, the sensory input was overwhelming. She focused on a single oversize white button on Hilda's suit, watched it draw nearer and then more distant as the room expanded and contracted. As though from a great distance, she saw Claude Larochelle pour himself a cup of coffee from the urn on the serving table. Half in and half out of her body, Faith floated, suspended somewhere just beneath the ceiling, observing the activity below like a Cheshire cat who'd forgotten its smile.

She dragged herself back to reality, focused harder on that white button. Around her, people clustered in groups, talking, talking, snippets of unrelated conversation strung together like beads. "Poor little girl…only fifteen…so I told him if he thought I'd be sitting there waiting for him to call, he had another think coming…board of selectmen need to do something besides sit around with their heads up their asses…State Police think she killed herself…was seeing Davy Hunter…"

Davy Hunter. Davy Hunter. Davy Hunter.

"Excuse me." A middle-aged woman in a yellow cotton sundress leaned into Faith's face and thrust a paperback book into her hands. "I don't suppose you'd mind autographing this? It's for my mother, Clarisse. That's C-L-A-R—"

Faith looked at her blankly. The woman's blue eye shadow had started to melt, and was clumped in the crease of her eye-lid. Faith studied it with grim fascination. The woman's mouth moved and words tumbled out, but they were indecipherable. Faith glanced at the book in her hand. *Head Games*. Her sixth book, the one where the killer nearly succeeded in drowning the heroine before the hero came along to rescue her.

Oh, God.

Panic wrapped elongated fingers around her throat and squeezed tight. "Excuse me," she said, standing so abruptly that the book landed on the floor several yards away. Ignoring the fallen jaws and the incredulous glances, she shoved past bodies toward the door, beyond caring about courtesy or about what they thought of her. If they wanted to call her Chelsea's crazy cousin, it was fine with her.

She burst out of the church into blessed fresh air. The concrete at the top of the stairs was cracked, and she caught the heel of her shoe in it and nearly went sprawling. She lunged for the iron stair railing, caught it and steadied herself. Took a hard, sharp breath and fled to Ben's car, tucked into the last row of the parking lot, in the shade of a huge weeping willow tree.

She leaned against the car for support. In spite of the day's warmth, the smooth steel exterior, shaded by the willow, was cool. She leaned over the roof of the car, wrapped her arms around her head and pressed her cheek to that velvet-smooth coolness. Behind her, an unfamiliar male voice said, "Deep breaths. Slow and deep. Ride it out. It can't hurt you, even if it feels like it will."

Even though he was a stranger, there was something soothing about his voice, something reassuring about his nearness. The man rested a hand on her shoulder, and that simple human touch was like a lifeline. She relaxed, rode the wave as she'd been taught, silently repeated the mantra Dr. Garabedian had taught her. *Breathe in, breathe out. Breathe in, breathe out.*

"Is there something I can do?"

"Pills," she managed to say. "In my purse."

She watched a pair of unfamiliar hands rummaging

through her purse. He pulled out a small bottle, opened it, dropped a single pill into his palm. He held out his hand and she fumbled with the little yellow pill, nearly dropping it before she got a good grip on it. Faith dropped it beneath her tongue, held it there for a long minute, then swallowed it without liquid. She'd gotten pretty good at this. Although it had been a couple of months since she'd had a panic attack, this wasn't her first time, and it probably wouldn't be her last.

The fear and the sense of suffocation began to recede. Her heartbeat gradually slowed, and she could once again hold herself upright. She took a deep, shuddering breath and raised her head to look at her savior.

It was the blond-haired man she'd noticed at the funeral. Up close, behind the sun-darkened lenses of his glasses, his eyes were a pale blue, and red rimmed, as though he'd seen more than his share of sleepless nights in the recent past. He recapped the pills and returned them to her purse. "You okay?" he said.

"I'm fine," she said, taking the purse back from him. "Thank you. How did you know?"

"My college roommate used to have panic attacks. I recognized it right away." He peered at her with open interest. "I'm Newt Rollins. I own the *River City Gazette*. Chelsea worked for me."

Of course. That explained why he looked familiar. His family had owned the local newspaper since the beginning of time. When she'd been a kid, the Rollinses had been Serenity's nod to the aristocracy. They lived on a fifty-acre gentleman's farm on the outskirts of town, in a grand house that overlooked the river. In those days, Newt had been a shadowy figure, one the local kids had speculated upon endlessly: the rich, brainy kid who attended expensive private schools and spent a good part of each summer at some camp in the Adirondacks. "I remember you," she said. "You used to work for your dad in the newspaper office whenever you were home."

"I'm surprised you remember me. You were just a kid the last time I saw you."

"And you were about to start your sophomore year at Yale. So you're running the newspaper now."

"I took over five years ago, after my dad died. You know, Chelsea talked about you all the time. She admired you. She wanted to—" Newt stopped abruptly, and his eyes filled with tears. He shook his head and turned away. Faith hesitated for an instant before laying her hand on his shoulder in an awkward attempt to reciprocate a fraction of the comfort he'd given her. This man had obviously felt more than friendship for her cousin, and his pain was so palpable she could feel it. Regret washed through her, for she understood that kind of pain, and wouldn't have wished it on her worst enemy, much less on this kindhearted stranger.

He took a deep breath and turned around. "I need to talk to you. About Chelsea. I imagine you've heard what they're saying about her."

Her breath caught in her throat, and his blue eyes narrowed. "Yes," he said. "I can see that you have. They're saying she killed herself." He grasped her arm, a little too hard. "Chelsea didn't kill herself, do you hear me? There's something else going on."

She wondered if he'd been drinking. What he suggested was so outlandish it was almost laughable. But there was no scent of alcohol on his breath, only a faint hint of spearmint. And his expression was dead serious.

Something hard and uncomfortable lodged itself behind her breastbone. "Are you suggesting that Chelsea was—" she had a hard time wrapping her tongue around the word. It came out as a whisper "—murdered?"

"I'm not suggesting anything. I'm telling you that what happened Sunday night wasn't an accident. And it wasn't suicide. Chelsea got too close to something she wasn't meant to be part of, and she paid with her life."

It was absurd. This wasn't New York, where murders were so common they barely rated mention in the newspaper. This was Serenity, where things were supposed to be serene. It wasn't possible that somebody here in this tiny town could have hated her cousin enough to want her dead. Was it?

A trickle of sweat rolled down her back, and her arm hurt where he still clutched it. "That's a serious accusation, Mr. Rollins. Why would anybody want to harm her?"

Newt glanced furtively around the deserted parking lot. "Because of a story she was working on. And I damn sure intend to find out who did it."

Faith let his words sink in, turned them over and around inside her head. No matter how she looked at them, they still seemed ludicrous. She wondered why he was telling her this far-fetched tale. Wondered if there were even a grain of truth to it. She wanted to believe that the entire yarn had sprung full-blown from his imagination. But if there was any possibility that he was telling the truth, she couldn't let it ride. She owed it to Chelsea to hear him out.

"All right," she said. "You have my attention. What kind of news story, in a place the size of Serenity, could possibly lead to murder?"

He finally released her arm. It tingled as the blood came rushing back. Beneath the wrinkled suit jacket, his shoulders slumped. "I don't know," he admitted. "She wouldn't tell me. That's what I was hoping you'd help me figure out."

Seven

It was the worst day of Jessie Logan's life.

The Day from Hell had started with a visit from a state trooper named Lemoine who, despite his kindly demeanor, had poked and prodded and asked all kinds of ridiculous questions about her mom's state of mind in the days before she died. The day had gone downhill from there, sinking so low that not even seeing Cooper Gates at McDonald's could make it any worse.

He sat at a table with Bruce Tandy and Jimmy Madison. All of them were juniors, all of them varsity football players, all of them doing what seventeen-year-old guys do in places like this: playing with their food, blowing through their straws and shooting the wrappers halfway across the room, laughing uproariously while they remained totally oblivious to Jessie and her group of friends. She watched in rapt agony. Cooper was wearing his green-and-white letter jacket, and he looked so incredibly hot with that lock of dark hair falling across his forehead that she wanted to just swallow him up.

"Idiots," Becca said as she unwrapped her sandwich. "They act like they're ten years old."

"But that Cooper sure is cute," Katey Berube said, opening her salad container and grimacing at the contents. Katey, who carried twenty extra pounds and was perpetually on a diet, was the boy-crazy member of their little clique.

"So's an orangutan," Becca said, "but that doesn't mean I'd want to bring one home. Cooper Gates is bad news."

Jessie remained silent. She would never dare admit to Becca that she had a huge crush on Coop. Becca would roll her eyes and remind her that although the guy was admittedly gorgeous, he had a reputation, and it wasn't a good one. Jessie didn't need any reminders. She'd already given herself enough grief over it. She'd told herself countless times that if she really had to fall madly, passionately in love with some guy, it should be with someone cerebral. Someone like Danny Addison, who played jazz sax in the high school orchestra and planned to go to Juilliard. Or Ahmed Abdallah, who had an IQ of 153 and was in all her classes.

Either of them would have been preferable to the studly football player, all-around jock, and bad boy of Serenity High. Falling for the star quarterback of the high school football team was so eighth grade. Not to mention that half the girls in town were in the same situation, for Cooper, whose father just happened to be a hotshot doctor, was as close as it came in these parts to royalty. Bad boy he might be, but he was a much sought after bad boy. Jessie might as well take a number and stand in line. Not that Coop would ever look at someone like her, some skinny, flat-chested girl with glasses and stick-straight hair, not when he could pick and choose—and undoubtedly already had—from the entire varsity cheerleading squad.

Even the mental picture of Coop's probable string of busty blond girlfriends didn't cool her ardor, for Jessie had it bad. She didn't just long for Cooper Gates, she ached for him with an intensity she didn't fully understand.

Not that she didn't know all about sex. She'd learned about it in her sixth-grade Health and Hygiene class, understood it all in a clinical, academic, tab-A-fits-into-slot-B kind of way. But until Cooper Gates first crossed her field of vision, Jessie had never felt it, had never experienced that exhilarating and terrifying rush of emotion combined with pure animal drive. The resulting internal uproar had rocked her prim little body to its foundations. She'd tried valiantly to ignore her feelings, because she didn't want to be like her mother, bouncing from bed to bed, changing men the way other women changed their underwear. Jessie was determined to remain a good girl, the kind of girl that boys wanted to take home to their mothers. Not, like Chelsea, the kind they wanted to take to bed.

She'd never been able to figure out her mother. In spite of her fickle ways with men, Chelsea always eventually ran back to Davy Hunter. He was the love of her life. She'd admitted as much, one evening as she was getting ready for a date, combing and fluffing her hair and brushing a deep rose blusher onto cheeks already as rosy as dawn. As if she'd needed makeup. Jessie's mom was the most beautiful woman she'd ever seen.

"We can't seem to live together," Chelsea had said, blotting her lipstick with a tissue. "But we can't seem to live without each other, either. Kind of crazy, isn't it, Beans?"

That had been her mother's nickname for her. Beans. And Jessie had called her mom Chelsea, had called her by her first name for so long she couldn't remember ever calling her anything else. Her friends thought it was weird. None of them would have dared to call a parent by his or her given name. If they'd tried, most of them would have ended up in trouble for it. But Chelsea had encouraged it, had said it was just their way of doing things, something that made them unique, set them apart from other families. Jessie had liked being different, and she couldn't imagine it being any other way.

As she leaned into the mirror to apply mascara, Chelsea had told her that night, "There's something between us… some slender golden thread…that binds Davy and me together. I can't explain it, and neither can he. But it's as though our hearts function as a single unit."

Her mother's words were so poetic, so romantic, that Jessie had never forgotten them. Sometimes, when Chelsea was feeling philosophical, the words that came from her mouth were like precious gems, something to be saved and savored. But her relationship with Davy was confusing. If they loved each other so much, why didn't they just get married and stay in one place? Why did they both keep trying to leave Serenity, only to come running back every time to each other's arms? And why, if she loved Davy so deeply, did Chelsea continue to sleep with other men?

Now that Chelsea was gone, Jessie had never been so frightened in her life. When she'd watched them lower her mother's coffin into the ground, she had been so frozen with fear, she couldn't breathe. Her lungs, hidden away beneath a pair of woefully inadequate breasts, had ached from lack of oxygen. Her mother had been her Gibraltar. Her anchor. The yin to her yang. Now that anchor was gone and she had nobody, and it was terrifying. Their song kept running through her head, the one that Chelsea used to sing to her at bedtime when she was little. "You and Me Against the World." Chelsea had called it their theme song because it fit them so perfectly. They always took care of each other, no matter what. No matter where they lived or with whom, there'd always been this special connection between the two of them. Even back when Chelsea was drinking, and Jessie'd had to be the adult, that connection had never faltered. They had loved each other unconditionally, and her fear of being alone was so paralyzing, she wasn't sure she could go on living. Not when she felt as though the other half of her had died.

The fear extended to practical considerations, as well. Where was she going to live? She was crazy about Davy, but she couldn't very well live with him. He was hardly ever home, and when he was, he spent most of his time in another world. Day and night, he was out in that wood shop of his, building furniture, his mind wandering to places nobody else could follow. His trailer was a hovel, and his friends, what few of them he had, were not the kind of people she wanted to associate with.

Becca's mother would have taken her in, no questions asked. She practically lived at Becca's house anyway. But living there on a permanent basis wasn't the same as staying over once or twice a week. The McLaughlins already had four kids packed into a tiny three-bedroom ranch. There was no room to squeeze another person into their already overcrowded household.

She knew what people expected. At least what Davy expected of her. He had pretty much laid it on the line and told her that she'd be living with her mother's cousin. But what if she didn't want to live with Faith Pelletier? Not that she disliked Faith. The woman seemed nice enough, in that faintly annoying way of adults who know zilch about kids but are afraid to admit it for fear of appearing uncool. She was probably an okay person. But she was still pretty much a stranger.

And the woman lived in New York City. Jessie didn't want to leave Serenity. This was home to her now. Familiar and comfortable. She loved playing in the school orchestra, loved poking around the shops on Water Street and knowing all the proprietors by name. She loved Grampa's house, loved the way the old place creaked and moaned every time the wind blew. And all her friends were here. Becca and Katey. Ahmed Abdallah. The Larrabee sisters, Gwen and Dawn, who were in her homeroom and lived just down the road. Danny Addison and his crazy jazz saxophone.

Davy who, aside from her mom, was the only person she considered family.

And Cooper. Especially Cooper.

She glanced down at the cheeseburger she'd taken just a couple bites of. It tasted like sawdust. Everything had tasted like sawdust since the morning she'd been called into Principal Lombardi's office, where Davy had told her that her mother was dead. She hadn't wanted to believe it, but Davy would never have lied to her about something like that, and he'd looked as stunned and heartsick as she felt.

"You okay, Jess?"

She focused on Becca's concerned face. "Just thinking," she said.

Becca sighed. "This really bites, doesn't it?"

"Yeah. It does."

"Maybe Mom will rent us a couple of movies for tonight. I hear Nic Cage's new one really kicks ass." Becca toyed with the wrapper to her chicken sandwich. "That is, if you want to. I mean, maybe it'll help take your mind off...you know."

"I know. Thanks, Bec. A movie would be great."

Jessie wrapped the burger back up neatly and stole a final anguished glance at Cooper. If only he would notice her sitting here. If only he'd come over and offer a few words of consolation, she wouldn't feel so bad. But Cooper didn't even acknowledge her. He didn't know her mom had just died, any more than he knew she'd give up anything—even her precious violin—for one kind word from him.

Despair, black and aching, wrapped itself around her already wounded heart. Coop had no way of knowing how much she wanted him because she'd never told him. And he would never, ever want her back, because Cooper Gates, the bad boy of Serenity High, didn't even know that mousy little Jessie Logan existed.

Newt picked up two cups of take-out coffee from the Big Apple and they sat on a bench in a small park overlooking the dam, where each day, thousands of gallons of water plunged in a spectacular fall, only to be crushed to death against the rocks below. There'd been a time when the dam provided water power to run the cotton mill. Now, it was nothing more than a tourist attraction. Not that Serenity had many tourists. It was too far off the beaten path, in one of those you-can't-get-there-from-here kind of locations, to attract tourists. Of the few who did drive through, most had taken a wrong turn at Rumford or Bethel and wouldn't stay long.

"So?" Faith nudged.

"So." Newt rearranged his legs and lifted the lid on his coffee. "She was working on a story she said would blow the lid off this town. But she wouldn't tell me what it was about. Me, her editor! You can't begin to imagine how much that ticked me off. I hounded the hell out of her to tell me. I even threatened to fire her. She just laughed at me. She knew I'd never go through with it because she had me wrapped around her little finger. That was Chelsea."

He took a sip of coffee and stared at the billowing water that frothed and foamed as it moved downstream. "I'd never seen her so intense. Coming to work early. Staying late. Working weekends. It wasn't like her. Generally, Jessie came first with her." His mouth thinned. "And Davy Hunter came second. Work always came dead last." He winced as he realized what he'd said.

"But?"

He sat up straighter. "But with this story, it was as though she shoved everything else aside. She was like a pit bull with a slab of sirloin. Relentless."

Faith considered his words. "I'm afraid I don't see how this is leading up to murder."

"She had something going that night. I don't know what, or who it was with. But she left a message on my voice mail, telling me to hold the front page because she was bringing in a story that couldn't be buried on page five. Those were her exact words. She sounded excited. I tried to call her back, but her cell phone was turned off. And she never showed. We finally put the paper to bed at one-thirty. I couldn't wait any longer. Of course, it wouldn't have mattered, would it?" His shoulders sagged. "She was already dead."

Faith leaned back against the sun-warmed wooden bench and took a long, thoughtful slug of black coffee. It did seem to be a rather large coincidence that Chelsea had died on the same night she'd planned to turn in a story that was bound to prove very troublesome for some unknown party. Her claim that the story would blow the lid off Serenity implied somebody important. Influential. Perhaps somebody with the means to do away with a woman who was about to ruin his—or her—life.

Oh, God. Now she was starting to sound as paranoid as Newt. That's all this was, the paranoid ramblings of a grief-stricken man who hadn't slept in days. Serenity was no different than it had ever been. Across the street, at the Dairy Queen, kids still ate vanilla soft-serve, just as she'd done years ago when she was a kid. Down on Androscoggin Street, the bars still catered to the local drinking crowd, which had once included her Uncle Cy. Homer Berube still rode his ancient three-speed Schwinn every day to his job as a ticket taker at the Strand. Serenity might not be the picture-postcard-perfect town that tourists imagined when they thought of Maine, but it wasn't the kind of place where people routinely killed each other in the course of their workday.

"Look," she said gently, "I think you should go home and get a good night's sleep." She gave his knee a friendly pat. "Things will look different in the morning."

"You don't believe me." There was accusation in his voice, and dismay. Beneath the wrinkled suit coat, his shoulders slumped. "You have to help me," he said. "I have to find out the truth. I was never the kind of reporter who dug up dirt, you know. I was the op-ed editor for ten years until my father died and I took over as editor-in-chief. Before that, I wrote a gardening column, for Christ's sake. I didn't do investigative reporting. The *Gazette*'s a small-town newspaper, the kind that people read to find out who won the bridge tournament at the community hall on Saturday night. I don't know anything about investigating murders. I thought you—" He stopped abruptly.

"You thought I what?"

"You write suspense novels. Whodunits. You're used to figuring out complicated plot twists and people's motivations. You solve mysteries for a living. I just thought—"

"Newt." She spoke gently, as she would have spoken to a

child. "There's fiction, and then there's real life. The lines don't usually cross."

"Nevertheless, you have the kind of mind that could come up with a solution if you applied it to something like this."

"I don't understand," she said. "If you really believe Chelsea was murdered, why are you talking to me? Why haven't you taken your concerns to Ty Savage?"

"Even you don't believe me," he said dully. "Why should the cops?"

"Because it's their job?"

"Right. I'm sure these rinky-dink small-town cops have lots of experience with homicide investigations. Besides, for all I know, Savage could be involved. There could be some huge conspiracy going on right under my nose."

"Now you're starting to sound crazy."

"I'm not crazy. I'm just frustrated. I don't have that kind of nose for news. I'm just this Joe Schmoe who writes newspaper articles about whose relatives are visiting from Cleveland and what went on at town meeting. Or what's playing down at the Strand this week. I always know what's playing at the Strand."

"Do me a favor," she said. "Go home. Get a good night's sleep, and if things don't look better in the morning, come talk to me again."

He heaved a long-suffering sigh. "Fine. But I can guarantee that things won't look better in the morning."

"Maybe not, but at least we'll both be clearheaded."

He walked her back to her car, still sitting in the church parking lot. She fumbled with her seat belt, shifted the car into Reverse, and gave him a brief wave. He waved back, looking bleak and pathetic and a little miffed.

She drove past the municipal building. The gray cinder block structure wasn't the most attractive building in town, but the pansies that lined the walkway were a welcoming touch. She wondered if Ty had gone back to work after the funeral, wondered if Newt's outrageous story was worth bothering him with. She decided yes on the first count, no on the second. It had been a rough day, and exhausted didn't begin to cover how she felt. She had the house to herself, and by now Buddy was probably starting to feel deserted. If she didn't get back soon to let him out, he'd be leaving little gifts all over the house for her to step in.

Morning was soon enough to deal with Newt Rollins and his runaway imagination. For now, she intended to feed Buddy and turn him loose to do his business. Then she was going to shower and take one of Dr. Garabedian's precious pills. Just one, just this once. Emergencies be damned. She'd had a terrible day, and she knew she'd sleep better once she was able to relax.

And tonight, for the first time since she'd heard the news about Chelsea, Faith Pelletier intended to sleep the sleep of the dead.

Eight

Late-afternoon sun spilled through Ty's office window, pooling in a golden pond on the cluttered desktop. At a sharp knock on the door, he glanced up from the stack of paperwork Dixie had given him for his signature. Before he could respond, the door opened and his sister Jolene breezed in. He suppressed a groan. This day had started out lousy, and wasn't showing signs of getting any better. First Linda, and now Jolene. That was zero for two. One more, and he'd strike out.

He rolled back his chair and threaded his fingers together over his abdomen. "What do you want?"

She'd obviously come directly from work; she was wearing her ultraconservative schoolteacher disguise, the one that didn't fool anyone who'd known her for more than five minutes. From the low-heeled shoes to the prim gray dress to the old-maidish bun at the back of her neck, her appearance screamed schoolmarm. The real Jolene, the one she'd never dream of showing to her students, was hidden somewhere inside.

"Is that any way to greet your beloved one-and-only sister?" she said.

"You show up at my office at—" he glanced at the wall clock "—four-fifteen on a weekday, I know you want something."

His sister was two years older than Ty, and still hadn't let him forget it. She'd been the perfect child, never giving their parents so much as a lick of trouble. Which was amazing, considering the hellion who lived beneath that ultraconservative schoolteacher facade. To his misfortune, the aforementioned traits had apparently endowed her with the inalienable right to tell him how to run his life, a right she chose to exercise on a regular basis. "You're such a cynic," she said, and plunked down on the corner of his desk. "How'd the funeral go?"

Ty propped his feet on the metal wastebasket under his desk. "You wouldn't have to ask that question if you'd been there."

She picked up the marble paperweight that Dixie had given him last Christmas. Turned it over in her hands and studied it from every angle. "Chelsea and I never had much to say to each other." She set down the paperweight and her full lips turned up in a silky smile. "Besides, I couldn't very well leave twenty-six tenth-graders alone just so I could watch Newt Rollins and Davy Hunter duke it out over the casket." She reached up and pulled the pins from her hair. It fell in a tumble of dark curls around her shoulders. She tossed it back, away from her face, the true Jolene at last. "My boss would've had something to say about that, I'm sure."

"I'm sure he would have. On the other hand, if you were hoping to see Davy and Newt duking it out, you would've been disappointed, since Davy didn't show."

Jolene raised a single eyebrow. "I'll be damned," she said. "I thought he'd be there with bells on."

"I guess he's suffering from grief. Or something. I didn't expect him to show anyway. He told Faith yesterday that he wouldn't be there."

The eyebrow went higher. "Faith Pelletier? She's been back for twenty-four hours, and already the two of you are all cozy with each other?"

A ball of fire ignited in his stomach. "For Christ's sake, Jo, I stopped by to talk to her. I figured she was probably starving and too tired to cook, so I brought her a pizza." He thought longingly of his bottle of Maalox, tucked away in the drawer, but he wouldn't give his sister the satisfaction of witnessing his vulnerability. She'd exploit it for sure. "I wanted to offer her condolences on her loss." He tried to remember whether he'd ever gotten around to offering those condolences, but he couldn't recall. He'd been too caught up in a pair of exquisite blue eyes clouded by exhaustion and something else, something he couldn't quite put his finger on. "We're old friends, in case you forgot."

"How could I forget? You spent most of your formative years living inside each other's pockets. I hear she's improved with age. Matter of fact, from what I hear, she's absolutely stunning."

He absently rubbed his stomach. "Where'd you hear that?"

"This is Serenity, *mon frère*. The buzz was all over town an hour after she landed. Besides, I do occasionally read a book. I've seen her picture on the back cover. Quite a looker. Does she know you had a wicked crush on her back in the old days?"

"Jesus, Jo, I was eighteen years old." It was time to change the subject. This one made him squirm. He dropped his feet to the floor, rolled toward the desk, picked up his pen and continued signing papers. Dix had stuck a little yellow arrow each place his signature was needed. Without her, he'd be lost. "I ran into Linda at the funeral," he said.

His sister rolled her eyes. "Lucky you. What did she have to say?"

Ty set aside the paper he'd just signed, frowned as he skimmed the next one, then scrawled his John Hancock. "Apparently she and Skip Lombardi are getting married." He glanced up from his work. "She wanted to make sure I heard it from her first, instead of from some third party."

"As if you'd give a damn. I seem to remember that you divorced her. Or is my recall faulty? She trying to rub your nose in her new romance, or what?"

He shrugged. "The Lord and Linda both move in mysterious ways."

"Skip Lombardi." She cogitated for a while. "I'd heard they were dating. It's pretty hard to keep anything secret in the hallowed halls of Serenity High. But I had no idea it was that serious. The local gossips haven't got hold of this one yet." Jolene studied his face with the unconcealed concern of a sibling much older and wiser. "And you're okay with this?"

"Me? I'm fine with it. Hell, I got over Linda and her fickle ways a long time ago." He felt little for his ex-wife now except mild irritation. Skip was welcome to her, and all the headaches that went along with her. Linda was a high-maintenance woman in every sense of the word. "Why don't you tell me why you're really here? Then you can yell at me over whatever I've done and still be home in time to make supper for Jack and the kids."

"I'm not here to yell at you. If you must know—" her expression sobered "—I'm worried about Dad."

It was the last thing he'd expected. Ty leaned back in his chair and let out a long breath of air. "Dad's fine," he said gruffly.

"I knew you'd say that. You're in denial, Tyrone. Dad's not himself. He hasn't been for a while. His behavior's erratic. He's cranky as a bull moose in rutting season, and he keeps forgetting things. It's just not like him."

Ty thought about the relish jar in the cupboard, and squelched the thought. "He's getting old. He'll be seventy-four in July. You can't expect him to act like a thirty-year-old."

"This isn't normal aging. At seventy-three, he should still be sharp as ever. Maxine's grandfather is ninety-six, and his memory is better than mine. Dad used to be like that, too, but his short-term memory's deteriorated over the past few months. Don't tell me you haven't noticed."

He tossed his pen down on the desk. "So he's forgetful. It happens. It doesn't mean anything."

"I stopped in yesterday morning. He was pacing the floor, muttering to himself. When I asked what he'd had for breakfast, he couldn't remember."

His insides tightened. "Hell," he said, "I forget what I had for breakfast, and there's nothing wrong with me. My head's too full of stuff."

"Christ, Ty, he didn't even remember whether or not he'd eaten! And that damn book he's pretending to read? He's still on the same page he was on three weeks ago. I think he's having trouble understanding it."

The Tom Clancy. Page 238. *Shit.* Ty rubbed the back of his neck and let out a hard breath. Reluctantly, he said, "He left an open jar of relish in the cupboard yesterday."

"This isn't normal," she repeated. "There's something wrong. I think it's Alzheimer's."

Stubbornly, he said, "Dad does not have Alzheimer's."

Jolene slid down off the desk. She wandered to his bulletin board and stood there studying a yellowed town meeting announcement. "Look," she said, "whatever it is, it's in the early stages. Most of the time, he's perfectly normal. But if it is some kind of dementia, it'll only get worse." She took a breath and turned to face him. "They have medications nowadays to treat this kind of thing. They're not a cure, but they slow down the progression of the disease. I think he should see a doctor."

"Good luck. We're talking about the invincible Buck Savage. I don't think the stubborn old coot's set foot in a doctor's office in forty years. You want to be the one to break the news to him that he needs to see a doctor, be my guest. I'm staying out of it. I have to live with the guy."

In spite of the seriousness of the situation, humor warmed Jolene's eyes. "You do have my sympathies there, kid. On the other hand, it was your choice to move back home. If I had to choose between Dad and your ex-wife, I probably would've opted to stay with Linda."

Ty grimaced. "Look," he said, "we're probably both over-reacting. I'll keep a closer eye on Dad. If the situation reaches the point where we decide something has to be done, we'll confront him together. The old strength in numbers routine."

He picked up the pen and tapped it against his desk blotter. "If that doesn't work, we can always pull out the big guns and sic Mom on him."

"And start World War III? I don't know about that."

"Jesus, Jo, if we insist on sending him to the doctor, we'll already have World War III on our hands. Throwing Mom into the mix couldn't possibly make it any worse. But she's one hell of a strategist. She could help us win the war."

Jolene sighed. "I suppose it's all we can do at this point, seeing as how Dad's the most stubborn man on the planet."

"It'll be okay. I promise."

"I'm going to hold you to that, Tyrone. You're the one who lives with him, the one who sees him the most. If anything happens to him, I'm holding you directly responsible."

After she'd gone, he ruminated for a while on the situation. He'd been aware, in a distracted way, of Buck's increasingly erratic behavior, but he'd placed the blame squarely on the aging process. Jo was right; he was in denial. He hadn't wanted to look at the situation too closely for fear of what he'd find. Buck had always been a man's man, proud and macho, powerful and in absolute control. It had been one of the biggest areas of conflict between them, that testosterone-fueled battle to be alpha dog. Ty had struggled mightily with it, but in the end, Buck had always come out on top. He didn't want to think about how his father would react if suddenly that control was wrested away from him.

The clock on the wall read four-thirty. Ty finished signing the sheaf of papers Dixie had left him and returned them to her desk in the outer office. The afternoon shift had just come on duty and were getting ready to go out on patrol. He exchanged greetings with both of his incoming officers, then went back into his office and called Buck.

"Everything okay?" he said.

"Why wouldn't it be?" Buck snapped.

Ty closed his eyes and counted to ten before responding.

"No particular reason," he said. "Just checking in. I won't be home for supper."

Outside, the agreeable spring day had cooled, and long shadows slanted across the century-old brick buildings that lined Water Street. Ty pulled out of the police station and into the block-long snarl of downtown traffic that was Serenity's version of rush hour. Raising two fingers in greeting to Ned Ouellette, who stood, clipboard in hand, at the gas pumps outside the Getty Quik Mart, Ty cruised the length of Androscoggin Street, checking out the activity at Walt's Tavern and Ace's Place and the River City Pub. Things were quiet, but it was early. Most of the brawling wouldn't start until after nine o'clock. Restless, he rolled down his window. Hanging a right at the red light where Androscoggin Street met Route 43, he headed out Bald Mountain Road.

It wouldn't be dusk for another couple of hours, but he could already make out the faint outline of the moon hovering over the distant mountains. This was God's country, unlike any other place he'd ever been. And he'd done his share of traveling. He'd gone to college in California. While he'd been in the military, he'd been stationed in Germany, Japan, Kuwait. Each of those places had possessed its own unique style. But none of them was home. Like Mellencamp and his small town, Ty had been born here in Serenity, and this was probably where they'd bury him.

He'd intended to drive by the Logan place, but Faith's car was sitting in the driveway, and somehow he found himself turning in and pulling to a stop beside it. Buddy wandered over, wagging a greeting. The dog sniffed him, no doubt on the lookout for any secret stash of pizza he might be hoarding. Ty rubbed Buddy's head and smoothed his hands over those velvet-soft ears. He probably ought to warn her about Serenity's leash law. But her dog was on private property, and unless Buddy wandered into the road and disturbed traffic, there wasn't much of anybody out here to complain.

The dog followed him into the shed. Ty rapped on the door

and waited. Inside the house, there was absolute silence. Buddy poked around, sniffed at the old aluminum snow shovel propped in a corner, stuck his nose in an open bag of concrete mix and let out a resounding sneeze. Quiet footsteps approached the other side of the door, and then it opened.

She'd just gotten out of the bath. Her feet were bare, and her shampoo held a faintly floral scent. He didn't recognize the scent, but it was nice, not cloying like some of the stuff Linda used to doctor herself up with. The shapeless red plaid flannel pajamas were a potent fashion statement. On him, they would have been butt-ugly. On her, they possessed a certain inexplicable charm. She hastily shoved a clump of wet hair behind her ear and crossed her arms over her chest. "Hi," she said.

"Nice lingerie."

She looked down at the ugly pajamas, and color flooded her cheeks. "They're Ben's," she said.

"Who's Ben?"

"My husband."

Buddy, tired of waiting for something interesting to happen, squeezed past their legs and disappeared into the house. It hadn't occurred to Ty that she might be married, and the disappointment that washed through him was all out of proportion to the situation. What did it matter? They were nothing more than old friends, and she'd be gone again in a week, two at the most. Casually, he said, "So you left him in New York, but you pilfered his pajamas?"

She raised her face, and those clear blue eyes pierced and held him until he had the damnedest urge to hang his head and shuffle his feet. "He died," she said. "A year and a half ago."

Ty winced. Open mouth, insert foot. He wondered guiltily if God would strike him dead for being glad her husband had died. "Shit," he said. "I'm sorry. I have a really big mouth."

"It's not your fault. You had no way of knowing. Come on in." She stepped aside, and he accepted her invitation. "We never got a chance to talk at the funeral," she said, closing the door behind him. "You were having this intense conversation with Linda Larochelle, and then you both disappeared."

He could have sworn there was something faintly accusatory in her tone. Could it be possible that she was prying in her oh-so-subtle way? Having been quite recently guilty of the same crime, he thought he recognized it, but wasn't one-hundred percent certain. "We used to be married," he said. "She thinks that still gives her the right to monopolize my time whenever the whim strikes."

Those blue eyes widened appreciably. "Ah," she said. "I see. But you're not married anymore."

She was definitely prying. "We're not married anymore."

They studied each other in silence. Jo had hit the nail directly on the head: Faith Pelletier had grown into a knockout. Her skin was smooth and flawless, her eyes an unusual shade of vivid blue. She was slender, but solid. Good, strong bones. But she was far too pale. And a little too thin. She looked as though she could use a good meal. He preferred his women to have a little meat on their bones.

His women. As though he had a half-dozen of them sitting on the sidelines, at his beck and call. Wondering if she'd been ill, he said, "Have you eaten?"

"Actually, I was about to rummage around in the cupboard and see if I could find a can of soup."

"Wait. I have a better idea."

She smiled gamely. "Better than Campbell's chicken noodle?"

"I was thinking about a nice, juicy sirloin. Why don't you join me? Jessie can come along, too, if she wants."

"Jessie's not here. She's spending the night with a friend." She brushed a wisp of hair back from her face. "I appreciate the invitation, Ty, really. But I wouldn't be very good company. I'm bone tired."

"A hot, hearty meal will do you good. I won't keep you out late, and it won't take that much energy for you to throw on a pair of jeans and a sweater. You don't have to dress up. I'll swing by the house and change out of my uniform and into jeans. Then we'll be a matched set."

He could see that she was wavering. She'd obviously been ready to settle down for the night, but something was tempting her to accept his offer. Maybe that juicy sirloin. Maybe the pleasure of his company. Or maybe it was best if he didn't analyze her motives too deeply.

"I didn't sleep much last night," she said. "I'd have to be in by nine at the latest."

"Not a problem," he said. "The place I'm thinking of is just a half hour away. The atmosphere's casual and the steaks are huge."

"Well, then." Her smile drove itself directly into his solar plexus. "Give me five minutes to change. The steak sounds terrific."

The restaurant's ambience was pure twentieth-century American steakhouse, complete with Heinz ketchup and A-1 steak sauce on the tables, wagon wheel lights hanging from the ceiling, and an assortment of dead animals tacked up on the walls. It had been years since Faith had been inside a place like this, and she studied the decor with the same interest she would have shown had she been in a foreign country. In a sense, she supposed, she was. After all, rural Maine was a far cry from Manhattan.

He was true to his word. The steak was massive, and it came with fresh-cooked asparagus and a heaping pile of cottage fries. "I'll never eat all of this," she protested as the waitress set her plate in front of her. "If I tried to cram this much food down my throat, I'd bloat up like a balloon and explode."

Ty cut into his steak. It was pink and bloody in the center. "Don't worry," he said as he sliced off a healthy portion. "I'll help you. There's never been anything wrong with my appetite."

"I remember that about you. And I can see that you're still just a growing boy."

She watched with appreciation as he dug enthusiastically

into his meal. She'd always enjoyed watching a hungry man eat. Ben had once possessed a healthy appetite, but as he'd grown increasingly sicker, it had gradually fallen by the wayside. Toward the end, she'd been lucky to get him to drink half a can of Ensure at mealtime.

But Ty Savage had a hearty appetite. He was a big man, probably six foot two and close to two hundred pounds, every inch of it rock solid. He needed all that food to fuel his body.

Which, she decided upon further inspection, was a most attractive body. Not attractive in the way of the men she saw every day in Manhattan, with their artfully disheveled hair and their designer suits and their expensive cologne. Ty's attractiveness was unassuming and basic. He smelled not of cologne, but of soap and water. His clothes were more L.L. Bean than Hugo Boss: leather work boots, a plaid flannel shirt, and tight jeans that clung like wallpaper to muscled thighs. She'd forgotten just how attractive red flannel could look on a man. His dark hair was neatly cut, falling just shy of his collar in the back. He smiled and, somewhere deep inside, she felt a stirring she hadn't experienced since Ben died. It was his eyes, she decided, that intrigued her so. Dark and liquid and soulful, they were eyes that a woman could fall into and disappear.

"You're not eating."

A flush crawled up her cheeks as she glanced down at her heavily laden plate. She'd been too busy admiring his male attributes to remember she was supposed to be eating. Time to shift gears and get her head down out of the clouds.

"Sorry," she said. "I'm tired. I zoned out there for a bit. But the meal looks wonderful." As proof that she meant what she said, she picked up her utensils and sawed off a tiny portion of sirloin. She took a tentative bite and closed her eyes in pleasure. "This is heaven," she said, suddenly ravenous. What she'd taken for exhaustion was actually starvation. Thinking back over the course of the day, she realized that, except for a few bites of tuna and one forkful of potato salad, she hadn't eaten since last night. No wonder she was weak and irritable. Her blood-sugar level had probably dipped to an all-time low.

They ate in silence, warding off those first hunger pangs. Once they'd each made a significant dent in their respective dinners, Ty set down his fork and reached for a dinner roll. "What do you plan to do about Jessie?"

Faith nibbled at a slender stalk of asparagus and watched him butter his roll. "I don't really have much of a choice," she said. "Once I get things settled here, I'll take her back to New York with me."

"No chance of you staying around here?" He tore the buttered roll in two and ate half of it in a single bite.

She picked up a French fry and swirled it around in a puddle of ketchup. "I don't see it working," she said. "New York is home."

"How long have you lived there?"

"Pretty much ever since I left Serenity. Ben and I rented for several years, but when I started making decent money from my books, we bought a town house. I've grown very attached."

"You know," he said as he sliced off another piece of steak, "I've read all your books."

"You have?" She was surprised, although she couldn't explain why. According to her publisher, her reading audience was sixty percent male. It wasn't unreasonable that Ty Savage might be one of them.

"Hey, it's not every guy who can say he used to have weekly sleepovers with a glamorous, bestselling author." There was humor in those dark eyes as they studied her. "I figured if I wanted bragging rights, I'd better know what I was bragging about. You're really good, you know."

She grimaced. "I *was* really good. Emphasis on the past tense."

He reached for another dinner roll and paused, his hand hovering over the bread plate. "You're not writing anymore?"

"I'm supposed to be working on my next book, but the

manuscript's two years overdue, and I can't seem to finish it. My publisher's given me one last chance to finish, with a very tight deadline. If I don't turn it in on time, all hell will break loose." She toyed with her napkin, twisting and turning and torturing it. "They paid me a lot of money for the book. Unfortunately, publishers aren't in the business of subsidizing authors." Her smile was wry. "I just couldn't write after Ben died. I guess you could say I lost heart."

"Tell me about Ben. Unless it bothers you to talk about him."

"It doesn't bother me." She took another nibble of asparagus. "We met during the first semester of my junior year of college. Twentieth-century American lit. He was my professor."

His eyes widened. "Yikes," he said.

"Exactly. Even back then, before political correctness became the rule *du jour*, that kind of thing was frowned upon. Poor Ben didn't know what to do. It was his first semester of teaching, and he wasn't much older than his students. He certainly didn't expect to fall in love with one of them."

Ty took a sip of beer. "So what happened?"

"Nothing, really. Not until the course ended. We spent the semester making cow eyes at each other and pretending nothing was going on. When he gave back our final term papers, he wrote a note on mine, asking me for a date. Since we'd just ended our teacher-student relationship, dating was no longer taboo. Three months later, we were married." The memory made her smile, even after all these years. "I still have that term paper kicking around somewhere, with his invitation written in red ink right next to my grade."

"Which was?"

"I got a B minus for the course. There was absolutely no favoritism involved."

"Glad to hear it." Ty poured A-1 sauce over his steak. "So you had a good marriage."

"We had a good marriage. We were happy together. We had a nice, stable life. Friends who ran in academic and literary circles. We entertained a lot. Traveled when we could. We had so much in common. And then he got sick. Leukemia." Her voice went flat, the way it always did when she talked about Ben's illness. She set down her fork and unconsciously rubbed at her wrist. "Sometimes, I feel as though the disease took him so quickly. Other times, it seems like those last few months went on forever."

"I'm sorry."

"Thank you." She wasn't willing to delve any deeper into her life tonight. There was no need to tell him about the panic attacks, the sleepless nights, the pills, the psychotherapy. No need to tell him she still wasn't over Ben's death and probably never would be. Those details were too intimate for a first date. If, indeed, this was a date. It had been so many years since she'd dated she wasn't sure, and it would be humiliating to ask. Better to play it by ear than to make an utter fool of herself. She'd very nearly done that once already with this man, eighteen years ago; she had no intention of allowing history to repeat itself.

"I want to hear about you," she said. "I want to know how a cop's son with a chip on his shoulder ended up becoming chief of police."

From the overhead speakers, Britney Spears sang coquettishly about not being that innocent. Ty leaned back in his chair and stretched out his legs, accidentally bumped a foot against Faith's, and quickly withdrew it. "Well," he said, "I didn't know what I wanted to do after high school. Mom and Dad insisted I go to college, so I went, for a year. It was a disaster. So I dropped out and enlisted in the Marines. I traveled all over the world, spent some time in Kuwait during the Gulf War. It gave me a whole different outlook on life. Grew me up, I guess you could say. When my enlistment was up, I went back to college and got a degree in criminology. From there, it was a pretty easy jump to working for my dad on the force here in Serenity. When he retired, I got his job."

"You make it sound so simple."

"It wasn't. In case you don't remember, Buck and I always

got along like oil and water. We grew to respect each other, but we've never seen eye to eye on much of anything. And he didn't make it easy on me. Matter of fact, he was tougher on me than he would have been on any other rookie. Nobody'll ever accuse Buck Savage of nepotism."

Remembering Buck's hardheaded ways, she grinned. "I can certainly believe that."

"He's still making my life hell. I think it's what keeps him going. Or maybe he's just paying me back for the hell I put him through during my wayward adolescence." Ty picked up his bottle of beer and took a sip. "Either way," he said, still holding the bottle, "when he retired and I took over, I got a lot of flack from people who weren't interested in change. I heard more than my share of 'Buck didn't do it this way,' and 'Buck would never say that.' It just about drove me crazy. It's damn hard to try to make your own way in a small town where everybody still sees you as Buck Savage's kid. A police chief needs to convey an authoritative image. Walking in Buck's shoes played hell with that image."

"Has it improved any?"

He set down his beer. "It's gotten better, but it took three years, and I still run into resistance every so often. It's inevitable, I suppose, but I don't much like it."

"What kind of resistance?"

"Take the Somalis, for instance. I've taken plenty of flack over that."

His words nudged at her memory. Something Hilda had said this afternoon. "Forgive me for sounding ignorant," she said, "but I have no idea what you're talking about. Hilda Larson mentioned something about Somalis during the wake today. Something about a series of stories Chelsea wrote."

"They're refugees from the civil war in Somalia. A number of them have settled in Maine."

"Why, for God's sake?"

He chuckled. "Good question. I guess for the same reason anybody moves here. They were living in Atlanta, and they decided it was a lousy place to raise kids. So they set their sights on Lewiston, of all places. About fifteen hundred of them settled there."

"Lewiston," she said in disbelief. "Lewiston, Maine?"

"I know. Not exactly your suburban paradise. They stirred up quite a stink just by showing up. The locals were worried they'd take up all the available apartments, not to mention all the available welfare money. And of course in a place like Maine, which has been whiter than white for three hundred years, there was bound to be racial tension. To top it off, the mayor sent their elders a letter saying the city's coffers were severely overextended and asking them to tell their friends and relatives not to move here. It started a firestorm."

"Yikes."

"I believe the man's intentions were good, but it was taken the wrong way and blown all out of proportion. It made the national news. Racism in little old Maine. People who'd never before known where we were could suddenly point us out on a map. Once the story hit the wires, out-of-state racist organizations sensed fresh blood and scrambled to stick their noses in where they didn't belong. A white supremacist group from Illinois scheduled an anti-Somali rally. The folks at Bates College decided to counteract by holding their own pro-diversity rally. I guess a couple dozen people showed up at the hate rally. Three or four thousand showed up for the other one. The fellow who was supposed to lead the racist rally was unavoidably detained in Illinois on charges of conspiring to murder a federal judge, so he had to send a replacement."

"Sounds like the plot to a really bad soap opera."

"Uh-huh. In the midst of all this chaos, five Somali families decided it was time to relocate someplace that wasn't making news headlines. So they settled here in Serenity. A lot of people aren't happy about it. I'm one of the few who welcomed them, so I was on shit lists all over town for a while."

"Good Lord. How could I have missed something like that?"

"I imagine it generated a lot more press here in Maine than it did at the national level."

"The black woman I saw at the funeral. She's one of them?"

He nodded. "Her name's Sahra Hassan. She and Chelsea became friends when Chelsea was working on the news stories Hilda told you about."

"I am absolutely dumbfounded."

He grinned. "Bet you never knew Maine could be such a hotbed of intrigue."

Remembering what Newt had told her, she pondered the possibility that there could be a grain of truth to his words. Might Chelsea's death somehow be tied to the Somali situation? "Speaking of intrigue," she said slowly, "how well do you know Newt Rollins?"

"Well enough, I suppose. Why?"

She debated how to word her question. "Has he always seemed rational and levelheaded?"

He gave her question serious thought. "Newt's social skills could use a little polishing," he said, "but he's smart as a whip. Valedictorian of his high school graduating class. Phi Beta Kappa. Graduated summa cum laude from Yale." Ty tilted his beer and took a sip. "You're leading up to something. What is it?"

Faith busied herself rearranging her silverware on her plate. "This afternoon," she said, "he came to me with an outlandish story. He seems to think that Chelsea was—" She paused, a little embarrassed at having to speak the ridiculous word aloud. Lowering her voice, she said, "Murdered. And he thinks it was connected to some news story she was working on."

His eyebrows lifted in unison. "Murdered?" he said. "Where'd he get an idea like that?"

"Newt says that the night she died, Chelsea left a message on his voice mail. Supposedly she was bringing in some story that she thought would rock Serenity right to its foundations, and she asked Newt to hold the front page for her. But she died before she could get to the newspaper office."

Skepticism etched in every line of his face, he said, "And Newt believes this indicates murder because…?"

"I know. It sounds crazy. I told him to get a good night's sleep and see how he felt in the morning."

"Sound advice."

"He was in love with her, you know. He didn't say so, but it was written all over him. There's a part of me that says he's just grief-stricken and grasping at straws. On the other hand…"

"Don't tell me you bought into his story. There hasn't been a murder in Serenity since 1947."

"I know it's pretty far-fetched. But then, so is the suicide theory."

"Look," he said, "I believe there's a perfectly reasonable explanation for how Chelsea ended up in the river, and I highly doubt that murder had anything to do with it. Sooner or later, the truth will come out, and we'll all feel foolish about the speculation we've engaged in."

"I suppose you're right," she said.

Ty uttered a long-suffering sigh. "How do I put this without sounding like a pompous ass?" He straightened in his seat and leaned over the table, his dark eyes somber. "I'm a cop. I deal with evidence. If it can be seen or heard or tasted or touched or measured, I'm your man. You, on the other hand, are a crime writer. You spend most of your time probing the darker reaches of the human psyche. It's not unreasonable that you'd be looking for bogeymen under every bed and in every closet. But that doesn't mean you're going to find them."

Heat erupted in a slow simmer just beneath her skin. "You think I'm a nutcase."

"I don't think anything of the kind. All I'm saying is that without any evidence beyond Newt's suspicions, there's no reason to believe that Chelsea's death was anything more than an unfortunate accident."

Her fledgling anger crashed and burned. "You're right," she

said. "I know you're right. I'm just looking for answers where there aren't any. It's frustrating."

"I know. But let's hold off on making any rash judgments just yet. Let the state police conduct their investigation. If they come up with something concrete, they'll notify me."

"And you'll notify me."

He leaned back again in his chair and ran his fingers up and down the neck of his beer bottle. "I'll tell you as much as I possibly can."

"Which isn't quite the same as telling me everything."

The subdued lighting softened and blurred the lines of his face. His eyes were kind, his smile so subtly seductive that she was drawn in without even realizing it until awareness sucker punched her directly in the gut. "I won't hold anything from you," he said, "unless it's absolutely necessary."

She wet her suddenly dry lips. "I suppose that'll have to do."

"Good," he said. "Now that we have that settled, how about some dessert? The apple pie here is the best I've ever had. But whatever you do, don't tell my mother that. She'd never forgive me."

An hour later, their bellies groaning, they said good-night at her kitchen door. Faith let Buddy out to do his business, and Ty climbed back into his cruiser. She stood in the doorway and watched his taillights until they disappeared, then she called the dog back in. He came running eagerly. She locked the door and snapped off the outside light, plunging herself once again into that eerie darkness and isolation that surrounded the Logan place.

Her exhaustion had returned full-force. She decided to forgo the tranquilizer. If she couldn't sleep without it when she was this tired, she had a bigger problem than she thought. And Dr. Garabedian, with his insistence that she learn to function without benefit of pharmaceuticals, would be pleased. She changed into pajamas and brushed her teeth, then crawled into bed with Buddy curled up at the foot.

She was asleep the instant her head hit the pillow.

Faith was dreaming, one of those bizarre dreams that seem perfectly logical until you wake up and try to piece it back together, at which point the whole thing disintegrates into meaningless gibberish. In the dream, she and Davy Hunter were delivering copies of the *River City Gazette*, riding double on Homer Berube's ancient Schwinn, Davy on the seat and Faith propped with surprising comfort on the handlebars. The front-page story was one Chelsea had written about the Somali immigrants, and as they rolled down Water Street, Davy pulled newspapers from a canvas bag at his hip and tossed one on the sidewalk in front of each business they passed.

As they neared the police station, she saw Ty Savage standing out front holding a leash attached to the biggest pit bull she'd ever seen. They both gaped at the dog, which had to be the size of a Great Dane. While his attention was otherwise engaged, Davy accidentally rammed the bike into a lamppost with a dull thud, and Faith tumbled to the ground.

The pit bull began growling and straining at its leash, trying to get to her. Ty struggled to hold it back, but the dog's strength, like its size, was immense. On hands and knees, Faith scrambled away, but the pit bull kept getting nearer, flashing razor-sharp teeth, its growl increasing in volume and intensity with every inch it gained on her.

She awakened with a jolt, her heart hammering. Beside her, Buddy was growling low in his throat. In the inky blackness downstairs, she heard what sounded like a single stealthy footstep on the hardwood floor. She rested a hand on Buddy. His hackles raised, he growled again, more ominously this time. Faith held her breath and listened. Again, she heard the hushed tread of a shoe on hardwood.

Somebody was in the house.

She'd locked the back door when she brought Buddy in. She was certain of it. Whoever was downstairs either had a key or had broken in. She reached for the telephone to call the police, then remembered that there was no phone in Chelsea's guest room. Her cousin apparently hadn't entertained many guests. And Faith no longer owned a cell phone because she'd canceled her service after Ben died. Who, after all, was she going to call? As soon as she got back to New York, restoring it would be her number-one priority. But for now, she and Buddy were on their own.

She sat up in bed and swung her legs over the side. "Stay," she whispered to Buddy. She shuffled silently to the door and peered down the stairs. A faint bluish glow, like that of a television playing with the volume muted, dimly illuminated the downstairs. Faith crossed her arms over her chest. Could it be possible that Jessie had grown tired of her friends and decided to come home in the middle of the night?

Behind her, Buddy growled again, and she immediately discounted that theory. It was unlikely that he'd be growling at Jessie; her scent was everywhere in the house. The intruder was someone else, someone Buddy didn't know. But who in their right mind would break into someone's house in the middle of the night to watch TV with the volume turned off?

With nervous fingers, she rubbed absently at her upper arm. More times than she cared to remember, she'd sat with Ben through some slasher movie whose dull-witted heroine opened the door to the cellar, peered down into the darkness, and, ignoring the audience's shouted warning of, "Don't go in the cellar!" went down there anyway. She had always wanted to shake those Hollywood dimwits until they got a clue. They might as well wear a huge red V for *victim* on their shirts. Faith Pelletier was no victim, and she wasn't about to follow their twisted logic or their predictably fatal actions.

But she needed to do something besides just stand here and wait. Whoever was down there was apt to carry off half the household belongings if she didn't stop him. She took a tentative step into the hall, uncertainty dancing in her belly. What was she expecting to accomplish? She had no means of calling for help, and no weapon except for a forty-pound mixed-breed mutt. She was a petite woman with no self-defense training, alone with an anonymous intruder in a house in the middle of nowhere. If he were bent on harming her, there was little she could do to defend herself.

On the other hand, he—or she—hadn't bothered to come upstairs. The flickering blue light and the furtiveness of the sounds coming from downstairs said that his business wasn't with her. If she could keep Buddy quiet, her safest option might be to stay right where she was until the intruder found whatever he was looking for and left.

She crept silently to the top of the stairs, knelt in inky darkness and peered through the banister rails. From this vantage point, she could see a sliver of the den, where Chelsea had set up a home office. The bluish glow came from Chelsea's computer monitor. In the faint light, she watched a pair of black-gloved hands shuffle through a stack of floppy disks.

Newt's words rushed back to her, and suddenly they didn't sound quite so crazy after all. She wrapped her fingers around a white wooden spindle and held tight while the intruder chose a floppy disk, inserted it into the computer's A: drive, and booted it up.

Buddy jumped down from the bed with a thud, and the intruder froze. The dog clicked his way across the hardwood floor toward her, every tick of his toenails sounding like cannon fire. He whimpered, and she threw an arm around him and rubbed his neck in a soothing motion, hoping it would be enough to keep him quiet. But Buddy took his duties as a guard dog seriously. The dog whimpered again, then let out a single, deep bark.

Inside the den, there was a loud thump. Buddy barked again and raced for the stairs as the prowler dropped the stack of floppies on the floor with a clatter and dashed out of the room. In the dim light, Faith saw little more than a blur. The prowler was an average-size man—or perhaps a woman—dressed all in black and wearing a ski mask.

Downstairs, the back door opened and then slammed shut. Barking frantically, Buddy began throwing himself against it.

Faith ran downstairs, shoved him aside, and threw the door open. Buddy raced past her, still barking, and sprinted down the driveway. Somewhere in the darkness, an automobile engine started up. The driver shifted the car into gear and took off with a squeal of tires, as Faith stood in the open doorway and watched the red glow of taillights racing down Bald Mountain.

Her heart thudding, she called for the dog, who was still at the end of the driveway, barking himself hoarse. After a couple of minutes, he gave up and came trotting back, looking self-satisfied and ready to go back to sleep now that the fun and games were over. She knelt and gave him a hard hug, her hands fisted in his soft fur as she tried to calm her racing pulse.

Slow, calming breaths. One after another. Feel your body relaxing.

She was almost certain the intruder had acted alone. Almost. She got up from the kitchen floor and turned on the overhead light, then crept through the rest of the house with Buddy at her side, turning on lamp after lamp, switch after switch, until the old farmhouse was ablaze with light. Only then, with the gremlins of darkness held at bay and her heart rate once again somewhere near normal, did she pick up the phone book, look up Ty Savage's number, and dial the phone.

His voice sounded sleepy when he answered. Not surprising, since it was 2:23 in the morning. "It's Faith," she said.

He went from sleepy to alert within seconds. "Faith," he said. "What's wrong?"

"Do you think you could come over?" She rubbed her elbow and shuddered. "Somebody just broke into the house."

Nine

The man was waiting for him in the weed-choked entrance outside the locked gates to the old mill. The boy drove up and parked, driver's door to driver's door. He turned off his lights and killed the engine, then rolled down his window. From the other car, he could hear the Judds singing softly and sweetly about the good old days. "What did you get?" the man asked.

In the shadows, all he could see of the man was the glitter of his eyes. "Nothing," the boy said.

"I suppose you realize that's not an acceptable answer."

"Easy for you to say. You're not the one who almost got your nuts chewed off by some big-ass dog. Why the hell didn't you tell me there was a dog?"

"I didn't know there was a dog."

"Yeah, well, maybe next time you should do your homework. Or better yet, do your own dirty work."

In the dim light, he saw the man glance furtively over his shoulder. "You know why I can't do it myself. There's too much at stake."

"Right. And if I get caught, I hang alone."

"You do unless you want me to blow the whistle on you and tell the entire world what I know."

The guy had him by the short hairs, and they both knew it.

"Look, dude," he said, "I don't much care for this sneaking around in the middle of the night. It gives me the creeps."

"You don't have a choice. This isn't a game. This is the real world. If certain information gets into the wrong hands, you can kiss it all goodbye. The football scholarship, law school, shagging the goddamn prom queen."

"Then come up with a decent idea next time, because this one almost landed me in the emergency room, getting my ass stitched back together. Now what?"

The man was quiet for a while, thinking. "What about the girl?" he said. "Jessie?"

The boy blinked. He had only a vague impression of her. Dark hair, scrawny. He thought she wore glasses, but wasn't sure. "What about her?"

"You're a good-looking young buck. Football hero, teenage heartthrob. She's an impressionable young girl. Turn on the charm. Pay some attention to her. Get to know her. Get invited over to the house."

"Where I can get my hands on the computer."

"Exactly."

"How am I supposed to do that without making her suspicious?"

"You're a smart kid. You'll figure it out."

The boy sighed, silently cursing the series of bad decisions that had gotten him involved in this mess in the first place. "I'll see what I can do."

"We have to find that information before anybody else does. Understand?"

The boy squared his jaw. "Yeah. I hear you."

"Good. And, Coop? Don't screw up again."

When Ty pulled into the driveway, she had every light in the house on. All she needed was a few colored beads and an ugly mask or two, and it would look like Mardi Gras. He climbed out of the cruiser, stopping to examine a lone footprint in the damp earth outside the shed. It wasn't much of a print, just a section of sneaker tread. In spite of the recent spring rains, the northeast wind that had blown so hard for the past couple of days had gone a long way toward drying the muddy ground. In the absence of any other sneaker impressions, he concluded that the prowler had headed down the lawn and across the field adjacent to the house. From there, it would have been easy to jump the ditch and hop into his waiting car, parked by the side of the road.

He went into the shed and knocked on the door. Buddy barked, and Faith lifted the curtain and peered out before she opened the door. She looked tiny and vulnerable in jeans and a Daffy Duck T-shirt, dark hair tumbling around a face as pale as moonlight. Her lower lip trembled as she raised a hand to brush a strand of hair away from her face.

His protective instincts, never far from the surface, kicked in full-force. It was a good thing he hadn't caught the son of a bitch in the act, because he would have ripped the guy to shreds with his bare hands. "Are you all right?" he said.

"I'm fine. A little shaken, but otherwise in perfect running order. Thanks for coming."

She didn't look fine. Her hands were trembling visibly, and she was whiter than his mother's best bedsheets. "He jimmied the lock," she said unnecessarily.

Scowling at the door, he said, "I can see that." He gave the lock a cursory examination. Around here, most people didn't even bother to lock their doors. They didn't need to. Those who did were only trying to keep out the honest folk. This lock wouldn't have kept out a five-year-old, not if he was intent on getting inside.

"I'm sorry to wake you," she said. "I could've called 911, but I felt a little foolish. What was I supposed to tell them, that some burglar had broken in and was trying to steal floppy disks? They would have carted me off to the funny farm for a psychiatric exam."

"You would've ended up getting me anyway, unless the County Sheriff had somebody nearby at the time you called.

After midnight, all our calls are routed through their dispatch. If they get an emergency call for us and they don't have a deputy in the immediate vicinity, they call me at home."

"Do you still believe I'm seeing bogeymen everywhere?"

Instead of answering, he said, "Let's go take a look at what we've got."

He followed her through the living room and into a small den. The computer on the desktop was running, a listing of its C: drive contents splashed across the screen. A thick dictionary lay on the floor beside the desk. Scattered around it were a dozen plastic floppies. He knelt and studied them. It looked as though the dog had scared the bejesus out of the guy, at which point he'd dropped everything and fled. Obviously an amateur. A pro would have already checked out the place, discovered there was a dog on the premises, and taken steps to alleviate the problem. Still kneeling, he said, "You didn't touch anything, did you?"

"I'm not an idiot, Savage. I write crime novels for a living. I know how this stuff works."

She sounded so indignant that he had to hold back a smile. "I'm sure you do."

"Don't bother to look for fingerprints. You won't find any. He was wearing gloves."

He looked up at her, then brushed off his hands and stood. "I'm pretty sure I don't want to hear how you know that, but I'm going to ask anyway."

"I was hiding in the upstairs hallway, watching him."

Christ Almighty. He closed his eyes and winced. Opened them and studied her through narrowed lids. "Don't look at me that way," she said. "It was dark. He couldn't see me."

It took great fortitude to bite back the words he wanted to say. Instead, he said, "Did you get a good look at the guy?"

"Not really. The door was open a crack, and I saw a pair of gloved hands rummaging through the floppies. When Buddy ran downstairs, I got a quick glimpse of him as he beat feet for the door." She must have recognized the guarded optimism in his expression, because she added, "Before you get too excited, I can't identify him. Even if it hadn't been dark—which it was—he was dressed all in black and he wore a ski mask."

"Size? Height? Build?"

"Average, average and average. No identifying characteristics that I could make out, except for those black gloves."

"Great. We'll bring you down to the station for a lineup. Trot out all our suspects and put black gloves on them. See if you recognize anyone."

"Ha-ha. Very funny. Look, Savage, it was dark, and the guy was dressed in black from head to toe. Give me a break."

He liked the way she called him Savage. It implied a certain intimacy between them. Apparently he'd ticked her off just a bit, like he'd done during supper. Good. Getting mad had returned the color to her cheeks.

"So?" she continued. "Do you still think Newt's crazy?"

"I think he believes what he's saying."

"And you don't find it rather coincidental that somebody breaks into the house and rummages through Chelsea's computer disks approximately twelve hours after Newt tells me he thinks she was killed because of a story she was working on?"

He found it damned coincidental and, as a cop, he didn't believe in coincidence. But he was obligated to explore every possibility. He glanced again at the scattered diskettes. "Do you think he got away with anything?"

"Not unless he stuffed it down his pants. His hands were empty when he left, and I'm pretty sure he was wearing sweats. No pockets."

He gave her a long, speculative look. "I thought you didn't see much."

She stared back at him, brazen as high noon on a hot day in July. "It was a quick impression."

The blazing lights he'd seen as he drove up told him she'd already checked out the rest of the house. But he'd feel a whole lot better if he saw with his own eyes that nobody was hiding in some dark corner. Not that there were many dark corners left, considering how fast the electric meter must be spinning. "I'd like to check out the rest of the house," he said.

"Good. I imagine if anybody were here, Buddy would let me know. But I'd feel more secure hearing it from you."

Good to know he rated higher on her reliability scale than the dog. She'd been right when she claimed she wasn't an idiot. Although hiding in a darkened hallway and spying on an intruder wasn't likely to show up on any list of safety tips he'd recommend to security-conscious homeowners, at least she had the good sense not to confront the guy. Invisible teeth gnawed at his stomach lining when he thought about what might have happened if she had.

With Faith and the dog trailing behind him, Ty spent twenty minutes looking in closets and under beds and in every other conceivable location that an adult could hide. The door to the attic was locked from the outside, and no self-respecting thief would hide in the cellar, which smelled of damp earth and mildew and looked like a dungeon. Once he'd given the house the all-clear, he asked her if she wanted to file a report.

"What's the sense?" she said. "Realistically, what can you do? You have no suspects, no fingerprints and only a partial footprint. I highly doubt you're going to run DNA sampling on a simple B-and-E where it appears that nothing was even taken."

She was right. His resources were limited, and this wasn't exactly the crime of the century. But he felt damned uneasy about its proximity to Chelsea's as yet unexplained death, not to mention Newt's allegations of homicide. Although odds were that the break-in wasn't related to either of these events, he couldn't be sure, and that was what bothered him. He wondered if Newt had told anybody else besides Faith about his suspicions.

"I'd feel better," he said, "if you filed a report. Just so we have something on record."

She glanced at the clock. "Right now?"

"It can wait until morning. Meantime—" he took a second

look at the broken door lock "—you need some way to keep the door secured until you can replace the lock with something that'll actually keep people out."

She raised a slender arm and impatiently shoved a clump of hair behind her ear. In the cartoon T-shirt, with no makeup and her bare toes peeping out from beneath the ragged hem of her jeans, she looked about fifteen years old. There was no trace of the bestselling author, no trace of the staunch survivor who'd watched her husband die a lingering death and come out of the ordeal intact. "I'll wedge a chair under the knob for tonight," she said wearily. "In the morning, I can call a locksmith. I imagine at this point, I'm about as safe as it gets. The guy took off like a jackrabbit once Buddy started barking. I doubt he'll be back tonight."

She was probably right. The knowledge should have comforted him. For some reason, it didn't. "You do realize," he said, "that this was probably just some kid intent on stealing the computer equipment? He most likely heard that Chelsea had died, and figured while the house was empty, he could break in and steal whatever's not nailed down."

He wanted her to believe it. He just wasn't sure he believed it himself.

"I thought most kids have their own computers these days."

"They do," he said, "but if you're looking for money to buy drugs, electronics are one of the easiest and quickest items to fence."

She raised an eyebrow. "Does Serenity have a drug problem?"

"Every small town in Maine has a drug problem." He glanced at the clock. It was nearly three-thirty, and he didn't want to leave her alone, didn't want to leave her vulnerable. Didn't want to leave her, period. Had she asked, he would have stayed until daylight. But she didn't ask. If she felt secure staying in the house with just the dog for protection, there was nothing left for him to do but make a graceful exit. And if he spent the rest of the night lying awake, worrying, she didn't need to know about it.

He cleared his throat. "So you'll come down to the station in the morning to file a complaint?"

"I have an appointment at nine-thirty with Chelsea's lawyer to go over the details of her will. I'll stop by after that." She glanced at the door. "And after I call the locksmith."

"Albert Paré, 13 Androscoggin Street. He's in the book. Tell him I sent you, and that it's an emergency. He'll be out here in a flash."

For the first time since he arrived, she smiled. Tiny feathers of pleasure tickled his insides. "My, my," she said. "You're a veritable font of information, aren't you?"

He leaned against the doorjamb and said, "I'm a cop. You know the slogan—to protect and serve. I'm just doing my duty."

They stood that way, studying each other in silence, while wispy memories and impossible dreams flitted through his brain. "Hey," she said, finally, softly. "Thanks."

It was time to make his exit, before he made a damn fool of himself. He tipped his Red Sox cap and stepped away from the doorjamb. "You're welcome. Don't forget to wedge that chair under the doorknob." He paused, hand on the knob. "And keep Buddy down here tonight. Just in case. Sounds like he makes a pretty good burglar alarm."

He waited until she'd turned off the outside light before he backed down the driveway. When he reached the end, instead of turning toward town, he headed in the other direction, down the backside of Bald Mountain. At the bottom, he took a right onto Toothaker Road, drove past the swamp, and pulled into Davy Hunter's driveway.

It took Davy a while to answer his hammering. Eventually, the outside light came on and the ancient metal door with its jalousie windows swung open. Davy stood on the other side, gaunt and pale and shirtless, swaying as he squinted into the light. "Jesus Christ, man," he said, "it's three-thirty in the morning."

"You're damn right it is." Ty shoved his way past Davy and into the trailer. Inside, it was shabby, but neater than he'd expected. A brightly colored Mexican blanket camouflaged the faded tweed couch. On the kitchen table, a wooden bowl held an assortment of ripe fruit.

"Great to see you," Davy said dryly. "Won't you come in?"

Fists clenched, Ty swung around to face his old friend. At the look on his face, Davy froze. "What?" he said.

"Somebody broke into the Logan place tonight."

Davy relaxed, moving with cool nonchalance toward the kitchen. He opened the fridge and took out a can of beer. Popped the top. "That so?" he said.

"Park it," Ty said. "You and I are going to have a little heart-to-heart."

Davy took a long slug of Budweiser. "At three-thirty in the morning?"

"You got it in one, champ. And I'm not leaving until you spill everything you know about what's going on."

Albert Paré was there by 8:00. "Ayuh," he said, examining the inadequate little piece of nothing that Chelsea had called a door lock. "This here would make a nice lock for the bathroom door. Keep your kids from wandering in while you're soaking in the tub. But it won't do much to keep out intruders."

He reached into his toolbox and pulled out a small cardboard box. "For that, you need a dead bolt. Like this one." He popped the box open, and a heavy-duty dead bolt lock fell out into his palm. "Be pretty tough to break through this little baby. Not impossible," he added, studying the thing with all the admiration most men would have shown for a good-looking woman. "But she's pretty tough to get past."

By eight-thirty, the lock was installed, and Paré was paid and on his way back to town. Faith took a quick shower and dressed in a pair of cream-colored linen pants and a teal silk blouse with an open collar. Her appointment with Louis Cunningham, Chelsea's lawyer, was at nine-thirty, and she didn't want to go there looking like a woman who'd only slept for four hours last night. Even if it was the truth.

After Ty had left last night, she'd picked up the scattered floppy disks and locked them in a drawer, shut down the computer, then spent the rest of the night on the couch with Buddy by her side. Although she made a feeble attempt to sleep, she'd been far too wound up, her mind churning with endless questions. Who was the man in black? What had he been looking for? Were Newt's suspicions correct? And what did the break-in have to do with Chelsea's death?

There was no doubt in her mind that the two events were related. It was just too much coincidence for her to swallow. Yesterday, she'd considered Newt Rollins a grief-stricken, delusional man. Today, she knew better. It was clear that, just as in a well-written novel, Event A had led directly to Event B. Chelsea, with her typical full-speed-ahead-and-damn-the-torpedoes approach to life, had stumbled onto something she had no business knowing about. She'd pried and snooped until she'd uncovered information that would have caused an uproar if it had made the pages of the *Gazette*. Somebody hadn't wanted that information to come to light, somebody desperate enough to kill to prevent it from happening.

It made her mad as hell. Considering that she'd spent the past eighteen months locked in a state of numbness, the rush of passionate anger felt wonderful. Dr. Garabedian would have called it a breakthrough. Faith didn't bother naming it, she simply reveled in the fact that something had finally broken through the wall of indifference that had surrounded her since Ben's death. She might not be cured, but it was a first step in the long journey back. For the first time in eighteen months, she had a purpose and a goal. Somebody had killed her cousin, deliberately and maliciously, leaving an innocent fifteen-year-old girl without a mother. And Faith Pelletier wasn't going back to New York until she knew who had done it—and why.

But that wasn't the only thing that had kept her tossing and turning until dawn. Scattered among her turbulent thoughts of homicide were fleeting images of Serenity's police chief.

There was something about those eyes of his, something about the way he looked at her, that made her insides quiver with awareness.

It came as something of a surprise. She'd truly loved Ben, and he'd been gone for a mere eighteen months. There was a part of her, the long-married part of her, that felt distinctly uncomfortable being drawn like this to another man. But she'd loved Ty Savage, too, once upon a time, loved him in that callow, all-encompassing way of an eighteen-year-old girl with a broken heart she was certain would never mend. And vestiges of those old feelings still lingered. How could she have known that when he came knocking at her door, she'd take a single look into those soulful brown eyes and be shaken and stirred like a dry martini?

Of course, it didn't matter. She wouldn't be here long enough for it to matter. She wasn't the kind of woman to engage in casual sex, and her life was too complicated right now for a real relationship. Sooner or later—most likely sooner—anything they might start would reach a dead end. What was the sense in even thinking about it?

But think about it she did. Like the old childhood game where you tried not to think about a pink elephant with purple polka dots, the more she tried not to imagine starting up something with Ty Savage, the more the possibility occupied her mind.

She'd still been thinking about it, hunched over her morning coffee like a drunk coming off a bender, when Dottie McLaughlin had called to tell her that Jessie was insisting she be allowed to attend school today. Since Jessie was undoubtedly the primary heir to her mother's estate, she probably should have gone with Faith to Cunningham's office. But their meeting would be little more than an hour of legal gibberish that would have bored a fifteen-year-old kid beyond belief. Jessie's life had just fallen apart, and it wasn't unreasonable that she'd cling to the one solid, familiar thing she had left. While everything else around her was disintegrating, school offered a structure and a comfort that existed nowhere else in her life.

So Faith gave her blessing. It was probably just as well if Jessie didn't come home for a few hours anyway. Maybe by tonight, Faith would have figured out just how much to tell the girl about the broken door lock and how much to keep to herself.

Louis Cunningham was fortyish and attractive in a lean, loose-jointed way. In spite of the three-piece suit he wore, Cunningham exuded an air of casualness she found appealing. She'd never liked stuffy, self-important lawyers, and she knew instantly why Chelsea had chosen him. He offered Faith coffee and then proceeded to explain, in simple and comprehensible language, the terms of Chelsea's will.

"It's pretty straightforward," he told her. "You've been named executor of the estate. That puts you in charge of everything, from paying bills to deciding whether or not to liquidate assets."

"What assets?"

"Primarily the house and its contents. Chelsea owned it free and clear. Her father left it to her, and she left it to Jessie. As executor, you have responsibility for managing the household. I'm assuming you're planning to go back to New York?"

"Eventually, yes."

"Then you'll have to decide whether to keep the house for Jessie's use later on down the road, or sell it and bank the money to give her when she comes of age." He propped his elbows on the desk and threaded slender fingers together in front of him. "That's a decision you and Jessie will need to make together. Also—and I assume you're already aware of this—Chelsea designated you as the person she wanted to raise her daughter in the event that anything should happen to her before Jessie reaches the age of majority. Is that something you're comfortable with?"

"I'm not sure *comfortable* is the right word," she said.

"Comfort may take some time, considering that Jessie and I are virtual strangers. Do I find the arrangement acceptable? Yes." She crossed her legs and smiled. "Of course, there are Jessie's feelings to be considered here, too. How legally binding is this arrangement? If Jessie doesn't agree to it, can it be changed?"

"Legally, it doesn't hold much water. In reality, it's little more than the mother's expressed wishes. The court doesn't have to recognize them. Should you and Jessie agree to the arrangement on a permanent basis, you'd want to petition the court for legal custody. It makes things a lot easier. Just let me know, and I can get that started for you whenever you're ready." He leaned back in his leather-bound chair and swiveled it in a lazy back-and-forth motion. "The other primary consideration is Chelsea's life insurance. Jessie was the primary beneficiary. The money will come to her, but you'll be expected to manage it for her until she turns eighteen."

"I have a question." This hadn't occurred to her until now, but the possible ramifications were frightening. "I've been told the police could rule Chelsea's death a suicide. Not for a minute do I believe she killed herself. But if that's the official ruling, once the investigation is complete, am I correct in assuming the insurance company would refuse to pay?"

The attorney considered her question. "I suppose it depends on the insurance company, but in my experience, I've never known one to pay out on a policy if the death was ruled a suicide."

"How much money are we talking?"

Cunningham riffled through a stack of papers, paused halfway through, frowned as he skimmed Chelsea's life insurance policy. "It appears that Chelsea took out a policy last year for two-hundred-thousand dollars."

"Good God." The amount astonished her. Chelsea had provided well for her daughter in the event of her death. That much money would easily pay for four years at just about any college Jessie might choose to attend. If the insurance company should refuse to pay, it would be the equivalent of steal- ing Jessie's future right out of her hands. Faith couldn't let that happen.

"One more question," she said. "You told me that Jessie was the primary beneficiary. That implies a secondary."

"That's correct. There were two beneficiaries named on Chelsea's policy. Jessie is the primary, which means that as long as she survives her mother, she receives the money. If Jessie hadn't outlived her mother, then the secondary benefi- ciary would have received the two hundred thousand."

Her stomach soured. Already knowing the answer, she had to ask the question. "Who is that second beneficiary?"

Cunningham stood the sheaf of papers on end, tapped them against the desktop to line them up neatly before he clipped them together with an oversize wire clip and set them back down on the desk blotter in front of him. "Davy Hunter," he said.

Ten

It was a lovely spring day, birds twittering and chirping, the air rich with the scent of ripening earth, and after she left Cunningham's office, Faith decided to walk to the police station at the other end of Water Street. She'd been away for a long time, and she wanted to see up close what changes had occurred since she'd walked these streets as a girl.

The number of vacant storefronts was troubling. The bakery was gone, as was the hardware store where her father used to take her when she was a child. She'd been fascinated by the big galvanized aluminum bins filled with bolts and washers and nails of every size and variety. If she closed her eyes, she could still remember the smell of the dusty wooden floorboards where she'd loved to crawl. Her mother would always scold her when her father brought her home looking like a dust mop. But it was worth the scolding, for Mr. Wilkins, the proprietor, always gave her a pink-striped peppermint lollipop. He kept a glass jar of them next to the cash register, to give out to all the kids who visited. She'd adored both the man and the place.

That had been thirty years ago, and she supposed Mr. Wilkins was probably dead by now. At the time, he'd seemed ancient to her, but in all probability, he hadn't been much more than sixty. It was amazing how thirty years changed one's perspective on aging.

Two doors farther down Water Street had been another of her favorite places, the fabric store where her mother bought material to sew her school clothes. As young girls, she and Chelsea liked to play hide-and-seek in the narrow aisles between brightly colored bolts of fabric while her mother shopped. Faith had loved the feel of the different fabrics: the nubby softness of corduroy, the smooth, raspy coolness of satin, the wonderful scratchiness of taffeta. There'd been something magical about that store, about the colorful yards of fabric that her mother magically transformed into the most beautiful clothes she'd ever seen. For Faith, the memory was bittersweet. Her mother had been dead for nearly twenty-five years. Now, Chelsea was dead, too. And the enchanted fabric store of Faith's childhood was just another empty storefront with a faded For Lease sign propped in the window.

Across the street, where Harrington's Drugstore used to stand, with its old-fashioned soda fountain frequented by generations of teenagers, a new business had opened. The building had been painted a warm shade of yellow. Across the top of the plate-glass window the words Halaal Variety were painted in red. Beneath them were more words, in what she assumed to be Somali. In smaller print beneath that it said, "Meats, produce, cigarettes, gifts." Inside, behind the counter, stood the woman she'd seen at the funeral. Sahra Hassan.

Faith lingered on the cracked sidewalk and watched the woman bag merchandise for a customer who stood just outside her line of vision. The customer handed Sahra a fistful of bills. She counted them, punched the cash register, and handed the change back to the customer.

For an instant, Faith was tempted to cross the street, to go inside and speak to the woman. Sahra and Chelsea had been friends. Ty had said so. What if the woman knew something about Chelsea's death? What if she was aware of some small detail that might not seem important to her, but which would lead directly to Chelsea's killer?

That was a lot of ifs. And she knew that Ty wouldn't approve if she started snooping around. He would remind her of his earlier advice: leave the investigating to the professionals. But the professionals, Ty included, didn't appear to be doing much investigating, despite the fact that things in Serenity were anything but serene. And when strangers started breaking into her house while she was asleep, invading her private space, no matter what the motive, Faith couldn't help but take it personally.

A man wearing a John Deere hat and a two-day growth of beard emerged from Halaal Variety and paused on the sidewalk in front of the door to light a Camel. A Somali woman in traditional dress, trailed by three small children, approached the store. The man stood his ground, blocking her entrance while he took his time lighting the cigarette. He tossed his match onto the ground, eyed the woman at length, and made a remark Faith couldn't hear from across the street. The woman stiffened, but her eyes remained downcast. After a moment, the man snickered and stepped aside, and the woman quickly ushered her children into the store. His eyes followed her with an expression of such loathing, Faith's throat tightened in response.

Then he adjusted his hat and sauntered off down the street. She let out a hard breath. What on earth had that been about? Did he know the woman, or was he simply responding to her color? Ty had said the Somalis weren't welcomed with open arms. Did this kind of thing happen every day, or was this an isolated incident? She had no idea what he'd said to the Somali woman, but her body language had clearly stated that she didn't care for it.

Faith decided she'd better educate herself before she attempted to approach the Hassan woman. Chelsea's series of articles would be the ideal place to start. They'd give her a frame of reference from which to start. A jumping-off place.

Once she'd read and processed those, she would go through Chelsea's computer files with a fine-tooth comb. Her mysterious midnight visitor had obviously been searching for something. She suspected it would behoove her to locate it before he did.

She could only hope she'd recognize it when she found it.

The police station was quiet on this weekday morning. The young woman at the dispatch desk was tapping furiously at her computer keyboard. She paused to squint at the monitor, backspaced, and made a correction. "Help you?" she said distractedly.

"I'm Faith Pelletier. I had a break-in last night. Ty told me to come down this morning and file a complaint."

"Right. He said you were coming." The woman abandoned her work in favor of studying Faith unabashedly. She was somewhere in her late twenties, with a fresh-faced, girl-next-door look, her blond hair pulled back in a loose ponytail and freckles lightly dusting her nose. "Through the door over there—" she pointed "—first office on the right. Pete'll take care of you."

Faith told herself it wasn't disappointment that rose up inside her. There was no reason she should have expected that Ty would handle the paperwork himself. But she'd expected it anyway. She was being ridiculous. He was the chief of police. He undoubtedly had more important things to do than routine paperwork.

Pete Morin was a bear of a man with coppery-red hair and an offbeat sense of humor. She vaguely remembered him as an upperclassman from Serenity High. It was hard to forget hair that color. "I heard about your break-in," he said. "Boss looked pretty heated up this morning." He studied her with open curiosity, much as the dispatcher had done. "I understand you used to be friends."

"Years and years ago," Faith said.

"According to Ty, the two of you used to have—" he paused, waggled his eyebrows suggestively, and grinned "—sleepovers."

"We were nine years old," she said. "Is this an interrogation?"

He chuckled. "No, ma'am. I just haven't seen him quite this animated since…well, since forever. He perked up considerably when you hit town."

"I see. So he's not naturally perky?"

"He lives with Buck Savage. Would you be perky?"

"Point taken."

"The fact is, since he divorced Linda Larochelle, he hasn't shown much interest in women at all. Except for the occasional—" He paused, realized he'd said too much, and blushed like a maiden whose defloration was imminent. "Let me just find you a copy of the complaint form," he said, swiveling in his chair and rummaging through a rack of papers on a shelf behind his desk.

So the police chief had a lady friend. Faith wondered if it was the sprightly young blonde behind the dispatch desk. It was inevitable, she supposed. This was a small town, and Ty Savage was an exceptionally good-looking man, with a quiet charm that crept up on you and caught you by surprise. Of course he had a lady friend. Maybe more than one. Based on what she'd seen so far of Serenity's male citizenry, he probably had women falling all over him. Most women knew a good thing when they saw it.

They filled out the paperwork, she signed her name and Pete stapled the documents together and stacked them in a gray metal basket on the corner of his desk. Suddenly serious, he said, "You be careful out there. You're in a real isolated location. You might want to think about getting a security system installed."

"I appreciate your concern," she said, "but I really don't think I'll be here long enough to justify the expense."

"Well, just be extra careful. Anything happens to you, I don't want to be there when the boss finds out."

The river was still running abnormally high, its rapid current carrying debris from upriver flooding. A tree branch floated by, followed by an orange plastic bucket, the kind kids use to haul sand at the beach. His nephews, Sam and Jacob, had owned buckets like that when they were little. Ty sat in his cruiser, parked at one end of the rest area, and watched grimly from fifty feet away as a DOT worker dug post holes for the new guardrail. Five other highly skilled workers lent assistance by leaning on their shovels and offering the occasional word of encouragement. He was thinking it was a good thing they weren't on his payroll when his radio squawked to life.

He picked up the mike and clicked it on. "Yeah, Dix."

"René just called in. Apparently your dad got himself involved in a little fender bender over in the Ames Plaza parking lot. René thought you'd want to come over and take a look."

"Shit. He okay?"

"René says he's fine, but madder than a wet hornet. You know Buck."

"Yeah." He knew Buck. Some days, he wished he didn't. "Listen, Dix, did Faith Pelletier come in?"

"Came in, took care of business, and left. She looked a little disappointed when she found out you weren't here."

He knew she was waiting for him to bite. Just to gall her, he didn't. "Thanks, Dix," he said, and signed off. He wheeled the cruiser around, turned on his flashers and roared off toward the far side of town.

When the Ames department store chain had gone belly-up a couple years back, leaving forty-thousand-square-foot carcasses like woolly mammoths all over the New England landscape, traffic at Ames Plaza had died down to a minimum. There was a health food store that saw few patrons, now that the big draw was gone. Radio Shack still did a pretty good business, as did the ubiquitous Rite Aid pharmacy. Over the past ten years, Rite Aid stores had sprung up on every other street corner in Maine. Sometimes it seemed to him as though they sprinkled Rite Aid seeds every night, and every morning a new crop of stores sprang to life, already in full bloom. But even taking their brisk business into consideration, it was hard to imagine how Buck could have managed to collide with another car when he had twenty acres of empty parking lot in which to maneuver.

He got the answer to his question when he arrived at the scene. A small crowd of curious onlookers milled about outside the empty Ames store, watching as patrolman René Bellevance, looking as though he'd rather be somewhere else—anywhere else—got publicly reamed out by Serenity's former police chief. Buck was waving his arms and shouting like a crazy man, his hair standing on end and his shirttails flapping. Beside the two men, its nose buried three feet inside the front of the health food store, sat a bright-yellow Ford F-150 pickup truck with temporary plates. The sticker on the back said Spencer Goodwin Used Autos.

Goddamn it. Goddam it all to hell.

Buck might be a civilian these days, but his men still deferred to him out of respect for his former position as chief. René, eyes bulging in fear, stood staunchly and took his abuse like a man. When he saw Ty approaching, he swallowed hard and shot him a look of never-ending gratitude.

Fire ants began to dance a tango in Ty's stomach. Rubbing his midsection absently, he said, "What the hell's going on here?"

"I'll tell you what's going on here," his father said. "This green-ass punk kid has the gall to suggest he's gonna take my driver's license away—"

"Shut up," Ty told him. "I wasn't talking to you."

Buck's mouth abruptly closed. Behind him, Ty could hear murmurs from the crowd. "René?" he said evenly. "Care to fill me in?"

René swallowed again and stood stiffly at attention, ever mindful of the onlookers. "Jesus, Ty," he said in a voice that was little more than a whisper, "your father was pulling out of a parking space when he saw a pedestrian crossing the street and he stomped on the brake. Except he hit the gas instead, and, well—" He turned and gestured toward the massive hole that the truck had made in the front of the building. The sidewalk was littered with shattered glass and splintered wood. A bottle of echinacea tablets rolled off the edge of the sidewalk and into the parking lot. The wind caught it and carried it away into the midst of the crowd.

Cleanup was going to be a bitch. But there didn't appear to be any blood. He supposed that was a good sign.

"It was an honest mistake," Buck muttered. "Could've happened to anyone."

Ignoring him, Ty said to René, "Any injuries?"

"Just the store," René said. "The clerk inside's a little rattled, but nobody got hurt."

"What about the pedestrian?"

"He saw the truck coming." René cast a quick sidelong glance at Buck, who'd slumped down onto the curb, still steaming and muttering to himself. "Guy jumped out of the way. Good thing for him that he did. Otherwise, he'd be part of that wall right now."

They both glanced at the front of the store. "Or part of what used to be a wall," Ty said. He let out a long sigh of frustration. "Can you handle things here?"

"You get your old man out of my hair, I can handle anything."

"You're a good man, René Bellevance." He clapped the patrolman on the shoulder and called to his father, still sitting on the curb, sulking like a kid who'd been caught with his hand in the cookie jar. "Hey, Dad!"

Buck glanced up, his expression at once both belligerent and bewildered. Sounding disgusted, he said, "What?"

"Into the cruiser. You and I are going to have a talk."

Halfway through first-period study hall, the principal called Jessie into his office. She went reluctantly, wishing she could find some way to avoid the face-to-face contact. School gave her something to occupy her mind so she wouldn't think too much about what had happened to her mom. It kept her busy so she could forget for a while. Mr. Lombardi would only stir up thoughts she was trying to keep at bay.

But there was no getting around it. A summons from the principal couldn't be ignored. She dragged her feet all the way to his office, hoping maybe he'd be busy and she'd have to sit for a while on the bench in the outer office where miscreants were forced to wait out their sentences. But no such luck; Mrs. Henderson, the school secretary, waved her right past. "Go on in," she said, "he's waiting for you."

She found him sitting in a pool of sunshine, hunched over his desk, writing something on a sheet of paper. Behind him, the windowsill was lined with houseplants, a veritable garden of greenery. Mr. Lombardi had a green thumb, and he fussed over those plants as though they were his children. Her mom had owned a houseplant once, a rubber plant that somebody at work had given her. They'd joked about it, saying that even she couldn't kill a rubber plant. But three months later, it had been dead. Chelsea Logan had been a great mom, but her nurturing skills had left a little to be desired. And Jessie missed her so much she ached with it.

The principal glanced up and smiled. He had blue eyes and the whitest teeth she'd ever seen, and he had this way of looking at you as though you were the only other person on the face of the earth. Some of the girls had major crushes on him. "Jessie," he said, and dropped his pen. "Sit down. How are you doing?"

How was she supposed to answer that question? "Okay," she said softly, perching on the edge of a chair. Truthful or not, there was no other possible answer.

"I'm so very sorry about your mother." His eyes were kind, and she felt tears beginning to gather behind her eyelids. She fought them back and prayed he'd finish with her quickly. Under other circumstances, she would have warmed to him. She'd always liked Mr. Lombardi. He was so nice. But all she wanted today was to be treated as though it were any other day. Otherwise, she wasn't sure she'd make it through. "I've spoken with all your teachers," he said, "just to make sure everybody's on the same page. We're all going to do whatever it takes to help you through this."

"Thank you," she whispered.

"You're a straight-A student," he said. "One of our best and brightest. You have a promising future ahead of you." He studied her speculatively. "We want to make sure this tragedy doesn't derail you. We want to help, because we care. If there's anything you need, anything at all—even if it's just to talk—my door is open. And every one of your teachers has told me the same thing. We're here for you, Jessie."

She nodded, unable to speak. He seemed to have run out of words, and for a long moment, silence hung in the air between them. Then he cleared his throat. "Well," he said, glancing at the clock on the wall, "you'd better get going. The second-period bell's about to ring."

With immense relief, Jessie made her escape. Thirty feet down the hall, she swung into the rest room, marched to the last stall, and closed herself in. Mr. Lombardi meant well. He was a good principal, tough but fair. The halls of academe were a jungle, and being a high school principal had to be one of the toughest jobs on earth. Mr. Lombardi performed it with grace and diligence. But she didn't want his kindness today. Like a ghost, she wanted to just float through the day with minimal social contact. The watchword was *survival,* and that was all that mattered.

She checked the toilet seat, then sat down gingerly and leaned forward to take a deep breath. Somehow, she would make it through this day. Jessie took another deep breath, then unzipped her backpack and rummaged around until she found the container of breath mints that she always carried. She popped one into her mouth, closed her eyes and concentrated on the red-hot glow of the mint against her tongue. The pain felt good compared to the pain she carried inside.

The second-period bell rang. Outside the rest room, the corridors came alive with pounding feet and lively adolescent voices. The door swung open, and two girls came in, talking animatedly about the upcoming prom. Jessie didn't recognize either of the voices. She sat very still, books on her lap, backpack and violin on the floor in front of her, and waited while they took their time using the facilities, combing their hair, fixing their makeup.

Eventually, they left. Jessie let out a hard breath and opened the door of the stall. She looked right, then left, just to make sure nobody was still here, then she walked to the sink and washed her hands and her face. The water felt cool and comforting against her skin. She dried off with a paper towel, then studied herself in the mirror over the sink. She looked ghastly. Her eyes were sunken and her cheeks were pale. If she were to look up the word *bereavement* in the dictionary, she'd probably find a picture of herself.

Outside, the corridors had quieted down. Second-period classes were underway. That meant she could sneak into the auditorium for orchestra practice without being accosted by hordes of sympathizers. Becca's mom had told her that each day it would get a little easier. She wasn't sure Dottie McLaughlin knew what she was talking about, but she hoped the woman was right, because she couldn't continue to function indefinitely carrying this kind of pain. Maybe coming to school hadn't been such a hot idea after all. Every time she started to forget, even for an instant, some well-meaning person would reopen the wound that she was trying to heal. But her only other option was to stay home, where there was nothing to distract her from the blackness of her thoughts.

No, she'd made the right decision. And now that the corridors were empty, she could go to her second-period class. People would be setting up their instruments, their music stands, pulling out their sheet music and organizing it. They'd be too busy to pay attention to Jessie Logan and her late entrance. She would have an entire hour to focus on the music, to lose herself in it, to let it take her to a place where nothing, not even thoughts of her dead mother, could interfere.

Band practice was a frenzied hour of intense work. The evil Simon Legree, disguised as a mild-mannered band instructor, drove them without mercy. When the hour was through, Jessie was limp and drained, but in a good way. Without speaking to anyone, she folded up her music and stuffed it in her backpack, put away her violin and escaped. Her head still overflowing with Mozart and the complex piece they'd been assigned to learn, she stopped at her locker to drop off the violin. She was spinning the lock, her mind elsewhere, when a voice said, "Hey, Jess." A voice so unexpected she thought she must have imagined it.

But she hadn't, for there he stood, leaning against the row of gray metal lockers just two feet from her elbow. Coop adjusted the stack of books he carried in the crook of his arm, like a football. "I heard about your mom," he said somberly. "I just wanted you to know how sorry I am."

His face was about eighteen inches away from hers. She'd dreamed of that face for months. Every night while she slept. Every instant she was awake. If anybody had asked her, she would have laid money on the certainty that Cooper Gates didn't even know her name. Yet here he stood, big as life, and those dark eyes of his were focused directly on her. Jessie didn't know whether to laugh or cry. All she'd wanted today was to be left alone. But this was Cooper, the man of her dreams—quite literally—offering his sympathies on the loss of her mother.

"Thank you, Cooper," she said softly, the first words she'd ever spoken to him.

"Listen, Jess, I was wondering." He rocked back and forth on the balls of his feet, as though he were nervous about something. But what would Cooper Gates have to be nervous about? "Would you like to see a movie Friday night? With me?"

She had to be hallucinating. There could be no other explanation for why Cooper Gates, star quarterback, would be asking Jessie Logan, band nerd, for a date. "I—" She stopped, swallowed. "I'll have to check. I mean—I might not—" *Moron*, she thought. *Are you crazy?*

She took a deep breath. "Okay," she said. "I mean, yes. I'd love to go to the movies with you."

"Great!" He flashed her the most incredible smile, one that turned her knees to rubber. "I'll pick you up at six-thirty. The movie starts at eight. We can get something to eat first."

"Do you need directions to my house?" She still couldn't believe this was happening.

"I know where you live." He glanced around the nearly empty corridor and said, "I'd better run. My next class is at the other end of the building. Algebra. Mrs. Detweiler." He rolled his eyes. "If I'm late, the old bat'll lock me out of the room. See you Friday."

And he was gone, sprinting down the hall as though he were running for a touchdown, leaving a dumbfounded Jessie Logan to stare in astonishment at his retreating back.

Eleven

The bell above the door tinkled when Faith entered the newspaper office. It was just a small storefront, with dusty wooden floors and an overhead fluorescent light that sputtered and flickered. If she had to put up with that on a daily basis, it would drive her crazy, but the receptionist sitting at the front desk, filing her nails and talking on the phone to somebody named Tina, didn't even seem aware of it. Behind one of those portable fabric dividers, somebody was typing slowly, hesitantly, as though he or she were unaccustomed to keyboarding. Somewhere in the back, a radio was tuned to WBLM, northern New England's home of rock and roll. The deejay finished his spiel and began to play Bon Jovi's newest hit.

"So I was like, right. I really believe that," the receptionist said into the phone. "Honestly, Tina, does he really think I'm that stupid? Jesus." She glanced up, said into the phone, "Hang on a sec," cradled the phone to her shoulder, and looked at Faith expectantly.

"Is Newt in?" Faith said.

"All the way to the back. You can't miss it." And she returned to her vitally important phone conversation.

Behind the reception area, Faith found four miniature cubicles, two on each side, arranged around a center aisle and marked off with portable wall dividers. Spare and lean, each space was furnished with a desk, a computer, a phone and not much else. In the right-front cubicle, a woman sat at her desk, talking quietly into the phone while she rhythmically tapped a pen against the side of her coffee mug. The other three desks were vacant. In the left-rear cubicle, proudly displayed on the desktop next to a cube of neon-colored Post-it notes, was a framed photograph of Jessie Logan. Faith sucked in her breath and came to an abrupt halt. So this was Chelsea's work space. Aside from the photo, there was little here to mark it as hers. The space was neatly arranged, no clutter anywhere. A cup of yellow pencils sat next to the computer, all of them freshly sharpened. Chelsea had pinned up notes on her make-shift wall. Faith stepped into the cubicle and quickly skimmed them, but she found nothing of any significance.

When she stepped back into the aisle, the woman in the other cubicle eyed her with suspicion. "Can I help you?" the woman said.

"Just looking for Newt," she said brightly.

Her eyes brimming with distrust, the woman said, "Back office."

"Thanks so much," Faith said, and flashed her a smile of such brilliance that the woman quickly ducked her head back into her cubicle and began click-clacking away at her keyboard. Probably checking her horoscope, Faith thought. Nobody around here seemed to be doing any real work.

She found Newt in his office, hunched over his computer. The sleeves of his white cotton shirt were rolled up tidily, and he'd shaved since she saw him last. He looked as though he'd actually slept last night. He wasn't a bad-looking man when he cleaned up.

"Hey," he said, leaning back in his chair and stretching his arms over his head. "Come on in."

"Feeling better this morning?" she said.

He lowered his arms to the desktop. "If you mean have I

given up my theory about—" he lowered his voice and glanced toward the door "—murder, then, no. I don't feel better."

"Maybe you will after you hear what I have to say." Faith closed the door behind her and sat on a hard wooden chair. "Last night," she said, "somebody broke into the house."

Behind the lenses of his glasses, Newt's blue eyes widened. He leaned forward intently. "Is everybody okay?"

"I was home alone. Jessie was spending the night with a friend. My dog scared him off." She paused. "He was going through Chelsea's computer disks."

"I knew it! Hot damn. I knew I was right!" Newt seemed almost gleeful in his rightness, until he remembered about Chelsea, and instantly regained his hangdog expression. "Did he get anything?"

"I don't think so. When Buddy went racing downstairs, the guy took off like he'd been shot from a cannon."

"Well, well. If I were conducting an investigation of some kind, I might think this was a clue. Do you believe me now?"

"I believe you. I suspect Ty does, too, even though he refuses to admit it."

"Ah, shit. You told Savage?"

"What was I supposed to do, Newt? As you so eloquently pointed out, this appears to be a clue. Somebody killed my cousin. And somebody broke into the house while I was sleeping upstairs. It's not difficult to add two and two together and come up with four. I don't know about you, but that comes a little too close to home for my comfort level." It actually came a lot too close to home, but she didn't know him well enough to admit it to him.

"Have you checked out what's on those disks? It must be something important for somebody to risk breaking into the house while you were there."

"My thoughts exactly. I haven't had time yet, but that's how I plan to spend the afternoon."

He leaned back in his chair. "Why don't you bring them

here? I'll do half and you do half. You could use Chelsea's cubicle. It would be quicker that way."

"I thought about that. But I want to be there when Jessie gets home. And it will probably be a better use of our time if I go over the home computer and you check out the one she used here. We can report back to each other if either of us finds anything of significance."

Newt swiveled lazily in his chair. "I already took a quick glance through her computer here. I didn't see anything that sent up a red flag, but I'll go over it in more detail this afternoon. I don't expect to find anything. She didn't want anybody, not even me, knowing the details of this story she was working on, so she probably kept her notes on her home computer."

"If we could find something, just one solid piece of evidence, we could bring it to Ty. Without it, his hands are tied. But he's not the kind of man to ignore hard evidence."

"That may be true," he said, "but I'm not sure I'd trust Ty Savage to find his own ass in the dark with a flashlight."

"You're questioning his competence?"

"It's not personal. I'm sure he's good at what he does, but he's a small-town cop. Not exactly Columbo. What he knows about homicide investigation would fit on the head of a pin. Besides, he doesn't even have jurisdiction over the accident investigation. It belongs to—"

"The State Police," she said. "I know. Detective Lemoine stopped by the house yesterday morning to talk to Jessie about Chelsea's frame of mind before she died. I realize he has to investigate, but I hated letting him talk to her. He's obviously still working the suicide angle."

"Then I guess it's up to us to prove him wrong."

"I'm glad we're on the same page. I'm going to need a couple of things from you. First, I want to read Chelsea's series about the Somalis. Second, I want a list of every story she's worked on since you hired her. Then we're going to put our heads together and see what we come up with."

* * *

The crowd had started to disperse, now that the Buck and René sideshow appeared to be over. Ty sat in the driver's seat of the police cruiser, fiddling with the keys dangling from his ignition, while beside him, Buck fumed silently. "I thought we agreed about the truck," Ty said.

"I didn't agree to anything," Buck told him. "In case you forgot, you told me not to buy from Goodwin, and I told you to keep your nose out of it."

A dull ache began to throb just behind his temples. "How much did he take you for?"

Buck reddened. "What I paid for it's my business, not yours. And he didn't take me for anything. Maybe you take me for a fool, but that's a whole different story."

"Damn it, Dad, there wasn't anything wrong with your car."

"I was tired of the damn thing! I felt like trading it! Last time I checked, that wasn't against the law!"

Ty ran his hands across his face and up to his temples, massaging them in a vain attempt to erase the pain that had lodged there. It didn't help that he'd only slept three hours last night. "What the hell happened here today?"

"I thought it was pretty self-explanatory. I hit the gas instead of the brake. It's not that big a deal. This kind of thing happens all the time. Don't you read the newspaper? I have insurance coverage. They'll pay for the damage."

"Yeah. They'll pay, all right. And then they'll cancel your coverage." Of course he read the newspaper. Buck was right; this kind of thing did happen all the time. And every time he read a news report about some driver who'd confused the accelerator for the brake pedal, that driver was, without fail, some elderly person who had no business being behind the wheel in the first place. "Christ," he said wearily. "What am I going to do with you?"

Buck reached for the door handle and opened the door. "You're going to stop treating me like a little kid, that's what!"

"Then maybe you should stop acting like one! And just where do you think you're going?"

"In case you forgot," his father snapped, "I have a new truck sitting over there, half in and half out of the granola store. It'll most likely leave here on the back of a wrecker. I'd like to be there when they take it away. If they hook it up wrong and blow the tranny, I'll sue the bastards."

Ty closed his eyes, counted to ten. "And how'll you get home?" he said, as evenly as a man could speak when his stomach was eating him alive.

"Don't you worry about that. If worse comes to worst, I'll make René give me a ride. He wouldn't dare to say no. I had the kid quivering in his boots until you came along."

Faith sat in Chelsea's tiny cubicle a few feet outside the door of Newt's office, hunched over the computer. The five-part piece titled "Taking Care of Business" was smoothly written, and sprinkled with the kind of colorful detail that brought the lives of the Somali immigrants into clear focus. Chelsea had spotlighted the difficulties the women in particular faced in assimilating into a new and strange culture. She had interviewed each of Serenity's Somali wives, but it had been Sahra Hassan who had been at the heart of the piece. Sahra's story held a universality that was immediately recognizable to any mother trying to raise a family in America at the dawn of the twenty-first century. Like all mothers everywhere, Sahra's single most important goal in life was to provide a safe and healthy environment in which her children could grow and prosper.

After escaping the civil war raging in Mogadishu with nothing but the clothes on their backs, Sahra and her husband, Omar Abdallah, and their five children had spent nearly two years in a refugee camp in Kenya before the opportunity arose to emigrate to America. Once there, like many refugees, they'd settled in Atlanta. The climate was relatively warm, and a large black population already lived in the greater Atlanta area. The Abdallahs had hoped to fit in.

But they'd quickly become disillusioned. Atlanta was a big city, rife with the problems that plagued all big cities. Sahra and Omar had started looking for a different place to raise their children, a place that wasn't overrun by drugs and gangs and urban crime. Through a friend of a friend, they heard about Lewiston, Maine, a small northeastern city where a number of their contemporaries had settled. Uprooting their family yet again, they'd pulled up stakes and moved to Maine.

But Lewiston hadn't been particularly welcoming and, in spite of its small size, its inner-city neighborhoods were no stranger to poverty, drugs and crime. After a few months there, five Somali families, including the Abdallahs, had made the decision to move upriver to Serenity. They'd liked the name of the town, liked the picture it evoked. Liked its location, in a rural area, but not so far from Lewiston that they couldn't shop the malls or visit their friends when they wanted. This, they had reasoned, would be their last move.

But it hadn't been easy. Although the college-educated Sahra spoke fluent English, some of the women spoke virtually none. Maine's harsh climate had taken its toll on them during that first frigid winter. The customs were different, the food was different, the lifestyle was different from what they were accustomed to. Their children wore American clothes, spoke American slang, and listened to American pop music. They'd left a nation founded on Islam and settled in one founded on Christianity. And the faces that surrounded them—nearly all the faces that surrounded them—were white.

The townspeople hadn't exactly rolled out the red carpet to greet their arrival. Still, they'd stood their ground, these people who had survived civil war and refugee camps and a move to a different hemisphere. They would do what it took to become Americans and fit in without losing their own cultural identity. And their children would grow up in a place where the air was clean, the streets were safe and the pace of life was slow enough so they could take the time to appreciate these things.

The article was uplifting. Faith might even go so far as to call it inspiring. Faced with the insurmountable odds these indomitable people had somehow managed to surmount, she wasn't sure she could have triumphed. Chelsea had done a superb job of portraying them on paper, and Faith's respect for her cousin, once crushed by Chelsea's irresponsible behavior, grew afresh. Perhaps Chelsea had been able to render the lives of the Somali women with such clarity of vision because she, too, had been to hell and back. Like them, she'd been a survivor, one who'd beat the odds and pulled her fractured life back together after she broke the hold the bottle had held over her for more than a decade. Chelsea Logan and Sahra Hassan might have been born a continent apart, but they'd been cut from the same cloth.

Chelsea's death was doubly tragic, coming as it had at a point when she'd finally turned her life around. Faith swiveled her chair back and forth while she pondered the wedge that Chelsea's erratic and irresponsible lifestyle had driven between them. It had been seven years since the blustery winter evening when Chelsea, broke and in trouble once again, had shown up at the door of Faith's Manhattan town house with eight-year-old Jessie in tow. Ben had answered the door—earnest, easygoing Ben—and, bless his soul, hadn't blinked an eye at the unexpected arrival of her hard-luck cousin. As far as Ben was concerned, family was family, no matter what the circumstances. Faith hadn't been so sure. She'd thought maybe a little tough love was in order. But there'd been Jessie to consider. She couldn't leave an eight-year-old girl out in the cold.

So she'd taken them in, fed them, given them a warm bed to sleep in. Chelsea, as usual, had made repeated promises. "I'll repay you as soon as I'm back on my feet," she'd said, over and over again, like a broken record. Faith, knowing just how much Chelsea's promises were worth, had tuned her out. What was the sense in having expectations of a woman who never failed to disappoint?

Inevitably, after a couple of weeks had passed, Chelsea had started showing signs of restlessness. She'd never been able to stay in one place for long. So Faith had written her a sizable check and strongly suggested that she get her act together, if not for herself, then for her beautiful, solemn-faced little daughter, who needed some stability in her life before it was too late.

Chelsea had left with money and advice in hand. After that, they'd made feeble attempts to stay in touch, exchanging Christmas cards and the occasional letter. Every year, Chelsea would send Jessie's newest school picture, which Faith dutifully hung on her refrigerator door. But something had changed between them. The time had come to break free of the old pattern they'd established so long ago neither could remember how it had started: Chelsea screwing up, and Faith bailing her out. The old pattern wasn't working, and they both recognized that this was the last bailout that would occur.

Not long after, Chelsea had quit drinking. Faith would never know whether her words had had the desired impact, or whether Chelsea had simply reached bottom and couldn't go any lower. Whatever the reason, Chelsea had exchanged her itchy feet for a secretarial job at the *Boston Tribune*. There, she'd somehow managed to work her way up the ladder to reporter. With a steady income and no liquor bill, she'd begun paying Faith back. Every few months, a check would arrive in the mail. Fifty dollars here, a hundred there. Chelsea was doing her best to fulfill her promise. And Faith, who'd long ago grown cynical about her cousin, had wanted desperately to believe that this time, the change was real.

But until she sat down today in the newspaper office to read Chelsea's work, she hadn't realized how deeply the rift between them had hurt her. They'd had an intense love-hate relationship, and her angry words, spoken in haste and frustration, had resulted in an empty spot inside her that couldn't be filled by anything or anyone else. Now that loss was permanent, and reading Chelsea's words was nearly unbearable. The article itself may have focused on the Somali women, but Chelsea's voice, her marvelous irreverence and her dogged individualism, had shone through clearly, bringing Faith a stab of regret so profound it nearly doubled her over.

She didn't know her face was wet with tears until Newt held out a tissue in front of her. She grasped it, embarrassed by her show of emotion. She hadn't cried after Ben died. Now that the floodgates had opened, all that repressed emotion came gushing out. While Newt hovered helplessly, awkwardly patting her shoulder and handing her tissue after tissue, Faith lay her head on her folded arms and wept. She wept for Sahra Hassan, who'd left behind the only life she'd ever known for an uncertain future in a strange and hostile land. She wept for Chelsea and for Ben, who had both died far too soon. She wept for Jessie, whose mother had been senselessly snatched away from her, and for Faith, both the little girl and the grown woman, who'd been left by everyone she ever loved. She wept until there were no tears left, until her nose stuffed up and her eyelids swelled and her breath came in short, staccato hiccups.

"Feel better?" Newt said.

"I'm so sorry," she said. "I never do that." Her stuffy nose translated it to *I'b so sorry. I dever do that.*

"It's okay. Yesterday I was the one who was a wreck. Today's your turn."

"Is it?" She wiped her eyes a final time, dabbed at her nose. "It's just that everything finally got to me. I lost my husband a little over a year ago, and now Chelsea, and then there was the break-in—"

"You've earned the right to cry." Newt's blue eyes, luminous in his hangdog face, wore an expression of grave concern. "When was the last time you ate?"

She actually had to give it some thought. Brushing her tangled hair away from her face, she said, "Well…this morning I talked to Dottie McLaughlin on the phone, then Mr. Paré stopped by to replace the lock. By the time he was gone, I had just enough time to get ready for my appointment with Louis Cunningham. After that, I stopped by the police station about the break-in. Then I came here."

"In other words," Newt said, "you haven't eaten since yesterday."

"Damn." She dabbed again at her nose. "I have to stop doing that."

He chuckled and patted her shoulder. "I'll get Debbie to run over to Lenny's for a couple of sandwiches."

Fortified with breast of turkey on whole wheat, she sat in Newt's office and perused the list of headlines that Debbie, his secretary-receptionist, had typed up. Brow furrowed in concentration, Faith said, "This is everything Chelsea worked on?"

"That's right." Newt took a bite of his sandwich. A slice of tomato, greased with mayonnaise, squished out the open end and landed with a plop on the front of his white shirt. With a sigh, he set down the sandwich, peeled off the offender, and dabbed at his shirtfront with a napkin. "Debbie pulled it directly from the files."

It was a long list. Chelsea had covered it all, from town meetings to auto accidents, from house fires to local politics, from drug arrests to the closing of downtown businesses. The list of news stories read like a biography of the town, in chronological order. "Did she ever get any mail in response to any of these articles?" Faith said.

"You mean as in hate mail from angry citizens? Not that I'm aware of. There's always mail, but that's generally in the form of letters to the editor. Somebody takes offense at something that was said, accuses the *Gazette* of being biased on some trivial issue. But most of that's aimed at me. Chelsea reported the news, and she wrote the occasional in-depth piece, like the Somali story. I'm the one who writes the editorials, so I'm the target of most of the poison darts."

"Do you see a lot of poison darts?"

He lifted his coffee cup. "No more than any other small-town newspaper taking a liberal stand in the midst of a solid block of right-wing conservatives. This is middle America. Not everybody appreciates freedom of the press. In the five short years since I took over as editor, I've managed to offend just about everybody at least once."

"Any enemies? Any offended citizen who may have made vague threats? Some politician who lost an election because the *Gazette* endorsed his opponent? Has anybody been royally pissed off because they felt you came down on the wrong side of some weighty issue?"

Coffee cup still suspended in midair, Newt considered her question. "There are always kooks out there," he said, "even in a town this small. But I can't think of any particular instance where anybody's been less than civilized in their disagreement with anything we've printed. For the most part, Serenity's conservatives and I have agreed to disagree."

Faith returned her attention to the list.

Fire Leaves 5 Homeless, Wood Stove to Blame. Break-In at Local Pharmacy Nets Undisclosed Amount of OxyContin. Heated Selectman Race Too Close to Call. Recount Demanded.

She nibbled at her bottom lip. "What's OxyContin?" she said.

"The drug of choice for a number of addicts." Newt took a sip of coffee and set down his cup. Warming to his topic, he leaned back in his chair and clasped his hands behind his head. "It's a powerful painkiller, extremely addictive. Doctors prescribe it for cancer patients and other chronic pain sufferers. It's a hugely attractive black-market item because of the high street value. It's become a major problem in parts of rural Maine. Five years ago, most of the robberies around here were convenience stores. Easy access, open all night. Pop in, wave a gun, and pop back out with whatever's in the register. Nowadays, it's the pharmacies that are getting hit, and it's OxyContin that the thieves are taking. They can make a mint selling it on the street. I've heard that a single tablet can go for as much as eighty dollars. You do the math."

She let out a low whistle. "Half the town is out of work, and most of the rest are working blue-collar jobs. How do people get their hands on that kind of money?"

"Any way they can, legally or illegally. In the places that are hardest hit, it's started a crime wave."

"And is Serenity one of those places?"

"I wouldn't go so far as to call it a crime wave, but we've had our share of problems. Enough to keep Savage and his cohorts from getting bored."

She considered that information at length. "And one of the local pharmacies was robbed?"

"Dowe's Apothecary. Angus Dowe. It's over on Route 237, in the Food City minimall. He's actually been hit twice. Once last year, and then again, back in February or March of this year."

"Did Chelsea cover both stories?"

"The first one happened before she got here. I think Candy covered that one."

"Candy?"

"Candace Dutil. Candace Aguilera now. I hired Chelsea to replace her when she got married and moved to Tampa."

Deep in thought, Faith tapped a fingernail against the sheet of paper she held in her hand. "You say this Angus Dowe's been hit twice?"

"That's right."

"What do you suppose happens when a pharmacy's robbed like that?"

Newt's eyes, behind his glasses, grew large and owlish. "What do you mean?"

"If the thieves got away with a large amount of the drug, we're talking a huge monetary loss to the pharmacy. How do they recoup that loss? Even if the drugs were recovered, they'd be useless once they'd been out of the pharmacist's hands and on the street. They'd have to be destroyed. Either way, it's a total loss. Do pharmacies carry insurance to cover scenarios like that?"

"Damned if I know, but it's a good question. You think Angus Dowe could have had a hand in robbing his own store?"

"I don't know. But it wouldn't be the first time a robbery was an inside job." She thought about it some more. "Can you pull it for me?" she said. "The story Chelsea did on the most recent break-in?"

It wasn't much, just the standard five-paragraph bare-bones news item outlining the details of the break-in, noting that this had been the second robbery at Dowe's pharmacy in less than two years, and quoting a police source who stated that the investigation was ongoing. When asked the street value of the drugs that had been taken, that same police source declined to comment.

"And that was that?" she said. "The *Gazette* did no follow-up? Chelsea moved on to something else, and the OxyContin theft was forgotten?"

"Not forgotten," Newt said. "But it's old news now. There's a saying among newsmen. If it bleeds, it leads. That particular flow of blood has clotted. There's nothing new to say about it. When there is, when the blood starts to trickle again, we'll print it."

"They've never arrested anyone for the robberies?"

"Nope. The police won't even tell us if they think the two robberies are related. And whenever we ask, our esteemed police chief gives us the standard song and dance. It's an ongoing investigation, and he can't comment on it."

She considered the possibilities. "I might know a way around that," she said.

"Oh? How's that?"

"Ty and I are old friends. We grew up together. Maybe he'll talk to me."

Newt scowled. "Good luck," he said. "Look, I hate to name names, but as long as we're laying all our cards on the table, I might as well. Davy Hunter."

"What about Davy Hunter?"

"He had opportunity," Newt said. "He and Chelsea were closer than Siamese twins. And he may have had motive."

It took her a moment to shift gears. "You think Davy killed Chelsea?"

"I think he's mixed up in this OxyContin thing. He seems to be intimately acquainted with a number of companions of questionable reputation. Plus, he has no visible means of support."

It was more or less the same thing Ty had told her. "He doesn't have a job?" she said.

"If he does, he's keeping it well hidden. Maybe he won the Megabucks and didn't bother to tell anyone. Mostly, he just stays out at that ratty old trailer of his all day, working in his wood shop. At night, he hangs around the bars down on Androscoggin Street with his low-life buddies. If you ask me, he's a complete waste of humanity. I can't imagine what Chelsea saw in him."

Deep in thought, she said, "Everything you're saying may well be true. But how does that lead to murder?"

"Maybe she found out what he was up to. Maybe they argued over it. Maybe she was going to print his name in the *Gazette*, or turn him in to the cops." Newt's voice grew somber. "I don't know about you, but if it was my ass on the line, I can't guarantee I wouldn't resort to murder to stay out of prison."

Twelve

There were fifteen disks in all, slender squares of black plastic, each with a white label on which a number had been written in black ink. They looked innocuous enough, Faith thought, considering that one of them might hold information somebody had been willing to kill for. She set up her laptop at the kitchen table, made herself a cup of tea, and started with disk number one. She scanned the directory, matched up file names with the list of stories Newt had given her, wrote a number beside each listing that noted which disk Chelsea had stored the story on. She opened files at random, skimming, looking for something, anything, that might have led to Chelsea's demise.

But there was nothing. The stories that came out of Serenity weren't exactly edge-of-your-seat page-turners. There just wasn't that much intrigue to be found. Chelsea had written about typical small-town events. A bottle drive put on by the fire department to raise money for some badly needed new equipment. Story hour at the library. She'd interviewed Skip Lombardi, who doubled as both high school principal and football coach, about his team's chances for winning the state Class C championship.

By the time the school bus pulled up out front, Faith was

on her third cup of tea, and she'd made it through twelve of the fifteen disks without finding anything of significance. She hadn't read every word, but she'd seen enough to know there was nothing on any of those twelve disks to point her in the direction of Chelsea's killer. Had she sent herself on a wild-goose chase? Was she paranoid, and seeing bogeymen everywhere, as Ty had implied? Or was she simply looking in the wrong place?

Jessie came in looking ashen, pale skin drawn tight over prominent cheekbones. Faith closed the file she'd been reading and scraped her tangled hair back from her forehead. Vividly remembering her first day back at school after her parents died, she said gently, "How'd it go?"

"Okay." Jessie opened the refrigerator door and studied its contents. Finding nothing to her liking, she closed the fridge and opened the freezer instead. Stretching on tiptoe, she rummaged around, her arm buried up to the elbow, and emerged with a cherry-flavored Popsicle.

Not exactly a balanced meal. "Let me make you something," Faith said. "A sandwich, a can of soup."

"No thank you," Jessie said. "This will hold me until supper." She peeled the paper off the Popsicle and deposited it neatly in the trash. Eyes trained on the Popsicle, she said, "I have a date. For Friday night. If it's okay with you."

Faith had been about to bring up the topic of her visit with Louis Cunningham. Sooner or later, they would have to talk about it. Sooner or later, they would have to make some decisions. But not today. Right now, this was more important. In a small way, Jessie had opened up to her. She prayed this meant there was hope for the future. But she needed to tread carefully. Otherwise, she'd trample this delicate beginning.

She searched for an innocuous question. "Do you date a lot?" she asked.

"No."

She waited for Jessie to elaborate, but trying to get Jessie

Logan to talk was like pulling teeth. Quietly, she asked, "What would your mom say about this date?"

Jessie shrugged. "I don't know," she said in a tiny voice just above a whisper. "Nobody ever asked me out before."

Oh, hell. She definitely wasn't prepared for this. Was there some kind of manual she could refer to, a Dr. Spock for parenting teenagers? Her first instinct was to put Jessie in a chastity belt and lock her in her room until she was twenty-five. Since that wasn't a viable alternative, she would have to pretend she knew what the hell she was doing. "Who's the boy?" she said, not knowing what else to ask.

The Popsicle was starting to melt. "Cooper Gates," Jessie said, licking away a sticky, cherry-colored rivulet.

Faith recognized the name immediately. She'd read it just a half hour earlier, in Chelsea's interview with Skip Lombardi. Cooper Gates was the team's star quarterback, and Lombardi's fair-haired boy. She wondered about his background. Had there been a Gates family living here twenty years ago? She couldn't recall. Casting about frantically for something intelligent to say, she tried to imagine what her own mother might have said. But she'd been twelve when her mother died. The issue of dating had never arisen. "Is he from a nice family?" she finally asked. It was a lame question, but the only one that presented itself to her.

"I guess. His dad's a doctor. They have lots of money."

Which didn't mean zip. There were plenty of psychopaths with healthy bank account balances running the streets. "How old is he?" To her own ears, her questions were beginning to sound remarkably like the Spanish Inquisition.

But Jessie didn't seem to notice. "Seventeen. He's two years ahead of me in school."

Faith realized she didn't even know what grade Jessie was in. "Which would be...?"

"He's a junior. I'm a freshman." The girl caught another Popsicle drip with her tongue, grabbed a paper towel from the roll by the sink, and balled it up in her hand to catch the remaining drippage.

"Am I asking too many questions? I don't know much about teenagers."

"It's okay."

"Look, Jessie…it's going to take us some time. We really don't know each other, and this situation, being thrown together like this, wasn't of our own making. I intend to try really hard, but I hope you'll forgive me when I screw up. It's inevitable that I will. I just hope you'll remember, when it happens, that it's not intentional."

Softly, Jessie said, "I know."

"There's one other thing I want to say, and it's really important." Faith picked up a floppy disk from the table and examined the writing on the label. "I imagine you think nobody understands what you're going through right now. And you probably resent the hell out of me for even bringing it up. You're probably wishing I'd just shut up and go away." She set down the floppy and met Jessie's steady gray gaze. "But I want you to know that I understand your pain. I've been there. I lost both my parents when I was twelve years old. It was painful beyond anything I could ever have imagined. So you see, I do understand. At least a little."

Jessie studied her without blinking. "My mom never told me that."

"I figured as much. That's why I'm telling you now. I'm not trying to be a meddling old lady—"

"You're not that old."

"Well," Faith said, smiling, "thank you." More somberly, she added, "I just wanted you to know that if you need to talk, to vent, to cry—whatever—there's somebody here who'll listen and understand and not pass judgment on you."

Like X-ray vision, Jessie's solemn gray gaze continued to pierce her. "I have to go now," Jessie said. "I have homework."

A little hurt by the rebuff, Faith watched her walk away. Backpack over her shoulder, Popsicle in one hand and violin in the other, Jessie paused at the doorway and turned. Caught in a ray of afternoon sunshine, the girl looked so much like

Faith's own mother that she was momentarily unable to draw breath.

"Faith?"

"What, sweetheart?"

"Thanks."

She sucked in a hard breath. Jessie's footsteps were surprisingly light on the stairs. Upstairs, the bedroom door closed behind her. After a brief delay, the music began, a little less haunting this time. *Mozart*, Faith thought. A difficult piece. Jessie played it flawlessly, the clear, sweet notes pouring from her instrument. Then she hit a false note, faltered, and came to an abrupt halt. Faith held her breath. The music began again, from the beginning. This time, Jessie played smoothly through the spot that had tripped her up the first time.

Faith's heart clutched in her chest. It happened every time she heard that damnable violin. She got up from the table and took the phone book from the drawer, looked up a number and dialed.

Dottie McLaughlin answered on the fourth ring. In the background, she could hear kids squabbling. Somebody had cranked the volume on the television, probably to compensate for the yelling. "You told me to call you if I needed anything," she said. "You probably didn't expect to hear from me so soon. But I desperately need some parenting advice."

"You came to the right place. Hold on." To somebody at her end, Dottie said, "Turn down that TV! And you two, stop fighting or you're both going to your rooms." Mercifully, the noise subsided to a manageable level. "Better," Dottie said, returning to the phone. "What can I do for you?"

"One of these days, when we both have time, you can give me step-by-step training on parenting teenagers. But we'll save that for another day. In the meantime, you can start by telling me everything you know about a kid named Cooper Gates."

After the debacle with his father, Ty spent the afternoon working on a B-and-E case that had been hanging around for way too long. The prints they'd lifted at the scene had finally come back from the lab, and wonder of wonders, they'd been a perfect match for Leroy Stultz. Stultz and his older brother, Teddy, shared the same last name and a single brain between the two of them. Ty figured that was a direct result of the booze their mother had swilled while she was carrying them. Neither brother worked alone, which meant that sooner or later, Teddy's sticky fingers would show up somewhere in this case. While they waited for that to happen, Ty and Pete decided now was as good a time as any to saunter down to the body shop where Leroy worked and slap the cuffs on him.

Leroy whined and bitched about his civil rights as they carted him away. He continued to piss and moan all through the booking process. They offered him the use of a phone, but he turned it down. There was nobody to call but his brother, and Teddy had been standing right there, slack-jawed and bug-eyed, while they hauled Leroy off. Undoubtedly sweating bullets while he tried to remember the phone number of the local bail bondsman.

They had to listen to Leroy's whining for another ninety minutes while they waited for a sheriff's deputy to pick him up for transportation to County Jail. When the county cruiser finally pulled up and Ty saw who climbed out of it, he grinned in spite of himself. Deputy Theresa Bourgoin stood six feet tall and weighed nearly as much as he did, every inch of it solid muscle. She was tough as any man, tougher than most, and if the scruffy, sniveling Leroy gave her any shit, she'd probably stuff his whiny little head up his ass. Tess the Terminator, they called her. It was a beautiful thing.

After Tess drove away with a scowling Leroy safely ensconced in the back of her cruiser, Ty tried to make a quick escape. But he wasn't quick enough to dodge Jo's call. He'd known it was coming, had known his sister's barbs would all be aimed at him, so he just sat back in his chair, propped up his feet, and let her spout off. Eventually, after reciting a litany of his failings that went all the way back to infancy, she ran out of steam and paused for breath.

"What do you expect me to do, Jo?" he said quietly. "Take away Dad's driver's license?"

"I expect you to take care of him! How could you let something like this happen? He could have been killed! I am so mad at you right now, I could throttle you. I don't even want to talk to you. I only called to tell you that Dad's having supper at my house tonight. You're on your own."

Good thing she didn't want to talk to him. Otherwise, she might have gone on for another fifteen minutes. It was harsh punishment for whatever offense he'd committed, being forced to endure an evening without the pleasure of Buck's company. But somehow he'd manage.

Undoubtedly, Jo would fawn over their father who, after all, had barely escaped with his life. She'd spoil him rotten and then send him home, pampered and smug, for Ty to try to tame. He might as well paint the town red this evening, while he still had the chance. Once Jo got through with Buck, life was going to get a whole lot more complicated.

He drove home, took a long, steamy shower and changed into jeans and a flannel shirt. Too bad there wasn't more of a town to paint red, he mused as he spooned canned tuna into a dish for the cat, who twined herself around his ankles and purred while she waited. There was bingo at the VFW hall and a teenybopper comedy playing at the Strand. It was league night at the bowling alley, liver-and-onions night at Lenny's. Such were the joys of small-town life. He'd probably end up at Walt's with all the other unattached guys, nursing a Rolling Rock and watching ESPN on the TV over the bar. One more red-hot evening in River City.

Or maybe he'd take a drive, out Bald Mountain Road and through the foothills. If he turned on all his charm, maybe he could convince Faith to take a drive with him, to bomb around the back roads like a couple of teenagers with nowhere to go. He could picture her now, dark hair flying in the wind that rushed through the open window, her face alight with laughter. He hadn't heard her laugh once since she got here. Not that she'd had much to laugh about. He was going to have to do something about that.

He was halfway down Androscoggin Street, headed for her place, when he spied Davy Hunter standing outside the River City Pub, talking intently to Teddy Stultz. Their body language, the tension between them, told him it wasn't just a friendly chat. As he drove past, Davy looked up and their eyes met. Grim and expressionless, Davy held his gaze for a few seconds. Then the moment ended. Ty drove on, and Davy returned to his conversation.

What the hell had that been about? What business did Davy Hunter have with one half of Serenity's petty-crime tag team? It seemed more than coincidental that he'd seen them together less than two hours after Teddy's brother had been hauled off to jail.

Ty let out a deep breath. What had happened to Davy? He'd been such a straight-arrow kid back in the old days. Now it seemed he was intimately acquainted with every low-life scumbag in a hundred-mile radius. What could have happened in his life to turn him to the dark side? It was impossible to guess; like Chelsea, Davy had spent years living elsewhere. Like Chelsea, every time he left, eventually Serenity had called him back.

He'd gotten nowhere with the guy the night before. Hunter had simply opened a beer, then sat down and played head games with him until finally Ty gave up and left. He hadn't for an instant believed that Davy was telling the truth when he said he had no idea who'd broken into the Logan place or why. He'd been lying, just as he'd been lying back in February when he claimed he knew nothing about the OxyContin that had been lifted from Angus Dowe's pharmacy. Something rotten was going on in Serenity, and Davy Hunter was smack in the middle of it. Ty hadn't yet found a way to prove it, but eventually he would.

His stomach soured. Stopping for a red light, he reached across the seat, flipped open his glove compartment, and fumbled inside for the package of Tums he kept there, a more portable alternative to the bottle of Maalox he kept in his desk. He managed to pop two of them into his mouth before the light turned. Crunching dourly on cherry-flavored chalk, he headed out Bald Mountain Road. The OxyContin theft wasn't the only thing rotten in Serenity. This Chelsea Logan thing stunk to high heaven. The more he thought about it, the more convinced he was that her death had been something other than an accident. Especially since last night's break-in.

But he had no evidence and no reason, beyond his own gut feeling, to justify opening an investigation into her death. Nothing to bring to Lemoine except intuition, and the stone-faced state trooper didn't look like somebody who put much stock in intuition. Lemoine wasn't a bad guy, but he was obviously a solid by-the-book type. He wouldn't be interested in anything but concrete evidence. And the evidence just wasn't there.

Davy was tied up in it somehow. There might not be any evidence connecting him—at least not yet—but somehow, he was connected. It made Ty sick just to think about it. They might have grown apart over the years, but Davy was still his oldest friend. Putting him away on drug charges would be bad enough. But a murder rap? It was beyond imagining.

When he pulled into her driveway, Faith was sitting on the back steps, feet flat on the bottom tread, elbows propped on her raised knees. Barefoot, she wore snug jeans and an oversize white cotton shirt with the tails hanging out. Her sleeves were rolled up to reveal slender forearms, her hair a wild tumble of ebony waves around a face so pale those blue eyes were vivid in comparison. She raised a hand to shield her eyes against the setting sun and watched him pull up beside her parked Saab.

A breeze swirled up, riffled her open collar and stirred her hair. As he looked at her, all those places inside him that were tightly knotted began to loosen, like a series of locked doors popping open, one after another. *Faith-and-Ty. Ty-and-Faith.*

The words echoed in his head, a childhood refrain that beat in tune with his heart. He wanted to take her in his arms and just hold her, feel that slender body against his. Sink into her comforting warmth and forget the world and its woes, forget everything but the way she felt in his arms.

He would never be the kind of man to set the world on fire. That wasn't what drove him. He wasn't interested in owning the universe. He just wanted to be comfortable in his small corner of it. He wanted a piece of earth he could call his own, a modest home, a wife he loved and a couple of kids. Maybe it was just wishful thinking, but he could imagine himself coming home to Faith after a hard day's work, could imagine crawling beneath the bedsheets and curling into her warmth at night. But Faith Pelletier was a woman of the world, smart and sleek and sophisticated. She could have her pick of men. Why would a woman like that want a man like him? There was no reason to believe she would, no reason at all. Except that nothing in his life had ever felt as right as it did now, sitting here watching her watch him.

He turned off the ignition. If it was meant to happen, it would happen. If not, the world wouldn't come to an end just because after all these years, he'd rediscovered her and she wasn't interested. He would go on as before, chasing crooks and handing out traffic citations by day, watching baseball and arguing with his father at night. Simple and straightforward and boring as all get-out, this narrow little life of his.

With a sigh, he released his seat belt and got out of the truck.

He looked tired. That was Faith's first thought as Ty climbed down from the cab of the pickup truck and she saw the lines of weariness etched into his face. Some of that was her fault. She'd dragged him out of bed in the middle of the night to come out here and play white knight. Now probably wasn't the best time to interrogate him about Serenity's drug problems. She didn't need to add to his burden. Her questions could wait until tomorrow. Instead, she said, "Nice truck."

He made himself at home beside her on the narrow wooden step and silently studied the classic GMC pickup he'd just parked in her driveway. "I drive the cruiser so much that my truck just sits in the garage," he said. "She gets lonely after a while. I thought I'd take her out tonight and blow off a little of the dust. Keep her from rusting solid."

"What year is she?"

"She's a 1977. I picked her up for a little nothing and restored her myself." He adjusted his feet on the bottom tread next to hers. "Did you get any sleep after I left last night?"

"Not much," she admitted. "You?"

"Not much," he admitted. He propped his elbows on his knees, lowered his head and ran his fingers through his hair. His hands were large, his long fingers ending in blunt, square tips. His nails were neatly trimmed. On his wrist, he wore a Timex with a silver stretch band. He was a simple man, nothing pretentious about him. He was flannel and denim, beer and pizza, bowling and barbecues. He probably didn't even know what an espresso machine looked like. He probably didn't even care.

The steps were narrow, and his knee accidentally brushed against hers. Neither of them bothered to rectify the situation. "Bad day?" she said.

"The usual." Again, he ran his fingers through his hair. "Chasing bad guys. Putting 'em in jail. Issuing speeding tickets to little old ladies."

"Ah, yes. Doing your civic duty, upholding the letter of the law."

"Which would be a lot easier if my old man would stop making me crazy."

"Buck?" She raised an eyebrow. "What's he done now?"

"He got in an accident this morning. Drove his truck right through the front of the health food store over at Ames Plaza." His eyebrows drew together. "The truck, I might add, that I told him not to buy. He went ahead and bought it anyway, behind my back."

"Good Lord. Was he hurt?"

"Fortunately, no." Ty's expression was grim. "But he's starting to scare me. He says he mistook the accelerator for the brake. Rational people don't do that. His behavior lately has been bizarre. Jo thinks it's the beginning of Alzheimer's. For all I know, she may be right." Leaning, he picked at a sliver of wood that was coming loose from the step, then adjusted himself to a more comfortable position. His thigh fell against hers, and he left it there. "She reamed me out good this afternoon for not keeping a better eye on him. But, hell—" he broke the sliver of wood into pieces and tossed them aside "—there's no way I can keep Dad under my thumb. Jo ought to know that. She grew up in the same house I did. Buck Savage listens to nobody but himself."

His thigh, resting against hers, was warm and distracting. Faith cleared her throat. "What about your mother? Doesn't she have any influence over him?"

"He and Mom divorced about five years ago. They barely speak to each other now."

"I'm sorry. I had no idea they'd split."

"It was just as well. I think they really cared about each other, but they were a lousy match. Both of them jackass stubborn." His smile was wry. "It wasn't exactly a marriage made in heaven."

"So where is she now? Your mother?"

He crossed his arms over his thighs and studied her intently. His elbow brushed her upper arm, and awareness began a red-hot tango in the pit of her stomach. "She's living across town," he said. "Shacked up with a younger man."

Picturing in her mind the motherly Glenda Savage who, even in her forties, had been the apple-cheeked, pie-baking grandma type, Faith said in gleeful horror, "I don't believe it! Not your mother."

"Believe it. Dad's having a kitten over it." He continued to study her intently, before he said, "How'd it go with Cunningham?"

"Jessie and I have to make some decisions. About the house, that kind of thing."

"She want to stay here?"

"I don't know. We haven't discussed it yet. She went to school today, so I talked to Cunningham alone. Which reminds me." A breeze blew a lock of hair into her face, and she brushed it away impatiently. "Do you know a kid named Cooper Gates?"

"I know of him. Why?"

"He asked Jessie out on a date. Dottie McLaughlin says he has a reputation for being fast with the girls. I'm a little nervous about this. I don't want to screw up royally during my first week of motherhood. I just wondered if you were acquainted with him. In a personal or professional capacity."

"If you're asking if he's ever been arrested, I can tell you he has no record here in Serenity. I'd know if he did. His father's head of surgery at Androscoggin Valley General. Good at what he does, but his perception of his own importance is greatly exaggerated. He's king of all he surveys at the hospital, and unfortunately, the God complex runs over into the real world. If I'd ever had the nerve to look cross-eyed at his lily-white baby boy, he would've brought the wrath of God down on my head."

"Sounds like a prince among men."

He grunted noncommittally. "The mother's active in various local charities, and she's the queen of what passes for polite society here in River City. Rumor has it—" he paused, rearranged his big feet on the bottom step "—that Delia Gates has more than a passing acquaintance with Mr. Jim Beam."

"Oh?"

"Like I said, that's just a rumor. I don't know that it's true. What I do know is that both parents are too busy to bother with their kid. He's been running wild and unsupervised for most of his life."

"That doesn't sound good."

"I don't think he's a bad kid. Just a neglected one. In spite of the lack of parental supervision, he's managed to make a name for himself on the football field. Kid's one hell of a quarterback."

"I suppose it should comfort me to know he's not a hoodlum. But Jessie seems so young, so innocent. She's never even been out with a boy before. Starting with a boy like that is a little like tossing a nonswimmer into a pool full of sharks. If he lays a hand on her, I might have to castrate him."

"I'd say you're settling into instant motherhood quite nicely."

The lowering sun moved through a bloodred sky as it approached the horizon. A crow flew overhead, wings spread as it glided on an air current, black feathers glossy in the glow of the setting sun. In the distance, a dog barked. Buddy, lying on the ground near their feet, pricked up his ears. "This is nice," Ty said. "Peaceful. Remember when we used to sit like this and talk for hours? We were inseparable. There wasn't a thing we couldn't talk about. How'd we ever manage to lose that?"

She turned her head and studied him at length. "You had sex with my cousin," she said, "and I stopped speaking to you."

He winced. "Ouch. You have claws."

"If you can't handle the truth, don't ask."

"Don't tell me you're still mad at me after all these years?"

"That was almost twenty years ago," she said, staring into the bloody glow of sunset. "I'd be pretty stupid to hold a grudge for that long." It wasn't really an answer, but apparently he didn't notice.

"Well," he said, "since you're officially speaking to me again, how about going for a ride with me? I promised myself I'd paint the town red while Jo's baby-sitting Dad. We can stop by the DQ for a soft-serve, then do something really exciting. Maybe boonie-cruise while we listen to oldies on the radio. Relive our lost youth."

She bit back a smile at the picture his words evoked. "It sounds enticing, but I hate to leave Jessie alone."

"Bring her along. There's plenty of room. My truck's a club cab. She can sit in the back."

"That's easier said than done. I need a crowbar to pry her out of her bedroom. She came down long enough to wolf down a sandwich, and then she went back up there."

"I'll go up and talk to her. I never met a kid yet who didn't like ice cream."

Somehow, he managed to charm Jessie into abandoning her violin and coming with them. Maybe it was the promise of ice cream. Or maybe it was his offer to let Buddy come along that did the trick. Jessie was a silent presence in the back seat, staring wordlessly out the window at the passing scenery, one hand tangled in Buddy's long fur. Several times, Faith opened her mouth to speak to the girl. But each time, she exchanged glances with Ty, and something in his eyes told her to keep quiet.

Studying his face surreptitiously, Faith wondered why he and Linda had never had children. It seemed an oddity, for he struck her as the kind of man who would have made an outstanding father. Just as Ben would have, had he been capable of fathering them. She and Ben had talked about adopting, but their life had been full, so full they'd decided against it. Since his death, she'd often wondered whether they made the right decision. If she'd had somebody else to focus on, somebody else to love, somebody whose very survival depended on her maintaining her equilibrium, would she still have gone off the deep end? It was a question without answer, but one about which she'd speculated endlessly.

Sometimes Ty reminded her of Ben. On the surface, they were nothing alike. Ben had worn the refined mantle of academe around him as if he'd been born to it. Which, in effect, he had, since both his parents were college professors. Ty was rougher around the edges, a man's man. But beneath the surface, where it counted, there was a similarity between the two men. Both were men of strong character, genuine and honest. Maybe that was part of what had drawn her to Ben in the first place. Maybe in some unconscious way, he'd reminded her of Ty.

The Dairy Queen was doing a brisk business. Now that the weather had turned, it seemed that half of Serenity had come out for ice cream. Ty parked beside a maroon Escort, and Jessie waited in the truck with the dog while he and Faith took their place in line.

The evening was warm, the line slow-moving. Everybody knew Ty, and everybody wanted to talk about Buck's accident. The town was abuzz with gossip, for it wasn't every day that a retired small-town police chief drove his vehicle through the front of a building. Curiosity and misinformation ran rampant. Had Buck been drinking? Had he passed out behind the wheel? Had he really suffered a fractured collarbone like people were saying? Or did he have some heretofore undisclosed medical condition that should have prevented him from driving?

Ty fielded the questions with grace and tact, smothering the gossip as best he could while at the same time revealing nothing. It was an art, and a useful one at that. Faith studied how he did it, just in case she ever needed to borrow his technique.

Some people, the ones who actually knew her, greeted her. The rest of them just stared. Even those who didn't know her personally still knew who she was, and not a soul in the place missed noting that Faith Pelletier had shown up at the DQ with Ty Savage. Faith knew she'd been the object of gossip before tonight. People gossiped in Serenity because there was nothing else to do. By now, everybody in town already knew what kind of car she drove and what time she'd pulled into town the night before the funeral. Her New York plates were a dead giveaway in a town that out-of-staters seldom passed through. Now she'd given the gossips new fuel for their fire, far more titillating than Buck Savage's fender bender. Phones would ring off the hook tonight as the locals speculated on the nature of the relationship between the lady novelist and the handsome, unmarried chief of police.

After what seemed eons, their turn at the window finally came. They returned to the truck carrying two vanilla cones, a hot fudge sundae for Jessie, and a dish of vanilla ice cream, sans cone, for Buddy. They'd just settled down to eat when a shiny new silver Cadillac pulled up in the spot just vacated by the Escort. The driver's door opened, and Ty's ex-wife stepped out of the car.

Linda Larochelle wore a splashy scarlet suit over a white silk blouse. Her blond hair was artfully disarranged, and showed a fashionable quarter-inch of dark roots. Linda smoothed her hair and slung her Gucci bag over her shoulder, then marched directly to Ty's open window.

"I was driving by," she said, "and I saw you sitting here." Pursing ripe lips painted the same color as her suit, she said, "I just heard about Buck. How frightening! So many rumors floating around. Is he really all right?"

"He's fine," Ty said woodenly. "But thanks for your concern."

Linda stood there looking at him, as though uncertain about whether or not she'd really been dismissed so summarily. Then she smiled brightly and turned to Faith. "Faith," she said, "it's good to see you. I'm so very sorry about Chelsea."

Faith, painfully aware of Jessie's presence in the seat behind her, gave Linda a strained smile. "Thank you."

"It's so funny that I should run into you like this. I've been intending to call you ever since you got home. I'm always amazed by coincidences like that."

She was all saccharine graciousness, and Faith's muscles began to tighten, one by one. It was truly amazing that suddenly they should be bosom buddies. Especially considering that in years past, Linda hadn't spoken to her even once.

Sweetly, Faith said, "Really? You were going to call me? Whatever for?"

"Since you asked, I might as well tell you. I'm not sure if Ty's mentioned it to you, but I'm in real estate." Linda reached into her leather purse and pulled out a business card. She held it out in front of Ty, who pointedly ignored it, choosing instead to focus his attention on his ice cream. Faith reached past his sugar cone and took the card from her. "It's my understanding," Linda said, suddenly all business, "that you may be looking to sell the Logan place in the near future."

In the back seat behind her, Jessie sat still as death. Even Buddy was silent, as though waiting to see what would happen next. Stiffly, Faith said, "I have no idea at this time what my plans are."

"Of course you don't," Linda said. "I completely understand. This has all been so sudden. I just wanted to ask a favor of you. If you do decide to sell, I'd appreciate you calling me first." She shot a quick glance at Ty, then took a breath before she continued. "Look, I'm not trying to drum up business. My fiancé and I want to buy a house, and I think the Logan place is just what we're looking for. He's been renting a place for the past couple of years, but it's just an apartment and there isn't even a yard. He's looking—" again, she shot a glance at Ty "—*we're* looking for a house in the country, something with lots of space, a few acres of land, room for his little girl to play. A place where she can have a dog, maybe a couple of horses."

Faith's ice cream was melting. "Jessie and I will think about it," she said. "We'll let you know."

"Thank you. Tyrone, please give Buck my love."

They watched Linda walk away. She got back into her car, started it up and backed rapidly out of her parking space, causing a motorist who had just pulled in from the street to lay on his horn to prevent a collision. "Well," Faith said. "Well."

"I absolutely refuse to take any responsibility for her," Ty said.

"You're the one who was married to her, my friend. How many years was that again?"

"Eight," he said. "Eight of the longest years of my life."

"You stuck it out a long time, champ."

"I pride myself on not being a quitter. Eat your ice cream. It's melting all over you."

Faith obediently caught the drips with a swirl of her tongue. "The real estate business must be booming," she said.

"Not the last I heard. Nobody's got any money, and who the hell would want to move here, anyway?"

"Then how do you explain the brand-new Caddy?"

"Linda's always believed in dressing for success, right up to and including the car she drives."

Faith tried to imagine Ty behind the wheel of that flashy Cadillac, but the image just wouldn't come. It explained a lot about the demise of his marriage. "Who's the lucky fiancé?" she said.

"That would be Skip Lombardi. He's the high school principal."

"Ah. I've met him."

From the back seat, Jessie said, "His daughter's sick."

Faith turned around to look at her. "What do you mean, sick?"

"She has something wrong with her. Some kind of cancer or something." Jessie stuck her spoon into the mountain of vanilla ice cream in her dish. "He's missed a lot of work because he has to keep taking her to specialists out of state."

"How awful," Faith said, thinking of Ben. "How old is she?"

"Eight or nine. He's a really nice man. All the kids like him." Jessie paused to reconsider. "Well, most of us do, anyway. He's always been really nice to me." Eyes focused on what was left of her sundae, she added softly, "Are we going to sell the house?"

Damn that Linda Larochelle! Faith could easily have wrapped her hands around the woman's neck and squeezed. On the other hand, Linda had been the catalyst for the longest speech she'd ever heard Jessie make. "Don't you worry about it," she said. "That's just one possibility among many. You and I have a lot to talk about, and we don't have to rush into anything." God only knew, the girl had already been through enough, and Faith was not about to be responsible for tearing her home out from under her.

Glancing in his rearview mirror, Ty said with robust cheerfulness, "Don't forget, ladies, we still have that boonie-cruising to do. So fasten your seat belts, because we're about to take off."

Flashing him a look of gratitude, Faith locked her belt with a loud click. Behind her, Jessie did the same. Ty shot her a quick wink before he pulled out onto the street and headed west.

They passed the mill, its weed-choked yard spooky with shadows, and crossed the river, tires singing on the grid work of the old iron bridge. When they reached the west bank of the river, Ty took a right onto West Mollyockett Road and headed up into the hills. Faith glanced into the back seat. Jessie was still working on her sundae, her expression pensive as she gazed out the window. Buddy had finished his ice cream in a single gulp. Now he sat directly behind Ty, his muzzle pressed to the open driver's window, mouth hanging ajar and ears billowing in the wind.

The sun lay heavy against the horizon, its bloodred orb reflecting in a 360-degree wash of pinks and golds and purples. They passed trailers and ranch houses whose mailboxes bore familiar names: Rideout and Cormier and Ouellette, names that reflected the French-Canadian ancestry of the people who dwelt within. Most of the homes they passed were modest but neat. On her left, she saw an old farmhouse surrounded by acres of rolling fields. The old white Cape Cod glowed golden in the sunset, its lawn rich and lush with deepening shadows. In the front yard, a blue-and-white plaster statue of the Virgin Mary, purest of the pure, watched over and protected the farmer and his family. In the driveway, a flock of fat white geese flapped their wings. Nearby, cattle grazed in a cluster near the old bathtub the farmer used as a watering trough.

A little farther down the road, they passed an old trailer with sheets of clear plastic duct taped over the windows to keep the heat inside and the cold outside. Concrete blocks lined the trailer's roof, and a half-dozen disemboweled automobiles littered the property.

"The Stultz place," Ty said dryly. "Some of our more colorful citizens."

"Good Lord. Isn't there some kind of municipal ordinance governing the number of inoperable cars people are allowed to keep in their yards?"

"Oh, for sure. And every so often, Pete and I like to drop by and roust Teddy and Leroy, just for the fun of it."

They drove for another mile in silence. Just as the sun slipped over the horizon, Ty slowed and pulled onto the left shoulder, parking at the edge of a field sprinkled with nodding daffodils. "Why are we stopping?" Faith said.

He turned off his engine. "I wanted to show you where I plan to build my house. I bought the land over the winter. Just closed on it a couple weeks ago."

They climbed out of the truck, and while Jessie picked wildflowers, Buddy cavorting at her feet, Faith and Ty walked the property. It was her favorite time of day, that still, windless hour between sunset and nightfall, when birds perched in the treetops and twittered a raucous goodbye to the day before settling down to roost for the night.

Situated atop a hill, the property had once been pastureland, and was marked by a crumbling rock wall that ran alongside a row of towering sugar maples. At the far end was a gurgling brook that meandered across the back of the property and down the hillside. To the west was the White Mountain Range, the distinctive peak of Mount Washington clearly visible in the crystalline evening sky.

"I thought I'd situate the house here," Ty said, "with the master bedroom at this end. Maybe install a double set of French doors overlooking a redwood deck in the back. I'll probably build it at an angle to the road. Living room here, kitchen over there, two more bedrooms here in the back—" He paused, as though picturing it in his mind. "Maybe a paved drive, winding along the front. That would be pretty. I'll tame a little of the yard, front and back, for lawn. The rest I'll leave the way nature intended it to be."

"It sounds wonderful," Faith said. "What does Buck think about it?"

Still admiring his imaginary house, Ty said brusquely, "He doesn't know."

"Oh." It was just one syllable, but it held a wealth of meaning.

Beneath the maples, Jessie walked the rock wall, arms spread like airplane wings for balance, a clump of wildflowers clutched in one fist. Beside her, Buddy loped along the ground. Ty tucked his hands into his pockets and jingled a fistful of change. "Look at those two," he said. "Already the best of friends." He fell silent for a time, then said, "I'm still trying to figure out how to break it to him. Dad's so damn touchy lately, he blows up at the littlest thing. How the hell am I supposed to tell him I'm moving out?"

She touched his arm. Through the flannel shirt, his skin felt hot and a little damp, as though he were running a mild fever. "You'll find a way."

Mildly, he said, "I don't know what to do. It's not working, the two of us living together. But if he really does have Alzheimer's, I don't see how I can just go off and leave him alone."

"What about Jolene?"

"Jo has her own life, too. She teaches high school, and she has a family. She's in no more of a position than I am to play full-time baby-sitter."

In the distance, Jessie, still walking the rock wall, lost her balance. She flailed around a little before she regained it. Eyes still trained on the girl and the dog, he said, "Mind if I ask you a question?"

"Go ahead."

"Am I having pipe dreams, or is there something going on between us?"

His words shouldn't have taken her by surprise. It was obvious that Ty Savage was the kind of man who spoke the truth, straightforward and without hesitation or embellishment. But she was still caught unprepared. His question was too sudden, too intimate. It was too soon to give voice to feelings she hadn't yet sorted out in her own mind.

His gaze, locked with hers, was dark and deep and steady, making her abruptly aware of her own heartbeat, a little rapid, a little erratic. Abruptly aware of her own breathing, of the sudden tightness of her own skin. There was no way she could lie to him. He wasn't the kind of man a woman lied to. Trembling inside like a willow in a gale-force wind, she wet her lips and said steadily, "You're not having pipe dreams."

Their gazes held, each of them seeking something in the other's eyes, each finding what they sought. Vulnerability, need, an undeniable bond. He nodded slowly, as though satisfied with her answer. Then Buddy came racing up with Jessie behind him, and the moment was lost.

By the time they returned to the truck, darkness had begun to fall. Ty turned on the radio to the promised oldies station. The music was a soft, soothing accompaniment to the steady thrum of her heartbeat as he drove smoothly and surely through the night, navigating the back roads of Western Maine as only a native could, taking turn after turn until she was completely lost and couldn't have found her way home even if somebody had handed her a road map and a compass. Yet she felt utterly secure, utterly content, for she already knew she could trust him with her life, this old friend who had suddenly and inexplicably become much more than a friend.

This was crazy. She'd only been back for three days, and she hardly knew the man. Until this past Monday, they hadn't spoken in eighteen years. But there was no denying the way those dark eyes of his had touched her, reaching deep inside her to a place she thought had died with Ben.

She wasn't ready for this. Ben's death had turned her world upside down, and she still hadn't been able to right it. Her husband had been gone for just a year and a half, and she was a broken woman. She couldn't even take care of herself, let alone maintain any kind of romantic relationship.

Help me, Ben. Tell me what to do.

But Ben didn't answer, just as he'd failed to answer every other time she'd appealed to him for help. Her rock, the one solid, dependable thing in her life, had deserted her. She'd been dependent on him for so many things. Now, she was truly on her own, and it was terrifying.

On the radio, the Cornelius Brothers sang about no turning back. In the darkness, Ty reached across empty space for her hand. A shiver raced down her spine as he brushed the tips of two fingers over her palm, around the base of her thumb and across the back of her hand. Everything inside her tightened like a coiled spring. She'd never thought of the hand as an erogenous zone, but the whisper-soft touch of those two fingertips, moving with slow, teasing motions up and down her palm, over and around and between her own fingers, was the most exciting thing she'd ever experienced.

He fitted his palm to hers, loosely linked their fingers. Anticipation thickened the air between them as the truck rolled through the night, riding leftover frost heaves like a demented roller coaster. Faith's stomach grew queasy from the bumpy ride, or maybe it was from nerves. She tried to concentrate on something other than their linked hands, something other than his face, silhouetted in the faint greenish light from the dash. But his features, burned into her memory, would have been clear to her even in absolute darkness: the strong jaw, so like his father's; the straight nose that flared slightly at the end, softening what might have otherwise been a harsh countenance; his full lips, generous but still undeniably masculine.

She turned away from him, pretending interest in what was out there in the darkness. They passed a farmhouse with lights ablaze, the hulking dark silhouettes of century-old maples lining the driveway, and she realized that by some circuitous miracle they'd driven full-circle, back across the river, and now they were approaching Chelsea's house from the north instead of the south. He must have crossed at one of the small upriver bridges, and she'd been too distracted to notice. They climbed the backside of Bald Mountain, then Ty slowed, released her hand to downshift, and turned into her driveway.

He pulled to a stop behind Ben's Saab, in a shadowy spot

beyond the reaches of the forty-watt bulb that dimly lit the area surrounding the back door, its weak illumination barely reaching the near wall of the dilapidated chicken coop. Turning off his engine and opening his door, Ty said, "You need a brighter light. At least sixty watts. A hundred's better yet."

Faith didn't answer him. She wasn't sure she could have answered even if she'd had an intelligent response. Instead she sat frozen, her heart hammering, while he stepped out of the cab and tilted forward the driver's seat to make room for the back seat occupants to exit. Buddy leaped out and began dancing around Ty's feet, dog tags rattling merrily. Jessie, exiting behind him, took time to study Faith before she got out. Seeming to sense the tension between the two adults, she said, "I'll be in the house," and climbed out of the truck. "Good night," she said primly to Ty. "Thank you for the ice cream."

"You're very welcome."

He closed the driver's door, and Faith sat in darkness, watching Jessie all the way to the house. She waited endless seconds for the kitchen light to come on. Behind the window curtain, Jessie's shadow moved about the room.

Ty walked around the front of the truck with slow deliberation, in no hurry despite the fact that Faith was ready to implode. He opened her door, and light filled the cab. He offered her a hand and she took it, sliding easily from the seat to the ground below.

He closed the door, plunging them back into darkness. Faith leaned against the truck, its smooth steel finish cool and silky against her back. The night had grown chilly; a breeze stirred her hair, and goose bumps peppered her skin. In shadowy blackness, he caught her other hand in his, circled long fingers around her slender wrists, and pinned them to the truck on either side of her head.

Behind his shoulder, the night sky was inky black and studded with stars. Anticipation was a heavy weight, low in her belly. Inside her chest, her heart pounded so hard she feared it would burst free and fly off into space to take its place among those stars.

"Alone at last," he said, and lowered his head to kiss her.

His mouth on hers was hot and exciting. He tasted faintly of vanilla, and he took his time with the kiss, tasting and exploring without haste, while exhilaration sang in her blood. She felt seventeen again as all those adolescent yearnings came rushing back. Impatient, she wanted more, wanted his hands on her body, her hands on his. Wanted him cradled between her thighs. But she was trapped, her wrists pinned to the truck with an iron grip, while he exercised amazing restraint, standing just far enough away from her so that his body heat, mingling with hers, filled her with crazed longing.

Frustrated, she pushed him to greater intimacy, opening her mouth to the exquisite slide of his tongue against hers. With a soft groan, he released her wrists and cradled her face with hands that were broad and rough, like fine sandpaper, incredibly exciting against her tender skin.

Ty skimmed the pad of his thumb along her jawline, down her throat and past her open collar. His knuckles stroked the skin over her collarbone, raising goose bumps on her sensitive flesh, before they came to rest on the swell of her breast.

She moaned, and his mouth caught and muffled the sound. Her heart stuttered, and she reached up, released the top button to her shirt, and then the rest, one by one, until her shirt, like her heart, lay open before him.

He broke the kiss. They stood in each other's arms, breath coming hard and fast. "Touch me," she whispered. "*Touch me.*"

With a single finger, he stroked the sensitive skin of her breast, and she shuddered in delight. Hooking that same finger around the strap to her bra, he slid the strap down her arm. With excruciating gentleness, he rolled the satin cup downward and his big, rough hand closed over her bare breast.

Time stopped. He kissed her again, open mouth to open mouth, his breath mingling with hers, her heart thudding against his open palm. They couldn't do this. Not here, not now, not standing in the driveway in full sight of the road, not with Jessie only a short distance away inside the house. But it was exquisite, the touch of his hand on her bare skin, and she wasn't ready yet to stop. He cupped her breast, lifted its weight in his palm, brushed his thumb across the swollen peak. The friction from his rough hands was maddening, and she bit her lip hard to keep from crying out.

His breath gusting hot against her ear, he said hoarsely, "Do you have any idea how much I want you?"

She ran a hand up his forearm. Breathlessly, she said, "Tell me."

"You've got me lying awake at night, like some teenage kid with his first crush, analyzing every look you give me, every word you say. Looking for signs that maybe you feel the same way I do." He dipped his head and dropped a kiss on her breast, and she shivered, her body humming beneath his hands, his mouth. "It was always you I wanted. Chelsea was just a substitute."

Lost in his touch, it took a minute for his words to sink in. "What?" she said.

"It didn't mean anything, what happened with Chelsea. I was eighteen years old, raging with hormones. She was hell-bent on getting revenge on Davy. She came on to me, and I caved. It wasn't exactly my finest hour. Davy was my best friend."

Inside her chest, her breath backed up, engorging lungs that couldn't seem to release their burden. "I know you were disappointed in me," he said. "I was disappointed in me. But it didn't mean anything. It wasn't Chelsea I wanted. It just happened, one of those damn-fool things that teenage boys do when they're thinking with what's between their legs, instead of what's between their ears." He paused, finally seeming to realize that she'd gone stiff in his arms. "Will you for Christ's sake say something?"

"Idiot," she said, and shoved him so hard he stumbled backward. "Get away from me." Her back turned to him, she began feverishly pulling herself back together. She crammed her breast, that wanton traitor that still yearned for the touch of his hand, back into her brassiere, yanking so hard on the bra strap that she heard something rip.

"What?" he said in bewilderment. "What the hell did I do?"

Furious with him, even more furious with herself for allowing him to touch her, she wheeled around to face him. Closing the front of her shirt with staccato movements, one button at a time, she said, "You're just as big an idiot now, Savage, as you were back then!"

Lit only by starlight, his face was a pale glimmer in the darkness. "Wait just a minute." He moved toward her and she shrank back against the truck, hands still clutching her shirt front, her heart hammering double-time. "I'm missing something here."

"Just like you missed it then!" Rage spewed from her, a complex and bewildering mishmash of the anger she hadn't allowed herself to feel when Ben died and the fury she still felt toward Ty Savage for what he'd done to her all those years ago. The intensity of her rage was preposterous, disproportionate to the situation. By now, her anger toward Ty should have faded. But it hadn't. It had been simmering for eighteen years, and now it was ready to let go. Ty Savage had owned her young heart, and he'd stomped all over it when he rejected her in favor of a one-night stand with her sluttish cousin. After all these years, it still hurt.

"You can stop talking in riddles," he said, "because this is getting old really fast, and I don't have a clue what the hell you're talking about. You have something to say, Pelletier, then go ahead and say it. But don't play guessing games with me."

"You want to know what I'm talking about, Savage? Fine, I'll tell you!" She reached up and scraped a fistful of wild curls away from her face. "Did you really think I turned my back on you because I didn't approve of who you chose to play tiddledywinks with? Did you really think I was that shallow?"

"I don't know. You tell me. What else was I supposed to think?"

"Are you really that stupid?" She laughed, but her laughter was brittle and humorless and thick with unshed tears. "I stopped talking to you because when you slept with Chelsea, you broke my heart."

"What? What the hell are you talking about?"

"I wasn't disappointed in you, you big, stupid oaf." She swiped furiously at a single tear that had somehow managed to escape. "I was in love with you!"

Thirteen

Fortified with a steaming cup of the strongest Colombian coffee that Food City carried, Ty sat in the wicker rocker on his screened-in front porch, cat purring contentedly on his lap, his bare feet propped on the windowsill. The rocker made a comfortingly familiar squeaking sound as he rocked back and forth. Taking a sip of coffee, he thanked God for the wonders of caffeine. He needed something to get his blood circulating. He hadn't slept worth a damn last night. If he kept this up, he'd be dead soon from sleep deprivation.

It had been close to midnight before he'd finally stopped thrashing around and fallen asleep. He'd been awake again at dawn, thanks to those wretched grackles who clustered every morning in the ash tree outside his bedroom window and started chattering before it was even daylight. He'd been tempted on more than one occasion to scare them off with a BB gun, but he could imagine what the good citizens of Serenity would have to say about the chief of police regressing to the maturity level of a fifteen-year-old delinquent. There'd be a solid core of old-timers who wouldn't be surprised at all—who had, in fact, predicted that he'd never amount to anything. Maybe he should get out his service revolver and use the damn twittering birds for target practice. He hated like hell to disappoint anybody.

Faith had dropped one whopper of a bombshell in his lap last night before she and her injured pride had gone flouncing off into the house without issuing him an invitation to follow. He was still reeling from the impact. What a pair of cretins they'd been back in high school. Two eighteen-year-old kids whose friendship had gone far beyond platonic, both of them afraid to admit to their feelings for fear of rejection, both of them missing out on what might have turned into a forever thing because they stubbornly insisted on heading in different directions on different tracks instead of meeting somewhere in the middle.

She was right about one thing. He was an idiot. All these years, he'd been too stupid to figure out the truth, too stupid to figure out that a woman didn't stop talking to a man just because she thought he was making an ass of himself. A woman stopped talking to a man when he hurt her deeply and then failed to show even a shred of remorse. He'd made a mess of things without even knowing it, and eighteen years later, he could only shake his head in disbelief at his own stupidity.

In the kitchen, Buck began rattling pots and pans. Ty closed his eyes and winced. He really wasn't up right now to a confrontation with the old man. Had it been a normal day, he would have already been out of the house and on his way to work. But it was his day off, and unless he wanted to start it on a sour note—more sour than it already was—his best option was to escape the house.

Choosing the lesser of two evils, he drained his coffee, scooped the cat out of his lap and onto the floor, and rummaged around on the porch until he found the Skechers he hadn't worn in weeks. It was a beautiful morning, shadows long and deep and dark, dew sparkling crystalline on the grass. Ty kept himself in shape, but it had been a couple of weeks since he'd found the time to run, and his muscles reminded him of that fact as he headed off down Lithgow Street and fell into an easy rhythm.

Next door, at the house where Faith had lived as a kid, a

massive chestnut tree overhung the sidewalk in front of the small gray bungalow. As kids, they'd run in and out of each other's houses with no consideration to knocking on doors or asking permission. He'd eaten as many meals at Faith's house as she'd eaten at his. They'd ridden their bicycles all over town, freely explored woods and fields and streams, wandered in and out of the stores on Water Street, secure in the knowledge that nothing and nobody here in Serenity would ever hurt them. Life had been simple and good, possessed of a sweet naiveté he sometimes wished he could regain. Skies had been cloudless, bearing no hint of the darkness that was about to descend like a thunderhead upon them.

He could still remember that Sunday morning, as clearly as though it had been yesterday, although it had happened nearly a quarter of a century ago. The call had come in just after daybreak. There'd been a rollover on Bald Mountain Road, a half mile this side of the Westerly town line. Two fatalities, a male and a female. Buck had grumbled about being dragged out of bed so early. If the accident had happened just a half mile farther north, it would have been Eddie Kendall, Westerly's police chief, who'd have been dragged out into the February cold instead of Buck. It would have been Eddie who earned the privilege of watching the EMT crew cart away some fool in a body bag, somebody who'd still be alive if he hadn't been driving too fast on that icy back road.

Three hours later Buck had returned, looking ashen and stunned. Even at the age of twelve, Ty knew that something was very wrong. Buck, who'd always seemed hardened to that kind of thing, looked as though he'd been hit by a wrecking ball. Ty had crept to the kitchen doorway in time to see his father take his mother into his arms. Buck wasn't a demonstrative man, generally saving such gestures of tenderness for the privacy of his own bedroom. But that morning, he'd hauled Glenda into his arms and held her as though he were a drowning man and she his sole hope for survival. With simple, straightforward words spoken in an unsteady voice, Buck had broken the news to his wife that the victims had been Meredith and Armand Pelletier. Their good friends and neighbors. Faith's parents.

Ty shook off the memory, nodded to Eleanor Fraser, who'd just picked up her morning *Gazette* from her front lawn and was standing on her cracked concrete walkway in curlers and a flowered housecoat, checking out the day's headlines. Two houses down, a chipmunk chattered and scolded from the privet hedge Ira Weinstein had planted two decades ago to keep the neighborhood kids off his lawn.

Damn, but Faith had been mad last night. He'd never seen her so furious. He wouldn't have been surprised if she'd drawn off and belted him a good one. Even in the dark, the bloodlust in her eyes had been clearly visible. He'd hurt her, right down to the bone, and she hadn't yet forgiven him. But Christ Almighty, it had been nearly twenty years. They'd been in high school, for God's sake. That was one hell of a long time for a woman to hold a grudge.

Maybe that was only part of her anger. Maybe some of it sprang from embarrassment over the intimacies they'd exchanged. He hadn't intended to take things so far last night. If truth be known, he'd had no intentions at all, beyond buying her an ice cream and taking her for a drive. But the sexual tension between them had been thick enough to swim in, and when she stood there in the starlight, her face turned up to his, all wistful and filled with longing, those blue eyes of hers practically devouring him, and said, *touch me*—

Holy mother of God. There wasn't a man on the planet who could have turned her down.

He reached the stop sign at the end of Lithgow Street and took a right onto Union without breaking stride. Here, the houses were larger, elegant older homes that had been chopped up into apartments during the seventies, when the cost of oil had skyrocketed to the point where homeowners could no longer afford to heat the monstrosities in which their families had lived for generations. Most of the houses needed work. A little paint here, some new shutters there. Toys littered the yards, and the once lush grass had been trampled by dozens of little feet. In one driveway, a tripod had been set up and somebody was pulling the engine from a 1972 Plymouth Duster.

And there was paper scattered everywhere. What the hell was that all about? Damn, he hated it when people littered. Serenity might not be much of a town, but it was his town, and he took pride in it. Lack of money didn't mean people had to be pigs. Ty bent and snatched up a snowy white sheet, limp with dew, and crumpled it in his hand. It was all over the place, scattered as though somebody had left out a ream of paper and the wind had blown it everywhere.

Except that the air this morning was dead still.

As he stood, sticky with sweat and breathing a little hard, he realized that the papers hadn't been randomly scattered by the wind. They'd been placed here by human hands, in a well-planned and methodical pattern. In front of every apartment building on the street, somebody had dropped five or six sheets of ordinary eight-and-a-half by eleven white paper, the kind used by computer printers and photocopiers.

Ty opened the sheet he'd crumpled and smoothed it out, quickly skimmed the text.

Support the Brotherhood for Aryan Unity

We are not racists. We are good Christian people who believe in preserving the values and morals upon which this great nation was founded, including the superiority and purity of the white race. In other parts of our nation, the white race is rapidly disappearing, its blood diluted by liberals who insist on forcing upon us such evil concepts as diversity and equal opportunity. We cannot let that happen here! The Somalis must leave Serenity before our purity is tainted by colored blood and we become just like so many other places in America, places where a white man can no longer hold up his head and take pride. Help us to prevent Serenity from being tainted by colored blood!

It went on for a little longer in the same vein, ending with a web address where like-minded individuals could go for further edification or to provide moral or financial support. Rubbing absently at his midsection, Ty turned his attention from the flyer with its hateful message to the crooked line of white that extended down Union Street for as far as he could see. If they'd covered this much of Union, they'd probably wallpapered the whole town.

Damn it all. Damn it all to hell.

Was this somebody's idea of a joke? If so, it wasn't very funny. The situation with the Somalis was already tense and uncomfortable. This was going to start a firestorm. And if it wasn't a joke, if it was serious, then the town of Serenity, and Police Chief Ty Savage, had a big problem on their hands.

Faith had never done mornings well. Ben used to tease her about it, saying that she never got all her cylinders running until after her third cup of coffee, and even then, she was pretty much useless until noon. It was an exaggeration, of course, but an exaggeration based on a hard kernel of truth. This morning was worse than usual. She'd made an utter fool of herself last night, and her head ached with the knowledge. Eventually, her fury had dissipated. But not before Newt had called, sometime around midnight, to find out if she'd made any progress with the computer files.

"The disks are a big disappointment," she'd told him. "A dead end. I went through all of them and I didn't find anything."

He let out a pent-up breath. "What about the hard drive?"

"I'm hoping to get to it tomorrow."

"I told you I'd help you with it. All you have to do is say the word. And I happen to know that you weren't working on it all evening. At some point, you managed to get to the Dairy Queen with Savage."

Indignation, spurred by embarrassment, reared its ugly head. "Who the hell told you that?"

"At least a half-dozen people in the past two hours. This is a small town. Don't ever make the mistake of doubting the power of the grapevine. Did you find out anything about the break-in at Dowe's?"

She sighed and rubbed her temple. "We never got around to it."

"Oh? So what *did* you get around to?"

"If I thought it was any of your business," she snapped, "you'd be the first person I notified."

Silence reigned at his end of the line. "I'm sorry," she said. "I'm in a foul mood, and I have a headache coming on. I shouldn't be taking it out on you."

"I don't suppose your foul mood would have anything to do with our esteemed police chief?"

It had more to do with him than she was willing to admit to anybody besides herself. "Newt?" she said with saccharine sweetness.

"What?"

"Go pound sand."

"That's pretty much what I thought. Do you have something to help you sleep?"

Thinking of the soothing properties of Valium, she said, "Yes, but Dr. Garabedian wouldn't approve of me using it."

"Who's Dr. Garabedian?"

"My shrink. He decided it's time I cut down on the happy pills and started facing reality. I tend to prefer my own version of reality, rose-colored glasses and all. He's not particularly sympathetic to that viewpoint."

"You've had a rough day, Faith. Hell, you've had more than one rough day. Take a damn pill and get some sleep. You can go on the wagon tomorrow. I'll call you in the morning, when you're human again."

She decided it was sound advice, so she'd taken a tranquilizer before bed. It had relaxed her enough so that she'd slept like the dead, but this morning she was paying. She'd been forced to claw her way through a pea-soup fog to reach consciousness, and there were no rose-colored glasses capable of taking away the muzzy feeling that clung to her brain like damp cobwebs. Only time would perform that miracle. In spite of her chemical hangover, she managed to scramble a couple of eggs for Jessie's breakfast, relieved that the girl didn't expect anything more taxing.

When she asked about school lunch, she learned that times had changed since the days when you handed over your fifty cents and either ate what was on your tray or faced starvation. Nowadays, according to Jessie, everything was à la carte, and kids had a number of nutritionally balanced options. All the major food groups were represented: pizza, French fries, tacos and ice cream bars. With immense relief, Faith handed Jessie a five-dollar bill to pay for lunch. Then she threw on a ratty old sweater she found in the kitchen closet and stood at the top of the driveway, arms folded against the morning chill, watching until Jessie was safely on the school bus.

To Jessie's credit, the girl didn't show the utter mortification she undoubtedly was feeling at being seen off like a kindergartner by this demented woman into whose hands her fate had been thrust. She simply got on the bus without looking back or waving goodbye, leaving Faith standing there feeling more than a little silly.

When she went back into the house, the phone was ringing. It was far too early for social interaction, but Faith answered it anyway. "Feeling better?" Newt said.

With the phone cradled between her ear and her shoulder, she poured herself a cup of coffee and absently stirred sugar into it. "I was," she said, "until you called. Didn't we talk just last night?"

"I have news I thought you might not have heard yet."

"Am I going to like this news?"

"You should find it interesting. Last night, some citizen of

this fair town decided to sprinkle racist literature all over people's lawns."

She sat up straighter in her chair. "You're right. I find this
extremely interesting. Go on."

"It supposedly came from some white supremacist group
that calls itself the Brotherhood for Aryan Unity. It seems
they believe that since this great country of ours was founded
on white Christian values, it's time for our Somali friends to
hit the road. They're trying to drum up support to convince the
black heathens to go back where they came from, so Serenity
can return to its former pristine state as a bastion of whiteness."

"I'll be damned. Did you get one of these on your front
lawn?" Phone in hand, she walked to the window, pulled back
the curtain and craned her neck, but she couldn't see far
enough down the drive. "I wonder if I got one?"

"Probably not. I didn't get one. I live too far out of town.
But I hear they papered the streets in town pretty heavily."

"Good Lord." She knew without asking that Ty must be
having a conniption right about now. "Does anybody have any
idea who might have done this?"

"Not a clue. Look, I know you were all revved up over the
OxyContin angle. But what if we're barking up the wrong
tree? Maybe this all revolves around the Somalis."

She thought about it. "Yesterday, I would have said you
were wrong. But now I'm not so sure." She sighed. "If only
I'd found something on one of those disks."

"I think we should be looking more closely at the racial
thing. These flyers will probably start a conflagration. Maybe
that's what Chelsea was talking about. Maybe she stumbled
across this little group while she was writing the series on the
Somali women."

"Hmm. Maybe. I don't suppose you have one of the flyers?"

"It just so happens that I do. Debbie brought one in to work
with her this morning."

"Hold on to it. I'm going to want to see it. And I'm not
quite ready to give up on the drug angle."

"I really think it's a dead end. I didn't think so yesterday, but after seeing this flyer, my instincts are telling me to look more closely into the Somali situation."

"Maybe so, but I need to clear up a few things before I'm convinced. Do me a favor. Deputize me."

"Excuse me?"

"Make me an honorary reporter. If I have press credentials, I have an excuse to ask obnoxious questions. All I need is for you to back me up if anybody questions me. Tell them I'm filling in for Chelsea until you can find a replacement. It's not that big a stretch. I am a writer, after all."

"I'm not sure it's a good idea."

"Why not, for heaven's sake? Yesterday, you were all for it."

"I've had time to think about it since then. Look, even if the drug trafficking had nothing to do with Chelsea's death, somebody's still supplying the local addicts with some heavy-duty pharmaceuticals."

"And your point is…?"

"People like that don't play by the rules, Faith. You get in their way, you could get hurt."

"Look, Newt, you dragged me into this, and I'm not about to budge until I either prove or disprove our theory."

He sighed. "Fine. Consider yourself deputized. I'll cover your ass if anybody calls to question your authenticity. Dare I ask to whom you're posing these obnoxious questions?"

"I thought I'd start with Angus Dowe and Davy Hunter. Poke around a little, see if I can start that scab bleeding again. See, I've already learned my first journalism lesson. If it bleeds, it leads."

By the time Ty got to the police station, Dixie had already taken a dozen calls from outraged citizens who wanted to know exactly who had dropped racist literature on their front lawns during the night. "Am I ever glad to see you!" she told him. "What on God's green earth is going on out there?"

Ty dropped a flyer, one of several dozen he'd picked up this morning, onto her desk. "This is what's going on," he said. "I'm sorry, Dix."

The phone rang again. They both stared at it. Then Dixie sighed. "I knew I should've bought that condo in Florida while I had the chance." She crossed her eyes and made a face at him, then picked up the phone and said sweetly, "Good morning, Serenity Police Department. How may I direct your call?"

The woman deserved a medal. As he went on into his office and tossed the stack of flyers he'd collected onto his desk, he made a mental note to send her a dozen roses. What she really deserved was combat pay. Like everybody else on the force, Dixie was overworked and underpaid. But with his limited budget, it looked as though she was going to stay that way for a while.

Pete wandered in, coffee cup in hand, and perched his considerable bulk on the corner of Ty's desk. Amiably, he said, "Thought this was your day off."

"That makes two of us." He eyed Pete's cup. "That coffee fresh?"

"Made just a half hour ago by Miss Dixie."

"That's fresh enough for me." Dixie's coffee wasn't very good, but it was strong enough, as the old-timers said, to grow hair on a man's chest. Ty turned toward the door, ready to holler to Dixie, but she was already there, a steaming cup in her hand.

"Thought you might need this," she said. "And it's Ms. Dixie to you, Officer Morin."

"Sometimes you scare me," Ty said, taking the cup from her, "the way you seem to read my mind. You keep it up, I might have to start calling you Radar."

Dixie grinned, and then the phone rang again. She rolled her eyes and headed back to the dispatch desk. Pete picked up one of the flyers and examined it. "Looks like somebody had themselves a little fun last night. Every house on my street had one of these babies on the front lawn this morning. These from Lithgow Street?"

"Union. They somehow managed to miss Lithgow."

"How convenient for them, to accidentally overlook the street where our venerated police chief resides."

"Isn't it?" Ty took a slug of coffee. It was god-awful, but loaded with caffeine, which was the real point of drinking coffee anyway. "The damn flyers are everywhere, and there's not a thing I can do about it."

"You could cite 'em for littering if you could figure out who did it."

"I can't do much else. They haven't broken any other laws. If we don't arrest the Jehovah's Witnesses for disseminating literature to unwilling recipients, we can't refuse these people, either." He picked up a flyer and shook his head. "The Brotherhood for Aryan Unity. What the hell is that all about?"

"Seems self-explanatory to me. We got our own little white supremacist group right here in River City. This ought to go over big with Omar and his people."

"Do you suppose it's for real?" Ty sipped coffee while he perused a flyer. "This Brotherhood for Aryan Unity? Or is somebody trying to get us all riled up over nothing?"

"I don't know, but even if it is phony, we got plenty of pea-brains around here that'll take it seriously."

"Jesus H. Christ." He rubbed his temple, slowly, as the significance of Pete's words sank into his brain. "Like the Stultzes."

"For starters. Serenity's got no shortage of stupidity walking the streets on two legs. That's where hate groups do their best recruiting. They like these feeble little minds they can mold, like modeling clay, into good little soldiers for the cause. Some of these morons, you hand 'em a case of beer and they're yours for life."

The phone on his desk rang. With a sigh, Ty picked it up. "Yo, boss," Dixie said cheerfully. "Got Edna Gerard on line one. She's ready to string somebody up over this Aryan Unity thing. Wants to know what *you* intend to do about it."

"Great," he said. "You might as well put her through. Hell,

you might as well put them all through. The way this day has started out, I don't see how it could possibly sink any lower."

The ancient, putty-colored Oldsmobile was backed in close to the trailer. Davy Hunter and two other men were huddled beneath the raised hood. All three men looked up as Faith parked behind a white Geo Metro with a missing rear bumper and a phalanx of rust spots the size of half dollars. At second glance, she realized that one of the three men was actually more of a boy. Sixteen, seventeen years old. Tall and dark and potentially handsome, if too many Budweisers, a nagging wife, and a trailer full of kids didn't ruin him before he ever got a chance to reach that full potential. She checked her watch. It was ten-thirty in the morning. Why wasn't he in school?

She focused on Davy's other companion and felt the shock of recognition. He was the same man she'd seen downtown harassing the Somali woman outside Sahra Hassan's variety store. No wonder Newt and Ty had said Davy kept company with people of questionable reputation. How could he associate with someone who would bully a woman and her children for no better reason than the color of their skin?

Davy eyed her without expression. He said something to the others and ambled over to her car. Faith rolled down the window, and he hunkered down and leaned his elbows on the opening. His hands were covered with engine grease. "What?" he said gruffly. "What do you want?"

She searched his eyes, desperately seeking some trace of the boy she'd once known, some trace of the man her cousin had loved. But it was as though the humanity had been sucked out of him. His eyes were flat and hard, without so much as a hint of warmth. "I have to talk to you," she said.

"About what?"

"About Chelsea."

Something flickered in those hard eyes, flickered so briefly she wondered if she'd imagined it. "Chelsea's dead," he said. "There's nothing to talk about."

"But there is. Damn it, Davy." She glanced at the two men standing by the Oldsmobile, watching them with interest. "I need to talk to you privately," she said. "Please."

"This is private enough. They can't hear us."

Faith studied his face, realized this was as good as it was going to get. She took a hard breath and said, "Chelsea didn't kill herself. I know that's what the police think, but somebody helped her over that riverbank." She waited for a response from him, but he just stared at her, unblinking, like a reptile. "I think it has something to do with drug trafficking, but I can't prove it. You knew her better than anyone, Davy. You have to help me with this."

"Who put this damn-fool idea in your head? It was Newt Rollins, wasn't it?"

"What if it was?" she shot back. "What difference does it make? The idea's there now, and it's too late to take it back!"

"And I suppose he conveniently pointed you my way as the lead suspect."

She had the grace to flush. "He thinks you're involved. That doesn't mean I share his opinion."

"Newt Rollins is an idiot. An overeducated fool without a lick of common sense."

"But there is a drug problem in Serenity. That much is true. I've heard it from more than one source. And knowing Chelsea, she probably ended up right in the middle of it, and that's why they killed her."

Without warning, his hand shot out and caught her by the wrist, squeezing hard enough to get her attention. "Listen to me, Faith," he said. "Stay out of it. Stop shooting off your mouth, stop asking questions and stop listening to Newt Rollins."

"Let go of me." Fear was a hard, tight knot in her stomach as she struggled to free herself. *"You're hurting me."*

"You're hurting yourself. Stop fighting me. Sit still and listen. Chelsea's dead. There's nothing you can do for her now. Nothing! But you keep on the way you're going, you'll screw things up for a lot of people. One of them might be you."

Her heart began to thump. Incredulous, she said, "Are you threatening me?"

"I'm warning you. Leave Newt to his delusions. Pack up Jessie and get your ass back to New York. Forget all about everything you think you know."

"Don't you give a damn?" Tears stung her eyelids. "She loved you!"

His hand tightened on her wrist in warning. She glanced toward the two men who still watched them. "Somebody killed her," she whispered. "Willfully and deliberately, and they tried to make it look like suicide. Why won't you help me?"

"I can't."

"You can't? Or you won't?"

"Both."

She looked at the hand that held her wrist so tightly. Looked at the face of the man she'd once known, and sorrow filled her chest. "You can't help me," she said, "because you're part of it. You're part of it and you know who killed her and why. And you're mixed up in it so deep that you're afraid you'll be next."

Stonily, he said, "Go back to New York, Faith. You hear me? Go back now, before it's too late."

He released her wrist, and without another word, turned and walked back to his companions.

Angus Dowe had a face like a ferret. His skin, wrapped tight around the bones of his skull, was pale, like a mushroom that grew in darkness and had never been exposed to daylight. His age could have been anywhere between forty and sixty. His watery blue eyes stared at her from behind thick lenses. "Faith Pelletier," he said blankly.

"That's right. I'm a reporter for the *Gazette*." She held out her hand, but he didn't take it. Smoothly withdrawing the hand, she tried not to stare at the prominent vein that throbbed at his temple. "I'd like to ask you some questions."

"There was a Faith Pelletier who grew up here in Serenity." As he spoke, his skeletal fingers, sheathed in purple latex gloves, counted tiny white pills, poured them into a bottle and attached a machine-printed label. "Became a writer. That wouldn't happen to be you, would it?"

"As a matter of fact, it would."

"I read one of your books. *Dead Something-or-Other.*"

"Death Match."

"That'd be it. Didn't much like it. Too gory for my tastes. Funny, you don't look like the type to write gory stuff."

It didn't seem the kind of comment that called for a response, so she waited until he spoke again. "Just goes to show," he said, "you really can't judge a book by its cover. Or an author by her books. What is it you want?"

"I'm following up on the robberies that took place here." While he counted pills, she leaned against the counter and allowed her gaze to make a slow sweep of the store. It was small compared to the chain pharmacies she was accustomed to. Small and dark, with the same tired, run-down air she'd seen in a number of businesses around town. Angus Dowe ran a bare-bones operation. If you needed a prescription filled, or you were looking for Epsom salts or Vicks VapoRub, Angus was your man. On the other hand, if it was lawn chairs or cold beer or Doritos you were wanting, you'd have to go elsewhere, because Angus didn't carry any of that stuff.

She removed an eyeglass repair kit from a rack beside the cash register. It held a tiny screwdriver and a collection of screws of various lengths. At just ninety-nine cents, it was a steal. Turning it in her hand, she said, "Have the police identified any suspects?"

Still counting pills, Angus said, "If they have, they didn't bother to tell me."

She returned the repair kit to the rack. "Would they do that? Tell you?"

"How the hell would I know? You want an answer to that question, ask Ty Savage."

"Maybe I will. So you have no idea who might have done it?"

"Do I look psychic to you?"

Faith was no stranger to interviewing people. Speaking to experts in various fields, picking their brains, was a regular part of the research she did for her books. But she'd never before tried to pry information out of somebody who was reluctant to give answers, and she tried to imagine how Diane Sawyer or Katie Couric would have gone about it.

They would ask hard-hitting questions. Make the man squirm a little. Taking her cue from them, she said, "I understand that a significant amount of OxyContin was taken. Would you mind telling me the dollar value of that loss?"

He fixed her with a cold, blue stare. "As a matter of fact, I would. It's nobody's business but mine. And you can go back to the *Gazette* and tell Newt Rollins I said that."

"Oh, but it is somebody else's business, Mr. Dowe. Several somebodies. The Serenity police, for starters. Followed closely by your insurance company."

"You just about done asking questions?"

"Not quite. I was wondering about that insurance company. When a place like yours is robbed, and the thieves get away with a large amount of, say, OxyContin, your insurance policy must cover the loss. Unless it's absorbed by the pharmaceutical company." She smiled. "Or you."

He continued to stare, unblinking, unsmiling. "You're accusing me of robbing my own store?"

"You have to admit, it's an intriguing premise. Joe Average, who owns a small pharmacy like this one, finds that business has slowed down to a trickle—" she ran her forefinger along the edge of a wooden shelf of diabetes supplies and blew off the dust "—because Rite Aid has moved in down the street and stolen all of Joe's customers. His money's disappearing faster than water swirling away down a toilet bowl. So he gets this idea. He'll stage a robbery. Make a few thousand dollars worth of OxyContin disappear. It's a good idea, a good way to make up for the money he's losing every day to Rite Aid, because who will ever know? He reports the drugs as stolen, collects from his insurance company to cover the loss, then turns around and sells the OxyContin on the street for five or six times its actual value. Nice gig if you can get it."

"If it wasn't so laughable," he said, "I'd be insulted." He peeled off his rubber gloves with a couple of quick snaps and tossed them in a trash can. "If you're looking for a real story," he said, "instead of one that sounds like the plot to one of those lurid novels you write, maybe you should be asking Ty Savage about the heroin."

Silence reigned for half a beat. "The heroin," she said.

"That's right, missy. OxyContin's not the only drug out there making the rounds. Heroin's cheaper, and it's easier to come by. It's everywhere. On the streets, in the schools—"

"Heroin's in the schools?" she said. "You mean the high schools? Here in Maine?"

Angus leaned on both elbows over the counter, his bony face lit by a slim ray of light that had somehow managed to work its way to the back of the store. Dust motes danced in the air between them. "High schools, middle schools," he said, warming to his subject. "It's even trickling into the grammar schools. It's an epidemic, all over Maine. I've talked to kids who say it's easier to get than beer. The heroin store's a cash-and-carry enterprise. Nobody's checking IDs."

"How does it get here? Where's it coming from?"

"Massachusetts, mostly. Places like Haverhill and Lawrence. Dealers drive down there and buy it cheap, then drive back up I-95 and into Maine, where they turn around and sell it for three times what they paid. The street-level markup is enormous."

"And it's on the streets here in Serenity? In the schools?"

"With a vengeance. If money's a problem, unless you're willing to turn to a life of crime, you're not about to pay eighty bucks a hit for OxyContin when you can pay ten or twelve for heroin and get the same high. It's popular with the kids because it's affordable. Problem is, from what I hear, the stuff they're selling is pure enough to cause fatal reactions in a percentage of the people who use it. There was a girl here in town who overdosed a few months ago. Stacey Beliveau. Nice girl. Varsity cheerleader, honors student. Worked at the Dairy Queen. Nobody knows how she got it. Or if they do, they're not talking. Made one hell of a stir when it happened."

"Dear God. Are the police doing anything about this?"

"They're trying. But it's a little like trying to hold back a flood. You stick your thumb into the dike to plug a hole, a leak pops up in another spot."

Her head was spinning. "Christ on crutches," she said.

"Ayuh," he said. "Welcome to Maine. The way life should be."

It was when the chips were down that you learned who your true friends were.

Jessie had never been Miss Popularity, but she had a number of acquaintances and a lesser number of friends, and since they found out her mom had died, many of those people— not her dearest friends, but those in the outer circle—had been avoiding her. Death being the sticky subject it was, they were probably afraid it might rub off on them. That was just fine with her, because she didn't want to talk to any of them anyway. Nose buried in her algebra book, she sucked too warm milk from a straw and tried to ignore the lunchtime chaos churning around her.

She was probably the only kid in the state of Maine who spent her lunch hour studying algebra. Then again, she had a straight-A average, across the board, so anybody who dared to scoff at her could go right straight to hell.

The chair across from her scraped hard on the floor as somebody pulled it away from the ugly gray cafeteria table. Annoyed, Jessie glanced up from her algebra text, ready to freeze out whoever had the audacity to join her. Couldn't they see that she was studying and wanted to be left alone? But her annoyance faded when she saw that it was Ahmed Abdallah.

He set down his lunch tray, plopped his bony hindside into the chair, and began opening the top of his milk carton.

"Hey," she said, and closed her textbook.

"Hey."

Ahmed was a tall boy, slender almost to the point of emaciation, with skin the color of dark chocolate and a full lower lip which right now was thrust forward in concentration. He was wearing the same outfit he wore every day: jeans and sneakers, a plain black T-shirt, and the New England Patriots jacket that was his most prized possession. It seemed to Jessie that no matter where a guy was born or what his ethnic background might be, if he was male he couldn't manage to escape the football gene.

Ahmed worked slowly and judiciously at the milk container, folding back first one waxy cardboard flap and then another. He straightened them at precise angles with his long fingers before moving on to flaps three and four. This was a highly unorthodox method of opening a milk carton, and Jessie watched in fascination as he tugged on each set of flaps until he'd created an opening at the center that was large enough to put his straw through.

"There's a hole in the side," she said.

"What?" He glanced up, questioning her with eyes so brown they were almost black. Around those dark centers, she could see the whites, all the way around.

"On the side of the milk carton. There's a hole. You just punch it with your straw, and the little thing pops out. You don't have to go to all that trouble."

"It is no trouble, man."

Ahmed spoke a language all his own. Based on the too formal English so common to foreign-born speakers, it was flavored with an accent that was part Somalia, part Atlanta and part MTV. His favorite television show was *Real World* and he watched it obsessively in an attempt to learn the proper way to speak, dress, and act like an American teenager. Ahmed had an IQ that was off the wall, and for the most part, he stayed in the background, listening, observing, learning.

But today he had something else on his agenda. "I am very sorry to hear about the death of your mother," he said solemnly. "Where I come from, untimely death is too common. We learn to live with it from an early age. But still we never make peace with the monster which steals our brothers, our fathers, our sisters. So to you, Jessielogan—" that was how he always spoke her name, as though it were a single word "—I offer my condolences."

She bit down hard on her lip to keep from crying. "Thank you, Ahmed."

He picked up his fork, looked at the gooey gray glop on his tray. "What is this?"

"Shepherd's pie."

"It is made from sheep?"

"No. It's beef and potatoes and corn."

"Beef? Then why not cowherd's pie?"

It was a good question, even if she didn't know the answer. "I couldn't say. I wasn't around to offer my input when they were naming it."

Ahmed nodded solemnly and took a bite. He chewed thoughtfully, swallowed. "Tastes better than it looks," he said, and scooped up another forkful. "I have heard something that troubles me."

"What's that?"

"Cooper Gates said today in gym class, 'Hey, peeps, I have a date on Friday night with Jessielogan. She is one hot chicken.'"

"Chick. Not chicken. One hot chick." The blush started at her collar and worked its way up her cheeks until everything, even her ears, burned. Had Cooper really said that about her?

Ahmed's distress was clearly written on his face. "It is true, then."

"It's only a date," she said. "It's not that big a deal."

Ahmed looked to his left, then his right. He leaned over the table. With quiet intent, he said, "He is bad, Jessielogan. Stay away from him. He'll bring you nothing but trouble."

"What do you mean? Are you talking about his reputation with the girls? I'm not worried about that. I can handle myself."

"No." The single syllable was so vehement, she momentarily recoiled. "No," he repeated, more gently. "Cooper Gates is involved in crap. Bad crap. Stay away from him before something happens to you."

Jessie's mouth went suddenly dry. It sounded completely deranged, but she could have sworn it was fear she saw in Ahmed's eyes. Now that she thought about it, he'd been acting weird for a couple of weeks now. "What crap?" she said. "What's he mixed up in?"

Ahmed's mouth clamped abruptly shut, his full lower lip protruding in a stubborn refusal to say more. He shook his head slowly. "Listen to me, Jessielogan. I am your friend. I speak the truth. I've lost many friends. In Somalia. In Atlanta. I do not wish to lose you."

Fourteen

Faith found Newt in his office, talking on the phone. He took one look at the fire in her eyes and quickly ended the call. "What?" he said. "What's wrong?"

"I have two words for you—*Stacey Beliveau.*"

Newt winced, closed his eyes, and sighed. Opening them again, he squared his jaw and began tapping a pencil against his desk blotter. "What about her?"

"Is there any special reason you neglected to mention her? Or the heroin that's apparently flooding the streets and schools?"

His mouth opened, then closed. "To tell you the truth," he said, "it never entered my mind."

"How is that possible, Newt? We were talking about drugs. How could it not occur to you that there might be a connection here?"

He leaned forward and planted both feet flat on the floor. "*You* were talking about drugs," he said. "I wasn't."

"Oh, for Christ's sake." She swept a lock of hair back from her face. "Are you telling me you really believe drug trafficking had nothing to do with Chelsea's death?"

"I didn't say that. There's still one hell of a lot that Davy Hunter has to account for. But I'm not convinced that Chelsea uncovered some nest of drug vipers, if that's what you're saying."

"Did Chelsea cover the story about Stacey Beliveau? I didn't find mention of it anywhere."

"No! Damn it, she didn't!" He rubbed his temples with both hands. Wearily, he said, "Stacey's parents are friends of mine. She was a beautiful girl with brains and a promising future. Bud and Judy were devastated by her death. How the hell do you get over losing a daughter?"

Newt's blue eyes grew sad, and he shook his head slowly. "You can't imagine the pain they went through. The pain they're still going through. It tears your heart in two, just thinking about it. The town was in shock. Pain and disbelief. How could one of our own, a nice girl from a nice family in a small town like Serenity, end up dead from a heroin overdose? We all knew Stacey, and we all loved her. We'd watched her grow up. It was even worse at the high school. It's so hard for kids to understand something like this. Skip called in grief counselors, but still the kids took it hard.

"And the cops—" his mouth thinned "—Serenity's so-called finest, couldn't manage to figure out how Stacey got her hands on the stuff. It was a terrible tragedy. Nothing the *Gazette* could print was going to bring Stacey back. And it wasn't as though anybody in town hadn't already heard the news. The whole town knew about it two hours after it happened. What was the sense in hashing and rehashing it? Bud and Judy had already been through enough, so I decided the only compassionate thing to do was to leave it alone. The *Gazette* didn't cover the story. Now the Beliveaus are trying to go on without their daughter. The entire town is trying to go on without her. Unearthing her ghost isn't going to help us find out what happened to Chelsea. The two deaths simply aren't related."

Some of her anger dissipated, like air slowly leaking from a balloon. "How can you be sure?"

"I can't be sure, not a hundred percent. But the *Gazette*

never covered Stacey's death, and if Chelsea knew her, it was only superficially. I'm a newsman. I deal in facts. And without any obvious connection, I'm not about to make that kind of assumption."

"Oh, hell." She slumped onto a chair. "I was so sure I was on to something."

"Maybe you are. But personally, I don't see it." He unearthed a piece of paper from a stack on his desk and handed it to her. "Take a gander at this."

It was the infamous flyer he'd told her about earlier. She read it, her disbelief growing with each sentence, each paragraph. "Who on earth would have done this?" she said.

"Damned if I know, but there's no end to what these hate groups will do if they're not stopped."

"But this is Maine, for God's sake. This kind of thing doesn't happen here."

"You might be surprised to know that a hundred years ago, Maine had one of the largest KKK populations in the nation."

"The Klan was in Maine?"

"In big numbers. Of course, back in those days, it was those nasty French-Catholics they were trying to drive out."

"They weren't very successful."

"Apparently not, or with a name like Pelletier, you wouldn't be here today. They're still around, in small numbers. Isolated splinter groups. Every so often, Klan literature will show up in some small Maine town just like this stuff did, scattered all over people's front lawns. There was even a cross burning a few years back in Augusta, but I don't know if that was Klan related or just somebody's personal vendetta."

"Good Lord. What kind of mess have I walked into?"

"Drugs, murder, racism. Take your pick. If I were you, and I had the option, I'd get back in my car and head back to New York so fast there'd be nothing left of me but dust."

"If that were a real option, it's what I'd do."

He played with a piece of paper on his desk. "So why don't you?"

"Because," she said grimly, "some newsman named Newt Rollins convinced me that somebody murdered my cousin. Now I can't leave until I've found out who."

Newt sighed. "You know, maybe you should leave. I shouldn't have dragged you into this. I'd hate like hell to see you get hurt. Maybe you and Jessie should just leave town and put it behind you. Forget you ever heard of Serenity, Maine."

"Maybe we should, but I can't. If I ran away, I'd never forgive myself. I have to do this for Jessie, for Chelsea, for myself. I nursed my husband through terminal cancer. It wasn't pretty, and it wasn't fun, but I did it. I'm not the kind to run away from my problems."

"No," he said, studying her face, "I can see that you're not."

Examining the flyer, she said thoughtfully, "Maybe there's some kind of connection."

"I already told you—"

"No. I mean a connection between the drug dealing and the Somalis."

"What kind of connection?"

She wrinkled her forehead. "I don't know. But something happened the other day, and I forgot about it until this morning. I saw a young man harassing one of the Somali women on the street in front of Halaal Variety. He was tall and thin, sort of lanky, with long, greasy blond hair and a few missing teeth."

"Sounds a lot like Teddy Stultz."

"Stultz," she said thoughtfully. "Why does that name sound familiar?"

"He lives with his brother, Leroy, in an old trailer out on West Mollyockett Road. Half a dozen dead cars out front."

She set the flyer back on his desk. "Of course! Ty pointed it out to me the other night."

"Stay away from the Stultzes. They're outlaws of the worst variety."

"That's pretty much what Ty said. The thing is, I stopped by Davy Hunter's place today. He wasn't overly friendly."

Newt leaned back in his chair. Sourly, he said, "People with things to hide seldom are."

"He doesn't think much of you, either."

"Now there's a surprise."

"He and a couple other guys were working on an old car. One of them was the man I saw downtown."

"Teddy Stultz?" he said, sounding surprised.

"Apparently so. The other one was a young kid. Dark-haired, good-looking, in a high-school-football-hero kind of way. Any idea who he might be?"

Newt considered her question at length, then shook his head. "I can think of a dozen different kids who fit that description. And I don't know all the kids in town. Whoever he is, his choice of companions could be improved upon."

"That's what I thought. He looked about sixteen or seventeen, but it was ten-thirty in the morning on a weekday and he wasn't in school. It bothered me."

Newt shrugged. "A lot of the kids around here get bored or discouraged and drop out. He could be one of those. No future, no hope, so they turn to theft or dope dealing to get by. Sooner or later, most of them end up doing time."

"It's a shame. There should be something, some kind of program, some incentive to keep them in school."

"I agree. But the school budget's sorely limited, like everything else in Serenity. Skip Lombardi has tried after-school volunteer programs, but even things like that cost money, and there just isn't any. So the kids who aren't serious about school, the ones who aren't college-bound, end up falling through the cracks and drifting away."

"Speaking of which, what do you know about Skip Lombardi?"

"We're not close friends, but I know him fairly well. He's an okay guy. Why?"

"Last night, Linda Larochelle waylaid me at the Dairy Queen. Apparently she and Skip are interested in buying the Logan place if Jessie and I decide to sell."

Newt raised an eyebrow. "Oh?"

"Personally, I don't see the attraction. The place needs so much work. It can't be worth much."

"*Au contraire*, my dear. Maybe the house isn't worth much, but the acreage is. I think Chelsea told me once that she owned twenty acres. If the town's economy ever comes out of the toilet, that land could be subdivided into house lots, which could make Skip and Linda a very wealthy couple."

Faith pictured Linda's Caddy, her red suit, her expensively disheveled hair, and suspected she knew who had the real interest in the property. "I never considered that," she said. "Linda gave me some song and dance about Skip wanting room for his little girl to play."

"I suppose that's possible, but twenty acres seems a bit of overkill for an eight-year-old kid."

"She wants to raise horses, or something like that."

"It takes a lot of money to raise horses."

"And Skip doesn't have money?"

"He's a high school principal. Lousy pay, lousier benefits. You don't do a job like that if you're looking to get rich."

"Maybe Linda's the one with the money."

"I suppose it's possible. But the bottom fell out of the real estate market in Serenity about the time the mill closed, so unless she's got something going that I haven't heard about, I doubt she's rolling in dough."

"Jessie tells me Lombardi's little girl is sick."

"Alyssa. That's what I've heard, but I don't know the details."

"Jessie seemed to think it was cancer."

"Oh, man. That has to be scary. Especially since he's raising her on his own."

"What happened to his wife?"

"I heard she died the year before he moved here, which would make it about three years ago. I don't know what she died from."

Thoughtfully, she said, "So Lombardi's not a local."

"No. He moved here from some place in Rhode Island. I

think it was the year before last. He took over as principal when Lester McKee retired." He leaned back in his chair and studied her. "What?" he said. "I can see those wheels turning in your head."

"Nothing," she said. "I'm just trying to fit all the puzzle pieces together."

"Well, just be sure that you don't get yourself killed while you're fitting them together. I don't want your blood on my hands."

Faith sat in a pink-and-turquoise window booth at Lenny's, stirring milk into her tea and watching a teenage boy in a driver's ed car try, without much luck, to parallel park behind a Nissen Bakery van that was delivering fresh rolls. The kid, his arm thrown over the seat and his head turned to check the car behind him, backed cautiously into the space. He missed the van by a hair. The car came to a sudden, rocking halt as the driving instructor slammed on his brake to prevent a collision. The kid looked up in surprise as the middle-aged instructor, a true hero in Faith's eyes, waved his arms and gestured for the kid to back up and try again.

Faith opened her purse and pulled out the steno pad she was never without. She opened it to a fresh page, then sat for a moment, watching the little drama unfolding outside while she collected her thoughts. It seemed that the more she knew, the less she knew. Each tidbit of information that she gained led to more questions. Picking up her pen, she drew a big question mark at the center of the page. Around it, she drew a series of lines radiating outward like the spokes of a wheel. At the end of each spoke, she wrote a name. *Skip Lombardi. Sahra Hassan. Teddy Stultz. Stacey Beliveau. Davy Hunter. Chelsea Logan.* Chewing absently on the tip of her pen, she studied her drawing. Somewhere, there was an answer to the question at the center of all those names. She couldn't prove it yet, but she knew it existed. Sooner or later, she would find the hub that connected the spokes.

When she did, she would also find the person responsible for Chelsea's death.

The buxom, red-haired waitress delivered her lunch to the table. "One club sandwich on rye," she announced. "With chips and a pickle."

Faith dragged her attention away from the drawing to smile up at her. "Thank you."

"No problem." The waitress, whose name tag read Maxine, glanced out the window and rested a hand on her hip, the other hand wrapped tight around the orange plastic handle to a pot of decaf coffee. "That's Vicky Mayhew's boy behind the wheel of that car," she said. "Simon. Why she let him take driver ed is beyond me. Kid's been a menace since he was two. If Clem doesn't move that van pretty soon, he'll be lucky to have any fenders left."

"It's a frightening proposition," Faith agreed.

Maxine left, and while Faith nibbled at her club sandwich, she made a list of everything she knew, or thought she knew, about what was going on in Serenity. Somebody was distributing heroin to schoolkids. Somebody else—or was it the same somebody?—had stolen OxyContin from Dowe's Pharmacy, and now that was for sale on the streets, too. Stacey Beliveau had died four months ago from a heroin overdose and, so far, the police had no idea where she'd gotten it. Somebody had helped Chelsea into the Androscoggin River, presumably because of a story she'd been working on, but nobody knew what story. Some unknown person had broken into Chelsea's house to steal computer disks. Davy Hunter, who had no visible source of income, knew more than he was telling, and he regularly associated with Teddy Stultz, a local small-time criminal. She'd seen Teddy harassing an unnamed Somali woman outside Halaal Variety, which just happened to belong to Sahra Hassan, who'd been Chelsea's friend. Linda Larochelle and Skip Lombardi seemed to possess an unusually strong interest in buying Chelsea's house. And last but not least, some hate group who identified themselves as the Brotherhood for Aryan Unity was doing their damnedest to permanently drive the Somalis out of town.

That was Serenity in a nutshell. It was downright incestuous, the way the threads mingled and interwove and doubled back on themselves. She supposed it would be that way in any small town where everybody knew everybody else—and their business—but in this case, those interwoven threads created a tapestry of drugs, death and violence.

The bell over the door tinkled, and Faith glanced up from her notes. The man who lingered in the doorway stood tall and straight, and wore a blue uniform that instantly identified him as a Maine state trooper. She recognized him immediately as the detective who'd stopped by the house the morning of the funeral to talk with Jessie. He glanced around the room, pausing when he located Faith. Removing his hat, he ambled directly to her table. "Ms. Pelletier," he said. "Mind if I join you?"

She set down her pen and closed the steno pad. "Detective Lemoine. Please. Sit down."

He slid his considerable bulk into the booth opposite her. Maxine bustled over, coffeepot in hand, and Lemoine flipped the heavy ceramic mug that was sitting upside down on the table. Maxine filled it, he nodded his thanks and she moved on.

He picked up a sugar packet and tore it open. Pouring sugar into his cup, he said, "I understand that you don't believe Chelsea Logan's death was a suicide."

Faith rubbed her wrist, which still chafed from the pressure of Davy Hunter's fingers. "Look," she said, "I realize you have to do a thorough investigation, cover all the bases, before you come to a solid conclusion. Granted, Chelsea and I hadn't seen each other in a long time, but I knew my cousin well, and there's no way she would have killed herself. It's just not possible."

Lemoine stirred cream into his coffee and set down the creamer. Picked up his coffee mug and took a sip. Studied her through vivid green eyes. Tiny wrinkles feathered out from the corners. "You seem adamant about that," he said.

"I am."

He took a second sip of coffee and set down the mug. "Tell me why."

"Chelsea wasn't a quitter," she said. "No matter how bad her life got—and there were times when it got really bad— she never gave up. She was the eternal optimist, always believing that happiness was just around the next corner. She always had some new idea, some new scheme that she was certain would make her an overnight success."

Lemoine leaned back against the vinyl cushion. "I understand she was quite the party girl."

"At one point in her life, yes. But she'd put that behind her. Chelsea had finally become a responsible adult. Besides—" she picked up her spoon and stirred her tea "—she adored her daughter."

"Jessie."

"Yes." She laid down the spoon and looked him in the eye, a direct challenge. "Chelsea's mother deserted her when she was just a little girl. She grew up motherless. My mother did her best to fill the gap, but then, when we were twelve, my parents were killed. Chelsea's father raised us both from that point on. He was a hard man."

Lemoine sipped his coffee and waited for her to continue.

"Try to imagine how difficult it was for two adolescent girls, both growing up motherless, with no maternal figure to bring their concerns to. Adolescence is so hard for young girls. Their bodies are changing so rapidly, hormones are kicking in, they're starting to be interested in boys. It's a confusing, vulnerable time. Uncle Cy was useless when it came to female issues. All Chelsea and I had was each other. I got through it relatively unscathed, but she ran wild. Drinking, smoking, sleeping around. She had nobody, you see, to rein her in. We were both marked by the experience, and neither of us would ever deliberately allow a teenage daughter to fend for herself through those turbulent years."

"Fair enough. What do you think happened to Chelsea?"

"Tell me. Have you checked the car yet?"

"We have. We didn't find any mechanical defects."

She raised a mocking eyebrow. "There's a surprise. Did you know that Chelsea was working on a big story for the *Gazette*?"

Lemoine never moved a muscle, but she saw the change in his eyes. "Suppose you tell me about it."

"I'd love to, except I don't know what she was working on. Have you talked to Newt Rollins?"

"Not yet. He's on my list."

"Talk to him. He knew she was working on a story, but he didn't know what it was about. Chelsea wouldn't tell him, and the story never saw print. She died before she could finish it. The timing seems suspicious, wouldn't you say?"

His green eyes carefully neutral, Lemoine said, "Are you suggesting homicide?"

"That is, I presume, one of the scenarios you have to consider."

"You have to admit that it seems far-fetched."

"No more so than your suicide theory."

"It's not *my* suicide theory. In the absence of any evidence pointing to another answer, it's all we have. You'd be surprised to know how many single-car accidents are actually suicides."

"Not this one." Faith cupped her mug of tea and leaned over the table. "Talk to Newt Rollins. Think about what he has to say. And then come back and tell me you still think Chelsea killed herself."

She was just finishing up her lunch when she looked up to see a scrawny young Somali boy, no more than five or six years old, standing beside her table. His skin was the color of dark chocolate, his eyes bright and inquisitive. He fidgeted, clearly uncomfortable being here, clearly wired with the same nervous energy that powered all six-year-olds. Yet he'd crept up on her so silently that she hadn't heard him.

She set down her pen and smiled at him. "Hello," she said. "Who are you?"

The boy glanced around cautiously, then handed her a folded piece of paper. "For you," he said. He lingered a moment longer, then turned and almost ran back out the door.

She watched him through the window. The boy paused at the curb, checked for traffic, then raced across the street and down the opposite sidewalk in the direction of Halaal Variety.

When she turned away from the window, she found every eye in the place focused on her. Some faces were curious, others hostile. But nobody had missed the transaction that had just taken place, including the red-haired waitress, Maxine, who stood stone-still behind the cash register, staring at her with a deliberately blank expression.

Somebody had distributed those racist flyers this morning. Perhaps even somebody sitting in this room with her. Faith made a slow, deliberate sweep of the room, meeting each pair of eyes in turn. A few people had the grace to flush and turn away. But others, the more hostile faces scattered around the room, stared back at her boldly. A challenge, perhaps?

A shiver ran down her spine. This wasn't the peaceful, friendly little town where she'd grown up. This was some alternate universe, some Stepford village, where nothing was as it seemed, and where safety and friendliness were no more than illusion.

The hand that held the note trembled the tiniest bit, and Faith struggled to hold it steady. She unfolded the piece of paper. It was just a brief note, the handwriting neat and flowing, clearly a woman's hand. "I must speak with you. S.H."

S.H. Sahra Hassan.

With the exception of the camel meat that was sold behind the spotless white counter at the back of the store, Halaal Variety wasn't so very different from the Big Apple or any other mom-and-pop variety store Faith had seen. Omar Abdallah and his wife Sahra Hassan sold Fritos and Budweiser, Marlboros and phone cards, *USA Today* and Megabucks tickets. Faith wasn't sure what she'd expected, but it hadn't been this

Americanized convenience store with its Pepsi displays and its exorbitantly expensive packs of Duracell AA batteries hanging on the wall behind the register. There was little here to indicate that the place was run by immigrants who'd only recently arrived from Africa.

Dressed in a brightly colored robe, Sahra Hassan stood behind the checkout counter beside a young Somali girl in jeans and a western-style shirt. The girl's head was completely covered by a plain black scarf. Sahra stepped out from behind the counter. "Thank you for coming," she said, shaking Faith's hand. "Please, come upstairs. My daughter will mind the store while we speak."

The little boy who'd delivered her message peeked out shyly from behind his older sister. "Morning kindergarten," his mother said fondly as she led Faith through a door at the back of the store and up a narrow staircase. "Ali is anxiously awaiting next year, when he can attend school full-time as his older brothers do."

Sahra opened the door at the top of the stairs. Her apartment was sunny and airy, with huge windows and spacious rooms. "Sit," Sahra said, indicating the couch. "Can I offer you a cup of tea?"

Her English was flawless, tinged with a faintly British accent. "Thank you," Faith said, "but I just finished lunch."

"Of course." Sahra sat in a plush chair across from her and folded her hands demurely in her lap. They studied each other with avid mutual curiosity. "Chelsea spoke of you to me," Sahra said.

Surprised, Faith said, "She did?"

"Yes. She spoke often of her cousin, Faith Pelletier, the novelist. Chelsea thought a great deal of you. She was very proud of your success."

"I'm proud of hers, too," Faith said. It was the truth. Chelsea had struggled with alcohol and won the battle, and she'd built a good life for herself and her daughter. The stories she wrote for the *Gazette* were insightful and stirring, and she'd managed to engender devotion from such diverse people as Newt Rollins, Dottie McLaughlin and Sahra Hassan. The flighty and fickle teenager Faith remembered had grown into a woman of substance. It had taken her a long time to get there, but Chelsea Logan had finally arrived, and it broke Faith's heart to realize she would never have the opportunity to know that woman.

"Yes," Sahra said. "Chelsea had fallen far in her young life, but she found her way back. Her death was truly a tragedy. Tell me, how is Jessie?"

"Jessie's an enigma. She's built this wall around her that I can't seem to penetrate. She speaks to me, but there's no real connection, no way of knowing at any given moment what she's thinking or feeling."

Sahra nodded. "So difficult for a young girl such as Jessie, just beginning to flower into womanhood, to lose her mother."

"Yes," Faith said, thinking of her own mother, her own loss. "Yes, it is."

"It is important for a young girl to be able to speak with a trusted older woman about female issues. In a man's world such as this, women must benefit from each other's strength. Perhaps I could speak to her. Offer my assistance and support."

"Perhaps," Faith said, feeling suddenly inadequate, "you could offer it to me as well."

"Raising children is difficult, especially during the years of adolescence when young people are testing the waters. Here in America, children of that age have so much freedom. This is not necessarily a positive thing. I would be happy to offer you whatever help you might need with Jessie. But I suspect that most of the time your instincts will lead you in the right direction."

"I've been intending to talk to you," Faith said. "I just hadn't gotten to you until now." The last few days were a blur, a confusing mishmash of people and situations, a roller coaster of emotional highs and lows.

"Oh?"

"About Chelsea. I know you were friends. I'd hoped she might have said something to you, something concrete that would lead us to…" She trailed off, not sure how to continue without sounding paranoid.

"You believe, as I do, that Chelsea did not kill herself."

"Yes."

"Perhaps we can help each other," Sahra said. "I asked you to come here today to discuss a matter of grave importance regarding my eldest son, Ahmed."

"Your son," Faith said.

"Ahmed has always been a good boy, a happy boy. He has many friends, among them Jessie Logan. He speaks highly of her."

"I see."

"This town holds many secrets," Sahra continued. "Things are not exactly as we might like them to be. There is something bad here, something tainted. Something in which I fear Ahmed has become involved. I see fear in my boy, where once there was joy."

The Somali woman leaned forward earnestly. "My family is most important to me," she said. "Above all else, my children are my primary concern. We came to Serenity to find a safe place to raise our children, but I fear there is no more safety here than in Atlanta or Kenya or Mogadishu."

Something in her words sent a shiver racing down Faith's spine. "Have you spoken to the police about your concerns?" she said.

Sahra shook her head. "My husband has forbidden me to do so. If he knew I was discussing this with you, he would be angry. He prefers that we deal with such problems ourselves, without outside intervention."

"But you don't agree with him."

Sahra's eyes flashed fire. "Not when the lives of my children are at stake. Omar is a good man, but sometimes misguided. And often stubborn. He refuses to believe the situation is as serious as I judge it to be. But dark things are happening here. Like you, I know in the depths of my heart that Chelsea, my dear friend, the warm, caring woman I knew, did not end her own life. And if whatever happened to her is connected in any way with what has stolen the light from my son's eyes, then I fear greatly for his life."

"Why are you telling me this, Sahra? I'm not the police, I'm not an investigator. What can I do?"

"I tell you this because I feel that I can trust you, when I trust nobody else in this town. You may not be the police, but you are an interested party and an ethical person. And I am a good judge of character. Our conversation has done nothing to change my initial impression of you from my discussions with Chelsea. I have no idea what you can do to help, but I felt the need to share my concerns with you. And I trust you—" Sahra's gaze was clear and penetrating "—to know what to do with them."

Bombarded by phone calls, Ty spent the morning working damage control in an attempt to keep the citizenry happy. Everybody wanted to know what he was going to do about the situation, as though whoever had printed and distributed those flyers had committed the crime of the century. Nobody was particularly pleased when he explained that as far as he could determine, the only real crime that had taken place was littering. People were out for blood, and they expected him, as chief of police, to fulfill their revenge fantasies.

Everett Newsom, who'd spent ten years as First Selectman and liked throwing his weight around, called to demand that he dust the flyers for fingerprints. Annie Beaudoin, a retired schoolteacher with too much time on her hands, suggested that he do DNA testing. They'd both obviously watched too many episodes of *CSI*, and he was sorely tempted to tell both of them that if they thought they could perform the duties of his job better than he could, they should come right down to the station and knock themselves out. He could use a couple of days off. Fishing season had opened six weeks ago, and he hadn't yet found time to bait a hook and drop it overboard.

Then there was Eleanor Choate, who was so adamant about the Somali family upstairs being a cell of al Qaeda terrorists that the only way he could mollify her was by promising to send Pete over to check out the situation. Calls from Eleanor weren't uncommon. She was eighty-two years old and lived alone, and she had a vivid imagination, helped along, no doubt, by the vodka she bought by the case at the local liquor outlet.

In between calls, he toyed with the possibility that the crime might fall within the purview of the Homeland Security Act. Could these flyers be construed as a form of terrorism? In days past, the idea would have been laughable. But since the September 11 tragedy, paranoia in this country had run at an all-time high and, as a nation, America's sense of humor had disintegrated right along with those falling towers. As a result, perspective had gone out the window. Some people nowadays had difficulty distinguishing between a kid brandishing a Popsicle stick and saying, "Bang, bang!" on the playground, and a terrorist flying a jetliner full of people into a skyscraper.

Still, he couldn't see any overt threat from the Brotherhood for Aryan Unity. Most of what they had to say was little more than foolish babbling, somebody talking just to hear the sound of his own voice. Not to mention that the so-called victims in this case, the Somali immigrants, were Muslim, and it had been Muslim terrorists who'd started all this paranoia in the first place. Although he hadn't waded through the voluminous text of the Homeland Security Act, somehow he doubted that he'd find anything written there that would pinpoint this particular segment of the population as endangered souls who needed governmental protection. Which left him right back where he'd started, with an unknown perpetrator who, in addition to being a racist, also happened to be a litterbug.

By early afternoon, the calls had died down to a trickle. He ate lunch at his desk: a soggy vending machine egg salad sandwich, a bottle of Pepsi, a bag of greasy potato chips and a chocolate bar. While he ate, he checked out the Brotherhood for Aryan Unity's Web site.

It was pretty basic, the kind of thing a twelve-year-old could have slapped together in a half hour, hosted on one of those freebie servers that paid for itself by throwing pop-up ads in the faces of everyone who stopped by. The site held little new information. Most of what he saw there was word for word what had been printed on the flyer. There was an e-mail link where people could sign up for the Brotherhood's monthly newsletter, but no means by which supporters could make donations. It was an amateur site, put together by amateurs, either ignorant rednecks bent on pushing their twisted views, or teenagers bent on a little creative mischief. At this point, it was a coin toss as to which of those it might be.

He glanced at the open door of his office. Outside, Dixie was typing a report, her fingers flying over the keyboard at lightning speed. He pulled up Google on the computer, typed in Faith's name and hit the search button. While he waited, he shot another glance at the door. Damned if he didn't feel as guilty as a fifteen-year-old kid secretly surfing porn sites while fearing that Mom would walk through the door at any moment. It was ridiculous. He was a grown man, and he had a perfect right to check out Faith Pelletier's Web site. He'd read all her books; he was a fan. It wasn't as though he were bent on ogling her photo.

If he was, he'd have been a disappointed ogler. Her full-color studio portrait looked somber and authorish. Not exactly the stuff of which oglers dream. Nor was it a photo he would have chosen. He'd have preferred a candid snapshot of her looking the way she'd looked last night, sitting on the back steps in an oversize man's shirt with the wind stirring that wild mop of ebony curls about her face. But of course, nobody'd asked him.

Hers was no thrown-together Web site. She'd obviously

had it professionally designed, and the result was worth whatever she'd had to pay. He bounced around the site, clicking links here and there, looking at her book covers and reading the synopses, skimming through her bio, which gave no personal information at all—master's degree in English, won the coveted Edgar Award for *Death Match*, loves to hear from readers. He pulled up her guest book and read through some of the entries, thought about making an entry of his own, but chickened out at the last minute. What the hell would he say?

Sooner or later, he supposed he would have to apologize for whatever it was he'd done wrong last night. If there was one thing he'd learned about women in his thirty-six years on this planet, it was that the man was always wrong. As long as a man learned the clever art of groveling, he could survive without being disemboweled or castrated. But any man who was fool enough to believe he had the upper hand deserved whatever he got for his stupidity. It had been that way since Adam and Eve, and would continue as long as the planet was populated by two opposing sexes.

The phone on his desk rang. Sighing, he crumpled up the candy bar wrapper and the cellophane from his sandwich, tossed them into the trash and answered the phone.

It was Tim Leavitt, who'd played football with Ty in high school and who'd succeeded Everett Newsom as First Selectman. "I'm calling a special selectmen's meeting for tonight," Tim said, "to talk about this Brotherhood for Aryan Unity thing and the Somali situation in general. Seven-thirty. I'd appreciate it if you could be there."

"Would this be in my official capacity as Chief of Police," he said, "or just because you haven't seen my ugly mug in a while?"

Tim's grin carried through the phone line. "I thought maybe you could come in and stir things up a bit."

"You don't think things have already been stirred up enough?"

"I think we're just getting started. I also invited Omar Abdallah, just for fun. I thought with him on one side of the table and Jeb Turcotte on the other side, the sparks'll be a-flying."

"Thanks a bunch for the invitation. I'll see you there."

He hung up the phone, got up and walked to the doorway that led to the outer office, folded his arms and leaned against the door frame, watching Dixie type at a speed that defied the laws of physics. "I'm leaving," he said. "I have some things to do, and now that it's quieted down, I might as well try to salvage what's left of my day off."

Dixie stopped typing. "Ten-four," she said. "If anything comes up—"

"Pete can take care of it. Unless it's on fire, bleeding copiously or toting a gun, I don't want to hear about it until tomorrow."

Late-afternoon sun slanted through the kitchen window when Jessie emerged from the downstairs bathroom, transformed from a plain-Jane schoolgirl into a glamorous young woman. She'd left behind the eyeglasses that made her look like a librarian. The mascara and eye shadow she'd applied with a steady hand had brought depth to eyes that had previously appeared unremarkable. Liquid foundation and pink blusher had given much needed color to her otherwise pale complexion. Her dress, a simple A-line in a pink-and-green cotton-polyester print, was becoming on her, if a tad shorter than Faith might have liked.

Amazed by the transformation, Faith said in genuine awe, "You look beautiful."

Jessie flushed and said, "Thank you." Tugging at her hem, she added, "I don't usually wear dresses."

"But for your first date with a special boy," Faith said, "it's perfect."

Jessie just smiled and shrugged, obviously embarrassed by the unaccustomed attention.

"Are you nervous?" Faith asked.

"A little."

"That's normal. After all, tonight is a landmark occasion."

Silence reigned between them as Faith reminded herself that Jessie's mother should have been here to see her daughter off on her first date. So many landmarks Chelsea would miss. Jessie's high school and college graduations. Her wedding. The birth of her first child. Chelsea should have been here for all these momentous occasions. Instead, somebody had seen to it that she wouldn't. Now it was up to Faith to pick up the slack. But no matter how supportive she was, no matter how hard she tried to fill that empty spot left by her cousin, it would never be the same for Jessie. She knew this from experience, for at every significant juncture in her life, she had mourned the loss of her own mother, who should have been there, supporting her and cheering her on.

Noting the hairbrush in Jessie's hand, she said, "Would you like me to brush your hair?"

Shyly, Jessie said, "My mom used to do that for me."

Yes. She could remember Jessie at eight years of age, sitting on the edge of the couch between her mother's knees while Chelsea brushed the long brown hair that hung nearly to Jessie's waist. "I don't mean to trespass on her territory," Faith said gently.

"No. You're not. I'd like you to brush my hair."

Jessie situated herself on a wooden kitchen stool, and Faith began dragging the brush slowly through the girl's long hair. This, she mused, was what it would have been like if she'd had her own daughter. That lack felt surprisingly poignant. "Your hair is so soft," she said.

"But it has no body. It's limp as a dishrag."

"Maybe you should try a body perm. It would add fullness and curl. But you wouldn't want it too curly. Just a little around the face, maybe, to soften its lines. Personally, I like your hair the way it is."

"Your hair is naturally curly?"

"The bane of my existence. I always wanted straight hair. I think it's universal among women to hate their hair. Straight or curly, we always want what the other woman has."

"Mom used to tell me I looked a lot like you. I've seen pictures of you at my age, and there's a definite family resemblance. But tonight, after I put makeup on, it was almost eerie. I looked into the mirror and could have sworn it was you looking back."

"Now that you mention it, you do remind me of myself at your age." Like Jessie, she'd been slender and dark, a little plain and far too serious. Like Jessie, she could be transformed by makeup into someone a little exotic and glamorous. "I guess that's just the way families are," she said. "I've known cousins who looked enough alike to be sisters, and sisters who looked so different they could have come from different families."

"I don't know who else I might look like. You're the only family I ever met. Except for Grampa. And I don't look anything like him."

"Let us hope not."

A smile slipped through Jessie's mask of solemnity. "He wasn't a very nice man," she said, gravity returned to its proper place. "I don't think he liked me much. I heard him arguing with Mom once. He didn't approve of me. Well, not me personally. But he didn't approve of her having a baby without a husband."

"He was from a different era, Jessie. A lot of people his age felt that way. Our value system has gradually changed. In his day, that kind of thing was considered a disgrace. Nowadays, nobody thinks twice about it."

"I was terrified of him."

"You, me and half the town. Cyrus was a hard man. He didn't have many friends, aside from his drinking buddies."

"But Mom loved him. Even though they didn't get along, she loved him. She cried when he died."

Guilt wrapped its fingers around her heart. She'd stayed away for her own selfish reasons. She should have been here to support Chelsea. But she'd been too wrapped up in her own disastrous life to realize that Chelsea had actually loved the old goat.

Faith swallowed hard in an attempt to dislodge the lump that had formed in her throat. "When we were kids," she said, "he was the only solid thing in your mother's life." A vicious, abusive alcoholic. No wonder Chelsea had taken so long to grow up. "Until you came along, he was all she had."

"She had you. And Davy."

"But I live so far away. We hardly ever saw each other as adults. And from what I gather, her relationship with Davy wasn't exactly solid."

"She told me they couldn't live together, but they couldn't live apart, either. I still don't understand it."

"I don't know, Jessie. Sometimes couples are like that. They love each other, but their differences are vast enough to make it impossible for them to live together on a permanent basis."

"It would have been different if my grandmother hadn't left. I know it would have."

"Maybe." But she wondered. Many times over the years, she'd pondered what kind of mother could have left a four-year-old daughter with a man like Cyrus Logan. No matter how she answered the question, it painted Adrienne Logan in a negative light. By leaving her daughter behind, Adrienne had demonstrated that she was no better at parenting than her good-for-nothing husband. As impossible as it sounded, Chelsea's life might have been worse if she'd gone with her mother instead of staying here in Serenity with her father. In spite of Cyrus Logan's ineffective parenting, at least, Chelsea'd had roots. A solid foundation. She'd grown up living in one place instead of moving all over the countryside. And she'd been fortunate in that her Aunt Meredith, Faith's mother, had done everything she could to compensate for the defection of her brother's wife. Meredith had treated Chelsea with the same affection she gave to her own daughter. It turned out to be a double-edged sword, for when Meredith died, for Chelsea it was like losing her own mother all over again. She'd taken it almost as hard as Faith did.

"Faith? How come you never had kids of your own?"

Lost in thought, it took her a moment to return to reality. Gliding the brush through Jessie's silky-soft hair, she said, "Ben couldn't father children. He had mumps when he was a boy, and it left him sterile."

"That's too bad." Jessie paused. "I remember him. When we visited you that time? He taught me to play gin rummy. And he used to take me for ice cream. I liked him a lot."

"He liked you, too." He'd bonded with Jessie during that brief couple of weeks. After Chelsea and her daughter moved on, Ben had seemed listless, a little bit lost. It was then that they'd discussed the possibility of adopting a child. Those weeks with Jessie had shown him just how much he was missing. But Faith had been busy building her career, researching and writing and revising book after book, and she was still teaching part-time. Ben had been promoted to English department chair, so he, too, was working long hours. They attended numerous functions as part of their professional lives, both in the publishing industry and the academic world. Faith had argued that neither of them had the time to offer a child the kind of attention he or she would need. And she wasn't the kind of woman to do anything halfway, especially a job as important as mothering a child. Going through adolescence without parents had taught her just how important that job was. So they'd decided against adopting.

But life, in its infinite wisdom, had chosen to get the last laugh on her. Ben, who'd wanted a child so desperately, was gone. Chelsea, who'd loved her daughter so deeply, was also gone. And Faith, who hadn't had time for a child, was left to raise Jessie alone.

The irony wasn't lost on her. And again, life had gotten the last laugh. When she'd come here, just a few days ago, the primary emotion she'd felt was resentment. She'd resented Chelsea for dying, resented her cousin for making yet another mess that Faith was obliged to clean up. She hadn't wanted her life complicated any further, hadn't wanted responsibility for Jessie or for Chelsea's estate. But in the course of just a few days, her attitude had undergone a 180-degree turn. She'd come to see her cousin in a wholly different light, not as an overgrown juvenile, tossed about by the wind, but as a woman who had worked hard to make a good life for herself and her young daughter. A woman who had died not as a result of her irresponsibility, but because of her ethics.

In those same few days, Faith had moved from resentment and apathy to sincere involvement. For the first time since Ben died, she cared about something besides her own misery, someone besides herself. Jessie Logan. Ty Savage. Sahra Hassan. Newt Rollins. She'd become inextricably entangled in their lives, emotionally involved to the point where she'd begun to question how she would possibly leave Serenity behind when it came time to return to New York.

Outside, a car pulled into the drive. "Looks like your date's here," Faith said brightly, giving Jessie's hair one final stroke.

Jessie slid down from the stool and said nervously, "Do I look okay?"

Studying her with maternal pride, Faith said, "You look beautiful. But can you see without the glasses?"

"Enough so I won't trip over my feet. I hope."

Contacts, Faith thought as footsteps sounded on the shed floor. *We'll have to get her contacts.* There was a knock on the door, and Buddy, who'd been sleeping in the corner beside the refrigerator, raised his head and growled. Jessie took a deep breath, smoothed her dress one last time, and opened the door. "Hi, Coop," she said.

A deep male voice on the other side said, "Hi. I brought these for you."

At the sound of his voice, Buddy's growl turned menacing. "Thank you," Jessie said to the boy who still stood in the shed. "They're lovely. Come on into the house for a minute." She turned from the door with a small bouquet of wildflowers in her hand. "Look, Faith. Aren't they beautiful?"

"They certainly are." As Jessie's date stepped into the

room, Buddy growled again, more loudly this time. "Buddy!"
Faith said to the dog. "Stop that!" Turning to the boy, she said,
"Ignore him. He thinks he owns the place. Let me just get a
vase for these—"

She locked eyes with Cooper Gates, and all the air left her
lungs. Football hero, doctor's son, high school lothario and
Jessie's date for the evening, Cooper Gates was the kid she'd
seen this morning, consorting with Teddy Stultz and Davy
Hunter.

Fifteen

It took every ounce of Faith's resolve not to shove Cooper
Gates out the door, slam it in his face, drag Jessie upstairs and
lock her in her room. If Cooper was hanging around with
Davy Hunter and company, Faith didn't trust him as far as she
could throw him. But could she really justify booting him out
on his backside for hanging with Davy when Davy himself
was probably Jessie's father?

So against her better judgment, she allowed Jessie to leave
with him. But not before she'd put him through an interrogation that would have done the Nazis proud. While Jessie stood
by, flushed pink with mortification, Faith grilled him brutally.
*Where are you going? Who are you seeing? What time will
you be back? What's your cell phone number? Do you drink?
Smoke? Take drugs? Have you ever been arrested? How long
have you had your driver's license? List all prior motor vehicle infractions on this sheet of paper and, oh, by the way,
you can leave your DNA sample at the door.*

She was probably overreacting. This maternal thing was
brand-new to her, and nobody had bothered to explain the
boundaries before Jessie was unceremoniously dumped in
her lap. Cooper Gates answered each of her questions politely
and without hesitation. How could she condemn him for no

better reason than having seen him at Davy's trailer? She couldn't. Instead, like any other mother, she set a curfew and made sure Coop knew there'd be hell to pay if he brought Jessie home even five minutes late.

Once they'd gone, the house felt barren. Cold. Agitated for no reason she could quite put a finger on, Faith crossed her arms and paced the kitchen, wondering if she'd done the right thing in letting Jessie go with the boy. It was impossible to tell. It was also a little late to change her mind now.

She needed a distraction. There was still the little matter of that humble pie. She had nothing better to do for the next— she checked her watch—four hours and twenty-three minutes. She might as well get it over with. Apologize for making a fool of herself, interrogate Ty about Serenity's drug situation and then make a sweeping exit from his life.

She pulled into Ty's driveway and parked the Saab behind the police cruiser. His GMC was there, tucked in the shadows of the musty old garage where they'd played hide-and-seek as kids. Parked directly behind it was the ugliest mustard-yellow pickup truck she'd ever seen, its temporary plates telling her it was undoubtedly the one Buck had driven through the front of the health food store.

Faith stepped out of the car, hesitated for a moment with her door still open, breathing in the rich scent of spring. The house still looked the same, neat and tidy and freshly painted the same shade of brick red it had been thirty years ago. Splashy spring flowers, Glenda Savage's pride and joy, still grew around the foundation. She wondered who took care of them now that Glenda no longer lived here.

Her gaze was drawn to the house next door, the house where she'd lived as a child. There'd been happiness in that house, and so much love she might have drowned in it. She'd missed that terribly after her parents were gone. Uncle Cy had done his duty by her, but she'd never harbored any illusions about the tenderness of his feelings toward his late sister's only daughter.

She closed the car door and straightened her shoulders in an unconscious attempt to shed yesterday's memories like an old, worn-out skin. She'd learned early that you couldn't go backward in life. There was no remote control with a handy rewind button. So she'd chosen, at the age of twelve, to live life to the fullest, and not waste time mourning for the family she'd lost. It was a healthy attitude, one of which her parents would have approved. Yet there'd always been a corner of her heart that held an emptiness, a void, that she couldn't seem to fill. Not even with Ben. He'd taken his own place in her heart, but no matter how happy she was with him—and she'd been very, very happy—that hole in her heart had remained.

She hadn't shared that knowledge with him, had kept it secret for fear he might misunderstand. She didn't really understand it herself. It wasn't loneliness she'd felt, not exactly. With Ben, she'd never lacked for companionship. He'd always been there when she needed him. It was more of a longing for something that no longer existed, a need for roots, for somebody who shared her history, her memories. Someone who could laugh with her and say, "Yes, I remember when your mother said such and such. We laughed for days afterward." For all his good intentions, that was something Ben could never be.

But she and Chelsea had shared that bond, had shared a childhood and a history, shared each other's memories. Now those memories were locked inside her, with nobody left to share them. At thirty-six, she was well and truly orphaned, and it was the loneliest feeling she could ever have imagined.

She took a deep breath and headed for the back door. Like so many other Maine houses, this one saw few guests through the front door, which was designated primarily for salesmen and people peddling religion. Family, friends and neighbors automatically used the back door, which, in spite of its name, was nevertheless the primary entrance to most small-town Maine houses.

The door itself was new, solid oak painted the same red

color as the house, inset at eye level with a lovely stained-glass window, a ruby-throated hummingbird hovering over a cluster of delphinium. As she knocked on the door and waited, she examined the window more closely, wondering where in Western Maine Buck had found something so lovely. It was obviously handcrafted, and she made a note to ask him for the name of the craftsman who'd designed it.

Inside the house, music was playing. Faith knocked again, then decided there was no sense in standing on ceremony. As a kid, she'd walked in and out of this house at will. Why stop now?

When she opened the door and stepped into the kitchen, memories assailed her. Not a thing had changed in this kitchen since the last time she'd set foot in it, eighteen years ago. The appliances were still the same ugly harvest-gold color, the floor still a brick-patterned inlaid, a little more worn from eighteen years of foot traffic.

Above the high-pitched whine of the vacuum cleaner, music was blasting. Tom Jones singing "She's a Lady."

"Hello?" Faith said, but there was no answer. Nobody could possibly hear her over the racket. She moved to the living room doorway, paused there to watch Buck—a little older, a little grayer than she remembered—attacking the drapes with one of the attachments to his Hoover upright. While he vacuumed, he sang along with Tom. It was an experience she wasn't likely to forget. Faith grinned as he hit a sour note. Then he turned and saw her, and his mouth fell open.

"I'm sorry," she said, shouting to be heard over the noise. "I didn't mean to startle you. I knocked, but you didn't hear me."

He turned around and silenced the stereo, then used one foot to switch off the Hoover. The sudden hush was overwhelming. "Meredith," he said in amazement. "Christ Almighty, Meredith."

She opened her mouth to protest, but he was already correcting himself. Shaking his head, he said, "No. That's not possible. Meredith's been dead for almost twenty-five years." He thought about it a moment longer, then his face lit up. "You must be Faith."

"That's right," she said, returning his smile. "How are you, Buck? I hear you had a little accident the other day."

"I'm fine," he said. "Don't know why everybody got so worked up over it, like I'm some piece of fancy china that might break if you touched it. And that truck of mine? She's a tank, that's what she is. Didn't get so much as a scratch." He sounded proud of his accomplishment. "You should see the hole she put in the front of that store."

"I saw it," she said. "I drove by this morning to check it out. They've covered it up with plywood and plastic sheeting."

They stood grinning at each other. Buck's hair was now an appealing shade of silver and he'd put on a few pounds, but all told, he'd aged well. At seventy-three, he was still a vital, handsome man. This, she thought, was what Ty would look like one day. A few more years, a few more pounds, a few more gray hairs. Her stomach clenched hard at the mental image that conveyed.

"You look just like your mother," Buck said, tilting his head to study her from a different angle. "When I looked up and saw you standing there in that doorway, I thought for sure I was seeing a ghost."

Regret flooded her heart. "Nobody ever told me that before," she said wistfully. "Sometimes, I'll look in the mirror and see a resemblance. But there aren't many people left who remember her. And it's been so many years now that my memories aren't as crisp as they used to be." It was heartbreaking, losing those precious memories of her parents. "Of course," she added, "I have photos. But it's not the same thing."

"You stand exactly the way she did. You even sound like her."

"Thank you for telling me that. You don't know how much it means to me."

Clearly uncomfortable with her show of emotion, he cleared his throat. Gruffly, he said, "I imagine you're wanting to see Tyrone."

"I am. Is he home?"

"Downstairs, in his workshop. I'd walk you down, but—" his mouth pulled together in a thin line, souring his benign expression "—he doesn't want to see me. Right now, I'm on his shit list."

As she descended the cellar stairs, Tom Jones started up again, followed immediately by the whine of the Hoover. Faith shook her head. Like Frank Sinatra, Buck had always done things his way.

By the time she reached the bottom step, butterflies had begun to cavort in her stomach. Apologies were always uncomfortable, but this one would be worse than most. She'd made an utter fool of herself last night, in such varied and multitudinous ways that she couldn't bear to think about them. Embarrassment brought a rush of hot blood to her face as she thought about the way she'd begged him to touch her, like some middle-aged, love-starved woman who couldn't get a man. What had she been thinking? What must he think of her? And then to admit the way she'd felt about him all those years ago. It was madness, madness that could only lead to utter humiliation.

She paused at the bottom of the stairs to look around. He'd set up one end of the cellar as a workshop, with a bright overhead light and a worktable. His dark head lowered over the table, he held a soldering iron in one hand and a shiny roll of solder in the other. He glanced up as she approached, studied her for a moment through plastic safety glasses, then returned to what he'd been doing.

It was a stained-glass piece, a complex arrangement of brilliant jewel tones in a pattern that at first glance appeared random, until her brain connected the dots and she realized it was a peacock, exquisitely rendered, its tail feathers splayed wide in a dozen stunning colors. She could only imagine the hours he must have put into the project, cutting and fitting hundreds of tiny pieces of glass and then soldering them into place to create a thing of excruciating beauty.

She'd answered her own question about the identity of the craftsman who'd created the stained-glass window in the back door. As he continued his work, she took a good look around the room. Exquisite stained-glass pieces hung on every inch of wall space, and were stacked carefully between soft cloths on shelves at one end of the room. He'd chosen to focus his art on birds and flowers. The end result was a riot of color that was simply amazing.

She paused before a winter scene, a pair of cardinals, male and female, perched on a snow-covered pine bough. The male's plumage was a flashy red, the female's a dull russet, her wings a few shades darker than the rest of her body. The pair looked real enough to take Faith's breath away. She tried to remember whether Ty had shown any artistic inclinations when they were kids, but nothing stood out in her memory. Who would have suspected the small-town cop possessed the soul of an artist?

He unplugged the soldering iron and pulled off the safety glasses. As he tidied up, she examined the piece he'd been working on. "It's magnificent," she said, awed by the hundreds of tiny pieces of glass that he'd so carefully and patiently anchored into place. "How long have you been doing this?"

"About five years." He opened a small refrigerator and pulled out a bottle of water. Opening it, he took a long drink and wiped his mouth with the back of his hand. "At first, it was an escape from reality after my marriage started heading south. After a while, I realized how much it satisfied something inside me, something I hadn't known existed until then. Expressing creativity, adding something new and beautiful to the world—it becomes an addiction after a while."

"Where did you learn the technique?"

He set the water bottle on the corner of his worktable. "I took a class. One night a week, for a whole semester, I drove to Portland—a three-hour round trip—over icy back roads. It was a royal pain."

"But obviously worth the inconvenience," she said, looking around at the evidence of that worthiness. "You're very talented."

He took another sip of water and shrugged. "It's just a hobby."

"Of course. Just like my writing." Imagining how much money his pieces would fetch in some Soho gallery, she said, "Do you sell them?"

Rolling the bottle between his palms, he said, "Once in a while. Sometimes I do pieces on commission. I've also been known to give them away as housewarming or wedding gifts. It's not about money."

No. With him, it never would be about money. Gazing into those soft, dark eyes, she took a deep breath and said, "I came here to apologize for last night."

His knuckles whitened as he gripped the water bottle. "There's nothing to apologize for."

"You're wrong. My behavior was appalling."

"You had a right to get upset with me. My timing couldn't have been worse. My heart was in the right place, but the delivery lacked that little thing we call finesse."

"Nevertheless." Her eyes searched his. "There's so much I need to say to you, but I'm not sure where to begin."

"I've always been partial to the beginning myself."

She took another deep breath and nodded. "Eighteen months ago," she said, "after Ben died, I had a breakdown." She met his gaze full-on to gauge his reaction, but he was simply waiting patiently for her to continue. "Dr. Garabedian—he's my shrink—said it wasn't uncommon, especially for overachievers like me, after that kind of loss." She turned away from him, focusing her attention on the peacock, running a fingertip over smooth, cool glass. "When Ben got sick, I put my life on hold. I was determined that I could heal him if only I did all the right things. I'm sure I must have made the last year of his life a living hell. I fussed over him, waited on him hand and foot, refused to let him out of my sight. I dragged him to all the best doctors, made sure he got all the best treatments. I was aggressive and demanding with all the medical people. I'm sure they thought I was the bitch from hell. And of course, it was all for nothing." She turned, smiled bitterly. "In the end, the leukemia got him anyway. After he was gone, it was as though I'd lost my purpose in life. I'd spent so long focusing exclusively on Ben, on getting him well, that once he was gone, I was lost. There was nothing left to focus on, just this big, empty hole in my life."

"That must've been hard."

"Yes and no. You see, I was enveloped in this tremendous apathy. My emotions were frozen into a solid block of ice, and I didn't care about anything. Or anyone." She rubbed her hands together. "The panic attacks started four weeks after Ben died. The first time, I thought I was having a heart attack. I was certain I was going to die. Of course, I didn't, and once I realized what it was, I tried to convince myself that it was a one-time thing, brought on by stress, and that it wouldn't happen again. I was right about the stress part, wrong about the rest. It did happen again. Over and over and over.

"Enter Dr. Garabedian. He told me I was depressed and needed to allow myself time to mourn, to adjust to my loss. He gave me pills—God! So many pills! Pills for depression, for anxiety, for sleeping, for waking. For months I just floated along in a drug-induced haze, doing what I had to do to get through each day, but still not giving a damn about anything. Eventually, the good doctor started weaning me from all those medications. And then Chelsea died."

She met his eyes again. "I didn't want to come here," she said. "I was irritated, a little angry at Chelsea for dying and leaving me to clean up the mess. I came here out of a sense of duty. I felt I owed it to her, owed it to Jessie. I knew I was in over my head, taking on a teenage girl, but what choice did I have? There was nobody else to do it." She took a deep breath and began pacing. "Then you walked through Chelsea's kitchen door, tall and good-looking and bigger than life, and that block of ice inside me started to crack. I started feeling emotions I'd buried nearly twenty years ago. And when Newt told me his suspicions that Chelsea'd been murdered, I just blew wide-open. So you see, that's why I reacted the way I did last night. For the first time since I lost Ben, I've been running on pure emotion. I'm really not a terrible person. Or as desperate as I must have seemed last night." The memory of what she'd said to him, of her heated response to his touch, brought a rush of blood to her face.

Softly, he said, "Faith."

Still hot with shame, she raised her head and said, "What?"

"I could never think bad thoughts about you." He took a step toward her, and her pulse quickened. His next step brought him so close she could feel his body heat. He cupped her cheek in his hand and ran his thumb along the corner of her mouth. Softly, he said, "You still don't have any idea how I feel about you?"

She stopped breathing. "You don't even know me," she whispered.

"That's where you're wrong. I know you the same way you know me. Eighteen years hasn't made a damn bit of difference for either one of us."

"But—"

"Do you think you were the only one with feelings back then? I was crazy about you. I was just too damn scared to admit it. Not that I did such a great job of hiding it. Everybody knew."

"I didn't know."

"You were the only one who didn't." He tilted her face up to his, studied it while her heart hammered against her ribs. "I carried you inside my head for so many years. No matter what I did, I couldn't get rid of you." A myriad of emotions played across his face. "At night, in the desert, in Kuwait, it was memories of you that got me through. Every time Chelsea mentioned you over the years, I hung on to every word. I read all your books because it was a way of being close to you even though you weren't really there. When I married Linda—" a shadow crossed his face "—I tried to convince myself that I was doing the right thing. You were a married woman, happily married as far as I could tell, and it wasn't going to do anybody any good for me to spend the rest of my life pining away for what I could never have. So I settled for second best. Of course, it didn't work out because I never loved her. It was always you that I loved."

Near tears, she said, "You never told me. Why the hell didn't you tell me?"

"Damn it, Faith, I'm telling you now."

Now he was telling her. Now that her life was a shambles, complicated by all the baggage she'd dragged here with her. Now that she had to deal with all the complications she'd stumbled across since her arrival. A needy teenage cousin. Heroin trafficking. Murder. Now, in the midst of chaos, he was telling her he loved her? What the hell was she supposed to do with that? A few dinner dates, a handful of stolen kisses in the dark were one thing. But he was talking about love, messy and exhilarating and thoroughly impossible at this stage of her life. "You're late," she said sadly, "by about eighteen years."

"So what?"

"I'm not the same person I was then. Neither are you. Even if we were, there are practical considerations. You live here. I live in New York. I have Jessie to think about. She's going to need a great deal of hand holding. You have Buck. He's only going to get older and more difficult to live with. Neither of us is free right now to start a relationship. Especially a long-distance one. It's an impossible situation."

"Excuses," he said. "Those are all excuses. If you're willing to give it a chance, to give *us* a chance, none of those things matter. They're just obstacles. If you let obstacles stop you from going after what you want in life, then you never really wanted it all that bad."

She looked into those dark eyes, and all her arguments disintegrated and blew away like dust. "I don't know," she whispered. "I don't know what to think."

"Look—" He glanced at his watch, and cussed under his

breath. "I don't have time for this right now. There's some-place I have to be. But we're going to talk this out. Tomor-row night. Just the two of us, with no interruptions. No Buck, no Jessie, no talk of murder or mayhem. In the meantime, will you please at least give it some thought?"

Now that he'd made such a monumental admission, how could she possibly not think about it? She'd come here pre-pared to talk to him about a multitude of things. Important things. She'd arrived carrying a mental list in her head. Now she couldn't for the life of her remember what any of them were. "It terrifies me," she admitted. "And I don't deal well with fear and anxiety."

"We'll deal with the anxiety together," he said. "Don't you think I'm scared, too? But I'm more scared of what'll hap-pen if we don't give it a chance. We've already wasted eigh-teen years. *Eighteen years*." He cupped her cheek again and leaned in close. For a single, breathless instant, she was cer-tain he was going to kiss her. But at the last moment, he backed away and left her wanting. "Tomorrow night," he said. "Are you willing to do that?"

"Tomorrow," she said. "Yes."

"I'll call you." And he left her standing alone in the mid-dle of the cellar.

Because she dreaded the prospect of being alone after dark in that spooky old house, Faith decided to kill time by taking a drive. Jessie wouldn't be home for a few more hours, and driving was a mindless activity that would allow her some much needed thinking time. With her sunroof open to capture the night air and her mind churning at warp speed, Faith crossed the railroad tracks and passed the deserted mill, drove across the old bridge, her tires humming on its surface, and headed downriver.

Tyrone Savage. The man who'd broken her heart so long ago. Who would have guessed that after all these years, they'd take a single look at each other and be drawn together like two heat-seeking missiles? She hadn't come here to fall in love. The very idea was ludicrous. Ben hadn't even been dead for two years, for God's sake. Surely, even in this day and age, there was a respectable period of mourning that lasted longer than eighteen months before a woman threw herself into another man's arms and begged him to touch her in ways that simultaneously shamed and excited her. Even if she hadn't broken some unwritten rule of widowhood, her life was a disaster. She was in imminent danger of being sued by her publisher, she'd just taken on responsibility for a teenage girl she barely knew and somebody had murdered her cousin. How could she even think about being with a man under those circumstances?

Yet being with him was all she could think about. The way his hands had felt against her bare skin, and the sense of loss she'd felt when he took them away. The words he'd spoken. *At night, in the desert, in Kuwait, it was memories of you that got me through.* Nobody had ever spoken words like that to her before, and already, in spite of the walls she'd built around herself, she was half in love with him.

The logical side of her, the mature, sensible woman who'd been Ben's wife, the woman who'd spent the last year trying to hammer composition skills into the hard heads of college freshmen, told her not to trust her feelings. It wasn't possible to fall in love so quickly. It was nothing more than physical attraction. Ty Savage was a stranger to her and, after eighteen years apart, it wasn't possible that they could start something up so quickly and expect it to work long-term. Any woman who believed in that kind of fairy tale was only setting herself up for failure.

The other side of her, the dreamer who believed in the fairy tale, the woman who sat down at the computer day after day and wove stories of love and hatred and betrayal, stories rooted in deep emotion, told her that only a fool would let this chance go by. He was offering her a second chance at a dream she'd given up on nearly twenty years ago, and if she let him get away this time, she'd spend the rest of her life regretting it.

Ben used to say that when his time came, he wouldn't regret the things he'd done, and only hoped he wouldn't regret the things he should have done. His time had come far too soon, but he'd left this world without regrets. Ben Feldman had lived his life full speed ahead, and had never missed a single opportunity that presented itself. She knew exactly what he'd have to say to her now: *Go for it, babe. Grab that brass ring and hold on for all it's worth.*

Maybe Ty was right. Maybe all the rest of it was just obstacles. Maybe it was time for the overly cautious, responsible woman inside her to forget logic and caution, and follow her heart instead. Maybe, if she listened with an open mind to what he had to say, he'd find the right words to convince that woman that her evil twin, the dreamer, the romantic, hadn't gone completely around the bend.

She crossed the river twenty miles downstream and headed back on the opposite side. At this time of night, there was little traffic here, except for the occasional pulp truck, noisy and ugly, its massive body outlined by yellow running lights. Alongside the highway, the river ran dark and smooth, moonlight dancing along the surface of the water, willow trees poking bony fingers into dark, empty space. A cloud crossed the face of the moon, momentarily obscuring it and darkening the water that had glowed with crystalline light just moments earlier.

Just outside of Serenity, she pulled into the rest area where Chelsea had died. Her headlights reflecting off the shiny new guardrail they'd installed after her cousin had plunged into the river, Faith killed the engine and sat there, her window rolled down, listening to the sounds that were the last Chelsea had ever heard. The river flowed past, nearly soundless, only the occasional splash or gurgle giving away its hiding place. In the tall grass along the riverbank, a lone cricket chirped.

Driven by some inexplicable inner curiosity to see exactly where Chelsea had died, she opened her door and got out of the car. In the beam of light thrown by her headlights, she walked to the guardrail, swung a leg over it and sat down.

Below her, the river rushed by, dark and deep and silent. She could see the tire marks where Chelsea had gone down the bank, could see the flattened area where the car had been dragged back up to solid ground. A candy wrapper lay crumpled on the muddy grass, left there by some bystander who probably hadn't even known her cousin.

An image formed in her mind, the two of them one Easter Sunday morning when they were six or seven years old. Somewhere, she still had the snapshot her mother had taken of the two girls in their finery, arms around each other and heads close together, wearing huge matching grins. They'd been so close. Like sisters.

Another image overtook that earlier one. Chelsea, a knockout at eighteen, bragging gleefully, telling Faith in graphic detail exactly what she and Ty had done that night behind the high school bleachers. Had she known the truth, that Faith was desperately in love with him? Had Chelsea done it deliberately, knowing it would hurt her? Or had it simply been one more example of her cousin's absolute conviction that the world revolved solely around her?

Did it really matter now? The past was just that, and the people they'd been in high school no longer existed. It was true that blood was thicker than water. No matter what Chelsea might have done to her in the past, Faith still loved her. Loved her, hated her and wanted to tear the heart out of whoever had killed her.

A breeze stirred her hair, and Faith tucked her hands into the pockets of her suede jacket. *I hope you know*, she thought. *I hope you know that I won't let the son of a bitch get away with it. Whoever he is, I'll find him, Chels. I'm getting so close, I can feel how near he is....*

Behind her, in the darkness, there was a crunching sound, like a footstep in the gravel. Startled, Faith swung around on the guardrail and listened. But all she could hear was the chirping of the crickets and the thumping of her own heart. Beyond the arc of her headlights sat darkness, thick and foreboding. "Hello?" she said. "Is anybody there?"

The only response was the sighing of willow leaves rustled by the wind. Yet she had the oddest feeling that somewhere out in that inky darkness, just beyond her vision, somebody was watching her. Waiting.

She took a deep breath, stood up. "Who's there?" she demanded. When there was no answer, she curled her hands into fists, so tightly that her nails bit into tender flesh. "I'm not afraid of you!" she shouted, the wind carrying her own voice back to her.

Fighting back terror, she walked back to the car. Once she was inside, she locked all the doors, checked the back seat, then leaned back against the headrest, hands resting on the steering wheel, limp and drained and more than a little embarrassed. It had been a long time since she'd allowed her imagination to take over, a long time since she'd allowed her paranoia free rein. Thanks to Dr. Garabedian, she'd learned to keep her rational side in control. Somehow, she'd slipped up. Perhaps because hormones had muddled her thinking to the point where she'd let her guard down. Or perhaps it was simply anxiety, anxiety that came from knowing Chelsea had taken her last breath in this spot.

Nobody was out there. It was possible that what she'd heard was a skunk or a raccoon venturing across the hard-packed gravel. It was equally possible that what she'd heard lived solely in her imagination. It wouldn't be the first time. Either way, she'd had enough of this place that held only negative connotations for her. What had once been a scenic turnout along the banks of the Androscoggin would now remain forever in her mind the place where some monster had killed her cousin.

And she needed to get back to civilization before her own imagination drove her off the deep end. She'd already been there once; she had no intention of visiting again.

Ten minutes later, driving down Androscoggin Street, she saw the beige Oldsmobile parked in a paved lot outside one of the nameless bars that lined the backside of downtown.

Making a split-second decision, Faith wheeled the Saab into the lot and parked near the front, under a flickering street lamp that was making a feeble attempt to illuminate the half-dozen cars that sat beneath it. When she turned off her engine, she could hear the music from inside the bar. Loud and hard and thumping, it poured from every crack in the old building.

Angry now, angry at herself, at Davy Hunter and Teddy Stultz, at whoever had helped Chelsea over that riverbank, she got out of the car slowly and tightened the belt to her jacket just as the antique clock atop the Key Bank building chimed nine-thirty. She still had ninety minutes before Jessie's curfew. That would give her plenty of time to poke a stick into their cozy little nest of adders and see what developed.

Nobody bothered to look up when she stepped inside the bar. There were maybe a dozen men scattered around the room. Most of them sat hunched over their beer, oblivious to the bored-looking bleached blonde who gyrated on the raised dais at the far end of the room. Clad only in a G-string and pasties, she had meaty thighs and soft, pendulous breasts. Beneath the heavy fall of blond hair, her face was hard, her eyes a little too close together. But nobody seemed to notice. Nobody even seemed to know she was there.

The place smelled of beer and stale cigarette smoke. Even though the state of Maine had banned smoking in bars and restaurants some time ago, no amount of disinfectant could erase the smell of tobacco that permeated the very walls of the building.

Faith sat at the bar. The bartender, a fat woman in a sleeveless shirt, was tattooed from her wrists to her shoulders. Her face was broad and square and dotted with pale freckles. She put down the *Portland Press Herald* she'd been reading and took her time getting to Faith. "What'll it be?" she said when she got there.

This wasn't the kind of place where you ordered white wine. Faith asked for a Rolling Rock without a glass. The bartender pulled one from somewhere behind the bar and popped it open, set it in front of her, and went back to the *Press Herald*.

Faith surreptitiously wiped the mouth of the bottle on the lining to her jacket, then swiveled on the stool and pretended interest in the dancer. Ben would roll in his grave if he knew she'd gone unescorted into a place like this. She imagined Ty wouldn't be any too pleased, either. A woman alone in this kind of place was asking for trouble. But Chelsea's killer wasn't exactly going to jump out in front of her and yell, "Here I am!" The only way she'd find him—or her—was by digging up every dirty little secret in town. And if digging included following that beige Oldsmobile to Serenity's dark side, then she was going to dig for all she was worth.

In a booth near the makeshift stage, Davy Hunter was deeply engrossed in conversation with Teddy Stultz. *Damn him.* Davy, the son of a bitch, had as much as admitted to her that he was involved in Chelsea's death, and she intended to haunt him mercilessly until she found out what he knew and just how deeply he was involved.

Davy looked up from his companion and saw her. His mouth thinned and his eyes, those hard, flat eyes, studied her at length. He said something to Stultz and got up from the table. As she watched him approach, she lifted her bottle of Rolling Rock and took a long, slow pull.

Davy stopped in front of her. "What the hell are you doing here?" he said.

She raised the bottle in silent tribute and said, "It's a free country."

"Damn it, Faith, I told you to go back to New York and stop sticking your nose into everybody's business."

"Chelsea's death is my business. You know more than you're admitting. And quite frankly, I intend to find out what you know. It would be a lot easier if you'd just tell me. But since you don't seem inclined to spill the proverbial beans, if finding out means I have to tail you all over town, then that's what I'm going to do."

"You're making a mistake, Faith. A big mistake."

"Don't be so reserved, David. Come right out and say what you're thinking."

Ignoring her verbal poke, he said, "Does Savage know you're here?"

His name brought a rush of heat to her neck, her face. She took a sip of beer and said, "He's not my keeper."

"No? Why don't we find out how he feels about that? I could call him right now." He reached into his pocket and pulled out a cell phone. "I have a sneaking suspicion he wouldn't be impressed. He always did have a thing for you, even back when we were kids. Pretty convenient for him that you're a widow now."

"Put your phone away, Davy. I don't answer to Ty Savage or to any other man."

"Go home, Faith. You have no business being here."

"I know you're involved in Chelsea's death. You and Teddy Stultz, and for all I know—" a wave of sudden, oxygen-swallowing anxiety coursed through her "—maybe even Cooper Gates."

His eyes narrowed. "Cooper Gates?"

"Don't play stupid with me, Davy. I saw him standing in your driveway just this morning. Or have you forgotten our little conversation?"

"How the hell do you know Coop?"

"I know a lot more than you think. And I met him when he picked Jessie up for a date three hours ago. Imagine how surprised I was to find out he was the same kid I'd seen with you earlier today."

He rocked back on his heels and gaped at her. "Jesus Christ, Faith, you let Jessie go out with that little shit? That was lousy judgment on your part. If anything happens to her while she's with him, I'll strangle the little son of a bitch."

She set down her beer with a thud. "I see. So he's a suitable companion for you, but not for your daughter?"

Stonily, he said, "Jessie's not my daughter."

Faith raised an eyebrow. "No? You're certainly acting the part of a father, making threats like that."

"Somebody has to do it."

"And you're just benevolent enough to step up to the plate and take on the job. What a hero you are. Tell me, Davy, if you're not her father, then who is?"

He squared his jaw. "Maybe you should ask Ty about that."

In the background, the music continued to play, deep and hot and funky, some kind of classic twelve-bar blues. Onstage, the bored dancer gyrated to its throbbing sexual rhythm. Heart pounding, Faith wet her lips. "What, exactly, are you saying?"

"I've already said more than I should've. Get the hell out of this place before something happens to you. You hear me? And keep Jessie away from Coop. The kid's trouble."

The drive back out Bald Mountain Road was long and dark, the moon hidden behind a bank of heavy clouds. Faith held the wheel in a death grip as she ran Davy Hunter's words over and over in her mind. *Maybe you should ask Ty about that.* Could it be possible that Ty was Jessie's father? He had sworn to her that he'd only been with Chelsea once. But if what Davy implied was true, there had to have been a second time. Jessie had been born two years after Chelsea graduated from high school. The thought that he might have lied to her was a heavy weight in her stomach. Even worse was the nearly unbearable mental image of the two of them, Ty and Chelsea, their bodies tangled in passion. She tried to erase the image, but it wouldn't go away. Instead, it played inside her head, over and over and over, until the contents of her stomach threatened to reverse direction.

Cold fingers of anxiety played up and down her spine. Tamping it down, Faith tried to remember whether Jessie and Ty possessed any similar features or mannerisms. But without the two of them standing in front of her for comparison, it was impossible to tell. The girl had dark hair, but that could have easily been inherited from Cyrus. In looks, she resembled Faith herself more than anybody else, and Faith closely resembled her own mother, clearly proving that the Logan genes had dominated Jessie's genetic makeup. Whatever she'd gotten from her father wasn't immediately obvious.

How well did she really know Ty Savage? The boy she'd grown up with had been molded by life into a man who bore little resemblance to the kid she'd climbed trees and ridden bikes with. He'd been to college. To war. He'd been married and divorced, and he'd spent years as a small-town cop. Those experiences had changed him, perhaps for the better, perhaps for the worse. Maybe he wasn't the man she thought he was. Perhaps, like so many others in Serenity, the face he showed the world wasn't his true visage. Perhaps, hidden from the world somewhere beneath that easygoing exterior, camouflaged by the man who created artworks of stunning beauty, there was a dark inner core. Perhaps he really was a man capable of refusing to acknowledge his own child.

No. It wasn't possible. She'd looked deep into those liquid brown eyes and seen nothing but goodness there. She considered herself a fair judge of character, and there was nothing about Ty's character to suggest deceptiveness, nothing to suggest he was anything less than what he appeared. If Ty Savage was Jessie's father, he wasn't aware of it.

Headlights rounded a curve behind her, the high beams reflecting in her mirror, blinding her. She reached up to adjust the mirror, then pumped the brakes a couple of times, hoping the quick flash of red would remind the driver to dim his lights. But the high beams remained steady as the vehicle drew closer. Probably some drunk on his way home from one of the downtown bars. Great. It would be better to allow him to go on his way than to remain in his path, one step away from becoming a statistic. She pressed down steadily on the brake pedal, lowering her speed by a good ten miles per hour, and waited for him to go around her.

But he didn't. Instead, he pulled up closer to her bumper, so close that his headlights illuminated the Saab's interior until it was as bright as midday. Faith stepped on the gas, accelerated a little, trying to pull away from him. But he stayed on her bumper, so close they could have touched. For the first time, she felt genuine fear. This wasn't some small-town Sat-

urday-night drunk who couldn't keep his car on the road.
This was somebody determined to deliberately frighten her.

And it was working.

Faith stepped down hard on the accelerator. He stayed glued
to her bumper, so close she didn't dare touch the brake pedal
for fear he'd go right through her trunk. The lights shining
through her rear window were so bright she couldn't tell what
kind of vehicle was following her. She rounded a curve a little too quickly and the Saab skidded toward the ditch. Faith
wrestled it back under control and stepped down on the gas.
But her pursuer was quicker. He slammed into her rear
bumper with enough force to snap her teeth together.

Her car lurched forward. Grimly, she tightened her grip on
the wheel as the other car pulled into the left lane and began
moving forward. Relieved, she let out the breath she'd been
holding and touched her foot lightly to the brake pedal, praying he was finally going to pass and leave her alone. Instead,
without warning, the other driver yanked his vehicle back into
her lane, clipping her bumper and sending the Saab into a spin.

She tried desperately to regain control, but it was useless.
Tires screeching on pavement, she spun around twice, maybe
three times, before the Saab left the soft shoulder and flipped
end over end, crashing into a stand of alders. The last thing
she heard was the sound of tearing metal and snapping
branches. Then something hit her head, hard, and the world
went black.

Sixteen

The man's voice was soothing and familiar. "Lie still," he said. "The ambulance crew's on the way."

Faith's eyelids fluttered open and she tried to get her bearings. Above her, the sky hung dark and heavy, without so much as a star to light the way. She was lying on the ground somewhere. It wasn't particularly comfortable, and her head hurt like a son of a bitch. She blinked to clear her vision and her eyes focused on a hulking shape a few feet away. It appeared to be a twisted pile of metal that in some macabre way resembled Ben's Saab. Or what Ben's Saab might look like after it had gone through the crusher.

Puzzled, she glanced up at the face of the man who knelt beside her in the grass. Blue eyes, rife with concern, gazed back at her, and she felt the shock of recognition.

"Davy," she said.

"Shh. Quiet. I don't think you have any broken bones, but you took one hell of a hit to the head when that airbag popped open. It probably saved your life."

She remembered then. The car that had tailed her up Bald Mountain Road and shoved her into a tailspin. The bumpy ride down the embankment. The god-awful screech of tearing metal as she rolled into the trees.

"You—" she said, but for some reason, her mouth didn't seem to be attached to her brain. Her thinking was slow, her speech slower. She tried again. "You—"

He shushed her again. "Will you for Christ's sake stay calm until we find out how bad you're hurt? Then if you want to piss and moan, knock yourself out."

"Hit me."

"Nobody hit you." He looked puzzled. "You had an accident. You drove into the ditch."

"No. Pushed."

"Pushed? What do you mean, pushed?"

"Pushed into ditch. Somebody…pushed into ditch."

His blue gaze suddenly sharpened. "Somebody drove you off the road?"

Tears filled her eyes. "You," she said.

"Me? Christ, Faith, what kind of animal do you think I am? We've known each other all our lives. I can't believe you think I'd ever hurt you."

"You—threatened me."

"Ah, shit." He ran a hand across his jaw. In the distance, she heard the faint shriek of a siren. "It wasn't a threat," he said. "It was a warning. Goddamn it, I told you to stay out of it. I told you if you didn't back off, you'd end up getting hurt."

The siren grew nearer. She closed her eyes and concentrated on making her words come out properly. "Did…you… kill…Chelsea?"

Davy took her hand in his big, grubby paw and folded his other hand over it. "No," he said. "And I didn't drive you off the road. I was on my way home, and I came along right after it happened. I pulled you out of the car." He glanced at the mangled pile of twisted steel and corrected himself. "What's left of the car. I'm not the bad guy here, Faith. You have to believe me."

For some crazy reason, she did. Faith closed her eyes hard, squeezing tears from the corners, and held on to his hand hard enough to cut off all circulation to his fingers. But Davy Hunter didn't complain, he just squeezed back.

* * *

The music was way too loud. Jessie'd always hated rap, and this rap was particularly offensive even before it got turned up to full volume. She wasn't even sure how she'd ended up at Kathy Cookson's house, in the midst of a major party while Kathy's parents were away at some conference for the weekend. Any minute now, the cops were going to come in and bust everybody for underage drinking. God only knew what else the kids were doing, but some of them were making out in dark corners—or even well-lit ones—and she'd already seen more than one drunken couple stumbling up the stairs to the second floor in hopes of finding a little more privacy.

Somewhere along the way, she'd lost Coop. He'd gone to the kitchen to find her a soda. It was going on twenty minutes now, and he still hadn't come back. All around her, kids were laughing and talking and having a wonderful time, while she sat here, a lone island of sanity in a sea of debauchery.

The evening had started out okay. He'd taken her to Lenny's for dinner, and then they'd gone to the Strand to see the latest big action-adventure film, the one the guys were all talking about. Coop had loved it, of course. It hadn't impressed her. But then, she hadn't expected it to. As far as she could tell, it was nothing more than some macho male fantasy of saving the world, complete with a full arsenal of explosives and a bunch of unlikely stunts that nobody with half a brain would ever attempt in real life. In other words, a guy flick.

But she'd sat through it without complaint because she was, after all, sitting there with Cooper Gates. She'd caught a couple of girls staring and whispering as they stood in line at the box office. When they saw her staring back, they'd shot her dagger-sharp looks, but Jessie had just smiled at them as though it were a beautiful spring day—which it was—and she were the luckiest girl in the world—which she was. She was out on a date with the man of her dreams, and nothing was going to burst her bubble.

It wasn't until after the movie that Cooper had sprung his

little surprise on her. "There's a friend of mine who's having a get-together tonight," he said. "I promised her we'd stop by."

Jessie wasn't very comfortable with the situation. Coop hadn't mentioned anything to Faith about a party, and she was pretty sure Faith wouldn't have granted permission if he had. But who was she to argue? He was Cooper Gates, and what Cooper wanted, Cooper got. Jessie reminded him of her eleven o'clock curfew, and he assured her that he would have her home on time. "Don't worry," he'd said. "I wouldn't want to rile up your—what the hell is she to you, anyway?"

"She's my mom's cousin."

"So that makes her, what? Your second cousin?"

"I guess."

"We wouldn't want to rile up your second cousin. Not after the way she read me the riot act tonight. That lady plays hardball."

"She's just watching out for me," Jessie said in defense of her second-cousin-cum-foster-mother, or whatever the heck she was.

"Yeah. Like a she-wolf with her pup."

She liked that image of Faith as a mother wolf doing whatever was necessary to protect her baby from harm. Now that Chelsea was gone, Jessie desperately needed someone to watch out for her, somebody for whom her welfare was of primary concern. Faith was an okay person. She would never take the place of Jessie's mother, but at least she knew better than to try. Instead, she was doing her best to build some form of communication between them, to find some common ground upon which to stand. And she didn't treat Jessie like a little kid. She didn't talk down to her. She treated her like an equal, and for that alone, Jessie would have liked her.

But liking her went deeper than that. She got the distinct feeling that Faith Pelletier understood her, in some primal way that couldn't be explained by something as simple as the fact that they both carried Logan blood in their veins. She trusted Faith absolutely. The only other person she'd ever trusted that way was her mom. Surely there had to be some significance to that.

The air in the room was so thick with cigarette smoke and the stench of burning weed that she could barely breathe, and the couple playing tonsil hockey at the other end of the couch were groping each other with total disregard for privacy or propriety. If they got any hotter, the couch would burst into flames. Jessie eyed them with distaste and decided it was time for some fresh air. If Coop ever returned—which she was beginning to doubt—he'd just have to come looking for her. She'd had enough fun and games for one evening.

Outside, the evening had grown chilly, but the fresh air was wonderful. Jessie opened her mouth and took huge gulps of it, like a drowning soul desperate for oxygen. Kathy lived in one of the few upscale housing developments in Serenity. Her dad was some kind of big shot over at UMaine Farmington, and the family wasn't hurting for money. The Cookson house was a custom-designed raised ranch, the grounds beautifully manicured. The houses here had been built a reasonable distance apart, but still the neighbors must be having a kitten. Every light in the house was on, and the steady boom-boom of the stereo was loud enough so she could imagine knickknacks dancing off the shelves of every house in the neighborhood.

Jessie wandered the flagstone patio that ran the length of the house. As she neared the corner where a walkway connected the patio with the driveway out front, the breeze carried voices to her, voices that were talking a little too loudly. One of those voices was Coop's. The music was too loud and she was too far away to hear what they were saying, but the deep timbre of his voice was unmistakable. Somehow, on his way to the kitchen to fetch her a drink, he'd gotten sidetracked and ended up out in the driveway.

Good. Maybe she could convince him it was time to leave. She didn't intend to let Faith down by blowing off her curfew, and it was already ten-thirty. Coop and some other guy had the trunk to his 1982 Chevy Citation open, and it sounded as though they were arguing. Under cover of darkness, Jessie drew nearer, trying to hear what they were saying.

"Come on, man," a voice whined, "you know how bad I need it." She recognized the voice as belonging to Zak Morrissey, one of Coop's football teammates.

"You still owe me for the last time," Coop said.

"Dude, I'm dying here. All I need is a little. Just enough to get me by."

Coop crossed his arms and leaned against the car. Examining his knuckles, he said, "No pay, no play."

"I'll pay you in a couple days," Zak wheedled. "I get paid on Wednesday."

"That's four days, Zak. How'd we get from a couple to four?"

"Four, then! Damn it, Coop, if I don't get it, I'm not gonna make it. Then you won't ever get paid."

"Wuss." At a leisurely pace, Coop turned and reached into the trunk. While Zak bounced nervously from foot to foot, Coop rummaged around a bit before he pulled out a small glassine envelope filled with some unidentifiable substance. Even from ten feet away and in semidarkness, Jessie could see the sweat rings under Zak's arms. "Here you go, loser," Coop said, and tossed the envelope carelessly in Zak's direction.

Zak reached out to catch it, but he missed. The envelope fell to the ground, and Zak followed it, scrabbling around on the pavement like some kind of wild animal until he located the envelope. Clutching it in both hands, he scrambled to his feet. He stood there for an instant, swaying. Then, without a word, he turned and marched unsteadily back toward the house.

With a soft snort of laughter, Coop watched him go. He wiped his hands on his jeans, turned and saw Jessie standing there. "Hey," he said.

"What was that?" she said.

Casually closing his trunk lid, he said, "What was what?"

"The envelope. What was in it?"

"Nothing."

"I saw it, Coop. What was it?"

He took a step closer to her, his features taking on a macabre appearance in the faint light from the backyard patio. "I said it was nothing."

A chill ran down her spine as they stared each other down, Coop defiant and Jessie determined. "It was drugs," she said. "I'm not a fool, Cooper."

"No," he said. "What you are is a baby. A naive little baby and a self-righteous prig, just like your mother was. I just hope, for your sake, that you don't have as big a mouth as she did."

A hard, cold fist closed itself around Jessie's heart. "What are you talking about?" she whispered.

His eyes went hard and flat. "Nothing," he said. "I'm talking about nothing."

"What about my mother?"

"Nothing," he said. "I spoke out of turn. It's nothing."

"What about my mother?"

Coop took another step toward her, a step that was clearly threatening. He grabbed her elbow in one powerful hand, squeezing it hard enough to bring tears to her eyes. "Leave it alone," he said. "You saw nothing, you heard nothing. We never had this conversation. Is that clear?"

Terrified, she closed her eyes and swallowed. Nodded.

"Good," he said, and released her elbow. Pins and needles, little shooting arrows of pain, danced in her tender flesh where his hand had squeezed her arm. "Now let's go back to the party."

"No."

He lifted a dark eyebrow. "No?" he said. "What do you mean, no?"

"I'm not going in there." Her stomach was threatening to lose all its contents. Struggling to hold back the bile that hovered just at the back of the throat, Jessie stood her ground. "I'm going home."

"Fine. Get in the car."

"No," she said. "I'm not going home with you."

"What the hell are you talking about? How else will you get there? Don't tell me you're going to walk?"

She squared her shoulders. "If I have to."

Cooper Gates snorted. "It's a good five miles, and it's ten-thirty at night. Nice little girls shouldn't be out walking around at that time of night. Bad things might happen to them."

Struggling to hide the tremor that ran through her entire body, Jessie said, "I'm not afraid of you." Of course it was a lie, but she wasn't about to let him know it.

"For Christ's sake, Jessie, get in the fucking car. It's too late for you to start hoofing it. Anything happens to you, your cousin will skin me alive. I'll take you home."

"You just threatened me," she said. "You think I'm stupid enough to get in the car with you? I'll find my own ride." Without so much as a goodbye, she spun around and began walking down that long, dark driveway.

His voice followed her. "You breathe a word about what you saw, Jessie Logan, and you're dead meat!"

Ignoring him, ignoring the thudding of her heart, she continued to walk into the darkness. Left foot, right foot. Left foot, right foot.

"You hear me, Jessie?" He waited for an answer. When there was none, he yelled, "I'll be watching you!"

The meeting that should have taken no more than an hour had dragged on for three, and still they'd reached no resolution. With Omar and his contingent on one side of the table, Tim Leavitt and his people on the other side, and a half-dozen copies of the infamous flyer in the center of the table, tempers were running hot. They were getting nowhere fast, and Ty was wishing he could become invisible and sneak away when his cell phone rang. "'Scuse me," he said, turning away from the table. He pushed the Send button and said, "Savage."

"It's Davy. I thought you'd want to know your girlfriend's on her way to the ER."

A volcano erupted in his stomach. "What?" he said. "What the hell are you talking about, Hunter?"

"Faith. I don't think she's seriously hurt, but somebody drove her off the side of Bald Mountain Road."

Ty didn't bother to explain to Tim and company, just mumbled something about a family emergency and sprinted from the room. The elevator was too slow, so he took the stairs, running down three flights to the ground floor of the municipal building. He burst out into the spring evening, took a couple of hard breaths of night air, and dashed across the wet grass to his cruiser.

The trip to the hospital seemed to take forever, although in reality, it couldn't have been longer than five minutes. He parked in a handicapped spot outside the ER doors and raced inside. "Faith Pelletier?" he said to the nurse at the desk.

"Examining room three. But you can't go in there!"

Sweeping past her, he said breathlessly, "Watch me."

The minute he stepped into the inner corridor, he could hear her arguing with the doctor. At the sound of her voice, his legs went weak, and for an instant, in order to stay upright, he had to brace his hands against the lip of a laundry cart somebody had left in the hallway. Mortified, he squared his shoulders and took a deep breath. He'd dealt with dozens of traffic accidents over the years, had attended a half-dozen autopsies during his police training. He'd been to war, for Christ's sake. None of those things had made him this squeamish. It would be a tad unseemly for the chief of police to pass out in the hospital corridor outside the room where they were treating his girlfriend. Or whatever the hell she was.

He pulled aside the curtain to the treatment room. She was sitting on the end of the examining table, flanked by a scrawny postadolescent resident and a middle-aged male nurse. All three of them looked exasperated as hell. When Faith saw him, relief blanketed her face.

"Thank God," she said. "Finally, somebody with some clout. Will you please tell these people that there's no way in bloody hell I'm spending the night in this place?"

He'd heard it said that in every great love affair, there was always a defining moment, a precise "Aha!" instant when everything fell into place and you knew, beyond the shadow of a doubt, that this person was The One. It wasn't the kind of thing guys talked about, wasn't the kind of thing they admitted, and he'd always wondered if it was truth or fiction. Now he had his answer. This was his defining moment, the moment when he realized that his entire life had been leading up to this point. He'd loved her when he was five years old, and he'd loved her when he was eighteen. Now that he was thirty-six, he still loved Faith Pelletier. And when, God willing, he was ninety, she'd still be the only woman he'd ever truly loved.

"You heard her, gentlemen," he said. "The lady says she's not staying here tonight."

She had a few bruises, a few minor cuts, and one particularly nasty bump on her forehead, but she was angry and beautiful and most important, alive. Her gaze hadn't left his face since he stuck his head around the curtain. "Hi," he said softly.

"Hi. How'd you know I was here?"

"Davy called me. He told me what happened."

"Oh, God, Ty. My car. It's gone. Totally demolished."

Tenderly, he said, "It doesn't matter. I'll buy you another one."

"It was Ben's."

"Ben's gone," he pointed out gently. "But I'm here."

"Yes," she said. "I keep noticing that."

"Look," said the underaged resident who'd been glaring at them throughout this little exchange, "that's a nasty bump on her head. She probably has a concussion, and we ought to do a CAT scan to make sure nothing's broken. After that, I'd really prefer to keep her here overnight for observation."

"Nothing's broken," Faith said. "I'd know if it was. I'm a little sore, and I have a whopper of a headache. I just want to go home and get in bed."

Ty turned his attention away from Faith and focused it on Doogie Howser instead. "How about a compromise?" he said.

"You run your tests, and then I take her home. I'll stay with her tonight to do the observing. You can tell me what to observe. That way, we can avoid a nasty little scene, and everybody wins."

"I don't want to be here," Faith said. "I hate hospitals."

"Look," he said, "we're trying to compromise with the nice doctor here." Turning to the resident he said, "How long's a CAT scan take?"

The resident continued to glare. "About a half hour," he said.

"See?" he told Faith. "Just another half hour, one little CAT scan, and then I'll take you home. Deal?"

She didn't look happy about it, but she caved. "Fine," she muttered.

"Good. Doc?"

"Fine," the resident snapped. "But she's signing herself out. I'm not taking responsibility."

Jessie was already twenty minutes past curfew when she finally reached downtown and a pay phone outside the Big Apple. She dropped in two quarters and dialed home. The phone rang and rang and rang, but Faith didn't pick up. That was odd. By now, Faith should not only be right there waiting by the phone, but checking the clock and pacing the floor.

She hung up, fished her change out of the box and tried Becca's house. Nobody answered there, either, and she remembered belatedly that Becca's family had driven down to Westbrook to attend a cousin's birthday party. They probably wouldn't be home for another couple of hours. She was on her own.

Feeling suddenly more alone than she'd ever felt in her life, Jessie hung up the phone, retrieved her quarters, and went into the store. The place was doing a pretty steady business, considering the time of night, but of course there wasn't anything else open. After nine o'clock, if you wanted a six-pack of beer or a gallon of milk, the Big Apple was the only game in town.

She bought a candy bar and a bottle of Coke. Ruby Bechard, behind the cash register, didn't even ask what she was doing out so late all by herself. Jessie went back outside and sat on a wooden bench to consider her options. She could call a cab, but there was only one cab company in town. At night, Bertie Snow drove for A-1 taxi. According to her mom, Bertie had been driving a cab for nearly forty years, and legend had it that he kept a flask of vodka under the seat for any alcoholic emergencies that might arise. Jessie decided she'd rather take her chances with the bears and the coyotes and the serial killers than get in any car with Bertie behind the wheel.

But the idea of walking home out three miles of dark, lonesome country road wasn't very appealing. Especially knowing that Coop might be out there somewhere looking for her. Cooper Gates. Her dream date. More like a nightmare. How could it be possible that Serenity's golden boy, the boy she'd spent so many months fantasizing about, was dealing drugs from the trunk of his car?

But she'd seen the evidence, had heard the hard edge in his voice when he realized she'd seen. Maybe everybody else already knew. Maybe she was the only one who lived under a rock and had no clue about what was going on right under her nose. But if his drug dealing was common knowledge, then why had he threatened her? Why had he seemed threatened by her? No, it was more than drugs that had Coop worried. The comment he'd made about her mother had to come from somewhere; it hardly seemed the kind of thing a seventeen-year-old boy would have conjured up out of thin air. Her mom's death had been an accident…hadn't it? She'd never questioned it, never even considered any other possibility. That kind of thing happened in movies, not real life. Who in this quiet, placid little town could have possibly meant her mother any harm?

Jessie shivered as Ahmed's words came back to her. *Cooper Gates is involved in crap. Bad crap. Stay away from him before something happens to you.* Ahmed knew something she didn't. It might be about Coop's drug dealing. Then again, it might be about something far more sinister. Tomorrow, she thought grimly, she was going to sit Ahmed down and have a long talk with him. She had to know what he had on Coop. Had to know if it was connected in any way to her mother's death.

It was a cool evening. She should have worn jeans instead of a dress. Goose bumps dotted her legs as she marched off stolidly in the direction of Bald Mountain. Past Food City, its windows darkened and its parking lot deserted. Past the silent Getty station, its gas pumps shadowy silhouettes that loomed like phantoms out of the darkness in front of her. Beneath a circle of weak light from a street lamp, she took a left onto Bald Mountain Road. The first half mile or so, the houses were tucked tightly together. But once the road crossed Clary Stream, she left civilization behind. Houses out here sat in deep, shadowy forest, marked only by the rural mailboxes that sat at the end of each driveway. There were no street lamps to light her way, only an inky, black darkness so thick she might have wandered off the road and not even been aware of it.

Three miles of solitary highway. Three miles of absolute blackness broken only by an occasional lighted window. Three miles of twisting, turning road, most of it uphill. She stumbled over a loose chunk of pavement and nearly fell. It was so dark, she hadn't seen it lying there. In the silence, her footsteps rang out on the hard asphalt surface of the road, bouncing and echoing back from the dense forest on either side.

She heard the car before she saw it, heard its engine whining in protest as it climbed the gradual incline behind her. Jessie stepped off the pavement and onto the soft shoulder. Her face averted, she kept on walking, praying that whoever it was would just drive by and leave her alone.

The car passed her, then its brake lights flashed, glowing red in the darkness. An instant later, the backup lights came on, and her heart began to hammer as the car backed toward her, transmission whining. It stopped beside her and the passenger-side window came down.

"Jessie?" said a male voice. "I thought it was you. What on earth are you doing out here?"

Relief was instantaneous. "Mr. Lombardi," she said. "I'm walking home."

He reached over and unlocked the door. "Hop in, I'll give you a ride."

She didn't hesitate, just climbed in and shut the door quickly, not even caring that he was about to give her the standard adult lecture about walking alone at night on a deserted back road. He didn't disappoint. The lecture was firm and pointed and blessedly brief. When it was over, and she was suitably chastised, he said, "How'd you end up out here?"

The heater's warmth felt so good against her bare legs. "I had a date," she said. "It didn't go very well."

"And this date of yours left you to walk home alone?"

"No," she said. "That was my choice."

"I see. Who is this paragon of virtue?"

Remembering that Mr. Lombardi coached the football team and was one of Coop's biggest supporters, she said, "I'd rather not say."

He sniffed the fumes wafting from her and said, "What's that smell? Is it what I think it is?"

"Yes. That's one of the reasons I left." Changing the subject, she said, "What are you doing out here so late? You don't live anywhere near here."

"My daughter," he said. "Tonight was her first sleepover at a friend's house. She got homesick and called me to come get her."

"Oh." Jessie thought about it for a while. "She'll get over that," she said. "I used to do the same thing. I'd be all excited about staying over, and then I'd end up homesick and crying. It'll be okay. You'll see."

They rounded a curve. Ahead of them, a phalanx of emergency vehicles blocked the road. Blue lights, red lights, yellow lights. "Must be an accident," Mr. Lombardi said, coming to a stop in the middle of the road.

On the shoulder of the road, she saw Davy Hunter's beige Oldsmobile. In the ditch not far from it, a car lay on its side, attached by a winch to a wrecker parked on the shoulder. As the winch tightened, the car—or what was left of it—slowly righted itself. It looked as though it was a red Saab. A late-model one, like the one Faith drove.

She saw Davy standing, arms crossed as he nodded gravely at something one of the cops was saying. Butterflies began to dance in the pit of her stomach as a somber-faced state trooper waved his flashlight in a low arc, indicating that they should go around. Jessie craned her neck to see as Mr. Lombardi inched his way to the left shoulder and began easing around the police car that was parked sideways across the middle of the road. As they passed the cop with the flashlight, she got a good look at the car. It was indeed a red Saab.

A red Saab with New York license plates.

"Stop!" she shouted.

"I can't stop here, Jessie. I have to go around—"

"No!" she screamed, nearly hysterical. "You have to stop! That's Faith's car!" And before his wheels came to a complete stop, Jessie threw open the door and took off running.

Seventeen

It took nearly an hour before the CAT scan was completed and the results interpreted. Faith was lucky; there were no broken bones and she had only a mild concussion. The doctor gave her a painkiller, and Ty took her elbow and guided her to the cruiser, still parked directly outside the doors to the ER.

Once he had her settled in the passenger seat, he got in the car and started it up. "Thank you," she said as he backed out of the parking spot and wheeled the car around. "You can't know how much I hate hospitals. When Ben died, I practically lived there. I'd be perfectly happy if I never had to set foot in another hospital."

Illuminated by the dashboard lights, she looked pale as death. Pale and wispy and delicate. Of course, the wispy and delicate part was a lie. Underneath that deceptively soft, feminine exterior lay a backbone of steel. Still, he hated to poke and prod at her anymore tonight. She'd been through hell in the last couple of hours, and he knew all she wanted was to climb into bed and sleep. But there were certain questions he couldn't leave unanswered. Somebody had tried to kill her. When he found out who was to blame, he was going to strangle the son of a bitch with his bare hands. "You look exhausted," he said.

She opened her eyes. "I'm fine. A little sore, but I'll survive."

"I have to ask you some questions."

"Of course." She smiled wearily. "The official interrogation. I'll tell you what I can remember, but it isn't much."

Pulling out into the street, he said, "Did you get a look at the car?"

She straightened, rubbed her eyes, and sighed. "No. It was pitch-black out there, and he pulled right up behind me with his high beams on. I couldn't see a thing. Except…" She trailed off, lost in thought. "It must have been either a truck or an SUV. Something that sits high off the ground. Part of the reason the headlights blinded me is because they were shining directly into my rear window."

A tall vehicle. A truck, or an SUV. That should make it easy. Every other household in Serenity owned a pickup truck. "Any idea when or where you picked him up?"

"I first saw him behind me about a half mile before the accident site. On that sharp corner just after Pilcher's dairy farm. But for all I know, he could have been behind me all the way from town. I wasn't paying attention that closely." She gave him a weak smile. "Next time, I'll know better."

Grimly, he said, "There won't be a next time. So tell me exactly what happened."

"It all happened so quickly. I saw him come around the corner, and then he accelerated and pulled up just a few feet from my bumper. His lights were blinding me, and I figured he must be drunk, so I slowed down to let him pass. Instead of passing, he rammed right into my bumper."

Picturing the scene, he felt his stomach clench even tighter. "What did you do then?"

"I tried to get away from him. But he kept right on me. Then he pulled into the left lane, and I thought he was going to pass. Except that he didn't. He pulled back in at the last minute and hit me at an angle. That's when I lost control of the car. I don't even know where he went. He must have sped off after I left the road."

She closed her eyes, and he knew she was reliving the memory of her car rolling and rolling. "The next thing I remember," she said, "I was lying on the ground, and Davy was there. He'd pulled me out of the car." She paused, gnawed on her lower lip for an instant. "I guess I blacked out."

"You left my house around seven-thirty. Where'd you go after that?"

"I went for a ride. Downriver about twenty miles, then back up the other side." There was something in her voice, some subtle change, that left him holding his breath in anticipation. But when she spoke again, it was gone. "I stopped by one of the bars downtown. Davy was there. I had a bit of a run-in with him."

Davy Hunter. Every time he turned around, Davy Hunter's name popped up. "What kind of run-in?" he said.

"I was prodding him about the drug dealing. He told me to leave it alone."

"Wait. Back up. What about drug dealing?"

"I think Davy's mixed up in heroin trafficking. I think that's why Chelsea was killed. She uncovered something that somebody didn't want printed in the *Gazette*."

"Where the hell did you hear about heroin trafficking? Was it Newt Rollins?"

"Actually, it was Angus Dowe. I went to ask him about the OxyContin thefts, and he told me that heroin was a bigger problem here than OxyContin. He told me about Stacey Beliveau. That's why I—"

"Christ Almighty on roller skates. I turn my back on you for a second and you're out there getting involved with drug dealers. No wonder somebody drove you off the road. I ought to strangle Newt for getting you mixed up in all this."

"He didn't get me mixed up in it."

He cocked a single eyebrow, and she capitulated. "All right," she admitted, "he did, but now he's trying to discourage me. I'm not sure what changed his mind."

"He's probably afraid you'll end up at the bottom of the

river. Did I or did I not tell you to leave the investigating to the investigators?"

"Nobody's doing any investigating! Damn it, Savage, she was my cousin, and somebody murdered her. Am I supposed to just stand by and let whoever did it get away with murder?"

"That's exactly what you're supposed to do. And there's no goddamn evidence that she was murdered."

"Oh, for Christ's sake." Her eyes accused him. "You're going to stick to the party line all the way, aren't you? Are you blind, or just stupid?"

He squared his jaw. "Neither. I'm looking out for your welfare."

"I can look out for my own welfare!"

"Damn it, Faith," he said, "don't look at me like that. Somebody tried to kill you tonight. Have you got that through your rock-hard head yet? You could have ended up dead!"

"Then find out who's behind this! This place isn't exactly Mayberry, RFD. There's something rotten going on here. Why the hell haven't you done anything about it?"

He clutched the steering wheel harder. "Are you accusing me of not doing my job?"

"If the shoe fits…"

He yanked the wheel hard to the right, applied the brakes, and came to a rocking, shuddering halt on the shoulder of Bald Mountain Road.

"What the hell are you doing?" she said.

Without answering, he crammed the shifter into Park, reached across the front seat, and hauled her into his arms.

There was a single, startled instant when she went rigid. Then her mouth turned hot and urgent against his. There was nothing tentative about this kiss, nothing tender or gentle. Fueled by fear and longing, by dark fury and the knowledge that they were both wonderfully, gloriously alive, they fed off each other like wild creatures too long deprived of sustenance. With his fingers knotted in her silky black hair and his lungs screaming for oxygen, he met her hunger with his own, lost himself in that hot, wet mouth and the pleasures it promised, kissed her until the earth shook, until fire threatened to consume him from the inside out, until the sky began to fall in splintered pieces around his head.

He broke away, gasping, and buried his face in that dark cloud of hair while her fingers drew erotic, mindless patterns against his back. "You're trembling," she said.

He cleared his throat and said weakly, "I thought that was you."

Her bright explosion of laughter was like the sun bursting through clouds on a dark day. He felt it against his chest, and inside his heart. Saw it, like little dancing bursts of light, in the darkness behind his eyelids. "What were we fighting about?" she said.

Ty raised his head and looked into her eyes, those incredible blue eyes that had caught and trapped him the first time he'd looked into them more than thirty years ago. "I forget," he said.

She took his face in her hands and drew his mouth to hers. This time, the kiss was tender enough to tear holes in his heart. "Christ, Faith," he whispered when he finally found the strength to stop. "Don't ever scare me like that again."

"I didn't mean to. Trust me on that."

"I know." A little disoriented, he struggled to regain his bearings, abruptly realizing that they were sitting here in his police cruiser by the side of the road, locked in a passionate embrace for all the world to see. How many people had driven by and seen them? Granted, late-night traffic on Bald Mountain wasn't exactly comparable to rush hour downtown. But he'd been so wrapped up in Faith that an entire fleet of loaded pulp trucks could have passed by and he wouldn't have noticed. He'd never wanted a woman so much in his life.

But not tonight. Not like this. When they made love, it was going to be in a bed, behind locked doors, where they could have some privacy. Furthermore, there'd be no rushing. Once he got her naked, he intended to keep her that way for a long, long time.

He brushed his thumb over the sunken dark hollows beneath her eyes. "I'd love to stay here like this all night," he said, "but if we don't get going, the Sheriff's Department is apt to come by and tell us to move along."

At the Logan place, Davy Hunter's beige Oldsmobile was parked in the driveway. Even before he'd stopped the cruiser, Jessie was bounding down off the back steps, her face pinched with worry. Davy followed at a more leisurely pace, his features rendered stark by the harsh illumination of the porch light.

Ty turned off the car as Jessie opened the passenger-side door. "Oh, Faith," she said. "I was so scared. I called the hospital and they wouldn't tell me anything. If Davy hadn't stayed here with me, I would have lost my mind. I was so afraid you'd leave me—" she paused and briefly closed her eyes "—just like my mom did."

"Oh, sweetie." Faith climbed gingerly out of the car and wrapped her arms around the girl. Wiping a tear from Jessie's cheek, she said, "That's not going to happen. I'll always be here for you." Over the top of Jessie's head, she exchanged a glance with Ty. "I'm not going anywhere."

"Except to bed," he said. "Jessie, can you help Faith into the house? I need to talk to Davy for a minute."

After Faith and Jessie had gone inside, the two men stood together in the windblown silence. "Faith okay?" Davy said.

"She'll live. But she's had one hell of a scare. What happened tonight?"

Davy tucked his hands into his pockets and rocked back on his heels. "Somebody drove her off the road. Or so she says."

"What do you mean, or so she says? If she says it happened, it happened."

"All I'm saying is that I didn't witness it. I must've come along right after it happened. The Saab's wheels were still spinning."

Ty studied his face, gauging his sincerity. "But you didn't see anybody?"

"Not so much as a squirrel crossing the road."

"Shit. This is serious."

"And it's not your only problem, my friend. I brought Jessie home tonight. Skip Lombardi dropped her off at the accident scene."

Ty eyed him sharply. "Lombardi? What the hell was she doing with him?"

"Apparently, she ditched her date and was walking home. Alone. Lombardi happened to come by, and he picked her up, gave her a ride."

"Great." Ty sighed, ran his fingers through his hair. He studied Hunter's face, gaunt beneath the scruffy beard. "I intend to sit down and talk with you," he said. "But not tonight." He glanced toward the house, and his mouth thinned into a grim line. "I have other things to deal with tonight. I'll catch up with you sometime tomorrow. I have questions for you, and this time, I'm expecting answers."

Inside the house, Faith was sitting on the couch. "What happened?" Jessie said. "I saw your car. It was completely wrecked. I thought you were dead."

"It was just an accident," Faith said. "A silly accident. I'm fine."

"Are you, really? You wouldn't lie to me?"

"She has a concussion," Ty said, "and the doctors said—"

"A mild one," Faith clarified, her eyes clearly warning him to back off on the gory details. "I imagine I'll be a little sore tomorrow, but the doctor wouldn't have released me if he didn't think I'd be okay." Her eyes, still fixed on his, defied him to contradict her. "All I want now is to fall into bed and sleep for about twelve hours." One arm around Jessie's shoulders, she said to Ty, "There's no need for you to stay. Jessie's here, and we can—"

Grimly, he said, "I'm staying."

She closed her eyes. "Fine. I'll have Jessie make up the couch for you."

"Wrong. I'm supposed to be keeping you under observation. I can't very well do that if I'm on the couch and you're upstairs. I'm staying with you."

"But—" She glanced nervously at Jessie. "It's not exactly—I mean—" She trailed off and shot him a meaningful glance.

"Oh, for Christ's sake," he said. "Listen, Jessie? Faith gave me one hell of a scare tonight, and I'm still not over it. I'm not letting her out of my sight for a while. Besides, the doctor's expecting me to keep an eye on her. I promised I would. But Faith's concerned about the propriety of the two of us sleeping in the same bed in front of you. You're fifteen years old, and in my considered opinion, if the sight of us sharing a bed offends your delicate sensibilities or otherwise does permanent and irreparable damage to your psyche, then you should keep your bedroom door shut, and it won't be an issue."

"It doesn't bother me," Jessie said. "There's just one thing."

"What's that?"

"Can I sleep in Faith's room with you? I'll bring my bedding and I can sleep on the floor. I don't want to be alone tonight."

"Of course you can." He turned to Faith. "There," he said. "It's all taken care of."

It wasn't quite the way he'd imagined it would be, sleeping with Faith, the two of them crammed into a narrow twin bed barely big enough for one person, both of them fully dressed, Faith in her ugly red pajamas and him in his jeans and T-shirt. She had a lump on her head the size of Rhode Island, not to mention numerous bumps and bruises, and a fifteen-year-old chaperon on the floor beside the bed. Not quite the scenario he'd painted for himself when he'd fantasized about sleeping with her.

But this was okay. Actually, it was better than okay. There was a coziness to the three of them being together like this, a sense of family that felt so right it was scary. It was easy to imagine, as he and Faith lay together, warmth pressed to warmth, that they were a long-married couple and that Jessie, curled up on the floor beside a snoring Buddy, was their daughter.

He'd missed out on something, not having kids. It was one of the issues—along with Linda's infidelity—that had ended his marriage. He'd tried, over and over, to make her understand how he felt, but she kept putting him off with her promises that they'd talk about it someday. Eventually, he'd gotten tired of her promises, tired of the way she constantly broke them. Especially that big one: *forsaking all others.* So he'd filed for divorce and moved back in with Buck.

He still wanted kids of his own. But he wasn't averse to starting out with a ready-made family. Of course, there was still Faith to be considered. She led a glamorous life in Manhattan, rubbing elbows with celebrities. Why would she be interested in making any kind of life with a small-town cop?

Lying in the darkness, listening to her even breathing, he pondered the twist of fate that had brought them back together. If it could be said that one good thing had come of Chelsea's death, this was it. He'd lost Faith the first time because he'd been too young, too stupid, too scared to face the truth about his feelings. But he wasn't young and stupid anymore, and this time, he wasn't letting fear get in his way. They were meant to be together. It was as obvious as the color of Buck's new pickup. He just needed to convince her.

But first, he had to keep her alive.

Somebody had tried to kill her tonight. Or maybe tonight had been a warning, a dress rehearsal for what would happen if she didn't stop asking so many questions. Somehow, in the process of trying to find out what had happened to Chelsea, she'd stumbled into a tangled mess of evil. Somehow, he had to extricate her before it was too late. Chelsea had paid with her life. He'd be damned if he was going to allow the same thing to happen to Faith.

God help him. He was in way over his head. What did he know about evil? About homicide? His experience ran mostly to breaking up bar brawls and putting the fear of God into shoplifting juveniles. He was coolheaded in an emergency, and he could hand out speeding tickets with the best of them. But his expertise ended there. His years as a cop in a town where nothing ever happened hadn't prepared him to deal with something like this. It didn't help that he'd had his head buried in the sand for so long it was a wonder he could still breathe. He hadn't wanted to believe that evil lived here in his quiet little hometown. But something malevolent was happening, and it was up to him to track it down and stomp it out.

In the morning, he was going to have a long talk with Davy Hunter. Sit him down and interrogate him. It was just too convenient that Davy had happened along when he did. Too damned convenient that he kept showing up everywhere. Whatever was going on, Hunter was involved in it up to his eyeballs. Maybe a little old-fashioned police brutality would loosen his tongue. Ty didn't generally believe in using violence as a crime-solving method, but in this case, maybe it was justified. Somehow, no matter what it took, he had to get Davy to talk. Even if it meant he had to shake the guy until his teeth rattled.

Considering what she'd been through, Faith wasn't nearly as lame as she'd expected to be. A hot shower took care of the worst of it, and a couple of Tylenol dulled what was left of last night's headache. She threw on the most comfortable clothes she could find, ran a brush through her tangled hair, and studied herself critically in the mirror. Her complexion was pallid. The bump on her forehead had gone down overnight. What remained of it, while much smaller than it had originally been, was already beginning to resemble a box of Crayolas. She looked like a cavewoman, wild of eye and hair and demeanor. The sensible, rational woman who'd lived inside her for the past twenty years had been replaced by some Bohemian stranger who bore no resemblance to the Faith Pelletier she knew.

She pinched her cheeks to add color, but it was hopeless.

She still looked as pale as the belly of a fish. Giving up, she raked her fingers through her hair in a final fruitless attempt to do something with it, then headed downstairs to face the dragons.

The aroma of fresh-brewed coffee, manna from heaven, reached her nose before she got there. Still wearing yesterday's jeans and T-shirt, Ty was at the kitchen stove, sprinkling Tabasco sauce over a huge skillet of scrambled eggs. The tantalizing smell of frying bacon came from a second, smaller skillet.

His hair was a mess, his clothes rumpled. He looked tired. Last night had obviously taken a toll on him. But when he turned to her, spatula in hand, and flashed her a world-class, heart-stopping smile, that smile wormed its way into all those soft woman places inside her, sending a heated rush of pleasure from her head to her heart to her pelvis. "Morning," he said.

"Good morning." She moved, zombielike, to the coffeemaker and poured herself a steaming cup. Eyes closed to better appreciate its rejuvenating qualities, she drank it black. It was the consistency of used motor oil, strong enough to remove the curl from her hair. "Good Lord," she sputtered. "Where'd you learn to make coffee?"

"From Dixie," he said, neatly flipping bacon, slice after slice, with a big, wooden-handled fork. "Our dispatcher. The guys all say her coffee could grow hair on your chest. Which in your case—" he eyed the aforementioned portion of her anatomy with interest "—would be a real shame."

The memory of his hands on her body sent heat rushing up her cheeks, undoubtedly giving them the color they'd so sorely lacked. "Where's Jessie?" she said, pointedly ignoring his remark. "Her room was empty when I came by."

"She took Buddy for a walk. I warned her not to leave the property. I want both of you where I can keep an eye on you until I figure out what's going on." He stirred the scrambled eggs, then lowered the heat under them. "How are you feeling this morning?"

"Nowhere near as bad as I'd imagined." She stepped to his side, reached past him and snagged a slice of bacon. "Did anybody ever tell you that you snore, Savage?"

"*What?*" The look on his face was priceless. "I do not."

"Oh, yes, you do." She bit off one end of the bacon. It was crunchy and salty, just the way she liked it. "Loudly and obnoxiously," she added. "I had to cover my head with the pillow, or I wouldn't have gotten any sleep at all."

"Well, damn," he said. "There goes my reputation as a stud."

Jessie came in with the dog, and the three of them sat down to eat breakfast. Just like a real family, Faith thought with a pang as she watched Jessie pass the grape jelly across the table to Ty. The thing she'd been seeking since she was twelve years old was right here, so close she could almost touch it.

But it wasn't hers. It wasn't real, just an illusion. Oh, she could pretend. For a time, she might even make herself believe in the forever-after fairy tale. But in the end, it lacked permanence. No matter how she felt about Ty Savage, she couldn't stay here in Serenity. Not permanently. She'd left eighteen years ago because there was nothing here for her, and that hadn't changed. She had a life—a good life—elsewhere. And after everything that had happened, she would never again feel safe here. Ty could take measures to protect her, but he couldn't be with her twenty-four hours a day. She refused to live a life entrenched in fear and anxiety. She'd already had enough of that. It was time to pull herself up by the bootstraps and move on.

But even if she couldn't have Ty, she still had Jessie. She couldn't wait to show Jessie the wonders of the city. Museums. Shopping. The opera. The symphony. After nearly two years of living in the dark, Faith was ready to burst out into the daylight. And she intended to spoil Jessie rotten. She might not be able to make up to the girl for the loss of her mother, but she was going to be one incredible auntie.

Jessie seemed quiet this morning, preoccupied. "With everything that's gone on," Faith said to her, "I completely forgot to ask. How did your date with Cooper go?"

Her attention on her scrambled eggs, Jessie said, "I think it's probably better if you don't ask."

Faith exchanged glances with Ty. He stared back at her evenly. Concerned, she said, "It didn't go well?"

"Let's just say we weren't compatible," Jessie said. "Can we talk about something else? While I was out walking Buddy, I did a lot of thinking. About the house, and all that." Jessie looked first at Ty and then at Faith. "I think we should sell it to Mr. Lombardi."

There was a moment of silence. "Well," Faith said, momentarily at a loss for words. "Are you sure? We haven't even had time to talk it over, honey. This house is your inheritance."

Behind the lenses of her glasses, Jessie's gray eyes were somber, and spoke of a knowledge far older than her fifteen years. "I know," she said. "But I've thought it over, and I'd rather have the money. It'll pay for college, right?"

"It should."

"That's what I want. I thought I wanted to stay here, in this house, in this town, but I was wrong. I think you should call that woman—" She glanced again at Ty. "Linda? And tell her we want to sell. The sooner, the better. Call her today. I know you want to get back to New York as soon as possible." She picked up a napkin and wiped her mouth. "May I be excused?"

"Of course."

Jessie carried her plate to the sideboard before she disappeared from the room, silent as a wraith. Outside the kitchen window, a flock of crows were making a racket. Ty picked a sliver of bacon from his plate and fed it to Buddy, who'd been waiting patiently at his feet just in case he dropped something. "I thought we'd made some headway," Faith said.

"Give her time." He reached down and gave Buddy's head a brisk rub. "Try to remember what it was like for you when your folks died. I think she's doing remarkably well, considering."

"Believe me, I remember what it was like. It was hell."

"Well, there you go. She'll come around." As he lifted his coffee cup, the violin music began upstairs, low and sweet and mournful. "I don't know much about music," he said, "but it seems to me she's pretty good at playing that thing."

"She's very talented." Faith took a sip of coffee. "There's a school," she said hesitantly. "In Manhattan. A performing arts school. It's just a couple of blocks from where I live. A lot of kids apply, but only the most talented get in. I think Jessie would have a good chance of being accepted. I have a friend on the board. He could get her an audition. It would be up to her to make the cut. But he could at least get her the audition."

Outside, the crows continued to screech and caw. Inside the kitchen, the refrigerator hummed. "Sounds promising," he said, picking up his coffee cup and draining it. He didn't say the rest of the sentence: *And what about us?* But she heard the words just the same.

"I have to go to work," he said. "I'd feel a whole lot better if I knew you and Jessie were safe."

Faith got up and began clearing plates from the table. "I have a solid lock on my door. I don't intend to let any strangers into the house. Besides—" she plugged the sink, squirted in dish detergent, and began filling it with hot water "—nobody's going to bother us in broad daylight."

He dropped his coffee mug into the hot suds. "Of course not. Nobody's ever been murdered during the middle of the day."

"Very funny. Look," she said as she scraped the remains of Jessie's uneaten breakfast into the trash, "maybe we're over-reacting. Maybe it really was just some drunk who saw a woman driving alone and thought it would be fun to play games with her. Maybe we're making something out of nothing."

"Maybe." But he didn't sound convinced. "You can believe I'm going to beat the bushes until I find out who it was. Promise you'll keep your door locked?"

She paused to look him in the eye. "I won't be a prisoner in this house. But I promise I'll be careful."

"I'll check in with you every couple of hours. I'm also going to make sure René cruises by a few times during his shift. I'll pick you up tonight at five-thirty."

"Tonight?" she said.

"I'm going to blame your forgetfulness on the concussion." The solemnity in his eyes belied his weak attempt at humor. "We have a date, remember? You and me. No interruptions. No talk of murder or mayhem. Just…us."

His eyes dared her to protest. "What about Jessie?" she said. "I can't go off and leave her alone right now. God knows what might happen."

"Already taken care of. Jessie's coming over to my house for the evening. She and Dad can keep each other company."

"You arranged all this before breakfast?"

"I don't believe in wasting time. Or in taking chances. If you see anything even remotely suspicious today, I expect you to call me immediately. I'll make sure Dixie knows she's to put your calls through no matter what I'm doing. And for Christ's sake, stay put."

"Where do you expect me to go?" she said. "I don't have a car anymore."

"Don't remind me." He caught a fistful of her sweatshirt and pulled her close. Her heart began to hammer as those dark eyes studied her as though he were afraid he might never see her face again. "You and I have serious business to discuss tonight," he said. "I'd like you to stay alive long enough to discuss it."

His nearness made her dizzy. She braced her hands against his shoulders to keep herself upright. "Ty—" she began.

"Shush." With his thumb, he traced the bow of her upper lip. Then he placed a kiss at the corner of her mouth, a kiss so tender, so light, that it left her trembling. "Five-thirty," he said. "In the meantime, behave yourself."

Eighteen

Ty's mood, which hadn't been particularly chipper to start with, showed no sign of going in any direction but south. "If Faith calls," he snarled at Dixie by way of greeting, "put her through." Dix stared at him as though he'd just grown little green antennae out of the top of his head. Ignoring her, he slammed the door to his office behind him. The resulting thud was so satisfying, he almost did it again.

Somebody had left a copy of this morning's *Gazette* on his desk. He set down his cup of coffee, plopped into his chair and opened the paper. The front page, above the crease, was dedicated to the mystery flyers scattered all over town by the equally mysterious Brotherhood for Aryan Unity. Newt had situated the other big story directly below the crease. Stomach acid slowly backed up into his throat as he studied the grainy black-and-white photo of Faith's Saab, looking as though it were the big loser in a demolition derby. Cussing, he tossed down the paper without bothering to read the story. He didn't need to hear the gory details. Faith had told him everything she remembered, and his own vivid imagination had filled in all the necessary blanks. He'd spent most of last night fighting off faceless demons in his sleep. Between that and Faith's announcement this morning that she was already making plans to put Jessie into some fancy performing-arts school in New York City, it was no wonder his mood—not to mention his stomach—was sour.

He picked up his phone and called Dixie. "Pete in?" he said.

"Last time I checked. Um…I know I'm not supposed to question your actions, since you're the big boss man, but why didn't you just call his extension?"

"I'm practicing being efficient. I need to talk to both of you. I called you, you call Pete. Grab anybody else who's hanging around. My office. Five minutes."

They filed in noiselessly, Dixie looking apprehensive, Pete resembling a big, amiable grizzly bear and Floyd Watson, who'd been on the force for as long as he could remember, reminding him of a slightly older Barney Fife. As Ty studied their faces, he realized for the first time how inadequate they were to deal with the kinds of challenges that the twenty-first century would bring. Their equipment, their methodology, their training, even their collective mind-set had been frozen in a time warp, somewhere around 1978. Granted, it wasn't all their fault; the town was small and the budget severely limited. Because Serenity was so tranquil, they'd had no reason to fight for expensive training and upgrades. Until now, the lack hadn't been noticeable. They functioned well as a team, effectively executing what little law enforcement was actually needed. But they'd also grown lazy and complacent. Faith was right. The Serenity Police Department was operating under the assumption that their quiet little town was another Mayberry, a place where nothing really bad ever happened. And the town itself, frozen in that same time warp, had cooperated in this little charade for so damn long that none of them had even noticed when those darker elements began to trickle in. Once this Chelsea Logan mess was cleared up and things went back to normal, he was going to have to do something to bring his department into the twenty-first century. In these days of terrorism and uncertainty, it was the only way they were going to survive.

He pushed the disturbing thought away and forced himself to concentrate on the here and now. "I imagine you've all heard what happened to Faith Pelletier last night," he said. "She's lucky to be alive. Meanwhile, somewhere out there, the son of a bitch who drove her off the road is having a laugh at our expense. We're going to find him, and I hope to Christ that when we do, one of you is strong enough to hold me back. Because I'm apt to beat him to a bloody pulp first and ask questions later."

Studying his knuckles, Pete said, "I might just have to be looking the other way when that happens."

"You're a good man, Pete Morin. Listen, I want you to go out and roust the usual suspects. Teddy Stultz, the Giroux boys, Eddie Haskell and his crew. Ask a few questions, find out their whereabouts last night between, say, nine-thirty and eleven, get a look at their vehicles. Ruffle a few feathers and see what happens. Floyd—and you'll want to listen to this, too, Dix, because you'll be radioing this message out to everybody who's on patrol—I want you to keep your eyes peeled for a large vehicle, probably a truck or an SUV. Year, make and color unknown. What we're looking for is fresh front-end damage. In particular, damage to the front bumper and/or the right front quarter. Look for red paint. You see anything, you radio it back to Dix, and she'll pass the info on to me. While you're on the horn, Dix, tell René I want him to keep an eagle eye on the Logan place today. He's to drive by there every half hour and make sure everything's copacetic. If he sees so much as a frigging blade of grass out of place, I want him to call for backup and investigate. Are we all on the same page with this?"

There were nods of assent from every quarter. "Good," he said, standing up in a gesture of dismissal. "I'm headed over to Sonny's to take a look at the Saab, see if this scumbag left any evidence behind. I'll let you all know if I find out anything."

Pete lingered after the others had left. "Just thought you'd want to know," he said. "Last night, while Greg Marston was on foot patrol, he happened across a couple of kids out back of Omar's store. They each had a can of neon green spray paint. Seems they were doing a little redecorating."

"Oh?"

"Report's on your desk. Jeff and Randy Stultz. Leroy's two oldest boys. Admitted that they were responsible for the artwork the other night."

He felt the keen edge of disappointment. In spite of their sketchy family background, neither boy had ever been in trouble with the law. "Damn it," he said, "they can't be more than eleven or twelve years old. Where do kids that young get these ideas?"

"The usual. They hear it at home, figure it's acceptable to spread their parents' particular brand of poison all over town." Pete clapped him on the shoulder. "You know what they say. The apple doesn't fall far from the tree."

"Ah, hell. Somebody remind me why I thought I wanted to be a cop."

"You got me there. It sure as hell wasn't for the highly coveted civil service benefits."

Faith loved the smell of wet laundry, loved the crisp snap of a clean bedsheet flapping in the wind. Living in Manhattan, she had no choice but to depend on her trusty Maytag dryer. But here, where there was an abundance of space, an abundance of fresh air, she took pleasure in hanging her laundry out to dry. She'd just pinned up the last bath towel when she heard a car pulling into the driveway. For an instant, her anxiety spun out of control. Breathing slowly, deliberately, armed with just an empty laundry basket and a mesh bag loaded with weathered clothespins, she walked around the end of the chicken coop to see who it was.

All her knotted muscles relaxed when she saw Newt Rollins sitting behind the wheel of the little silver Acura. He climbed out of the car and made his way through the tall grass to where she stood holding the laundry basket. "That's one hell of a lump," he said, examining her forehead.

"You think it looks bad now, you should have seen it last night. Come in the house. I'll pour us some lemonade."

"I'm sorry," he said, once they were settled at the kitchen table with icy glasses of lemonade. "This is all my fault. I'm the one who got you involved in this, and I could kick my own ass from here to kingdom come."

"Stop beating up on yourself. Think about it. Are you the one who killed Chelsea? Are you the one who drove me off the road? Look, Newt, all you did was nudge me in a direction I would have eventually stumbled across by myself. You made it easier for me, that's all."

He took a sip of lemonade and tapped his fingers on the table. "Still," he said, "I egged you on. I had no business doing that. No business pushing you to get involved in what should have been a police matter."

"The police weren't doing much."

"No," he admitted. "They weren't."

"They will now. Ty's finally seen how serious this is."

"Has he?"

"He's got René Bellevance driving by every half hour. You could set your watch by him. He stopped in on the first go-round this morning and introduced himself. He's a nice kid. I'm not sure how effective he'd be at stopping someone bent on doing me in, but his heart's in the right place."

"Look, Faith." With his thumb, Newt caught and dammed a drop of moisture that had rolled down the side of his glass. He glanced up at her, blue eyes earnest behind the lenses of his glasses. "I've given this a great deal of thought. I think you and Jessie should leave town."

"Leave town?" she said, appalled. "Just pack it in and let the bad guys win? Surely you jest."

"I'm dead serious. There's something really nasty going on here, and you're sitting right in the middle of it. I think you should get the hell out before it swallows you up. Take a Caribbean cruise. Travel to Egypt and visit the pyramids. Or check into some luxury hotel in Cannes and spend a couple of weeks lying on the beach. Go anywhere, just as long as you get away from this place. I'd be willing to bet good money that your cop boyfriend would agree with me. He doesn't want to see you hurt any more than I do."

"He's not my boyfriend."

It was an idiotic remark. Of all the things he'd said to her, why was that the one she'd chosen to take exception to? "Besides," she said, getting up and going to the refrigerator just to keep her hands busy, "I can't just pull Jessie out of school like that." She took the pitcher of lemonade from the fridge and returned to the table with it.

"Why not? A brainy kid like her, a couple of weeks wouldn't even put a dent in her grade point average. She pulls straight A's. Besides, you're planning to take her back to New York with you in a few weeks, aren't you? Changing schools will disrupt her school year anyway. What difference does it make if you do it now or later?"

She leaned over the table and refilled first his glass, then hers. "I'm not sure yet."

The fluorescent light reflected off his glasses when he raised his face to study her quizzically. "Not sure you're taking her with you?" he said.

"Not sure I'm going back to New York."

His face mirrored her own surprise. Until this very instant, she'd had no idea that she was even remotely considering the possibility of staying here in Serenity. There'd been nothing here for her eighteen years ago, long before the town began its gradual decline. Now that it was on its deathbed, Serenity held even less for a woman like her. It wasn't as though she had some sentimental attachment to the town or its citizens. She hadn't been all that popular in school. She hadn't even bothered to attend her ten-year class reunion. There was nobody she wanted to see. Her parents were buried here, but she'd long since made her peace with that. The past was the past, and the six years she'd spent planning her escape from this town had been the worst years of her life.

And it wasn't as though she'd been welcomed with open arms when she came back. Certainly there were people who'd been kind. Dottie McLaughlin came to mind immediately. But others had been less than welcoming. Davy Hunter had been downright rude on more than one occasion. Angus Dowe hadn't exactly been warm and fuzzy. And some unknown person had tried to kill her, for Christ's sake.

She had a satisfying life in Manhattan. Or at least she'd had it before Ben died. She'd been guilty of neglecting that life for too long. But it didn't have to be that way. She could go home and blow the dust off, polish things up a little. Make a few phone calls, reach out to the friends she'd withdrawn from when widowhood took the light out of her life. She could recreate the life she'd found so satisfying. With Jessie to fuss over, she could make it even better than before. Richer, fuller. There wasn't a reason on God's green earth why she would want to stay here in this pathetic excuse for a town, situated at the far end of the universe, a single step away from the falling-off place where monsters dwelled.

No reason at all, except that Ty Savage called this place home.

Quietly, Newt said, "Does Savage know how you feel?"

"It's not like that," she said. "It has nothing to do with him."

"Of course not. That's why you're wearing that deer-in-the-headlights look. I'll say this for him, he's a lucky son of a bitch. What it is about him that draws the women, I can't fathom. Maybe it's pheromones. All I know is that sooner or later, they all fall dead at his feet."

"I told you, it's not like that."

"And I repeat my question. Does he know how you feel?"

"Oh, shit." She wheeled around, flung open the refrigerator, and returned the lemonade pitcher to its shelf. Closing the door, she said desperately, "How could he? *I* don't even know how I feel."

"This complicates things," Newt said. "My advice is to take a couple of aspirin and go to bed. Maybe by morning, it'll pass."

"Very funny."

"I apologize. Look, your safety should still be the number-one priority for both of you. If he cares about you, he must know that. Get out of town until things quiet down. If you still want to play kissy-face with the guy a couple of months from now, go for it. But until the cops figure out who drove you off the road, you should get as far away from this place as you can get."

Before she could respond, Jessie came into the room, quiet as a shadow. There was a pinched look about her mouth, and Faith wondered how much of their conversation she'd overheard. "I'm riding my bike into town," Jessie said, "to spend the day with Becca."

Alarm bells went off in Faith's head. Newt must have recognized the distress on her face, for he said smoothly, casually, "It's a long haul, Jessie-belle. I'm about ready to head back. I'll give you a lift."

"Thank you, Mr. Rollins," Jessie said somberly. "Just let me get my backpack."

"I don't want you wandering around town alone," Faith said. "Ty and I will pick you up around quarter of six."

She'd expected at least a token protest. But Jessie just nodded solemnly and headed upstairs to get her backpack, leaving Faith to wonder if Jessie knew more about what was going on than she'd thought.

Newt drained his lemonade and stood up. "How's she doing?" he said.

Faith shrugged. "She's a teenager. A chameleon. She runs hot and cold. I suppose I must have been the same after I lost my parents, although I was a little younger when they died. At twelve years old, I lost both of them. I thought my life was over."

"I'm sorry."

She crossed her arms. "It's been a long time. I just wish I could figure out what Jessie's thinking. Last night, she had a date. She was so excited. But this morning, when I asked her how it went, she wouldn't even talk about it. I have no idea what went wrong, but quite clearly something did."

"Who's the boy? Maybe I know him."

"As a matter of fact, he's the same boy I was asking you about. The one I saw at Davy's trailer. His name's Cooper Gates."

Newt's eyebrows shot up. "Coop was hanging out with Davy Hunter?"

"So you do know him."

"He worked for me all last summer. He did odd jobs around the office, ran errands, basically played gofer. He's not a bad kid, but I can't imagine that hanging with Hunter and his cronies will do him any good."

"Funny," she said, "when I mentioned him to Davy, he told me the kid was bad news and I should keep Jessie away from him."

Newt snorted. "Why am I not surprised? Hunter and I have yet to see eye-to-eye on anything. Of course, if Coop's spent much time with him, being the lousy influence that he is, the kid probably *is* bad news by now. Hell, Hunter's probably proud of himself for corrupting the kid." His mouth thinned. "Looks like I'm going to have to have a little talk with Cooper Gates. I hate like hell to see a good kid like that, from a good family, go wandering off the straight and narrow path." He glanced toward the doorway and his face relaxed into a smile. "Here comes Miss Jessie. Ready to roll, kiddo?"

"I'm ready. Will you be okay by yourself, Faith?"

"I'll be fine. Remember what I said. No running the streets alone."

"I won't." Jessie turned to go, but halfway to the door she stopped, spun around, and came back to give Faith a bone-crushing hug. "You take care of yourself," she said fiercely. "I don't know what I'd do if anything happened to you."

When Newt backed down the driveway, one hand out the window to wave goodbye, Faith's mouth was still hanging open.

The Saab was locked up in Sonny Gaudette's impound lot, safe from prying eyes and larcenous hands. Anybody with ideas about contaminating or stealing evidence was, as the kids liked to say, SOL. Sonny's impound lot was double-protected. Not only was it surrounded by an eight-foot chain-link fence topped with barbed wire, but it enjoyed an added accessory: the biggest, meanest Doberman in three counties. Nobody got past Othello unless Sonny gave the okay. Even then, it was chancy. More than one insurance adjuster had been bitten on the ass trying to squeeze past Sonny's Dobie.

Ty wasn't afraid of the dog. They'd come to a mutual understanding years ago. Othello didn't take to many people, and even with Ty, the dog didn't let down his guard until Sonny gave him the signal. But once he knew that his guard duties were over for the time being, the dog always came trotting over to sniff around and poke his muzzle into every pocket of Ty's clothing until he found the inevitable dog biscuit, his reward for his honorary status as a member of Serenity's finest.

This morning, Ty spent a couple of minutes renewing his acquaintance with Othello before he and Sonny approached the mangled Saab. The vehicle had seen better days. It wasn't likely to see them again. Little more than a pile of twisted steel and broken glass, the car looked worse in real life than it had in the newspaper photo.

Ty reached into his pocket, pulled out a roll of Tums, peeled back the foil wrapping, and popped a couple of them into his mouth. Chewing absently, he replaced the roll and walked around the Saab, studying it from every possible angle. Probably an accident reconstruction expert could have explained the origin of every one of its numerous dents and scratches, but to him, it just looked like somebody had taken a sledgehammer to it.

He knelt by the left rear quarter. When one vehicle collided with another, there was always evidence. But he couldn't find a damn thing. No stray flakes or chips that didn't match the Saab's red paint. "No paint residue," he said thoughtfully. "At least none that's visible to the naked eye."

When Sonny hunkered down beside him, Ty got a whiff of the unmistakable scent of *eau de l'auto*, a piquant mixture of gasoline, motor oil and axle grease, that always surrounded Sonny. "Nope," Sonny agreed, closely examining the crumpled fender. "That's kinda funny."

"What do you suppose it means?"

"We-e-l-l…" Sonny pulled off his John Deere cap and rubbed his forehead. Replacing the cap, he drawled, "I'd say whoever hit her must've had a solid chrome bumper."

"Solid chrome." Ty raised his eyebrows. "Been a few years since they made vehicles like that."

"Ayuh."

"So you think it was an older vehicle?"

"That would be my bet. Some old pickup truck from the days before they started calling these damn fiberglass and rubber contraptions bumpers."

Ty chewed on it for a while. Sonny's assessment made sense. Unlike today's toy-car bumpers that disintegrated with a five-mile-per-hour impact, bumpers in years past were designed for maximum protection in a collision. They could do some pretty heavy damage to another vehicle, but left no paint residue because they were solid chrome.

He and Sonny spent another twenty minutes examining the vehicle, but the only foreign substances they found were mud, dead leaves and tree bark, all of them pretty self-explanatory. Hoping that he'd pick up some kind of vibes from the Saab that would enlighten him, Ty hung around a little longer. But there were no vibes. The Saab just sat there, mortally wounded. If it had been a horse, he would have shot it to put it out of its misery. Since it was a car and there was nothing left for him to do, he rubbed Othello behind the ears, watched Sonny lock the gate behind them, and went back to the cruiser to radio Dix with the information he'd gathered.

Davy Hunter was next on his list. He took a shortcut, bypassing Bald Mountain Road altogether, circling around the backside of the mountain and approaching Hunter's place

from the opposite direction. The woods here were so thick
with pine and spruce that he saw occasional patches of snow
in spots where the sun seldom reached. Mid-May, and still the
snow hadn't completely left the woods. Pretty soon, blackfly
season would be underway. Then the mosquitoes would come
out, and before he knew it, winter would be back for a return
engagement. Any man who willingly remained in this climate
had to question his sanity.

When he pulled into Davy's yard, the place looked deserted. Hunter's rusty Oldsmobile wasn't sitting in the driveway, its absence compensated for by a dark stain in the dirt
where the Olds had leaked a significant amount of oil. He
climbed the steps and knocked repeatedly on the trailer door,
but nobody answered. Hunter wasn't home.

So far this morning, he was zero for zero. He had a shit-
load of questions, and Hunter had a great deal of explaining
to do. He'd been the only witness to last night's incident. And
it was entirely possible that Davy'd been more than a witness.
That he'd been the one who drove Faith off the road. His timing was damn convenient. Ty hadn't wanted to say it aloud to
Faith for fear of starting a firestorm. But he knew that even
though she didn't want to admit it, the same possibility had
occurred to her.

A dull throbbing sprang to life behind his temple. Rubbing
at it, he sat down on the decaying wooden steps to wait.
Maybe Hunter'd simply gone into town to pick up groceries.
Or to visit his granny, who was eighty-three and legally blind,
and lived by herself in a low-income apartment complex on
the other side of town. It couldn't hurt to kill a few minutes
waiting. It was a gorgeous spring day, sunny and cloudless and
warm, if you didn't mind the occasional gust of wind. Out
here in the woods, birds flitted from tree to tree and sang so
much more melodiously and pleasantly than those infernal
grackles that screeched and chattered outside his bedroom
window at the crack of dawn every day. He counted at least
a half-dozen different bird calls, recognized them all. Cardi-

nal, robin, chickadee. A pair of goldfinches darted past, immediately recognizable for their swooping flight pattern as well as their bold coloring. He even caught a quick flash of orange as an oriole, rare in this region, flew over the roof of the trailer and landed in a birch tree at the edge of the woods.

It was peaceful out here. Tranquil. Relaxing. He'd always assumed that Davy stayed here because, tucked away in the woods, he could do whatever he wanted and nobody would notice. The thick evergreen forest was useful for hiding a multitude of sins. But there were other advantages Ty had never considered. The trailer itself might be a dump, but its location was a little slice of heaven. How did that Robert Frost poem go? Something about the woods being lovely, dark and deep? That was the way this place felt. No wonder Hunter stayed.

After a half hour he gave up, wrote Hunter a message on one of the yellow sticky notes he always carried, and stuck it to the trailer door. There was no sense wasting any more time sitting here. He wanted to give Lemoine a call, see if those tox screens on Chelsea Logan had come back yet. It was highly doubtful. It had only been six days; even under the best of circumstances, that kind of thing could take weeks. The state police detective seemed determined that Chelsea had done herself in, but Ty's instincts kept telling him something else was afoot, and he generally trusted his instincts. Was Chelsea's death tied into what had happened to Faith last night? If it was, he needed to know. And if it wasn't, if Chelsea's death truly had been either suicide or an accident, he'd feel a hell of a lot better knowing the truth. As it was, he'd become so paranoid, he was starting to see bogeymen behind every corner and under every bush. He'd criticized Faith for that kind of thinking, but he was beginning to understand where it came from.

As he approached the Logan place on his drive back to town, he thought about stopping. But he'd already wasted a half hour waiting for Davy, and if he stopped, he'd end up

staying for an hour or two that he couldn't afford to waste.
He was expecting a call from Tim Leavitt about last night's
meeting with the Somali elders, and he wanted to stay close
by the station in case anything interesting came to light. If and
when the vehicle that had forced Faith off the road surfaced,
he wanted to be there.

She'd been washing clothes. The evidence hung on the
line, fluttering in the breeze. White cotton bedsheets, brightly
colored towels. Women's dainty unmentionables. His throat
went dry and his internal thermostat shot up a good twenty
degrees as he pictured Faith in those wispy little scraps of fabric. And then pictured himself removing them, one lacy
morsel at a time.

Jesus H. Christ. He couldn't take much more of this. There
had to be something seriously wrong with him. What kind of
dementia drove a man to thoughts of hot, steamy sex just because he saw a woman's lingerie drying on the line? Zero to
sixty in .02 seconds. But ever since Faith came back to town,
he'd had sex on the brain more often than not. And truth be
known, if he thought there was any chance of a little daytime
dalliance, he'd stop for those couple of hours anyway, and let
Dix track him down if anything important came up.

But a dalliance was out of the question with Jessie in the
house. Not to mention that dallying, daytime or otherwise, involved two parties, and if the other party wasn't interested, it
was pretty much a moot point.

Except that she was interested. He'd seen it in her eyes, felt
it in her touch. When they'd kissed last night, he wasn't the
only one who'd gone up in flames. Faith Pelletier was ripe for
the plucking. Ripe for him. If the circumstances last night had
been different…if she hadn't been fresh out of the ER and shot
up with painkillers…if they hadn't been parked in his cruiser
by the side of a state highway…if Jessie hadn't been home…
he'd have spent the night in her bed doing something a hell
of a lot more interesting than sleeping.

Shit. There was only so much of this a man could take. He

pulled out his cell phone and punched in the number to the station. "Hey, Dix," he said when she answered. "I need you to look up a phone number for me."

Ty's ex-wife was dressed casually today, in a powder-blue turtleneck sweater, jeans and L.L. Bean boots. "I was surprised when you called," Linda said. "I wasn't sure I'd hear from you at all, and certainly not this soon."

"It was Jessie's idea," Faith said, ushering Linda and company into the kitchen. "She told me this morning at breakfast to call you, that she's ready to sell the house. You know, sometimes it's easier to run away than it is to face the memories of somebody who isn't coming back." She understood only too well that there was running away, and then there was running away. Running didn't always involve distance.

Lombardi was also dressed casually, in jeans and a blue athletic shirt. He and Linda made a stunning couple; even in jeans, he was eye candy of the highest order. If nothing else, Ty's ex-wife had good taste in men. In his arms, propped against his left hip, was a bright-eyed little girl. Slender of build, she had short, wispy blond hair and enormous blue eyes. The child looked to be about four years old, but if Jessie's information was correct, she was closer to seven. Small for her age, but still a bit of a load for her daddy to be carrying.

Smiling at the child, Faith said, "Skip. It's nice to see you again. And this would be…?"

"Alyssa," he said. "Light of my life. Lys, say hello to Ms. Pelletier."

The child responded by burying her face in his shoulder. Smiling indulgently, he said, "She's a little shy."

"I think we can take care of that. Hi, Alyssa, I'm Faith, and I bet if we looked hard enough, we could find a couple of chocolate chip cookies with your name on them. Does that sound good?"

Lombardi joggled the girl a little higher on his hip. "What do you say, pumpkin? Want a couple of cookies?"

Alyssa turned her head to look at Faith, but still kept it pressed against her father's chest. "Yes, please," she said softly. "Can I pat your dog?"

"You most certainly can. His name is Buddy, and he loves kids." At the sound of his name, Buddy, who'd been lying in the corner of the kitchen, raised his head and wagged his tail. "Come on, Bud," she called. "Come meet Alyssa."

Buddy got up and stretched, then came over, still wagging. Lombardi put the girl down and she crouched in front of the dog. She touched his head tentatively, then ran her hand down his muzzle. "He's so soft!" she exclaimed.

"We can't have pets where we live," Lombardi explained. "Alyssa's at that age where she wants a dog, a cat, a horse." He smiled down at his daughter as though she were the most precious creature on the planet. "Last week, she saw one of those Vietnamese potbellied pigs on TV, and she begged me for a solid three days to let her have one."

Faith grinned. "I bet your landlord would love that."

"For sure. He won't even let us have a guinea pig, let alone a real pig."

They left Alyssa and Buddy together in the kitchen to get acquainted over cookies and milk while Faith showed the place to Lombardi and Larochelle. "It's an old house," she warned as they wandered through the downstairs rooms. "Nothing fancy, just a good old solid American farmhouse."

Linda linked her arm loosely with Skip's. "That's what we're looking for. Something big and solid, with plenty of room for Alyssa and all her friends. Something we can fix up a little at a time. We're not afraid of hard work."

It was a good thing, because Cyrus Logan had been a tight-wad, and Faith doubted he'd ever spent a penny on updates. "It will probably need work," she said as they climbed the stairs to the second floor. "I suspect the wiring will need replacing, and possibly the furnace. But there's certainly plenty of room." She opened the guest room door, and Linda stuck her head in. "Four bedrooms upstairs and, as you've already seen, one downstairs."

"Two baths," Linda said. "That's a plus."

"That's right. A full bath up here, a three-quarter bath downstairs."

"That would make mornings easy, wouldn't it, Skip?"

He grunted noncommittally. Linda peered into Jessie's room, where the bed was made neatly and not an item was out of place. "This room is darling," she said. "It would be perfect for Alyssa. Sunny and bright, and the wallpaper is so dainty and girlish."

"Chelsea recently redid all the upstairs bedrooms," Faith said. "She was working her way through the house, one room at a time." Something tightened painfully in her chest. "She died before she could get to the downstairs."

Lombardi glanced passively into Jessie's bedroom and then closed the door. "How much land is there?"

"I believe it's twenty acres, give or take."

"Lys could have a dog, Skip. We could get horses." Linda's eyes shone with excitement. "I could teach her to ride."

"Which is fine, as long as you don't expect me to get on one."

They went back downstairs and spent a few more minutes examining the kitchen and the bathroom before trooping outside into the bright sunshine with Alyssa and Buddy in tow. "The property extends all the way to the woods out back," Faith said, "plus all the open fields you see."

"What about the water supply?" Skip said. "Dug well or artesian?"

"Artesian. At this elevation, the water's pretty far below the surface."

"Come on, Lys," Linda said, holding out her hand. "Let's go check out the barn." She flashed an intimate smile at Lombardi. "I'm sure Daddy's more than happy to let us do that without him."

They marched off, leaving Skip and Faith alone in the driveway. "I'm a city boy," he explained with a sheepish grin. "Show me a spider, and I'm out of here."

"I don't blame you a bit. So you're not from around here."

"No." He leaned against the fender of Linda's Caddy and crossed his arms. "I grew up in Stamford, Connecticut. I've moved around a bit in my career, teaching here and there. Before I came here, I was principal at a high school just outside of Providence." He watched Linda and Alyssa disappear into the dark interior of the barn, then rested his gaze on the crumbling chicken coop. "What's that thing?"

Faith's smile was wry. "A monument to my past."

"Come again?"

"It's a chicken coop. I used to have to feed them when I was a kid. I hated the damn things."

"Ah. I see." He studied her speculatively. "I know this is none of my business," he said unexpectedly, "but you might want to keep a tighter leash on Jessie."

Thinking of the quiet girl who spent most of her life locked in her room with her violin, Faith raised her eyebrows. "Why? Is there some kind of problem?"

"I'm not sure. But I picked her up last night a couple miles down the road. It was past eleven o'clock, and she was walking home from town."

She felt the blood drain from her face. "She was walking? That late at night?"

"It seems she'd had some kind of disagreement with her date, and she walked out on him."

"Good Lord. I had no idea. When I got home last night, she was here and Davy Hunter was with her. I just thought... oh, my."

"Yes. Apparently she and her date were at a party and things started to get a little intense. She didn't like what was going on, so she left. She's lucky I was the one who came along. At that time of night, on a deserted country road, a young girl like Jessie's just asking for trouble."

"That little shit. Wait until I get my hands on him. He should have insisted on driving her home."

"She may have been safer walking. Depending on the kid,

and what kind of illicit substances he may have ingested. What's his name?"

"Cooper Gates."

Something flickered in his eyes. "Yikes," he said.

"You know him," Faith said. "Did I make a mistake, letting her go out with him?"

He stretched his legs, dug his heels into the dirt beside Linda's whitewall tire. "Coop's not a bad kid," he said. "He's like a lot of teenage boys. High-spirited, and pumped up with testosterone. It's why football's so good for them. They get to work off some of that energy on the field instead of taking it out caveman style on the girls that flock around them." He hesitated, then said, "Jessie was pretty shook up when she saw your Saab crumpled like an old tissue. That's how she ended up with Hunter. I handed her over to him at the accident scene."

"That poor kid. No wonder she was so wound up when I got home."

"When she recognized your Saab, she jumped out of the car before I could even come to a stop. I had to park on the shoulder and go back to find her."

"Thank you," Faith said. "Thank you for taking care of her."

"Hey, I have a little girl of my own. That's sacred territory."

"Skip…can I ask you a question?"

"Shoot."

"Is the heroin problem really as bad in the schools as people are telling me?"

He sighed and ran his hands over his chiseled face. "Do I really have to answer that question?"

"Isn't there something you can do? My God, they're just kids. Babies."

"Short of frisking every one of them when they walk in the door each morning? Not really. Some schools have actually tried that, but this is the age of political correctness, the age when you have to be careful not to offend anyone. Some kid comes home crying to his parents that you violated his civil rights by going through his backpack and confiscating a couple of joints, they'll slap a lawsuit on you so fast your head will spin. Besides—" he shifted position again, crossed his legs "—if the kids aren't getting the drugs at school, they'll find them on the street instead. There's no way you can whitewash the whole town."

"It's changed so much from when I went to school here. Poor Jessie."

From somewhere in the dusty interior of the barn, a peal of delighted laughter rolled free. A bittersweet sadness washed over Lombardi's face. "You can't know," he said, "how it does my heart good to hear that. There wasn't any laughter for such a long time."

"Jessie told me your daughter's been ill."

"She has a rare form of leukemia. We've been battling it for two years."

"I'm so sorry. I've been there. My husband died of leukemia eighteen months ago."

"Then you understand how agonizing it is when nothing works."

Remembering Ben's gradual downhill slide, she said, "I understand. Believe me. But Alyssa doesn't look sick. She's a little thin, but her cheeks are full of healthy color."

"Yes. I've come to believe in miracles. She has a wonderful oncologist in Boston. Dr. Perlman. He started her out on the standard treatment, and for a while, it worked. Then it stopped working. Everything they tried stopped working. Perlman said that sometimes it happens that way, and nobody knows why. Last summer, we almost lost her."

"Oh, God." Losing her husband had been a nightmare. She couldn't even begin to imagine the pain of losing a child.

"I've never been so scared in my life. Not even when my wife died. You can't know what it's like, watching your child grow weaker and weaker, watching her slip away right in front of your eyes, and there's nothing you can do to help her. To save her." He paused, shook his head. "Do you have kids?"

"No."

"As a parent, you're supposed to be omnipotent. No matter what hurts, you're supposed to be able to kiss it away and make it all better. When you can't do that, you feel useless. You want to lash out at somebody, something, find a scapegoat, a place to lay the blame for your own inadequacy."

Something stirred inside her, deep at the core. Until he put it into words, she hadn't recognized how deeply she'd been affected by her inability to prevent Ben's death. Was it possible that she'd gone off the deep end not because of grief, but because she'd been incapable of handling the brutal glimpse she'd been given of her own impotence? She, who had so highly prized control, had been rendered powerless. Maybe Ben's death had been the universe's way of showing her who was really in charge.

Fiercely, Lombardi said, "I'd do anything for that kid. Anything! Dr. Perlman told me about these experimental treatments they were doing in Mexico, using drugs that aren't FDA approved. They only take on the most hopeless cases, the cases that aren't responding to conventional treatment. He said they'd been having amazing results. So I took my daughter to Mexico. She was so weak, she could barely walk. We spent two weeks there. The treatments were hell on both of us, but the end result—well, you can see for yourself."

Another giggle floated from the recesses of the barn. "Are you telling me that she's cured?"

"Not cured. But she's in remission. We've made two more trips to Mexico since that first one. The treatments are renewed every six months. And she still goes to Boston twice a month to visit Perlman. He's encouraged by her progress. None of us knows how long the remission will last. She could live for another sixty years, or she could catch some virus and die next week. But as long as she's alive, I'm determined that she'll have a normal childhood. I intend to spoil her rotten. If she wants to ride horses, then by God, she'll ride horses. If she wants them dyed green with pink polka dots, I'll find a way to do it. I might not have the final say in what happens to her. That's in the hands of somebody a little more powerful than me. But whatever I can manage while she's still with us, I intend to do. No matter what the cost."

Faith blinked back tears as Alyssa and Linda emerged from the barn, hand in hand, arms swinging gaily between them, Buddy trotting cheerfully alongside. "Daddy!" the little girl shouted. "There's enough room for three horses! One for each of us!"

"That's wonderful!" he shouted back. Then, in a soft aside to Faith, he said wearily, resignedly, "I suppose this means I'm going to have to learn to ride."

"All right," Becca said when they were settled cross-legged on the bottom bunk with the door barricaded against her pesky little sister Heather, who slept in the top bunk and always tried to listen in on their private conversations. "What's going on? You sounded hysterical on the phone. What happened last night?"

Ever since Jessie'd seen Faith's car crumpled like a piece of aluminum foil in the ditch, she'd had trouble breathing. If Chief Savage hadn't spent the night, she wouldn't have slept at all. There was something about him that comforted her. He was big and solid and she felt safe when he was around. And he was nuts about Faith. It was obvious, even if Faith did pretend not to notice. She knew he'd do everything in his power to keep them both safe from harm.

"You have to promise," she told Becca. "You have to promise that what I tell you won't go beyond this room. You're my best friend, and I don't know who else to tell. Promise me, Bec?"

Becca's wide, freckled face took on a somber cast. "I swear on my life," she said.

"There's something going on. Something bad. I think it has to do with drugs. Coop's dealing, Bec. Right out of the trunk of his car."

Becca looked skeptical. "Are you sure?"

"I saw it with my own eyes. Some kind of powder in little plastic envelopes. It could be coke. Maybe heroin. I saw him selling it to Zak Morrissey. When he found out I'd seen, he threatened to hurt me if I told anyone."

"Oh, man. I told you Coop was bad news."

"That's not all." She took a deep breath. "He said something about my mom. About how he hoped I didn't have a big mouth like she did. God, Bec, I hope I'm wrong, but I think somebody murdered my mother. And I think Coop was involved."

"Come on, Jess, that's crazy talk."

"That's what I tried to convince myself. Until Faith drove off the road last night. She totaled her car, but she's okay. Thank God."

"I heard about her accident. My mom and dad were talking about it."

"Except that it wasn't an accident."

Becca's blond eyebrows went sky-high. "What do you mean?"

"This morning, I heard her talking to Newt Rollins about it. Mr. Rollins was trying to convince her to leave town. He told her she should go away until the police find out who drove her off the road. Somebody tried to kill her, Bec. What if somebody drove my mom off the road, too? Maybe that's how she ended up in the river."

"But your mom wasn't mixed up with drugs. Why would they kill her?"

"She was a newspaper reporter. She was always sniffing around, looking for a story. I think somebody killed her because she knew something."

"Holy crap," Becca said. "What are you going to do?"

"I'm not sure yet. I have to talk to Ahmed first. He knows something. He told me that Coop was mixed up in something bad, but he didn't tell me what. He's afraid. But I have to get it out of him somehow."

"I think you should go to the police."

"I think the police already know. They just don't know

who's to blame or what to do about it. Ty Savage stayed at our house last night. He said it was because Faith had a concussion and he was supposed to watch her, but that's not the real reason. It was so he could protect us."

Becca chewed on her lip while she thought it through. "Do you trust him?"

"Absolutely."

"Then talk to him, Jess. This is serious stuff. You're only fifteen years old. There isn't a thing you can do about any of it. Tell him what you know, and let him do his job."

"But I don't know anything! Not without talking to Ahmed. He's at work today. He always works on Saturday. Will you come with me to talk to him?"

"My mom would kill me if she knew I was getting mixed up in something like this."

Faith's warning rang in her ears, and she deliberately blocked it out. *No running the streets alone.* "Never mind, then," she said. "I don't want to get you in trouble. I'll go by myself."

"I don't think so. You're my best friend, and whither thou goest, I'm not far behind."

They took the bikes, Jessie on Becca's purple mountain bike, Becca on her brother Kenny's silver-and-black eighteen-speed racer. It was just a short hop downtown, where kids were lined up outside the Strand for the afternoon matinee. Hard to believe it had been less than twenty-four hours since she'd sat in the packed movie house, elated because she was on a date with the larger-than-life Cooper Gates. Today, some of the boys who lingered on the sidewalk smoking forbidden cigarettes tossed out catcalls and insults because she and Becca were riding bicycles instead of driving cars. Jessie ignored them, her mission too important to waste time squabbling with morons. They'd get their comeuppance one of these days. In the meantime, they were too insignificant to even acknowledge.

When they entered Halaal Variety, the bell over the door

rang. Sahra Hassan, Ahmed's mother, looked up from behind the counter. Cool and elegant as always, she said in her distinctive, soft voice, "Good afternoon, girls. Jessie, I'm so glad to see you. How is Faith? I heard about her accident."

"She's okay. I guess she has a mild concussion, but she seems fine today." Thinking of her mother, she said, "It could have been so much worse."

"Yes," Sahra said, and Jessie knew the woman had followed her train of thought. "It could have."

"We're looking for Ahmed," Jessie said, glancing quickly around the store. She didn't see him anywhere. "Is he around?"

"Ah. I'm sorry that I must disappoint you. Ahmed has gone out of town with his father. He'll be back late tonight." Sahra studied her with eyes that seemed to bore all the way into her soul. "Is there anything I can help you with?"

"No," Jessie said. "It's not that important. I can talk to him tomorrow."

"Jessie? May I ask you a question?"

Her heart rate accelerated. "Of course," she said. "What?"

"You and Ahmed are friends. You see him every day at school. Has he seemed troubled lately?"

Jessie's mouth went dry. She couldn't lie to Ahmed's mother. She was a terrible liar, and even if she'd been the queen of prevarication, the way Sahra was looking at her, she couldn't have pulled it off. "He hasn't been himself lately," she said.

"So it isn't my imagination?"

Jessie shook her head. "It's not."

"And you, Jessie. Has he told you what troubles him?"

"No. He hasn't." It was the truth. She might suspect she knew what bothered him, or at least some of it, but he hadn't said anything to her. Nothing beyond his warning that she should stay away from Cooper Gates because he was mixed up in something unsavory.

If she'd listened to Ahmed in the first place, she wouldn't

be in this mess right now. Because she felt incredibly guilty, as though it were all her fault, she found herself making promises to his mother. "I'll talk to him. It's probably nothing. But I'll see what I can find out."

"Thank you," Sahra Hassan said. "Will you do one more favor for me? Will you give Faith a message?"

"Of course."

Sahra's eyes, like dark pools, held an emotion Jessie couldn't decipher. "Tell her to be careful," the Somali woman said.

Nineteen

Ty showed up at precisely five-thirty, looking handsome in a snowy white dress shirt, a charcoal tweed suit coat, and a charcoal-and-blue striped necktie. Everything Faith thought she knew about Ty Savage told her he should have appeared uncomfortable and overdressed, for he wasn't a jacket-and-tie kind of man. Yet he wore the semiformal attire with the same casual flair he brought to flannel and denim. The suit coat fit as though it had been designed for him, and the end result was breathtaking.

She had no idea what this evening would bring. But like him, she'd acknowledged its importance by taking pains with her appearance. She'd tamed her wild mop of curls into a classic upsweep that left the nape of her neck bare, giving her a wispy, Audrey Hepburn look. And then she'd done something that was so out of character she didn't dare to examine her motives.

She'd raided Chelsea's closet.

She hadn't really expected to find anything suitable, but nothing she'd brought with her seemed appropriate. They'd always been able to fit into each other's clothes, and she was desperate. So, praying that the gods would forgive her, she did the unthinkable and ransacked the closet of a dead woman.

Chelsea's exquisite and expensive taste surprised her. After thumbing through a rack full of lovely designer outfits, she finally settled on a cream-colored silk pantsuit with a vaguely Asian flavor. The slender pants were a perfect fit, and the button-front top flowed, caftan-style, nearly to her knees, its mandarin collar a tasteful accompaniment to her upswept hairdo. As long as she'd already committed the sin of raiding the closet, she figured she might as well go for broke, so she'd finished off with a quick brush of color to her cheeks, a touch of cherry-red lip gloss and a hint of eye shadow. She knew somehow that Chelsea, who'd easily shared her clothes and her cosmetics when they were teenagers, wouldn't have minded. As a matter of fact, somewhere out there, her cousin was probably cheering and whistling and applauding her.

It had been so long since she'd dressed for a man. After Ben got sick, she'd been too busy. After he died, there'd been no reason. But tonight, she'd taken that terrifying first step out of the prison cell she'd built around herself the day her husband died. Tonight she'd dressed with just one goal in mind: to please Ty Savage. Not provocatively, for that wasn't her style. She was more the cool, elegant type. Ben had always told her that her innate elegance was her most attractive feature, that it was what had drawn him to her in the first place as she sat in his classroom, a quiet island of cool grace amid a swarm of flashy, scantily dressed college coeds.

Tonight, she didn't feel quite that cool. Her emotions were chaotic, confused. Last night, she'd come close to dying. Then Ty had taken her in his arms and kissed her as though he were afraid she might disappear forever, and his kiss had left her breathless and stunned. He'd driven every thought from her mind but one: She was amazingly, gloriously alive. And she wanted him with a ferocity that terrified her.

He'd slept in her bed last night. She'd been so exhausted that she'd fallen asleep the instant her head touched the pillow. Aided by a powerful hit to the head, she'd slept hard and deep. She had no memory of another body lying beside her in the narrow twin bed. When she woke, he was already up, frying bacon and eggs in a skillet. There was no evidence that he'd even been there. Except that when she cradled the spare pillow to her chest and buried her face in it, she could smell him on it. And his scent, there amid her rumpled bedding in the early-morning light, had been a potent aphrodisiac.

She wasn't the same woman, numbed by loss and fear, who'd driven into Serenity a week ago, a week that now seemed like years. That woman was undergoing a rapid metamorphosis as light and color and feeling returned to her life. The old Faith Pelletier, the woman who'd gone to pieces when her husband died because it was easier than facing the truth, had disappeared forever. Tonight, she intended to explore the possibilities open to the new Faith.

On the way to Ty's house, they swung by Becca's to pick up Jessie. Faith got out to let the girl into the back seat of the pickup. As Jessie passed her, those soft gray eyes took Faith in from head to foot, missing nothing. She had to have recognized the outfit from her mother's closet, but Jessie said nothing, simply fixed Faith with a long, penetrating stare and then climbed into the truck.

At the Savage house, Buck was cooking. Butter crackled and spit in a frying pan that simmered over low heat. The kitchen counter was littered with fresh produce, peppers and mushrooms and cloves of garlic. He'd lined up a half-dozen cans of tomato sauce beside the can opener and pulled as many jars of spice from the rack above the stove. A fat onion squatted on the cutting board, awaiting Buck's attention.

In his hand, Buck held a carving knife big enough to dismember a rhinoceros. He raised it to eye level and studied it. Glanced back at the onion, then returned his attention to the knife.

Faith and Ty exchanged glances. Ty cleared his throat and said, "What you up to, Dad?"

His father wheeled around, his expression puzzled, as though he wasn't quite sure what he was supposed to do with the knife, wasn't quite sure how it had ended up in his hand. "What's it look like I'm doing?" he said, without much conviction. Then he saw Faith, and his entire face lit up. "Evening, Meredith," he said. "You're looking lovely tonight."

She felt a tiny jolt of shock that quickly turned to pain when she recognized the distress on Ty's face. Returning his father's smile, she said, "Why, thank you, Buck. You're looking rather handsome yourself. Is that spaghetti sauce you're making?"

"Yep. Soon as I cut up this honker of an onion." He turned back to the cutting board, looked again at the carving knife, turned it over in his hands a couple of times. Then he set it down—Ty's relief was so palpable, she could actually feel it—picked up the onion, and began prying at its skin.

The knife lay on the counter, gleaming in the light from the overhead fluorescent. Buck fiddled with the onion's stubborn outer layer for a while before he gave up, picked the knife back up and poked at the onion with the tip of its slender, razor-sharp blade.

Faith held her breath, not sure what to do. Buck was an accident about to happen, and it was terrifying to watch. He seemed to have totally forgotten how to use a knife. The blade he was mismanaging looked lethal, and the way he was poking and prodding at that onion, it was only a matter of time before the blade slipped and sliced off one of his fingers.

Indecision froze her in place. Should she step forward and help him? He wasn't her father, and it wasn't her place. Ty might not appreciate the interference. But she couldn't allow Buck to injure himself. She shot Ty a quick glance. He stood rigid beside her, his own fear and agitation clearly reflected in his eyes. Faith opened her mouth to speak, but before she could get the words out, Jessie brushed past her to stand at Buck's elbow.

"Let me help you with that, Mr. Savage," she said, smoothly removing the knife from his hand. "I love to cook."

Buck turned to stare at her, and Faith's pent-up breath left her lungs in a huge rush. "I'm Jessie," the girl said to Buck, "in case you didn't know."

"I know who you are. Pretty hard not to know in a town this small."

"This knife's pretty big," she said, casually returning it to the wooden rack on the counter and selecting a more appropriate substitute. "We don't want to mutilate the poor onion, just chop it. A friend of mine taught me a neat trick. Watch." As oxygen reentered Faith's lungs, Jessie cut off the ends of the onion and peeled away the skin, then swept the leavings into the trash.

"You just cut it crosswise—" Jessie held the onion steady with one hand, while with the other she made several deep cuts with the knife. She swiveled the onion and repeated the motion, cutting this time directly across the first set of cuts. "Then you turn it, like this—" she rolled the onion onto its side "—and you slice. See how easy it is?" With the onion on its side, she sliced all the way through, top to bottom, working her way from left to right. When she was done, she had a huge pile of onion that she'd expended almost no effort to chop.

"That's pretty amazing, young lady," Buck said. "I can't wait to see what you can do with a green pepper."

"Well, you see, first you have to wash them—" She shot a glance at Faith, who flashed her a relieved smile. Jessie returned it, faintly, but at least it was a smile. "Don't worry about us," she said to Faith. "We'll be fine. Won't we, Mr. Savage?"

He was at the sink, diligently washing the peppers and mushrooms. "Of course we will. You two kids go on and have a good time." He turned toward them, a fistful of dripping wet mushrooms in his hand. Waggling his eyebrows at Faith, he said, "Don't do anything I wouldn't do."

Once they were in the truck, Ty started up the engine and let out a harsh, ragged breath. "What the hell am I going to do with him?" he said. "I'm afraid he's a danger to himself. Did you see the way he was handling that knife? Christ Jesus. And he thought you were your mother. I had no idea it'd gone this far." He turned his head and studied her. "Thanks for just rolling with it."

"If there's one thing I've learned to do, it's roll with it." She took a breath. "Look, Ty, I don't want to stick my nose in your family business, but I really think your father should have a checkup. When was the last time he had a physical?"

"Probably never."

"Somebody needs to take him by the hand and lead him to a doctor, even if he kicks and screams and drags his feet the entire way."

"Yeah?" His smile was faint, and tinged with resignation. "Who's going to do it? You, me and what army?"

"Maybe Jessie can convince him. He seemed to take to her right away."

Backing out of the driveway, he said, "That kid is amazing. There we were, two adults, both of us frozen in place, and she just stepped in and took over, so smoothly the old man never knew what hit him. Fifteen years old going on thirty-five."

"Jessie's had a lifetime of experience at being an adult. Back when Chelsea was drinking, there was a lot of role reversal going on. Jessie never had a snowball's chance in hell of having a normal childhood."

"It's a shame. But she seems to have come out of it relatively unscathed. At least as far as I can see."

"Sometimes they do," Faith said. "And sometimes…" Thinking of Chelsea, she trailed off without finishing her sentence. "So tell me," she said instead, "how'd you manage to get Jessie and Buck together for the evening without anybody squawking?"

His grin was devilish. "Easy," he said. "I told her she'd be baby-sitting him, and I told him he'd be baby-sitting her."

"What a brilliant plan."

"I thought so. They'll watch out for each other, neither one is home alone, and Pete'll be driving by every half hour to make sure the house is still standing."

"Which leaves us with…"

He checked his watch. "A good five hours before they send out the bloodhounds." Stopping for a red light, he glanced over at her. "I made dinner reservations at this rustic old inn a few miles west of here. There's a mill pond and an old waterwheel and ducks swimming around. The food's out of this world. I think you'll like it."

Downtown Serenity was deserted. The town really did roll up its sidewalks at the end of every day. The only businesses left open on Water Street at six o'clock on a Saturday evening were the Strand Theater and Halaal Variety. Gazing blindly at the Somali convenience store as they drove past, Faith said distractedly, "I have to talk with Jessie first thing tomorrow. I found out this afternoon that Coop didn't bring her home. Skip Lombardi told me he picked her up last night on Bald Mountain Road. She was walking home from town at eleven o'clock at night."

"I've already talked to her about it. This morning, before you got up. Davy told me about it last night—that's why he was there at the house with her. Lombardi was giving her a ride home and they came across the accident scene. Davy brought her home from there."

"I can't believe she'd do something that stupid. She's a smart girl."

"It's a small town, Faith. She feels safe here."

"At eleven o'clock at night on a backcountry road? I hope you clarified that for her."

"Don't worry. She won't be pulling anything like that again. But you probably should let her know how you feel about it. Reinforce what I already told her."

"Believe me, I intend to. By the time I'm done, she'll probably think I'm the queen of bitches, but her safety has to come first." Faith sighed. "I'm walking such a fine line with Jessie. I don't want to be the enemy, especially now that we're starting to build some kind of relationship. I'll probably knock it right back down like a house of cards. But that kind of behavior isn't safe under the best of circumstances. And with all the craziness that's gone on around here lately, walking alone at night like that could be deadly."

"Well, she's safe enough tonight. Nobody'll bother her at Dad's house."

"Let's hope so." They drove past the town sandpit, where three orange snowplows, put out to pasture until the return of winter, were parked in a row. "Did you have any luck trying to find out who was playing bumper cars with me last night?"

He squared his jaw. "I thought we agreed not to talk about any of that stuff tonight."

"Last night shook me up more than I want to admit. Humor me, Ty. Please."

"We didn't get anywhere with it," he said. "It appears to be a phantom vehicle. I had every one of my officers looking for it, but nobody turned up anything. It was that kind of day."

"Bad day?"

"Nothing went right. I spent the whole damn day spinning my wheels. I left a message for Lemoine, hoping he might have something back from the lab. But when I left for the day, he still hadn't called back."

"Does this mean you're finally coming around? You finally believe that somebody killed Chelsea?"

Grimly, he said, "I believe that somebody tried to kill you last night. I know that your cousin died under mysterious circumstances just one week ago. I know you've been asking too many questions of too many people, prying into matters that aren't your business, just like Chelsea was doing before she died. I don't believe in coincidence." His eyes still on the road, he tapped his fingertips on the steering wheel. "Which is why I tried to talk to Davy Hunter again, but he wasn't home. I left a note on his door this morning. The last time René cruised Bald Mountain Road this afternoon, he swung by Hunter's to check. Nobody was home, and the note was still on the door. Christ only knows where he went." Ty's mouth thinned. "Probably to Massachusetts on a drug run."

"I'm not so sure."

He glanced at her from the corner of his eye. "You know something I don't?"

"Not really. It's just a feeling. And before you remind me that you're a cop and you deal with facts instead of intuition, hear me out. Last night, after he pulled me from the car, I asked him if he'd killed Chelsea. It's all sort of vague. That airbag hit me pretty hard, and I was still seeing stars. But he said something to me, and every time I think about it, I get shivers up and down my spine. He told me he's not the bad guy here. It was something about the way he said it that made me believe him. That, and the hurt I saw on his face when he knew I thought he'd been the one to drive me off the road. He couldn't believe I'd think so little of him. It would be hard to fake that kind of response."

"Hard, maybe, but not impossible. And maybe his definition of *bad guy* doesn't quite match yours."

She gnawed on her lower lip. "Maybe. But I also seem to remember hearing it said that a man's supposed to be innocent until proven guilty."

"Technically, yes. But try working in law enforcement for a while and then tell me how you feel about that particular topic." He was silent for a time before he said, "How'd you happen to talk to Skip Lombardi?"

"He and Linda came out to look at the house today. They're very interested. They're planning to make a formal offer on Monday."

He raised his eyebrows and said, "I'll be damned."

"They brought his little girl with them. Alyssa. She's so sweet, Ty. It just breaks my heart when I think of everything that poor child has gone through. He's been taking her to Mexico for experimental treatments, the kind of treatments she can't get here in the U.S. It seems to be helping. Skip says her leukemia's in remission. You should see her. She doesn't look sick at all. It's a disgrace, the way our health care system treats people. Denying treatment to sick people because the drugs that might help them aren't approved by the FDA. What are we supposed to do, give up and die because our own government is failing us?"

"Don't even get me started on that topic. The health care system in this country is a mess. Goddamn HMOs have taken over our lives. Pinheaded bureaucrats making medical decisions that should be made by doctors. Last year, my sister's gynecologist recommended that she have a hysterectomy. She'd been having female troubles because she was loaded with fibroids. Her damned HMO denied her because there was no evidence of malignancy and, under their guidelines, she wasn't old enough to qualify for a nonemergency hysterectomy. Jo went ahead and had the surgery anyway. She and Jack are still paying it off."

He slowed the truck, blinked for a left turn, waited for an approaching car to pass and then pulled into the crushed-rock parking area of the Mollyockett Inn. Killing the engine, he turned to her and said, "From this point forward, murder and mayhem are off the table. Agreed?"

With a soft smile, she said, "Agreed."

The inn was magnificent, an old Federal-style, three-story structure surrounded by acres of rolling green lawns, elegantly landscaped with flower beds, wild rosebushes and Japanese maples. The building's exterior was simple and unadorned, painted a soft yellow, with glossy black trim highlighting its massive twelve-over-twelve double-hung windows. A flagstone path led to the mill pond, where they stopped to watch a pair of mallards, babies in tow, waddle up onto the grass, hoping for a handout. The two-hundred-year-old mill wheel still turned, and the soft trickle of water was soothing. A hummingbird flitted among the bluebells that grew near the water's edge. Faith took a deep breath and said, "This place is wonderful. I remember it from when I was a kid. We used to drive by on the way to my grandmother's house. But we never stopped."

"Wait till you see the inside."

The dining room sported hand-hewn exposed beams, a polished pine floor and a massive fieldstone fireplace. Birch logs crackled on the hearth, and soft jazz spilled from invisible overhead speakers. The hostess seated them at an intimate booth tucked into a shadowy corner near the tiny dance floor. Faith slid across soft leather and leaned to sniff appreciatively at the apple-scented candle that flickered at the center of the table. The waitress took their drink orders, and then Ty excused himself. "I'll be right back," he said. "There's something I have to take care of."

He walked away with that distinctive smooth, confident gait that she so admired. Hers weren't the only pair of admiring female eyes following his progress across the room and into the reception area. Every woman in the room between the ages of twelve and ninety watched him with rapt interest. Tamping down a sharp little pang of jealousy, Faith deliberately turned her attention to the handful of couples on the dance floor.

She loved to dance. In college, she'd attended every event the small, private university held. With or without a date, it hadn't mattered, for it wasn't uncommon to see the college girls dancing with each other, or even by themselves. All that mattered was having a good time, cutting loose in an exuberant celebration of life and youth. Of course, slow dancing was a different matter altogether. For that, she'd required a man. Dear, easygoing Ben had tried to be accommodating because he knew how much it meant to her. But every time she'd managed to drag him out onto the dance floor, he'd looked like a man headed for the guillotine. He'd had two left feet and no sense of rhythm. Eventually, out of respect for his feelings, she'd stopped trying. It hadn't really mattered all that much. She was a settled, married woman and dancing was for kids. She'd found other ways to express herself, other ways of celebrating life that were more appropriate for a young faculty wife. But she'd never lost the urge to get up there on the dance floor and lose herself in the music.

The drinks arrived, a white wine for her, a Rolling Rock for Ty. He arrived right behind them. When he slid back into the booth across from her, his knee bumped hers. He left it there, a sizzling reminder that he was male and she was female and something hot and exciting and frightening was happening between them.

Deep breaths, she reminded herself. *Slow, deep breaths*.

He reached across the table, brushed a stray wisp of hair away from her forehead and examined the lump on her head. "The swelling's gone down," he said.

"Yes." She should have said something more eloquent, something that showed there was a brain inside her hard, unbreakable skull. She never found herself wordless, never ran out of things to say. But his long fingers, so gentle against her skin, left her unable to breathe, let alone think.

"Is the headache gone?"

"Yes." God help her, she sounded like a parrot with a monosyllabic vocabulary.

Those chocolate eyes studied her closely as his hand glided across her temple and down her cheek. "Last night," he said, his thumb brushing the corner of her mouth, "when Davy called me, I thought for sure you were dead. You can't begin to imagine how that made me feel."

The intensity that surrounded them was suddenly uncomfortable. "Hey," she said with false lightness, "I'm pretty close to invincible."

"You're not invincible. You're flesh and blood and bone. A little too fearless, a little too careless."

"I'm not careless," she said defensively, her heart thudding against her ribs because of what his touch was doing to her nervous system. "I was just driving home. I can't live my life inside a box."

Amazing to think that she'd referred to that old wreck of a house as home. Her home was in Manhattan, not in the house where she'd spent six heartbreaking years of adolescence. But old habits die hard, and truth was truth. She might have hated every minute she spent living there with the old tyrant, but Cyrus Logan had put a roof over her head. Technically, the old farmhouse was home.

He sought her hand, clenched in a hard fist on the tabletop. He laid his hand over it and gently uncurled her tightly clamped fingers. Bringing it up to his mouth, he placed a gentle kiss on each of her fingers, one by one. "Are you hungry?" he said.

Hungry? When she was shaking so hard she could barely speak? She'd probably never be able to eat again. "No," she said.

"Good. Then let's dance."

Maybe dancing would be easier. Dancing, after all, didn't require intelligent conversation. But the instant he took her in his arms, she recognized her mistake. It all came rushing back to her, the way she'd thrown herself at him, the stolen kisses under a star-studded sky, the thrill of his hands touching forbidden places. Her throat went dry. She should have taken a couple sips of that white wine before she left the table. Hell, she should have slugged down the whole glass.

God, he smelled good. Just the faint fragrance of some subtle, unrecognizable cologne, and beneath it the scent of warm, sexy man. He smelled like something she wanted to swallow alive. She was getting light-headed just from his nearness. This whole thing was just a smidgen over the top. She was thirty-six years old, not sixteen. Wasn't sex supposed to be a little less turbulent and a little more dignified at thirty-six?

Then again, who'd said anything about sex?

The music wasn't helping. Etta James, singing "I'd Rather Go Blind." Faith recognized the song because Ben had owned an extensive jazz and blues collection, and the sultry-voiced Etta had been one of his favorite artists. The hot, steamy blues number just screamed sex, and Faith was liquid and boneless in Ty Savage's arms, her breasts pressed up hard against that rock-solid chest. She laid her head on his shoulder and gave herself over to his lovely, lovely heat, and to his hands, those incredibly talented hands, that moved slowly up and down her back.

He lowered his head and brushed his cheek against hers. A shudder rippled through her. They were intertwined so tightly that when he swallowed, she felt the movement against her cheek.

"Faith," he said softly, so softly she could barely hear him over the music.

She wet her lips and said, "What?"

"We can end this torture right now if you want."

Yes. She could leave his arms right now, stumble back to the table, try to gather the scattered pieces of herself and glue them back into a coherent whole. Put their derailed agenda back on track. Dinner. A serious talk about their relationship. Or their non-relationship. Whatever the hell this thing was that had flared up out of nowhere and was devouring her from the inside out. "Of course," she said, surprised by her ability to form the words, equally surprised by the wave of disappointment that flattened her.

He caught her chin in his hand and raised her eyes to his. "In the pocket of my jacket," he said, "there's a key to one of the rooms upstairs. It's ours for the night. All you have to do is say the word." Something flickered in those beautiful dark eyes of his. "If the word's no," he added, "I won't be offended. Disappointed, yeah. But not offended."

Suddenly, it all made sense. His disappearance while she'd waited for their drink order. The way he'd arranged for Jessie to come to the house to stay with Buck. He'd planned this in advance, had set up this evening with the intention of seducing her. Breathless, she waited for the sensible woman inside her, the college professor, the bestselling author, the widow, to tell her that she hardly knew this man and couldn't afford the risk. That there was no chance for a future with him, and she'd only end up getting hurt.

But that inner voice remained stubbornly silent. She did know him, damn it, knew him in every way that mattered. Knew that he was a good man, an honest man, a man who would never deliberately hurt her. If there truly was no future in it, well, later on down the road she couldn't say that she hadn't known it in advance. If she accepted the risk, she'd be prepared to pay the price.

And there it was, right on schedule, the voice of her conscience. But it wasn't the voice she'd expected. Instead of the sensible Faith telling her to cut and run, it was Ben's voice that echoed inside her head. *Don't be a fool, Faith*, he said. *You know what you want. Go for it.*

Ty was still waiting for her answer. Patiently, but the rigid line of his shoulders told her that his patience came at a cost. "What will the waitress think," she said with forced lightness, "if we just disappear without ordering dinner?"

His voice was soft and husky. "Do you really care?"

And to her utter amazement, Faith Pelletier, who wasn't into taking chances, who'd probably never taken a chance in her life, said, "Not particularly."

"Beat you again," Buck said cheerfully. "That's three for three in my favor. Ready to call it a day, Miss Muffet?"

Jessie'd been ready to call it a day after the first round, when Buck's red checkers had swept her black pieces right off the board. But he'd seemed to be really into it, and Jessie didn't want to disappoint him. Chief Savage—she kept forgetting, he'd asked her to call him Ty—had explained to her that his dad was having some memory problems and that he was a bit nervous about leaving him alone. Except for the episode with the knife, and when he'd called Faith by the wrong name, Buck had seemed fine to Jessie. He certainly hadn't forgotten how to play checkers. The man was unbeatable.

Besides, she didn't really mind keeping him company. There was something warm and grandfatherly about him. Not like her own grandfather, who'd been mean and unpredictable. When she was a little girl, she'd been terrified of Cyrus Logan, with his gruff, whiskey-drinker's voice and that thick black beard. He'd reminded her of Popeye's nemesis, Bluto.

Compared to him, Buck Savage was a marshmallow.

"Can we turn on the TV?" she said. If she was lucky, maybe MTV would be running an episode of *Real World* or *Road Rules*.

"Fine with me. My old bones are getting tired. Mind if I turn in?"

"I don't mind." He probably wouldn't want to watch MTV anyway.

"If you need anything," he said, "my bedroom's just down the hall."

She settled in a comfy chair with the remote and began channel surfing. It was still early, and it would probably be a while before Faith and Ty came back. If they came back. There was definitely something heavy going on between those two. Jessie's eyes had nearly popped out of her head when she saw Faith earlier tonight, dressed in one of Chelsea's most elegant outfits, with her hair up and her face painted on. She was Hot-with-a-capital-H. And the way Ty had been looking at her…oh, man. He obviously had it bad.

Jessie hadn't yet decided whether that was a positive or a negative thing. It looked as though she and Faith were joined at the hip for the foreseeable future. Not that she minded. She missed her mom so bad she ached with it, but if she'd ever been given the choice of a mother, Faith would have come in second. There was just one thing that worried her. If Faith and Ty hooked up, where would that leave her?

Her life was such a muddled mess. Finding out the truth about Coop, that he was a total jerk and a criminal, had been a real kick in the teeth. She'd worshiped him from afar for so long. Half the town worshiped him. Mister football hero. If they only knew the truth. God, she'd been such a fool to think he was worth her time. Last night had been totally humiliating.

She heard a car coming down the street. It slowed, and the headlights made a wide sweep of the living room as the car turned into the driveway. It couldn't be Faith and Ty coming back, not yet. Not unless their idea of a hot date was burgers and shakes at Mickey D's and a half hour making out at lover's lane. The idea of the two of them steaming up the windows of his truck seemed absurd. They were so old. Did people really have sex after thirty? She couldn't imagine it, but she knew her mom had slept with a lot of men. Chelsea hadn't exactly been secretive about her love life. So if she did it, maybe a lot of older people did. Jessie knew that they'd kissed the other night, out under the stars, after they'd come back from the Dairy Queen. Faith had come into the house all flustered, her hair and her eyes wild, her lips swollen and a stunned expression on her face. It was pretty obvious that something had happened between them.

Outside, the car that sat idling in the driveway shut off. Jessie got up and peered out the window, but it was too dark to identify the vehicle. Footsteps sounded on the back steps, and then whoever it was knocked on the door. Jessie hesitated, glancing in the direction of Buck's room, but he was already snoring like Grampa used to do when he'd had too much to drink. It was up to her to deal with it. The knocking came again, louder this time, and Jessie set down the remote and went to answer the door.

When she opened it, she wasn't sure which of them was more surprised. Davy Hunter had his fist raised, ready to strike the solid wooden door a third time. "Jessie," he said, lowering his arm. "What are you doing here?"

"I'm supposed to be baby-sitting Mr. Savage. But I have this funny feeling he thinks he's baby-sitting me."

His smile was warm and easy. They were comfortable together because they'd been part of each other's lives since she was a baby. He was the closest thing she'd ever had to a father. "Is Tyrone home?" he said.

She shook her head. "He's out for the evening. With Faith. On a date. That's why I'm here. Do you want to come in? Mr. Savage and I made a sensational spaghetti sauce. I could heat you up a plate of spaghetti."

The smile remained, but his eyes looked troubled. "No, thanks, Skeeter," he said. "I've had a long day. I'm dead on my feet. Can I take a rain check?"

"Of course. You can always take a rain check. You know that."

"You behaving yourself?" he said, blue eyes boring deep into hers. "Staying out of trouble?"

What was he asking? She always stayed out of trouble. He knew that. Was it possible he knew about Coop? Had her humiliation spread that far? "Of course I'm behaving," she said.

"Good. Listen, when Ty comes in, tell him I got his note and we need to talk. If he wants to call me tonight, I'll be up for another hour or so. If I don't hear from him tonight, I'll catch up to him tomorrow."

He turned to walk away, and she felt a pain inside that was so strong it nearly doubled her over. "Davy!" she said.

He stopped, turned. "Yeah?"

His hair was all scraggly and he hadn't shaved in weeks. His clothes were threadbare, like the clothes of a homeless person. But he was family in a way that nobody else would ever be, and the love she felt for him was fierce and genuine.

He recognized the look on her face, took two steps back toward her, and she threw herself into the warm, safe haven of his arms. He hugged her back, patting her shoulder awkwardly with one hand. "It'll be okay, sweetheart," he said. "We'll get through this."

But she wasn't at all sure that she would. Her mom had been dead for a week, and she hadn't even cried yet, hadn't shed a single tear. Now, her broken heart cracked wide open as she stood here on Buck Savage's back steps. While he held her close and murmured soft words of comfort, Jessie Logan spilled out her grief in Davy Hunter's arms.

Twenty

A single squat candle burning in an amber-colored glass threw indistinct shadows into every corner of the room. Ty tossed his jacket across the foot of the antique four-poster bed and pulled off his necktie. Across the room, Faith discreetly checked her reflection in the mirror, smoothing a strand of hair away from her forehead and frowning at the wrinkles that were gradually embedding themselves in the pale flesh above her brow. *Your hands will not tremble*, she silently reprimanded her reflection. *Your hands will not tremble!*

On the bureau in front of the mirror sat a hand-painted wooden music box designed to look like a miniature carousel. Faith picked it up and admired it from all angles. She carefully wound the crank, and a tinny rendition of a Strauss waltz began to play as the tiny wooden horses went round and round. Ty came up behind her and slipped his arms around her, and she set down the music box and twined her arms around his. Leaning back against the solid wall of his chest, she met his eyes in the mirror. "Hi," she said softly.

"Hi."

That bothersome strand of hair had fallen once again from her tightly coiled upsweep. While they both watched, he reached up and smoothed it away from her face. His hand lingered, and he brushed his knuckles against her cheek. Near her ear, in a husky voice, he said, "Faith."

Breathless, she said, "Yes?"

Instead of answering, he fumbled with her hairpins, his big hands awkward as he pulled them out and tossed them on the bureau. Combing his fingers through the hair that tumbled loose around her shoulders, he said, "That's one hell of a lot better." He drew the heavy fall of hair aside and with exquisite gentleness, placed a whisper-soft kiss against the nape of her neck.

"*Oh,*" she breathed, unable to say more as he continued his onslaught of delicate, feathery kisses. She watched in the mirror as he kissed her neck, her jaw, her shoulder.

While she watched, mesmerized, his hands glided northward, rough and raspy against cream-colored silk. They skimmed her breasts, and tiny barbs of pleasure needled through her. Faith threw her head back against his shoulder, still watching as with agonizingly slow deliberation, he unbuttoned the silk blouse. One. Button. At. A. Time.

Oh, God.

The blouse fluttered open, slid from her shoulders and fell to the floor, and she was left standing there dressed only in Chelsea's narrow-legged pants and a wispy, barely-there sheer lace bra. It left nothing to the imagination, and he let out a hard, sharp breath. "Jesus," he said. "You are so damn beautiful."

She couldn't see it. All she saw was a woman who was railthin. Beneath those magic hands that stroked her bare midriff so delightfully, she could see the outline of her ribs. Could count every last one of them. She'd lost about twelve pounds after Ben died, and no matter how hard she tried, she hadn't been able to put those pounds back on.

But Ty didn't seem to notice that she looked like a poster child for the walking dead. His breath hot on the back of her neck, he groped at the clasp to her lace bra. It sprang loose and he peeled it off. Dropped it on the floor. Their eyes met in the mirror, brown gazing intently into blue, as he slipped his arms back around her waist. "I've dreamed about you," he said. "But you're so much more beautiful than my imagination painted you."

In spite of her reservations about her body, there was something incredibly erotic about their mirrored reflection, something incredibly exciting about his arms encircling her, his hands splayed on her abdomen. The candlelight concealed a multitude of sins, and it had turned her skin a burnished gold. Her breasts were firm and high, the nipples dusky in the hazy light. Her belly was flat, her hips narrow. All things considered, she could have looked a lot worse.

Then he moved his hands up to cup her breasts and she forgot everything else. Enthralled, she watched in the mirror as he lifted and shaped and stroked and—oh, God!—it was the most incredible sensation, those marvelous hands of his, rough against her sensitive skin, sending wave after wave of pleasure coursing through her. Faith closed her eyes, drew in a ragged breath and made a soft, strangled sound deep in her throat, praying that this moment would go on forever.

"Feel good?"

Her eyes fluttered open. He was watching her face intently. "Do you have to ask?" she said.

With a soft laugh, he turned her in his arms. Burying his face in her hair, he inhaled her scent. "Christ, Faith," he said brokenly, "we have so damn many years to make up for."

"It doesn't matter," she murmured against the warm flesh of his throat. "We're not the same people we were at eighteen. We're so much more."

"You mean we're smarter?" He lifted her chin and ran his mouth down the long column of her neck.

Oh, yes. "And stronger," she said breathlessly, resting her hands on his shoulders.

His mouth reached the dark cleft between her breasts. "You make me feel so damn good," he said against her skin. "You always did. I've missed that. I never realized how much I missed it until you came back." His tongue climbed a heated trail along the curve of her breast, and anticipation tangled her breath in her throat. He reached the sensitive peak and lingered there, his tongue teasing her with wet, lazy strokes.

A billion nerve endings came to screaming life inside her. She clutched at his shoulders, not sure she could continue to stand on her own. He closed his mouth over her breast and furthered his sweet torture. Her fingers tangled in his hair, hands opening and closing of their own volition, tugging and knotting and urging him on.

He paused for breath, then resumed his torment on her other breast. Faith closed her eyes and swayed dangerously, clutching frantically at his shirt so she wouldn't fall flat on her ass. "Bed," she gasped. If she didn't lie down soon, she was going to fly apart into a million pieces.

He was a big man, and she weighed far too little. Like Rhett carrying Scarlett up that staircase, Ty scooped her up as though she weighed nothing at all. They fell across the bed, legs dangling over the side. Chest heaving, he paused to study her face. Then he kissed her, a hot, openmouthed kiss that held nothing back. Faith groaned as their tongues moved together in a mating dance that shot waves of desire directly to her pelvis, pressed snugly against his, leaving her absolutely no doubt about the state of his arousal. Dizzy and reeling, barely able to remember her own name, she tugged at his shirt buttons, managed somehow to free them. She tore off his shirt and tossed it, freeing all that sleek, hard flesh to her touch.

He broke the kiss. Sticky skin to sticky skin, breathing hard, she lay beneath his heavy weight, hands skimming his bare back, breasts crushed against that wonderful, rock-hard chest. "I want you," she said breathlessly. "Inside me. Right now."

"Oh, yeah." He scrambled to his feet and unbuckled his belt. She peeled off the borrowed pants and the wispy scrap of lace that passed for undies. Lying there on the bed, she watched as he stripped off the rest of his clothes and stood before her, gloriously naked, impressively erect.

He took her breath away. Hard and sleek and sculpted, exquisite in his nakedness, inarguably male, inarguably hers. His shoulders were broad, his chest smooth and hairless, his belly flat and hard. His thighs were strong and his hips narrow. While she watched, he bent and rummaged in the pile of clothing at his feet, emerging with a small foil packet. He tore it open and sheathed that impressive erection. She held out her arms and he returned to her, kneeling on the bed and settling between her open thighs. Eyes focused on hers, with a single thrust he smoothly filled her with his heat.

Oh. My. God.

She closed her eyes, arched her back, enthralled with the sensation of hot, slick friction. He made a ragged sound of pleasure as he withdrew, then, with agonizing slowness, plunged deep again. Her fingers worked the muscles of his back like a kneading cat, nails biting into his flesh. His mouth sought hers and they kissed, until she was gasping and incoherent and lost in the pleasure of this intimate connection they'd forged.

"Look at me," he rasped.

She opened her eyes, looked directly into his. They were dark and hazy with passion. "I just want to make sure," he said hoarsely, "that you remember who it is that's fucking you blind."

She ran a fingertip over his shoulder, marveling at the smooth, sleek skin pulled tight over hard bone and solid muscle. "As if I could forget," she said breathlessly, "when I've been thinking about this ever since the night you walked through my door…looking like walking sex…and smelling of pepperoni pizza."

"Jesus, Faith." His struggle to maintain control was clear on his face. "You're trying to kill me, aren't you?"

She rocked beneath him, torturing them both with the exquisite sensations her motions caused. "If Buddy hadn't been there that night to chaperon…I think I would've jumped you…right then and there."

He squeezed his eyes tightly closed. "Oh, fuck," he muttered. "Oh fuck oh fuck oh fuck."

"Tyrone," she breathed, "why are you holding back?"

"I'm trying to wait…don't wanna rush you."

In response, she rolled out from under him and reversed their positions, knelt over him and straddled his hips, her dark hair brushing his chest and shoulders as she impaled herself.

She watched his face in the shadows as she took control with a steady, fluid rhythm. It was the most exciting thing she'd ever experienced, watching his face and knowing she was the one responsible for the look of tortured ecstasy she saw there.

His breath came out in a hard rush and he clutched convulsively at her hips. "Christ Jesus," he breathed.

"You like?" She leaned forward to kiss his neck, shrouding him with her dark cloud of hair.

"Faith," he said harshly. "Baby?"

She closed her eyes, threw her head back, moved against him with slow deliberation. "What?" she said.

"You only think you're in charge." He lifted himself on his elbows. Thrown off balance, she clutched at his shoulders for support. "Wrap your legs around me," he ordered, and before she knew what was happening, he'd raised himself onto his knees and tumbled her over backward on the mattress. She lay beneath him once again, gasping, shocked, secretly thrilled by his domination, even if it wasn't politically correct.

She tried to smother a giggle, but wasn't quite successful. He kissed her neck. Her ear. Was that really her, giggling again? "God, I love it when you laugh," he said.

"And I love it when you—*oh*."

"Huh. You actually *like* that?"

"Shut up, Tyrone…I—oh, Jesus, yes."

"And that?"

"*Oh, please.*"

"Oh, please, what? Oh, please stop?"

"Damn you, Savage…you sadistic bastard…"

He laughed. "Maybe you'll like this even better," he said, and she clung to him desperately so she wouldn't tumble off the face of the earth as he rocked her, hot and noisy and hard, so hard the bedsprings screamed in protest.

She caught a frantic breath. "...old house...walls are thin...somebody will hear...."

"Fuck 'em."

She snorted, most indelicately, and then she was beyond caring, beyond the point of no return. She pulled his mouth down to hers, kissed him hard to smother her cries as her body shattered and that sweet rush of ecstasy flooded her. Locking her legs more tightly around him to prolong the bliss, she continued to rock him hard until, with a smothered groan that sounded more like a sob, he followed her into paradise.

They fell back to earth together, limp and depleted and gasping. She wasn't sure how long they lay there, tangled to the point that she couldn't tell where she left off and he began, but eventually, he lifted his head and gazed solemnly into her eyes. "I don't think we've been properly introduced," he said. "My name's Savage. Tyrone Savage."

She groaned. "There's a joker in every crowd. And lucky me, I got this one."

"And may I add, hopefully without any danger of being labeled a sexist pig, that you are one hot mama?"

"You're not so bad yourself, Savage."

"So was it good for you?"

"Stop. It hurts when I laugh. And you're as heavy as a gorilla."

"But a lot less hairy. I'm crushing you, aren't I?"

"Not at all. We're designed to fit together this way. I like it. You know—" she pressed her lips to his shoulder and tasted salt on his skin "—I had this vision of you in my head after we talked on the phone that first time."

Humor danced in his eyes. "Is that so?"

"I kept imagining you with a beer belly and a receding hairline, a shrewish wife and a half-dozen kids, living in squalor in some rickety old trailer."

"Gee, thanks. I'm totally underwhelmed by your high opinion of me."

"It was a defense mechanism. There was a part of me that just knew you were still going to be this hot stud muffin I wouldn't be able to resist. Besides, I was still mad at you for breaking my heart."

"Christ, woman, it's been eighteen years. Are you ever going to let me live that down?"

"Check with me again in another ten years and we'll see. Maybe by then, if you're really, really nice to me…well, you never know what might happen."

Suddenly serious, he said, "I've missed you, Faith. You were the most important person in my life for so many years. Then you were just gone. You left a hole nobody else has ever been able to fill."

Thinking of those two kids who'd run in and out of each other's houses on a daily basis for nearly two decades, she felt tears forming beneath her eyelids. "I know," she said.

"If I'd had any brains, I would've come after you. Tracked you down and told you I was crazy mad in love with you. Hounded you until you gave in and came home with me, where you belonged. But eighteen-year-old kids don't have brains. I was a fool, and I let you get away. It's been the single biggest regret of my life."

A lone tear welled up and rolled down her cheek. "I had a good life with Ben," she said. "But there was always a corner of my heart that belonged to you."

"Aw, Christ, Faith, don't cry. My ego can't take it. I brought you here to release a little of the steam that's been building up between us. To have a good time. Now look at what I've done."

"I am having a good time." She reached up and swiped the tear away. "You can't tell?"

He chuckled. "I think you're a trouper." He rolled onto his side, taking her with him, and cradled her head to his chest. "Look at everything you've been through. And you're still walking upright."

"But you're my reward for all that pain and chaos." She raised her head and gazed into his eyes. "The pot of gold at the end of the rainbow."

"Beer belly and all."

Running a hand over gleaming, rock-hard abs, she said, "Beer belly and all."

"Hang on a second. I have to take care of something." She moved aside and he swung his legs over the side of the bed. Clutching the sticky used condom, he said, "Be right back," and disappeared into the adjoining bathroom.

Faith sat cross-legged on the bed, gathered up the spare blanket from the foot and wrapped it around her shoulders. In the bathroom, the toilet flushed, and then she heard the sound of running tap water. "Ty?" she said. "Am I stepping on anybody's toes?"

"What do you mean?"

"Something Pete said the other day led me to think you might have a girlfriend."

The splashing inside the bathroom ceased. "A girlfriend," he said blankly. "Are you talking about Maxine?"

Maxine. The red-haired waitress from Lenny's. "He didn't name any names," she said, "but I got the distinct impression that he wished he'd kept his mouth shut."

"Maxine and I are old friends," he said over the sound of the running water. "I like her, she likes me. And yeah, once in a while, we get together and have sex." He turned off the tap. "But it's not a serious thing."

"You're sure? I don't want to be known as anybody's other woman."

"Trust me." He came back into the bedroom, climbed into the bed and tucked the blanket around them.

She cuddled up to his warmth and rested her head against his shoulder. "There's one other thing we need to talk about," she said.

"Oh, boy, here it comes. The old 'where do we go from here?' speech."

"Actually, that comes later. This is something else. Something Davy Hunter said to me last night."

He sighed, his breath riffling her hair. "Why does that name keep popping up?"

"Because, like it or not, he's a big part of our lives. He always has been. Look, I'm not sure how to say this. I'm not even sure it's any of my business. But I have to know."

"I don't have any secrets, Faith. Certainly not from you." He rubbed his cheek against hers and tightened the blanket around them. "What you see is what you get. What the hell did he say to you?"

"I accused him of being Jessie's father, and he said he wasn't. So of course I couldn't resist asking if he wasn't her father, then who was? And he told me that if I really wanted to know…I should be asking you."

"Me?" He looked at her as though her words were spoken in Mandarin Chinese. "Was he implying what I think he was?"

"It sure looks that way to me."

"Faith…my God. I've told you, I was only with Chelsea once. Jessie was born years later. You do believe me, don't you?"

"I just needed to hear you say it again."

"I'm saying it again." Beneath the blanket, he took both her hands in his and looked her directly in the eye. "I am not Jessie Logan's father. I was with Chelsea just once, when we were eighteen years old and in high school." Still holding her hands, he grew silent, thoughtful. "Hell," he said, "even if you didn't believe me, I could prove it's not even remotely possible. I was stationed in Germany when Jessie was conceived."

"I'm not doubting you," she said, ashamed of the rush of relief that told her a tiny part of her had indeed doubted him. "I just needed to hear you confirm it."

"Where the hell do you suppose he got a crazy idea like that?"

"Maybe he's still resentful about what happened back in high school."

"Or maybe Chelsea lied and told him it was me."

"Why would she do that?"

"To make him jealous? To cover up the fact that she didn't know who the father was? Hell, I don't know. Chelsea did whatever she had to do to get by. She wasn't above lying to get what she wanted."

"It doesn't matter now. We both know the truth. Life's too short to waste it talking about a dead issue when we could be taking advantage of a couple more hours of privacy and all this lovely nakedness."

"What a brilliant conclusion. You and I, Faith Pelletier, are a match made in heaven. And if you play your cards right, I might just call Jessie and tell her we're staying until morning."

Bright morning light filtered in around the shades. She was wrapped tight in Ty's arms, her backside pressed against his heat. Her body humming with satisfaction, she drifted in that lazy, comfortable state that wasn't quite sleep, wasn't quite full awareness. Like a movie shot slightly out of focus, pictures and words floated in and out of her mind. Making love until she ached in muscles she'd forgotten she owned… the terrifying car crash…Davy Hunter's surprising kindness…Ben's Saab crumpled like a foil candy bar wrapper… Jessie's aborted date with Cooper Gates…Alyssa Lombardi's trips to Mexico for cancer treatments…the HMO crisis… Buck Savage and that lethal-looking butcher knife.

In her semiconscious condition, Faith frowned. Something in that filmy, drifty list was out of whack. *"One of these things is not like the others."*

Alyssa Lombardi. The HMO crisis…

Suddenly wide awake, she sat bolt upright in bed. "Oh, my God," she said. "Skip Lombardi."

Beside her, Ty rolled onto his hip. "Skip Lombardi?" he said sleepily.

"Remember what you told me about Jo and her lousy HMO?" Faith reached up a bare arm and scraped back a fistful of wayward hair from her face. "She teaches school, right?

Skip's the high school principal. Wouldn't he be covered by the same lousy HMO?"

He stretched, adjusted the bedcovers and waited for her to continue, his eyes suddenly alert.

"What do you suppose it costs to travel to Mexico for experimental cancer treatments?" she said. "No HMO is going to pay for that. And no high school principal from Serenity, Maine, earns that kind of money. So how did he pay for it? Even if he'd gone into debt, wiped out his life savings, it still wouldn't have covered the cost. And now he wants to buy Chelsea's house. Where's the money coming from? It doesn't add up."

Ty sat up slowly, his mouth drawn tight in a frown. "Heroin trafficking," he said, thinking out loud. "Makes for a nice little second income, doesn't it?"

Excited, Faith said, "He told me yesterday that he'd do anything for Alyssa. My God, Ty, it would be so easy for him to filter the heroin into the school system. All he needs is one or two confidants. Kids he can trust. Kids like Cooper Gates."

"His star quarterback. Someone with whom he's really tight."

"He told me he takes Alyssa to Boston twice a month to meet with her oncologist. It wouldn't take much effort to make a side trip to Lawrence or Haverhill on the way back."

"Where he meets his contact, picks up the goods, and then drives home to Maine."

"Where everybody feels sorry for him because his kid is sick."

"It's one hell of a cover," Ty said. "Who'd suspect a high school principal of dealing drugs?"

"And he knew Chelsea. She interviewed him for the *Gazette* a few months ago." Something else suddenly occurred to her. "Ty, he was out that night. He picked Jessie up and drove her home. That places him in the vicinity just a short time after I was driven off the road."

"Son of a bitch," he said. "Son of a fucking bitch."

He rolled out of bed, rummaged through the pile of clothes on the floor until he found his cell phone. Naked, he stood there and punched in a number. "Pete," he said, "I need you to give Judge Townsend a call. I want a court order to look at Skip Lombardi's financials ASAP." He paused, listened. "Goddamn it, I know it's Sunday morning. I don't give a damn if you have to drag him out of the front pew of the First Baptist Church. Track him down. If you can't get Townsend, try Bernier. Keep trying until you find somebody. While you're at it, send René over to drive by Lombardi's place. Make sure his car is there. I'll meet you at the station in a half hour."

His eyes met Faith's over the bed. "It'll be quicker," she said with a flirtatious little smile, "if we shower together."

His gaze flickered downward, paused at her breasts. Swept past her belly and down her long legs before moving back up to her eyes. "Pete?" he said. "Make that forty-five minutes."

On Sunday mornings, downtown Serenity looked like a ghost town. The bars on Androscoggin Street, always tacky even under cover of darkness, looked seedy and downtrodden in the light of day. Church bells pealed atop the massive gray stone cathedral that topped the steep hill east of downtown. Walking quickly, Jessie took a shortcut through an empty lot where the Androscoggin Hotel had sat until fire gutted it a few years back and the town razed what was left standing.

Water Street didn't look any livelier than Androscoggin had. There were a couple of cop cars parked in front of the police station, and a big yellow dog who shouldn't have been running loose was sniffing at a pot of geraniums outside the door of the shoe repair shop.

In front of the newspaper office, Newt Rollins was washing windows with a bucket of soapy water and a long-handled squeegee. His sleeves were rolled up and he was wearing a pair of faded jeans. He spied her, waved and she crossed the street to talk to him. "Hey, Jessie-belle," he said. "What're you doing in town all by yourself? I distinctly remember Faith telling you not to run around alone."

Guilt brought a warm flush to her cheeks. She'd promised Faith to stay put, but this was important. Ahmed knew something about what had happened to her mother, and she had to get to the bottom of it. A breeze caught a wisp of hair and tossed it in her face, and she brushed it back and tucked it behind her ear. "I'm going to see my friend Ahmed," she said.

"Ah," he said. "Omar's boy." He stretched up to his full height and drew the squeegee down the glass with a loud squeak. Rinsing it in the bucket, he said, "How'd you get here? Faith hasn't bought a new car yet, has she?"

Thinking of what the Saab had looked like after she'd rolled it a couple of times, Jessie felt her stomach tighten. "No," she said. "She's driving Chief Savage's truck today while he's at work. I walked over from his house. I spent the night there." She watched him for a minute before saying, "She's picking me up later. I can give her a message if you'd like."

He stretched again, ran the squeegee down another section of window. "Any particular reason you spent the night there?"

"They were out on a date, and I don't think they wanted to—"

"Out on a date?" he said with interest. "Faith and Savage?"

She didn't like the way he said Savage, like it was some kind of insult. "That's right," she said. "They didn't want to leave me alone all night, so I stayed with Buck."

His eyebrows went sky-high, and she realized she'd said too much. She really wasn't comfortable discussing Faith's sex life with Newt Rollins, no matter how close he'd been to her mother. And it was pretty clear that Faith had spent the night doing something more exciting than driving around the back roads of Serenity. The way she and Ty had looked when they'd come rushing into the house this morning, it couldn't have been any more obvious if they'd taken out a front-page ad in the *Gazette*.

A flush crawled up Jessie's cheeks. "I don't think I was

supposed to tell you that," she said. "I mean, Faith didn't tell me not to, but it is sort of personal."

"Don't worry. I won't breathe a word to anybody. So they're, ah—" he paused, seemed to search for the right word "—dating," he finally said. "Seriously."

It had looked pretty serious to her, especially right before Ty went flying back out the door to work, when he'd leaned over and kissed Faith, really, truly kissed her, right there in front of his father and Jessie. And Faith had kissed him back with equal enthusiasm.

"I have to go now," she said primly to Newt Rollins. "I have important business with Ahmed."

"Ten-four, Jessie-belle," he said. "Just be careful. When you see Faith, tell her I'll probably stop by to visit her this afternoon. I want to hear the latest gossip directly from the source." And dipping his squeegee once more into the bucket of water, he went back to washing windows.

"What do you mean, you can't find a judge?" Ty tossed his pen down on the desk. "Keep trying."

Pete leaned against the door frame and crossed his arms. "It's Sunday morning, Ty. They're all in church. Or out on the golf course."

In disbelief, he said, "They can't all be playing golf."

"This is the twenty-first century, boss. The age of caller ID. If you were in their shoes, you wouldn't be answering your phone on Sunday morning, either."

He muttered an oath. If he had his way, he'd be spending every Sunday morning for the rest of his life buck-naked and tangled in the sheets with Faith. Not here, following yet another wild goose. He'd already checked Lombardi's DMV file, and he didn't own a truck or an SUV, just a ten-year-old Volkswagen Jetta. Which, at this precise moment, was parked in his driveway, right next to Linda's Cadillac. Good to know that some people got to stay in bed on a Sunday morning.

"What in hell's eating you?" Pete said.

"Other than the fact that for every step I take forward, I take two steps back? Not a damn thing."

"Christ, boy, you're bitchier than my wife when she's PMS-ing. And if you tell her I said that, you're dead meat. What you need is to get laid."

Ty threaded his fingers together, propped his size thirteens on the wastebasket beneath his desk, and leaned his chair back. He kept his face deliberately neutral as he gazed silently at Pete.

"I'll be goddamned," Pete said. "You and Faith? When?"

"Last night. And again this morning, although I don't know if you can technically call that particular instance getting laid, since we weren't lying down at the time."

"You sneaky little shit." Pete's grin was a mile wide. "So…was she, uh—" he cleared his throat "—as good as she looks?"

"Shut up or I'll throw my marble paperweight at you and knock you out cold. You're talking about the woman I intend to marry."

"And have you mentioned that tiny little detail to her yet, or are you waiting for the right moment at some point in the distant future?"

"I'll get around to it."

"When'll that be, precisely? About the time hell freezes over?"

"Shut up, Morin. I'm in complete control of the situation."

"Uh-huh. Just like you were the first time you let her walk away from you."

The phone on his desk rang. "I was in high school, for Christ's sake," he said, reaching for it. "Cut me some slack." He lofted the phone to his ear and cradled it against his shoulder. "Savage."

"Morning. Lemoine here. I wasn't sure I'd catch you, but I see you're working on Sunday morning, too."

"To protect and serve, that's our motto, 24/7, eight days a week."

"Tell me about it," Lemoine said. "I have a kid. Eight years old. He plays Little League. You think I've been to even one of his games so far?"

"I hear you," he said, thinking of Faith and the warm bed he'd been forced to abandon. "So we got anything?"

"Well, here's the thing. I did my nosing around, just like I promised I would. Everybody I talked to in your idyllic little town said the same thing. Logan wasn't suicidal. Something about the whole scenario bothered me. So I called up my sister-in-law. She works at the state lab in Augusta. I promised her a six-month supply of Godiva chocolates if she'd put a rush on it for me."

He glanced up at Pete, still hovering in the doorway. "And did she?" he said.

"Oh, yeah. She called me this morning with the results. The official paperwork is on its way, but she told me over the phone what she learned. I think you'll find it interesting."

"Go ahead. Make my day."

"Logan had been drinking. Not a lot. A glass or two at best. Not enough to send her off that highway and into the river. Not an experienced drinker like her. It was the other stuff that did her in. Are you familiar with Rohypnol?"

"Rohypnol," he said. "The date-rape drug?"

"You got it in one. Her system was loaded with it."

He sat up straighter in his chair as the ramifications struck him. "Somebody added a little extra oomph to her drink?" he said.

"You mix that stuff with alcohol and it's all over. Somebody poured enough Rohypnol in whatever she was drinking to down a six-hundred-pound gorilla. Then he put her behind the wheel of a car. Seems to me the intent's pretty clear. Dope her up, put her behind the wheel while she's still cognizant, then let her drive away, an accident waiting to happen. It takes twenty to thirty minutes for Rohypnol to kick in. If he timed it right...well, let's just say that if I wanted to kill somebody, it would be a pretty reliable method of doing it. We're looking at manslaughter here at the very least. My money's on murder one."

Jessie found Ahmed behind the counter of Halaal Variety. When he saw her, he darted a nervous glance toward the curtain that separated the retail space from the back storeroom. Jessie quickly checked the store for customers. When she verified that there were none, she approached the counter. "I have to talk to you," she said.

"I am working, Jessielogan. We can talk later."

"No," she said. "I need to talk to you now."

He turned his back on her and began rearranging a display of Kodak film that didn't need to be rearranged. "Tomorrow," he said. "We will talk tomorrow. At school."

Setting her jaw, Jessie walked around the end of the checkout counter and stepped behind it. Grabbing his hands to still them, she said softly, near his ear, "We…will…talk…now."

Ahmed darted another glance toward the curtain. She wouldn't have thought it possible for the expression *green around the gills* to apply to a person the color of chocolate, but maybe the expression had less to do with color than with facial expression. "My father is in the back room," he said. "If he hears us—"

"We'll be quick and quiet. Now talk."

"What are we talking about?"

"You already know, Ahmed."

Ahmed swallowed, his Adam's apple bobbing up and down. "I cannot go there, Jessielogan. You must leave it alone."

"Leave it alone," she said. "Leave it alone! That's all anybody ever tells me, to leave it alone!" She grabbed his sleeve and tugged hard enough to pull him around. "Listen, Ahmed, I have to know what you're hiding. It's important. What is it you have on Coop? If it's the drugs, I already know. I found out Friday night that he's dealing. But he said something that really bothered me. Something about my mother. Something about—" she paused, lowered her voice "—her big mouth. Look, if there's something you know that I don't, you have to tell me."

The boy closed his eyes. When he opened them again, she saw resignation in those ebony depths. "Do you remember Stacey Beliveau?" he said.

"The girl who overdosed on heroin," she said. "Yes. What about her?"

"She bought it from Cooper. The lethal dosage."

Jessie's stomach lurched, and for an instant, she was certain she'd lose her breakfast. "Are you sure?"

"I'm sure. And Cooper has threatened to kill me if I tell."

"Well," she said, "there seems to be a lot of that going around."

Ahmed glanced again toward the back of the store. "But there's more," he said. "I know who his supplier is." Terror brought a wildness to the boy's eyes. "I found out who is smuggling heroin into Serenity." He closed his eyes and swallowed hard. When he opened them again, she saw tears forming at the corners. "I have already done enough damage, Jessielogan. If I tell—if anything should happen to you—don't you understand? It is my fault. My fault that your mother is dead!"

The cold began at the tips of her fingers and inched its way along her limbs. Her chest aching with the effort to breathe, she said hoarsely, "Why? How could it be your fault?"

"Because I told her," he said miserably. "Your mother. I told her everything I know."

Faith parked Ty's pickup truck next to the house. Buddy was ecstatic to see her. And wonder of wonders, he hadn't left her any little surprises. Faith dropped her purse on the kitchen table and let him out to do his business. It was another splendid, sunny day here in Northern New England, full-blown spring at last, and she began flinging open windows to let winter's last vestiges out of the tired old house.

Laurie Breton

She felt energized. Reborn. Ready to climb mountains Like a butterfly emerging from its chrysalis, she was ready to give life a chance. Maybe it would work out between them maybe it wouldn't. But she wouldn't go down without a fight Whatever it took for them to be together, whatever obstacles she had to hurdle, she was willing to make the attempt. Last night had been magic, and she intended to hold on to that magic for as long as she could. Maybe even forever.

Amazing. Until last night, she thought she'd stopped believing in forever.

She was ravenous. They hadn't taken time for breakfast Ty was in too much of a hurry, and the little interlude in the shower had taken up a few more minutes than they should have allotted to it. But it was worth the starvation, this glorious feeling of being alive again. Humming an off-key rendition of some old Broadway tune, its title long since forgotten, Faith popped a couple slices of wheat bread into the toaster and went to check the answering machine, which was blinking furiously.

When she pushed the button, Marie Spinelli's voice floated out. "Faith? It's me. God, I hate these generic answering systems with the canned voices. You don't even know if you've reached the right number."

The toast popped up, and she went to butter it. "Where the hell are you?" Marie continued. "You headed out a week ago to East Bumfuck and disappeared off the face of the earth. I hope to God your silence means you're writing like crazy, because the deadline isn't getting any farther away." A moment of silence. Then, "I miss you. Call me!" As an afterthought, Marie added, "And if you're not Faith, please disregard this message."

She opened the refrigerator and poured herself a glass of cranberry juice. Poor Marie. She'd intended to call her agent, but she'd completely forgotten. She would have to call now and tell Marie…what? That she was too mixed up in murder and intrigue and instant motherhood right now to even think about her deadline? That she'd fallen head over heels in love with a man whose roots ran deep in the rocky Maine soil, and that her entire future was one giant question mark? None of that was anything Marie wanted to hear. But she couldn't just leave her hanging. She had to tell her something.

Glancing at the clock, she decided it was still too early to call. Anybody who possessed the audacity to disturb Marie Spinelli before noon on a Sunday deserved whatever they got. She'd call this afternoon. Maybe by that time, Ty would have something solid on Lombardi. Maybe by then, the worst of this nightmare would be over.

She took a bite of toast, and the phone rang. Swallowing quickly, she washed it down with cranberry juice and rushed to answer the phone.

"You were right," Ty said in lieu of a greeting.

Melting at the sound of his voice, she said, "Right about what?"

"About Chelsea. I just got the results of the toxicology tests. She'd had a couple of drinks that night. Somebody loaded them with a date-rape drug called Rohypnol and then put her behind the wheel of the car."

She sat down hard, gasping, struggling to get her breathing back under control. She'd known, almost from the beginning, that sooner or later they'd find something concrete. Some sliver of evidence that would prove beyond the shadow of a doubt that some monstrous person had been responsible for her cousin's death. But knowing wasn't the same as hearing it said out loud. She set down the cranberry juice and absorbed the impact.

"Faith?" he said. "Are you all right?"

"Just give me a minute. Oh, God."

"Damn it, I shouldn't have called you."

"I'm okay." Slowly, like a swimmer with a stomach cramp, she straightened back up. "It's just—oh, Ty, how could somebody do this to her? What am I going to tell Jessie?"

"Jessie's tough as shoe leather. She just looks puny and weak. We'll tell her together."

"Yes." She took a deep, hard breath, grateful, for once in her life, to be able to lean on somebody else's strength. "All right."

"You okay? You got your breath back?"

"Yeah." She took a series of long, slow breaths. "I'm okay."

"Jessie there with you?"

"No. She's at your house, with your father. I told her to stay put."

"Good. Look, I don't want you staying out there alone. Right now, it looks as though Lombardi's at home. But he won't stay there forever. I want you to pick up whatever you and Jessie need and come back to my house. I'm sending Pete out to pick you up."

"No. That won't be necessary. Pete has better things to do. I'll gather up a few things and drive back into town. Ty, do you have anything at all to connect this to Lombardi?"

"Not yet. But we're working on it."

"There's still one thing we haven't gotten to. Her computer hard drive. I checked out all the disks after the break-in, and I intended to go over the hard drive, but with everything that's happened—the last week has just been a blur."

"We'll pick it up later, bring it to the house, go over it together. Look, I can't talk right now. Lemoine's on his way over. Looks like I just had a murder investigation dumped in my lap. You gather your stuff together right away and get the hell out of that house. Call me when you get to my place. If you don't reach me in person, leave a message with whomever you talk to. I want to know that you're safe." He hesitated, the open phone line crackling between them. "I love you," he said.

Before she had a chance to respond, he hung up.

She ran outside to pull yesterday's laundry off the line, cramming towels and bedding into the yellow plastic laundry basket without bothering to fold them. Back inside the kitchen, she quickly sorted what was hers, then left the rest of the pile sitting in the basket on the kitchen table. She could fold the laundry later. It wasn't going anywhere.

Upstairs, she pulled her suitcase from the closet and set it on the bed, popped the lid open and began hastily pulling garments from hangers and cramming them into it. She didn't need much, just enough to get her through a couple of days. If she had to stay in town longer than that, she could always come back for more. She opened the top drawer of the dresser, selected a couple changes of undergarments, and tossed them into the suitcase. Then she sprinted down the hall to Jessie's room, where she gathered an armload of jeans, T-shirts and underwear. She carried it all back to the guest room and arranged it with more speed than grace in the suitcase before she closed the cover and snapped the locks. There were probably other things Jessie needed. Schoolbooks, for instance. She was just going to have to go without them for a couple of days. Knowing Jessie, she was probably the only kid in the state of Maine who'd be unhappy about having to leave them behind.

Suitcase in one hand and laptop in the other, Faith went downstairs and carried them out to Ty's truck. She whistled for Buddy. He came running and launched himself up into the cab. Shutting the door behind him, she said breathlessly, "Be right back," and flew back into the house to get his bag of dog food.

She paused to run a hand through her hair. There was one more thing she'd forgotten. Jessie might have to go without her schoolbooks for a few days, but she wasn't going without her violin. Faith dashed back up the stairs and grabbed up the violin case that Jessie kept right by the side of her bed, then she paused to take a quick look around. The room was spotless, the bed made neatly, the walls plastered with travel posters. Places Jessie had never had the chance to visit. Was it her dream to see London, Paris, Rome? If it was, Faith could make that dream come true for her.

If she ever finished *Blood Sport*.

At a more leisurely pace, she went back downstairs for the last time. Outside, in the cab of the truck, Buddy was barking like crazy. He loved to ride, but he hated being closed inside a vehicle alone for any length of time. Violin in one hand, dog food in the other, Faith snatched up her keys—Ty's keys, actually—from the kitchen table and slung her purse over her shoulder.

She was standing at the door, her hand on the doorknob, when somebody knocked on the other side, startling her so that she nearly dropped the violin. She hadn't heard anyone drive up, but that explained why Buddy was barking. The knock came again. She hesitated, then hefted the bag of dog food higher. Heart still pounding from the fright she'd been given, she opened the door, breathing a sigh of relief when she saw who stood on the other side. "Good God," she said, opening the door wider. "You scared the daylights out of me."

And then she saw the gun. A shiny little silver revolver, not much bigger than his hand. It didn't look terribly menacing, but as a crime writer, she was familiar enough with guns to know in graphic detail just how much damage it could do. And its business end was pointed directly at her.

She took an involuntary step backward, and he moved smoothly into the room. With the gun still trained on her, he closed the door, made a half turn and shot home the dead bolt.

"Hello, Faith," he said. "Going somewhere?"

Twenty-One

Ty was sitting at the computer, typing up his report for a judge Pete still hadn't tracked down. He made a typo, hit the backspace key, and corrected it. He wasn't much of a typist; he must have been hiding behind a door somewhere when they passed out Keyboarding 101 skills. But he'd picked up speed from years of writing endless reports, and using a computer had to be one hell of an improvement over the way they'd done it back in the old man's day.

Somebody rapped on his door frame and he glanced up to see Davy Hunter standing there. "I got your note," Davy said tersely. "We have to talk."

"I'm a little busy right now."

"It can't wait."

"Neither can this. Where the hell were you yesterday, Hunter?"

"In Augusta. Arguing until I was blue in the face." Davy glanced over his shoulder. "Mind if I shut the door?"

"You might as well. If I said no, you'd just go ahead and do it anyway."

Davy quietly closed the door behind him and crossed the room. He pulled a slender black leather sleeve from the breast pocket of his shirt and tossed it down on the desk. Ty glanced at it, glanced back up at him and opened it. He studied it at length before folding it up and sliding it back across the desk.

"DEA," he said. "You're fucking DEA."

"That's right. I've been working undercover for the last eighteen months."

Ty grasped the edge of his desk until his fingers went white. He could feel the surge of anger climbing, could feel the blood pooling in his face. "And you just randomly made the decision that it was more beneficial to your case to keep the local authorities in the dark?"

"It wasn't my choice," Davy said. "I was following orders."

"Jesus H. Christ." He was on his feet now, putting every ounce of his fury into his voice. "What in hell ever happened to law enforcement agencies working together? Goddamn it, Hunter, you've been right at the top of my fucking suspect list! Do you have any idea—any idea at all—of the kind of clusterfuck this could've turned into if something big came down and my men didn't know we were working the same side? Somebody could've ended up dead!"

"Don't give me any shit, Savage. I'm already up to here with it." Davy made a slicing motion across his throat. "I spent six hours yesterday sitting in an office in Augusta, trying to convince my boss, and his boss, that if we didn't come clean with you now, more bodies were going to start piling up. One of those bodies just might belong to your girlfriend."

With quiet fury, he said, "Leave Faith out of it."

"I'm not the one who dragged her into it, and I don't like it any better than you do. But in it she is, right up to her pretty little ass, and if you don't put a leash on her damn soon, she'll end up like Chelsea did."

"Who the hell are you to offer advice? Seems to me you didn't keep such a good eye on your own woman!"

They glared at each other, both of them breathing hard. "Do you think I don't know that?" Davy snapped. "Do you think I haven't told myself a hundred times that if I'd put Chelsea ahead of my job, she'd be alive now? I have to live with that."

Looking defeated, he ran his palms up and down his face. "Listen," he said wearily, "what happened the night before last wasn't an accident."

"No shit, Sherlock." Still furious, Ty crammed his fists into his pockets to keep from strangling Hunter with them and stalked across his office to the window. He had a spectacular view of a five-foot section of the iron bridge and one wall of the old mill. Looking out, he said, "I suppose you know who drove her off the road?"

"I can't prove it yet, but my list of suspects is damn short."

He turned, crossed his arms, and stood with his legs braced apart. "Any names you'd care to share?"

"If I share names, I compromise my entire case." When Ty's steely expression didn't alter, Davy sighed. "Look, I've been working this investigation for almost two years," he said. "We knew Serenity was a hub for heroin distribution all over this part of the state. We knew there was a network of small-time dealers, but we wanted to nail Mr. Big, the guy who was actually carrying it across the border and networking it out to the little guys. The only way we could do that was to send somebody in under deep cover. I got chosen for obvious reasons. I grew up here, so nobody thought anything of it when I came back and settled down out there in the swamp. I had to act like one of the boys, worm my way into their good graces, curry their favor, win their trust. That kind of thing doesn't happen overnight. You can't imagine the hours I've put into this. But it worked. I found out who he is, and I've been waiting for him to make that one fatal mistake. He's smart, and he's sly, and he knows how to keep his nose clean, but sooner or later, he'll trip up. They all do eventually. The end result was worth what I've been through." He grimaced. "Or it was, until Chelsea got mixed up in it."

Ty closed his eyes. When he opened them again, he said, "What happened?"

"She found out. Not about me, but about him. Mr. Big. I'm not sure how. She refused to reveal her source. But she came to me with it, and I tried like hell to talk her out of pursuing it. She wouldn't listen to anything I had to say. She had this one-woman crusade going on. She was going to be the one to bring him down, via the power of the press. She had this fantasy that it would send her career as a journalist into outer space. We had a hell of a fight over it. She couldn't understand why I was dead set against her getting involved, and I couldn't tell her the truth without blowing my cover. We were at an impasse. So off she went one rainy night, overflowing with dreams of justice and glory." He squared his shoulders, and his mouth thinned. "And she ended up at the bottom of the Androscoggin."

Ty's anger had dissipated, like air leaking slowly from a balloon. There was little sense in holding on to it. They both had a job to do, and unfortunately, stepping on each other's toes went along with that job. "Can you prove she was with him that night?"

"I can't prove it. But I know what I know."

"If you can find evidence, we can put him away on something bigger than drug charges. I just got the toxicology results back this morning. Whoever Chelsea was with the night she died gave her alcohol laced with a massive dose of Rohypnol. Somebody murdered her. Are you ready now to give me names?"

Davy's eyes were hard, unfeeling. Indecipherable. "Cooper Gates," he said. "Ernie Belanger. Teddy Stultz."

"Now there's a surprise," Ty said. "And let me guess. It was Lombardi who masterminded the whole thing."

"Lombardi?" Davy looked confused, and Ty's stomach took a sudden swoop. "Skip Lombardi? Not unless you know something I don't."

"Lombardi's not involved?" he said. "He's not Mr. Big?"

"Hell, no. Not even close. Maybe that's why Chelsea was so determined to bring him down herself, because they'd been so close. She trusted him. She thought they were friends."

"Then who—"

"Newt Rollins."

He simply stared at Davy as his befuddled brain tried to make sense of what he'd just heard. "Newt Rollins," he said. *"Newt Rollins?"*

"She went out that night to have dinner with him, and she never came back."

"Oh, Christ," he said, as the blood drained from his extremities. "I have to tell Faith."

"Congratulations," Newt said. "I hear you succeeded in bagging our illustrious chief of police."

Faith took a step away from him, then another. "I don't understand," she said, looking in disbelief at the gun in his hand. "I'd like an explanation."

"You know, I really like you, Faith. I didn't want it to turn out this way, but you just wouldn't let it go. Once you get an idea in your head, you're a pit bull. Just like Chelsea. And once you stumbled onto the drug connection, I knew that sooner or later you'd figure it out and rat me out to your boyfriend. Still, I tried my damnedest to refocus your attention from your self-appointed mission as Wonder Woman. When Floyd and Roland sent out their flyers, I thought to myself, why not piggyback on the work they'd already done? It would have been a brilliant plan if it'd worked."

"Floyd and Roland," she said. "Eugley and Moody? Those two old codgers?"

"AKA the Brotherhood for Aryan Unity. Change comes slowly in a place like this, Faith, and not without conflict. It's the old-timers who have the most trouble accepting it. But their little papering job was a perfect opportunity for me. I thought if I could convince you that Chelsea's death had something to do with them, you'd back off on the drug sniffing and start looking elsewhere for your killer. Unfortunately, it didn't work out."

"You killed Chelsea," she said, incredulous. "Why, for God's sake?"

"The thing is, I loved her. I mean, I really, really loved her. I would have married her in a heartbeat, if she would've had me. But she didn't want me." His face darkened. "Your beautiful cousin had a mean streak a mile wide. She was heartless. I let her know, in so many different ways, that I'd lay down my life for her. But did she appreciate it? Hell, no. To her, I was still the nerd, the weirdo, the brainy kid that all the other kids laughed at. She took advantage of my love, every chance she got. She teased me. Tormented me. Toyed with my affections, then went running back to Davy Hunter to laugh at me behind my back. The thing is—" he paused to shove his glasses back up his nose "—we could have been so damn happy together, if only she'd given me a chance. She could've had half the money. Not to mention the prestige. The Rollinses have run this town for seventy years. Marrying me would have taken some of the stink off that unsavory background of hers, and that drunken fool she called a father. But she wasn't interested. I didn't want to have to kill her, but what the hell was I supposed to do? She was going to splash all my dirty little secrets right across the front page of my own newspaper. I didn't have a choice, Faith. Just like I don't have a choice now."

"I'm missing something." Her heart thudded in her chest. "You're the one who got me involved in this witch hunt in the first place. Why would you set me on the trail of a killer, if the trail was going to lead right back to you?"

"I made a tactical error. I underestimated you. There you were, swallowing tranquilizers like they were candy, having panic attacks in public. It was the perfect setup. I was sure you'd be easy to manipulate. I needed your help to get my hands on what I wanted, and I thought you'd hand it to me without even realizing what you had in your possession. Haven't you ever heard the old saying about keeping your friends close, and your enemies closer?" His smile was grim. "But it backfired on me in a big way when you turned out to have a mind and a will of your own. I realized then that I'd created a monster, and unless I stopped it, that monster would turn on me and destroy me."

The bag of dog food tucked under her arm was getting heavy. "So this was all just a setup. What about the call Chelsea made to you the night she died?"

"You know, Faith, I've learned that when you lie, it's best to stick as close to the truth as possible. I knew Chelsea was planning to write up the story. But of course, she wasn't going to tell me about it ahead of time. That was a total fabrication. I think I should win an Oscar, don't you? I certainly had you convinced."

"But why? What could you possibly have wanted so bad you were willing to take a chance like that?"

"The computer, sweetheart. I know she had information tucked away somewhere. We tried to get the disks—"

"We?"

"My associate and I. It doesn't matter who. If it hadn't been for your goddamn dog, we'd have erased everything from the hard drive, and that would have been that. Case closed. You'd be on your way back to New York right now, and you wouldn't have to die. So if you're wondering who to blame for this unfortunate turn of events, blame that stupid mutt. It's all his fault."

He was going to kill her. It was an amazing fact, and she almost laughed at the irony of it. All these years it had taken for her and Ty to rediscover each other. And now, it looked as though they weren't going to get that second chance after all. "It was you," she said. "You're the one who drove me off the road Friday night. And the next morning..." Her stomach began doing flip-flops when she realized she'd put Jessie in the car with him, thinking he was a friend instead of a monster.

He followed her thoughts. "I'd never hurt Jessie," he said. "Now put all that stuff down, and toss me your purse. Gently."

She would have liked to heave it at his head with all her might, but the gun he was pointing at her was lethal, and a lot quicker than her pitching arm. She set down the dog food and the violin. "Here," she said, and tossed the purse in his direction.

He caught it in his free hand. "Good girl."

She clasped her hands into tight fists, wanting nothing more than to wipe that supercilious smirk off his face. Newt set the purse on the table and rummaged through it one-handed. Pulling out her bottle of pills, he said, "Women are so predictable." The gun still trained on her, he quickly scanned the pharmacy label. "They keep everything in their purses. God, I love it when people do my work for me."

The telephone rang, and they both froze. "Don't move," he said. He strode across the kitchen and yanked the plug, and the phone went abruptly silent. Moving to the sink, he turned on the tap, opened the cupboard, and took out a glass. "This will be a lot less painful if you do what I tell you," he said, filling the glass with water.

"I just bet."

"Look," he said, handing the glass to her, "I really don't want to have to hurt you. I'm not a sadist. I don't get off on hurting women. I'm only protecting my interests."

"Oh? And what interests might those be?"

"The *Gazette*'s been in my family for four generations. My great-grandfather founded it." He popped open the bottle of pills and poured the contents into his palm. "This town is dying," he said. "The economy's in the toilet. Subscriptions are down. A lot of businesses have folded. The paper's been struggling for years. I've been pouring my own money into it just to keep it afloat. Even so, things were going pretty smoothly until the last stock market crash. It damn near wiped me out." His blue eyes little-boy earnest, he said, "The *Gazette*'s my birthright, don't you see? My family legacy. I couldn't just sit by and watch it go down the tubes. I had to find a way to pump money into it. A transfusion to keep it healthy. I'd like to think that Great-Granddad would be proud."

"Oh, I'm sure he would. I bet Stacey Beliveau's parents would be impressed, too."

"I'm not responsible for Stacey Beliveau. That was Coop's

screw-up. If I ran a gun shop, you wouldn't hold me responsible for Joe Schmoe going out and shooting his neighbor with one of my guns. Same thing applies here. I just supply the merchandise. I'm not responsible for what happens after it leaves my hands."

"Maybe we should give you a medal. Or a gold star to wear on your forehead."

His face darkened. "Shut up," he said, holding out his hand, "and start swallowing pills."

She looked at the cluster of tiny yellow tablets he held out in front of her. "So this is how you're planning to kill me?" she said, furious. "With an overdose of my own pills?"

"Sweetheart," he said, "you've got this all wrong. I'm not going to kill you." His smile, cold and heartless, chilled her to the marrow. "You are."

"She's not answering," Ty said. "The phone just rings and rings." He met Davy's eyes, saw his own concern reflected there. "Maybe she's on her way already. Damn it, I should've sent Pete out there to get her. Or insisted that she stay with Dad until I got home. But she's a stubborn woman."

"It runs in the family," Davy said.

Ty tapped his fingertips against the desktop. Impatient. Worried down deep in his gut. He picked the phone back up and dialed home. "Dad," he said when Buck answered. "Is Faith there?"

"Nope. Haven't seen her since she left this morning."

"She should be on her way. When she gets there, have her call me. It's urgent."

"Everything okay?"

"Oh, hell, I'm probably just paranoid. I just wish I hadn't let her go back out to the Logan place alone."

At a knock on the door, he glanced up. The door opened and Pete stuck his head into the room. "Sorry to interrupt," he said, "but I have Judge Bernier holding on line two."

Shit. How the hell was he supposed to explain this one? Ty

pinched the bridge of his nose and nodded to Pete. "Dad," he said into the phone, "I have to go. Things are hopping here and I need to take another call. Make sure Faith calls me when she gets there." He hung up, punched the button that was flashing. Leaning back in his chair, he took a deep breath. "Your Honor," he said. "I apologize for disturbing you on a Sunday."

"As well you should," David Bernier said in the no-nonsense voice that had struck terror into the hearts of two generations of wayward teenagers, not to mention a multitude of attorneys, law enforcement officers, hardened criminals, and employees of the Department of Corrections. "I understand you called regarding a search warrant you're in a big rush to get your hands on. So much of a rush that you couldn't wait until Monday morning."

Ty rubbed his temple in anticipation of the headache that was about to hit. "Actually, Your Honor, I just received new information that may render that warrant unnecessary." His stomach started gnawing, and sweat pooled beneath his arms.

Dead silence. "Oh?" the judge finally said. "Perhaps you'd care to explain that."

"Well, you see, sir, although all the evidence we'd gathered so far pointed toward a particular suspect, information I received this morning from another law enforcement agency has convinced me that we were, in effect, ah…barking up the wrong tree."

More silence. Then, "I see. Does this mean I can get back to my golf game now, Chief Savage?"

He cleared his throat. "Yes, Your Honor. It does."

"Good. Don't call me again on a Sunday, young man, unless you have all your facts gathered in advance."

A click, and the judge was gone. Across the desk, Davy Hunter grinned. "Chew you a new asshole, did he?"

"Man, I feel like I did when I was nine and got reamed out by the principal for turning those frogs loose in the classroom."

"I remember that incident."

"I bet old lady Hodges hasn't forgotten it, either." In spite of the tension in the room, or perhaps because of it, they both snickered. The snickers turned to deep belly laughs. "Shit," Ty said, wiping the corner of his eye. "I haven't laughed like that in months."

"Neither have I."

"Look, I need something on Rollins. Something good enough to hold him for twenty-four hours. Long enough so I can convince Faith that she and Jessie should get out of town for a while. You must have something."

"I don't know if I have anything that'll stick. If he has a good lawyer, the best you can hope for is three or four hours. And if we spook him, this whole house of cards could tumble."

Ty returned to tapping his fingertips. "What about his minions? Any one of them you think might crack under the right amount of pressure?"

Davy chewed on it for a bit. "Maybe Cooper Gates. He pretends to be a tough guy, but underneath it all, he's just a scared kid."

"We drag him down here, his old man will have a shit fit."

"Yep."

They eyed each other for a minute, then he picked up the phone and dialed Pete's extension. When Pete picked up, he said, "I want you to run out and pick up Cooper Gates. Bring him in for a little chat."

At the other end, Pete said, "What about his old man? He won't take too kindly to us questioning his precious offspring."

"We can only pray he's in the operating room right now, performing an emergency appendectomy. Or maybe on a Caribbean cruise. Maybe you'll get lucky and find the kid out driving around in that shitbox car of his. There must be something you can find wrong with it."

"Oh, yeah," Pete said with obvious glee. "A car that old, I can probably find half a dozen things wrong with it."

"Knock yourself out, my man."

* * *

Buck Savage knew that his memory was failing.

It had started about five years ago, before he and Glenda had split. She'd send him to the grocery store to pick up dish soap, and he'd come back with twenty-five dollars worth of stuff, but no dish soap. She always got crazy over it, was forever ragging him about what she called Senior Moments. At first, he thought it was just because he was getting older, but as the condition gradually worsened, he began to suspect it was more serious than that. That was the real reason he'd retired three years ago. A police chief had to stay on top of things, and once his brain turned to Swiss cheese, he'd realized it was time to let somebody else take over before he screwed up something really important.

So far, he'd done a pretty good job of hiding it from everyone. Except possibly Jo, whose eagle eye never missed a trick. And now Tyrone. After that little incident with the truck, his son thought he was ready for the old folks' home. Thought he wasn't playing with all his marbles anymore. Well, maybe so, but he wasn't completely useless. Not yet anyway. That business yesterday of calling Faith by her mother's name… well, hell, he wasn't a fool. He knew the difference. It was just that once in a while, things got a little muddied, and he'd say something stupid. Or do something stupid, like hit the gas pedal instead of the brake, and drive through the front of a building.

Okay, so he wasn't as sharp as he used to be. But his cop instincts hadn't disappeared yet. Nor had his common sense. He knew that Tyrone was worried about Faith. He could hear it in his son's voice. And Ty didn't worry without good reason. The kid was still a little green, but he had the makings of a good chief. There were nasty things going on in Serenity. Buck heard the rumors, saw the tension on his son's face when he came home every night. Chelsea Logan, for instance. Something smelled fishy there. And now somebody had tried to kill Faith. Sweet, beautiful Faith, who looked so much like her mother it brought tears to his eyes. Tyrone hadn't even bothered to tell him. It had been Jessie who spilled the beans.

Last night was the first time he'd ever spoken to Jessie Logan, although he'd watched her grow up, had spent years, in fact, studying her facial expressions, her mannerisms, the shape of her jaw. Wondering. Every once in a while, he thought he saw a glimpse of his mother in that somber little face. But every time he did, he told himself it was just the pointless speculation of a foolish old man who'd been an even bigger fool when, in his late fifties, he'd recklessly taken up with a woman half his age.

It hadn't lasted long. When it was over, he'd come crawling back to Glenda. With that incomprehensible radar that women seem to have, she'd known about it all along. She forgave him for reasons he had yet to comprehend, and he'd tried to put it behind him. Except that eight or nine months later, Chelsea had given birth to a dark-haired little girl who was the spitting image of Jo at the same age. And he'd spent the next fifteen years wondering if that baby was his daughter.

It was pointless to speculate. Chelsea was dead, and he'd probably never know the truth. Right now he had other, more pressing things to concern himself with. Faith still wasn't here, and his instincts were telling him it wouldn't hurt to take a drive out Bald Mountain Road and find out what was taking her so long. He'd probably meet her somewhere along the way. If he did, he'd flag her down, deliver Tyrone's message, and continue on his way.

But just in case he didn't, just in case there was some kind of trouble…

He went to the wall safe and spun the dial. His mind might be going, but he hadn't yet forgotten the combination. He took out his service revolver, its heaviness familiar in his hand, and relocked the safe. He'd locked the gun away the day he turned in his badge. Now he took it out every couple of months to clean and polish it. He'd been one hell of a shot in his day, even though he'd never once, in thirty years of service, had to fire it in the line of duty.

Not that he expected to need it now. But thirty years as a cop had left him with the philosophy that it was never a bad idea to carry a friend.

The streets of Serenity were deserted. Everybody was either at church or sleeping in. On his way out Bald Mountain Road, Buck passed only three cars. He scrutinized each of them closely, but they were all familiar faces, people who probably didn't even know Faith Pelletier. Jerry Haskell was undoubtedly headed into town to buy the Sunday paper, just like he did every Sunday morning. Margaret Owens and her daughter were headed to the ten o'clock service at the First Baptist Church, which she'd attended for some forty years, and Zeke Murray's kid was on his way to his job sweeping floors and cleaning tables at McDonald's.

Cyrus Logan's place sat in the open near the top of the hill, clearly visible from a distance. Tyrone's pickup truck was parked in the yard. Beside it sat some kind of little silver car, one of those newfangled things that looked just like every other new car on the road. Back in his day, you could tell at a glance not only what make and model a car was, but what year. Now, they all blended together into a single Japanese-compact body style, and who the hell knew?

He slowed as he approached the driveway, saw her dog dancing around and barking inside the cab of Ty's pickup. That seemed a little odd, and something told him to drive on past. He parked a quarter-mile up the road, got out, tucked his revolver into his belt and walked back. A hundred feet from the house, he jumped the ditch—he still had it in him, by God—and crossed the damp and muddy field to the backside of the old farmhouse.

The sun hit the windows on that side directly, turning them opaque. He tried to peek inside, but he couldn't see a thing. So he circled the house, came around by the driveway, where that damn-fool dog was yapping and carrying on. Shooting a quick glance at the house, he meandered over to the truck, silently opened the door, and let the fool loose. The dog raced around the yard, circled back to him, and started jumping all over him, guaranteeing that his clean pants would be covered with dog hair and he'd spend the rest of the day sneezing.

He rubbed the mutt behind the ears to calm it, and slunk to the nearest window. Shading his eyes, he peered in. Through filmy curtains, he saw a couch, a television set, a couple of easy chairs. He moved on to the next window, glimpsed movement inside and ducked. If anybody driving by saw him, they would think he'd lost his mind. Here he was, a grown man with a gun in his pocket, skulking around like some kind of common criminal. But until he'd completed his surveillance, until he knew who was in there with her and what they were doing, he didn't intend to make his presence known.

Slowly raising his head, he peered cautiously through the glass. The room was an office of some sort, with a big, L-shaped desk. Faith was sitting at the computer, fingers poised on the keyboard. Newt Rollins leaned over her shoulder, studying the monitor. Buck could hear the murmur of voices, but couldn't make out what they were saying. Then Rollins shifted position, and he saw a flash of silver.

Wait a minute. Was that a gun Newt had in his hand?

Faith's dog whimpered and nuzzled his feet. Buck shoved it away. Crouched in the grass, he moved to the opposite corner of the window and tried to get a better look from a slightly different angle. Newt's hand rested on Faith's shoulder, but there was nothing friendly about their body language. Newt's knuckles were white, as though he were restraining her in the chair, and she sat stiffly, clearly uncomfortable. She said something Buck couldn't make out. Newt responded with a burst of anger. Then he raised the gun—and it definitely was a gun—and held it against the back of Faith's head.

Breathing hard, Buck slithered away from the window and sat on the grass. Well, well, well. Wasn't this interesting? He'd known his instincts were right. Inside the house, something was very, very wrong.

Now he just had to figure out what the hell to do about it.

Twenty-Two

He and Hunter were strategizing, planning how they were going to handle Cooper Gates, when Ty heard a commotion out in the hall. Voices raised in argument. Through the closed door, he heard Floyd Watson's voice rising above the fray. Then Floyd was overridden by another voice. Young. Female. Excited.

And indisputably Jessie Logan.

He and Davy exchanged startled glances, then he got up and walked around the desk. Opening the door, he said, "What's going on out here?"

"Sorry, Ty," Floyd said. "I told these two kids you were busy, but they wouldn't take no for an answer."

Jessie wore an expression of steely determination. Beside her stood a tall, gawky Somali boy he recognized as Omar Abdallah's oldest son. The boy looked terrified. "We have to talk to you," Jessie said in a voice as resolute as that of the judge he'd just spoken with. "Faith may be in trouble. And it's all my fault."

His heart took a sharp leap. "Into my office," he said brusquely, and both kids scooted past him.

"I didn't know," Jessie said, her words coming out so fast they rolled and tumbled over each other. "He was out washing windows and I told him Faith was home alone, but I didn't know until I talked to Ahmed. I think he killed my mother, and now he's—"

"Stop!" he said. "Calm down. Take a deep breath." Turning to the boy, he said, "Think you can tell me what's going on?"

"Newt Rollins," Ahmed said. "I told Jessie's mother that he was dealing drugs, and then she died. I believe he killed her. This is all my fault. I should have kept what I knew to myself."

"Son of a gun," Floyd said from the open doorway. "I forgot all about the truck."

All eyes turned to him. "What truck?" Ty said.

"The old quarter-ton Chevy pickup that Newt Rollins keeps in his barn. It's about forty years old. His old man used to use it for farm work. I never thought of it when you had us beating the bushes, looking for the vehicle that drove Faith off the road."

Ty and Davy exchanged glances. "Please," Jessie said, "you have to do something. He knows that Faith's home alone. What if he goes out to the house? What if—"

"Get over to Newt's place," he told Floyd. "Check the truck out for forensic evidence. Front-end damage, red paint, whatever. Let me know what you find." He picked up the phone and dialed the Logan place. It rang six times, seven. Nobody picked up. His stomach doing flip-flops, he clicked the button, met Davy's troubled gaze and called his own house again. But his dad didn't answer, either.

He hung up without leaving a message. "She's not home," he said, "and now nobody's answering at my house, either. I think it's time to leave Cooper Gates cooling his heels and go find Faith. Hunter, you come with me. And you," he said pointedly as he turned to the kids, "stay here."

Jessie immediately protested. "But—"

"No buts. Stay the hell here. Get a soda from the vending machine, find a magazine to read and don't move an inch. If you're not sitting right here when I get back, I'll have your hides. Both of you!"

He strode toward the front door with Hunter a step behind him. "If Lemoine shows up," he told Dix as he blew past her desk, "have him wait in my office."

"You might want to hear this before you leave."

It was her tone, as much as her words, that stopped him midstride. He paused, breathing hard, the half-open door in his hand. "What?" he said.

"I just had a phone call from Buck, asking for backup."

"Backup? What in hell is he talking about?"

"He called from his cell phone. He's at the Logan place. I couldn't make it all out, but he said something about Newt Rollins and a gun. Want to tell me what's going on?"

The fear that he'd kept in check until this instant sprang to instantaneous, full-blooded life. Panic-stricken, he met Davy's eyes. "Shit," Davy said.

And they were out the door and running.

She'd swallowed twenty-seven pills. Faith knew how many there were because she'd counted them as they went down—twenty-seven five-milligram Valium tablets. She wasn't sure what a lethal dosage was, but she suspected twenty-seven was enough to do the job. She was already starting to feel the effects. She wasn't quite tipsy, but her reflexes were slowed, her thinking processes a little gummed up.

Her fingers fumbled on the keyboard. "Start deleting files," Newt said, and nudged her with the gun. "We don't have time to read this stuff. Just get rid of it all. Nobody'll ever know the difference, except you and me." He paused. "Oh, I forgot. You'll be dead. I guess that just leaves me."

She started dragging folders into the trash, wondering how she'd manage to get out of this alive. Even if it was possible to escape from Newt, there were all those pills she'd taken. She tried frantically to recall what she'd learned about overdoses. How much time did she have before she passed the point of no return?

"You do realize," she said, trying to hide her terror, "that a computer professional could probably resurrect everything I'm deleting?"

"But nobody will have any reason to dig into the computer's innards. What happened to Chelsea was an unfortunate accident. And you, just recovering from a breakdown, poor thing, were so distraught over your cousin's death that you took your own life. Pretty devastating for me, to stop by for a visit and find you dead, just a week after losing Chelsea."

"Ty will know I didn't kill myself," she said, still deleting files. "He'll come after you."

"He'll never figure it out. Why should he? I have a solid reputation in this community. My great-grandfather was one of the town founders. I'm respected here. Nobody would even think to suspect me. Besides, your medical history should be sufficient evidence to prove your death was a suicide. A major breakdown after the loss of your husband. Clinical depression with accompanying anxiety disorder. Psychotropic medications." He waved the gun in a circle near her head for emphasis. "Nobody will be surprised to hear that your cousin's death was the straw that broke the proverbial camel's back."

The Valium was starting to kick in. A little woozy, she said, "You're crazy, Newt. But I bet you already knew that."

"Like I care." He nudged her cheek with the barrel of the gun. It was cool and smooth and lethal, and her heart rate accelerated. She had to stay calm. Maintaining calm meant maintaining life. The faster her heart pumped, the more quickly the Valium would work its way through her system. Remembering the relaxation exercises Dr. Garabedian had taught her, she let herself go limp. *Slow, deep breaths*, she reminded herself. Slow, deep breaths would ease her into a relaxed state that would slow down all her body functions. It was probably already too late for her, but she wouldn't go down without a fight. While half her mind was focused on those slow, deep breaths, the rest of it was scouting around, looking for some kind of weapon. A ballpoint pen. A small ceramic ashtray. A heavy-duty stapler...

"Empty the trash," he ordered. "I don't want anything accidentally left behind."

She clicked the Empty Trash button. For an instant, the screen went blurry before her, and she shook her head to clear her vision. "Move it!" he said. "I don't have all day."

Grimly, she said, "Neither do I."

He'd already tried both doors and found them bolted. Now Buck crept around the back of the house, looking for an open window. A back door. Any kind of access he could find. What he found was the basement bulkhead. Built on a concrete foundation and held together with a padlock, the old wooden doors looked as though they'd barely hold the weight of a good-size man. A little muscle was all he needed. That, and something to pry them open with.

He crept soundlessly back around the house and into the shed, rummaged around until he found a crowbar. He took a step back toward the door and a floorboard creaked. Buck froze, waiting for Rollins to open the door and catch him. But there was no sound from the house. After a moment, once his heart rate slowed a little, he began working his way, one silent footstep at a time, back toward the shed door. Then he was on the grass, and moving at a pretty damn good clip for an old duffer who was slowly losing his marbles. Back at the bulkhead, he stuck one end of the crowbar under the edge of one of those rotted wooden doors and pried with every ounce of strength he possessed.

The wood gave a creak they probably could hear all the way to Lewiston, and he silently cussed it. He shifted position, stuck the crowbar in at a different spot and tried again. Again the wood groaned as though it was suffering the tortures of the damned. Then, with a suddenness that almost catapulted him onto his rump, it gave, tearing loose from its rusty hinge and splattering him with splinters. Buck tugged a little more, lifted the door and folded it back over the other one, then took a deep breath and started down the concrete stairs.

The dog tried to follow him. "Stay!" he snapped, in a voice barely more than a whisper.

To his surprise, the dog lay on the ground beside the bulkhead, ears flattened against its head, muzzle pressed to its paws. "Good dog," Buck murmured, and continued down the stairs, swiping away cobwebs and trying not to think about what might have created them. There wasn't much in this world that Buck Savage was afraid of, but spiders were pretty low on his list of favorite things.

It took a minute for his eyes to adjust to the darkness. A thin stream of daylight came in through the open bulkhead, but the narrow cellar windows were so dirty that only minimal light filtered through. He circled the furnace, a hulking monster that looked to be about fifty years old. The water pipes overhead were corroded and ugly. He placed his hand on a metal beam that Cyrus must have put in to keep the place from caving into the cellar. Something ran across his hand, and he jumped, beads of sweat popping out on his brow. *Holy Jesus*. It was enough to tempt him to turn tail and run. Except that he had to save Meredith.

No. Not Meredith. Faith. He had to remember that. *Concentrate, you old geezer*, he told himself. *Her name's Faith. Not Meredith. Faith.* She was Meredith and Armand's daughter. The one Tyrone had been in love with since he was eight years old. *If you don't save her, she'll never get to be your daughter-in-law. And if that doesn't happen...*

If that didn't happen, all the light would go out of his son's eyes.

He found the stairway that led upstairs, grabbed the railing in the darkness and started climbing, praying the door wasn't locked at the top. He heard a noise behind him, realized that the goddamn dog had followed him. "*Git*," he whispered through gritted teeth. "Get the hell out of here!" But the dog just stood there beside him, wagging and whining. It looked like Buck didn't have a choice. They were a team whether he liked it or not.

He reached the top, put his hand on the doorknob. It squeaked when he turned it, but the door popped open. Before he could make a move, the dog pushed past him into the kitchen, toenails clicking on ancient linoleum. So much for the stealth approach. Might as well have hired a brass band to announce his arrival.

He caught up with the dog in the kitchen when it stopped to lap water from a plastic dog dish. "Shh!" he hissed. "Heel." The dog stopped drinking and fell into step with him.

In another room, two voices were raised in argument. "This is taking too long," Newt Rollins complained. "Move a little faster."

"I'm sorry," Faith said. "Amazingly enough, I tend to be nervous when somebody's holding a gun to my head."

"Cut the wise-ass remarks and speed it up."

"If I'm too slow for you, maybe you'd rather do it yourself."

"I don't think so, sweetheart. I'm not stupid enough to leave my fingerprints on the keyboard for your boyfriend to find. Now, come on! Move faster or I'll use the gun."

"To do what, shoot yourself in the foot? If you shoot me, your little suicide scheme will be out the window, and you'll be the number-one suspect in my murder."

Buck stepped silently to the doorway of the den. Raising his gun, he said, "Let her go, Newt."

With amazing cool, almost as though he'd been expecting him, Newt turned. He took in the gun that was pointed directly at his heart, and smiled. "Well, well," he said. "If it isn't Buck Savage, come to join our little party." The gun he held to Faith's temple gleamed silver in the light from the window. "It looks as though we're at an impasse, Mr. Savage. You have a gun and I have a gun. If you shoot me, I'll put a bullet through her head. Is it really worth it?"

"I'm dead anyway," Faith said. "He made me swallow—"

"Shut up, bitch." The gun still pressed to her temple, Newt forcefully wrapped his free arm around Faith's throat and yanked her to her feet. Using her as a shield, he said to Buck,

"Drop the gun, Mr. Savage, or she's dead. You may succeed in killing me, but—" his smile was chilling "—I'll kill her first."

Her eyes wild with terror, Faith struggled ineffectually to break Newt's iron grip. Buck had no doubt that Newt was serious. If he didn't drop the gun, Newt would kill Faith. If he did drop the gun, they were probably both done for. It was one hell of a choice.

"I'm waiting," Newt snapped.

With overwhelming reluctance, Buck set his gun on the floor. Behind him, the dog growled again, a low rumble in his throat.

"Wise choice," Newt said with a smile.

"Now what?"

"Goddamn meddling old coot. You threw one hell of a monkey wrench into my plans. Now I have to kill you both."

"Ty will rip your heart out," Faith said.

"Shut up."

"What's wrong, Newt? Afraid of the truth?"

"I said, shut up!"

Newt shook her, hard, her head flopping back and forth like a rag doll. Beside Buck, the dog made a fierce, feral sound and launched itself at Rollins, its sharp white teeth clamping down on Newt's ankle. Newt let out a high-pitched screech and tried to shake the dog off without losing hold of Faith. "Get him off me!" he screamed. "Get him off me!" He danced and kicked, but the dog was a snarling, whirling frenzy. "Call him off or I'll shoot the little bastard!"

Faith met Buck's eyes. She raised her arm, then thrust it backward, driving her elbow hard into Newt's stomach. With a startled sound, he doubled over, releasing his hold on her. With lightning speed, she grabbed the heavy-duty stapler from the desk and slammed it down with all her strength on top of Newt's head.

He swayed, and then his legs buckled, and he went down, his gun dropping from his hand and skittering off across the floor. Buck dived for the gun, landing with a thud on the rock-hard floor, cussing as his sciatic nerve violently protested the abusive treatment. He was too goddamn old for this Indiana Jones stuff. Tomorrow, he'd pay dearly. He scooped up the shiny silver revolver, stuffed his own gun back into his belt, and stumbled to his feet, holding on to his aching ass with his free hand. It would be a miracle if he didn't end up in traction.

Rollins lay on the floor in a crumpled heap. Buck hoped to Christ Faith hadn't killed the son of a bitch. But no, he was alive; dead people didn't moan and bleed. What the hell was taking Tyrone so damn long? He needed a little help here. "Run out to the truck and get me Ty's spare set of handcuffs," he told Faith. "I'll feel a lot better once we have this guy restrained."

She didn't answer. Kneeling beside Rollins, he glanced up at her, saw the odd expression on her face. "Faith?" he said. "You okay?"

"Pills," she said. "Valium. Twenty-seven." She took a single step forward, swayed like a blade of grass in a windstorm, and slithered to the floor.

Ty brought the cruiser to a shuddering halt at the foot of the driveway and they both stepped out and moved stealthily toward the house. Past his pickup truck, past Newt's silver Acura, past Buck's hideous yellow F-150. The kitchen door was locked with that infernal dead bolt he'd insisted she install, and he cussed himself for ever suggesting it. Ty put his face up to the window and peered inside. The house was silent, the kitchen empty. He glanced at the gun in his hand, then at Davy, and said quietly, "You ever tried shooting a door lock?"

"Not while I was sober," Davy said. "I think that kind of thing only works on TV."

Ty glanced around the shed, spied a roll of duct tape. The universal tool. He picked it up, tore off a few strips, and stuck them to the window. Then he turned his gun around backward, grasped it by the barrel, and swiftly drove the butt of it against the duct tape.

The window broke soundlessly. "That'll do it," Davy said. "It's always worked for me." Ty peeled away the duct tape, and the broken glass came with it. He set it aside, then reached inside the opening and fumbled around until he located the dead bolt. It turned with a sharp click that resounded like a gunshot in the stillness. They both froze, but the only sound he heard was the low murmur of conversation coming from somewhere in the depths of the big old house. Ty eased open the door and stepped into the kitchen. Behind them, Davy silently closed the door. Guns drawn, they quickly checked the kitchen, the bathroom, and found nothing.

Toenails clicked on hardwood, and Buddy sauntered into the kitchen. The dog saw Ty, wagged his tail, and whimpered softly. "Hey, boy," he whispered, and knelt to pat the dog.

That was when he saw the blood. It dotted Buddy's face and was spattered all over his white ruff. Ty's heart lurched. *Faith. Jesus God, Faith.* If that bastard Rollins had harmed so much as a hair on her head—or on Buck's, for that matter— he was going to strangle the son of a bitch with his bare hands.

He gave Buddy a final pat, signaled to Hunter, and stepped farther into the cool darkness of the house. The living room lay still, dust motes dancing in the sunshine that pooled on the hardwood floor beneath the windows. He could still hear the murmur of conversation. It sounded like Buck talking, but he heard no response, just that single voice, droning on and on. Buddy squeezed past him and trotted off in the direction of the den. Cautiously, moving one step at a time, Ty eased toward the sound of his father's voice.

Behind him, Davy stepped on a squeaky floorboard. Ty froze, waited. Conversation inside the den abruptly ceased. Buddy walked to the door of the den and stood there, wagging his tail tentatively. Muscles rigid, Ty raised his gun, and with a single movement, stepped into the doorway.

Newt Rollins sat on the floor, propped against the wall beneath the window, his hands and ankles tied with what looked to be a lamp cord. A nasty gash on his head dripped blood, and his crimson-streaked pants looked like they'd been through a shredder. He glared at Ty, but didn't speak.

Across the room, Buck leaned against the opposite wall, his gun pointed directly at Newt, his cell phone in his free hand. Ty let out all his breath. Faith sat beside his father on the floor, bowlegged and floppy, her head cradled in her arms like some sorry-ass drunk. But she was alive.

"About time you got here," Buck said. "Check the medicine cabinet for ipecac." When both Ty and Davy just stared at him, he barked, "Now!"

Davy took off running while Ty knelt on the floor in front of Faith. "Babe?" he said. "You all right?"

She raised her face to his, and his heart sank. Her eyes were wild and drifty, the pupils dilated. "Ty," she said thickly. "I'm so sorry."

"She swallowed a whole goddamn bottle of Valium," Buck said.

"Jesus Christ on rollerskates. How many?"

"Twenty-seven. I just got off the phone with poison control. They told me to give her ipecac as long as she's still conscious, then get her to the hospital ASAP. But I didn't dare to leave Newt, so I've been waiting for you. Ambulance is on its way. Damn good thing you bought me that cell phone for Christmas."

For a heartbeat, he just stared at the old man, stupefied. "What?" Buck said irritably.

He shook his head, scooped Faith up in his arms and carried her to the bathroom, where Davy waited with a bottle and a spoon. Ty knelt on the floor in front of the toilet, his hands shaking so hard that Davy had to open the bottle for him, had to pour the stuff into the goddamn spoon. "Faith, honey," he said, terrified by her lethargy, "you have to drink this. Do you hear me?"

"I hear." Her words were thick and slurred, but at least she was responsive.

He took the spoon from Davy, spilling only a little. "Open

your mouth, sweetheart. This'll make you better." He had no idea if it would, but he couldn't let her see that. If he fell apart now, where would that leave her?

She opened her mouth. He drizzled in the ipecac, and she grimaced. "Oh, God," she said. "Awful."

"I know. But you have to swallow it. You have to do it for me."

She swallowed, retched, and he held her head over the toilet as she vomited violently. It was the most beautiful sound he'd ever heard. Over her head, he said brusquely to Davy, "Call Pete. Tell him to drop whatever he's doing and meet us at the hospital. If Lemoine's there, he should bring him along, too. Once the doctors are through with Rollins, somebody needs to book him. I'm staying with her." As Faith continued to upchuck the contents of her stomach, Davy stood up, laid a hand on Ty's shoulder and squeezed it.

In the distance, he heard the shriek of a siren. He found a washcloth, wet it and gently bathed her face with cold water. "Faith?" he said. "Stay with me. Talk to me, baby. Talk to me!"

"Don't…leave…me."

"Are you kidding? I'm not going anywhere. You're stuck with me. For the next fifty years at least."

She smiled. "Oh, good." She lay her head against his shoulder and closed her eyes.

"Faith? Wake up." He shook her, and her head flopped limply. "Don't you leave me," he said, his heart squeezing so hard he couldn't breathe. "Don't you dare to leave me!"

She didn't respond. Frantic now, he scooped her up again as though she weighed nothing and ran to meet the ambulance as it turned into the driveway.

Her dreams were bizarre. Nightmares, really, hazy images of faceless people committing unspeakable acts of torture upon her body. Mingled with those were the all too clear visions of three-headed monsters and other creatures never found in nature, half man and half beast, stalking her relentlessly.

She moved beyond the creatures, flew through a long,

black tunnel toward some unseen destination. Arms reached out to her, dozens of arms plucking at her, poking and patting and touching. Faces floated in the darkness above her head. Familiar faces, smiling at her, arms reaching out to greet her. Grandma Pelletier, who'd died when she was three. Meredith and Armand, her parents, younger now for eternity than she would ever be again. Uncle Cyrus, his face softened into a mask of benevolence. Chelsea, young and beautiful, gazing at her with an expression of such profound sadness it took her breath away.

Home. She couldn't see her destination, but she could feel it. She was headed home, and her heart sang with the joy of it.

Stop!

Ben's voice. Ben's face, looking fierce. Beautiful. So many things she wanted to tell him. So much he needed to know. *I'm okay*, she tried to tell him. *I'm okay.*

He never opened his mouth, just looked at her with that inscrutable expression, but still she could hear his thoughts. *Go back, Faith. It's not time yet.*

But it feels so right here, she told him. *So beautiful.*

No. You have to go back now. He's waiting for you.

With no warning, she was sucked back through that black tunnel, back past all the smiling faces, past the man-creatures. She drifted for a time in utter blackness before easing into a deep and dreamless sleep.

It could have been hours, could have been weeks, that she slept. Eventually, she awoke to find herself lying flat on her back on a rock-hard surface. Her throat hurt, she had the mother of all headaches, and she was hitched up to enough tubes and wires to run the moon shuttle.

Hospital. She was in a hospital bed.

She blinked against the harsh light, fumbled with the sheet that covered her, turned her head and saw him, sprawled awkwardly in a chair that wasn't designed for comfort, unshaven and dressed in a sweatshirt and wrinkled jeans. Ty's eyes were closed, but somehow she knew he wasn't sleeping.

She shifted position on the stiff mattress, and he opened his eyes. Soft, melted-chocolate eyes, filled with a mixture of worry and relief and something else, something that made her heart beat a little more quickly. She reached out to him, and he left the chair, kneeling at the side of her hospital bed. He kissed her outstretched hand, and she touched his cheek. "Hey," he said.

She wet her parched lips and said, "You look like something the cat dragged in."

"I thought I'd lost you. We almost did. I've never been so scared in my life. But you came back."

Exploring his face with her fingertips, she said, "I know. He sent me back."

"Sent you back?" he said, looking confused. "Who?"

"Ben. He told me it wasn't time yet, and—" She saw the expression on his face and stopped. "Never mind. I guess I was dreaming." She closed her eyes, drifted for a bit. "Where's Jessie?" she said.

"Outside, in the waiting room. Dad's there with her. You've had a lot of visitors. Davy's been by, and Skip and Linda. Jo stopped in, and so did Dottie McLaughlin. But Dad and Jessie have stayed here around the clock, right along with me."

She looked past him then and saw the cards, the flowers, the balloons that overwhelmed the tiny private room. "Wow," she said.

"Your agent sent flowers," he said. "Those yellow ones. The red roses—" He cleared his throat. "They're from me."

"Good Lord, how long have I been here?"

"A couple of days. You were in intensive care for a while, but they moved you up here this morning after your vital signs stabilized."

She searched his eyes. "Your dad," she said. "If it wasn't for him…"

"I know." His voice was hoarse, his eyes intent on hers. He cleared his throat again. "He says it's Buddy who deserves all the glory. I've already decided that when I build our new house, Buddy's having his own room and a lifetime supply of Milk-Bone dog biscuits."

Had he really said *our* house? She thought that was what she'd heard, but she was still a little woozy, still a little slow.

"Of course," he continued, "you didn't do too bad a job yourself, cleaning Newt's clock with that stapler. It's a wonder you didn't kill him."

She gave him a faint smile. "Turnabout is fair play," she said, then sobered. "What happened to him?"

"Our good buddy Newt's got his own private room in County Jail, where he's recuperating from a hole in the head and some pretty nasty dog bites. He won't be bothering anybody again for a while."

She took a breath and let it out. "Ty?" she said.

Her hand tightly wrapped in his, he kissed her knuckles. "What?"

"Did you really mean what you said…about sticking around for the next fifty years?"

"Oh, yeah. I sure did."

Her mouth felt like the Sahara Desert. She wet her lips again. "Does this mean we're getting married? Because there's no way I'm living in sin with you, Savage."

"I guess if I have to marry you…well, it's a hardship, but I'll face it like a man."

"Ben didn't just send me back," she said. "And stop looking at me like that, because I'm not crazy. He sent me back to you. He told me I had to come back because you were waiting for me."

She felt a shudder run through him. Visibly shaken, he turned his face heavenward and said in an unsteady voice, "God bless you, Ben Feldman."

"Come here," she said.

Cautiously working his way around the tangle of wires and tubes, he eased up onto the narrow bed beside her and took her in his arms. She rested her head against his chest, reveling in his warmth, his solidity, the incredible sense of belonging she felt in his arms. "Welcome home," he said.

Faith tightened her arms around him. *Fifty years*, she thought. *Maybe more*. And she smiled. "Yes," she said. "Welcome home."

New York Times Bestselling Author

SUSAN WIGGS

Grace Bennett is a woman standing at the crossroads—of her life and marriage. But when the unthinkable happens, Grace is left to face a navy wife's worst nightmare—the cold truth that life's biggest chances can slip away while you're looking for guarantees.

THE
OCEAN
BETWEEN
US

"A human and multilayered story exploring duty to both country and family."
—Nora Roberts

Available the first week of March 2005 wherever paperbacks are sold!

MIRA®

www.MIRABooks.com

MSW2147

The *USA TODAY* bestselling
author of *Twilight Hunger*
brings you the newest book
in her Wings in the Night
series, *Blue Twilight*.

MAGGIE SHAYNE

A mysterious vampire has a
town in thrall and female tourists
are disappearing. Maxine Stuart,
a private investigator specializing
in the paranormal, takes the case
when a friend's daughter goes
missing. But she finds herself
up against a force she might not
be ready for....

BLUE TWILIGHT

"A tasty, tension-packed read."
—*Publishers Weekly* on
Thicker Than Water

*Available the first week
of March 2005 wherever
paperbacks are sold!*

www.MIRABooks.com   MMS2150

If you enjoyed what you just read,
then we've got an offer you can't resist!

Take 2 bestselling novels FREE!
Plus get a FREE surprise gift!

Clip this page and mail it to MIRA®

IN U.S.A.
3010 Walden Ave.
P.O. Box 1867
Buffalo, N.Y. 14240-1867

IN CANADA
P.O. Box 609
Fort Erie, Ontario
L2A 5X3

YES! Please send me 2 free MIRA® novels and my free surprise gift. After receiving them, if I don't wish to receive anymore, I can return the shipping statement marked cancel. If I don't cancel, I will receive 4 brand-new novels every month, before they're available in stores! In the U.S.A., bill me at the bargain price of $4.99 plus 25¢ shipping and handling per book and applicable sales tax, if any*. In Canada, bill me at the bargain price of $5.49 plus 25¢ shipping and handling per book and applicable taxes**. That's the complete price and a savings of over 20% off the cover prices—what a great deal! I understand that accepting the 2 free books and gift places me under no obligation ever to buy any books. I can always return a shipment and cancel at any time. Even if I never buy another The Best of the Best™ book, the 2 free books and gift are mine to keep forever.

185 MDN DZ7J
385 MDN DZ7K

Name	(PLEASE PRINT)	
Address	Apt.#	
City	State/Prov.	Zip/Postal Code

*Not valid to current The Best of the Best™, Mira®,
suspense and romance subscribers.*

Want to try two free books from another series?
Call 1-800-873-8635 or visit www.morefreebooks.com.

* Terms and prices subject to change without notice. Sales tax applicable in N.Y.
** Canadian residents will be charged applicable provincial taxes and GST.
All orders subject to approval. Offer limited to one per household.
® and ™are registered trademarks owned and used by the trademark owner and or its licensee.

BOB04R   ©2004 Harlequin Enterprises Limited

MIRABooks.com

We've got the lowdown on your favorite author!

☆ Read an excerpt of your favorite author's newest book

☆ Check out her bio

☆ Talk to her in our Discussion Forums

☆ Read interviews, diaries, and more

☆ Find her current bestseller, and even her backlist titles

All this and more available at

www.MiraBooks.com

MEAUT1R3

LAURIE BRETON

32025 MORTAL SIN	___ $6.50 U.S. ___ $7.99 CAN.
66660 FINAL EXIT	___ $6.50 U.S. ___ $7.99 CAN.

(limited quantities available)

TOTAL AMOUNT	$ _____
POSTAGE & HANDLING	$ _____
($1.00 FOR 1 BOOK, 50¢ for each additional)	
APPLICABLE TAXES*	$ _____
TOTAL PAYABLE	$ _____

(check or money order—please do not send cash)

To order, complete this form and send it, along with a check or money order for the total above, payable to MIRA Books, to: **In the U.S.:** 3010 Walden Avenue, P.O. Box 9077, Buffalo, NY 14269-9077; **In Canada:** P.O. Box 636, Fort Erie, Ontario, L2A 5X3.

Name: _____

Address: _____ City: _____

State/Prov.: _____ Zip/Postal Code: _____

Account Number (if applicable): _____

075 CSAS

*New York residents remit applicable sales taxes.
*Canadian residents remit applicable GST and provincial taxes.

MIRA®

www.MIRABooks.com

MLB0305BL